Yashar Kemal

Memed,
My Hawk

Translated from the Turkish by
Edouard Roditi

FLAMINGO

Published by Fontana Paperbacks

This book was first published under
the title of *Ince Memed* by
Remzi Kitabevi, Instanbul
First English edition published by
William Collins Sons & Co. Ltd
and the Harvill Press 1961
Second impression January 1970

This Flamingo edition first published
in 1984 by Fontana Paperbacks,
8 Grafton Street, London W1X 3LA

Printed in Great Britain by
Richard Clay (The Chaucer Press) Ltd,
Bungay, Suffolk

Memed, My Hawk

YASHAR KEMAL was born in 1922 in a small village in Southern Anatolia, the descendant of landowners on his father's side and bandits on his mother's. He had a very hard upbringing and when he was only five years old, saw his father shot dead in a mosque. After this incident he developed a stutter which he overcame a few years later by the singing of folk ballads, and in time became a master of this rich tradition whose influence can be felt in the haunting quality of his writing.

When he was nine, Kemal decided to learn to read and write. He had to walk daily to a distant village to do so and eventually went for three years to a secondary school at Adana. He held a variety of jobs, working in the local rice and cotton fields, and in a factory. As champion of landless peasants, he was hounded out of every job. Yet he managed to save enough money to buy a typewriter and set himself up as a public letter writer in the small town of Kadirli. Later he went to Istanbul and became a journalist. In 1952 he published a book of short stories and in 1955 came his first novel, *Memed, My Hawk*. This book won the best novel of the year prize in Turkey and its hero has since become a living legend among the peasants of Anatolia. It has been translated into eight languages.

Now considered the greatest living Turkish author, Kemal has been nominated for the Nobel Prize in Literature several times and was on the shortlist in 1982. That same year, he won France's prestigious Del Duca Literary Award for his overall output of ten novels.

Yashar Kemal lives with his wife in Istanbul.

I

The slopes of the Taurus Mountains rise from the shores of the Eastern Mediterranean, on the southern coast of Turkey, in a steady ascent from the white, foam-fringed rocks to the peaks. They then spread inland, at a tangent to the curve of the coast. Clouds in white masses always float over the sea. The coastal plains between the mountains and the shore are of clay, quite smooth, as if polished. Here the soil is rich. For miles inland the plain holds the tang of the sea, its air still salt and sharp. Beyond this smooth ploughed land the scrub of the Chukurova begins. Thickly covered with a tangle of brushwood, reeds, blackberry brambles, wild vines and rushes, its deep green expanse seems boundless, wilder and darker than a forest.

A little farther inland, beyond Anavarza on one side and Osmaniya on the other, on the way towards Islahiye, begin the broad marshes. In the summer months they bubble with the heat. Filthy, unapproachable because of their stench, they reek of rotting reeds and rushes, rotting grass and timber, rotting earth. The surface of the water is then hidden by the decomposing vegetation. In winter the whole area is covered by the sheen of stagnant flood-water, unrolling like a carpet. Beyond the marshes there are more ploughed fields. The earth is oily, shining, warm and soft, ready to repay forty-fold, fifty-fold, the seed that it receives.

Only beyond the low hill-tops crowned with heavy-scented myrtle do the rocks suddenly begin to appear, and with them the pine trees. The crystal-bright drops of resin ooze from the trunks and trickle down to the ground. Beyond the pines are plateaux where the soil is grey and arid. From here it looks as if the snow-capped peaks of the Taurus are very close, almost within arm's reach.

Dikenli, the Plateau of Thistles, is one of these highland plains, with five small villages clustered on it. The inhabitants of all five are tenant farmers, the land belonging only to Abdi Agha. Dikenli is a world by itself, with its own laws and customs. The people of Dikenli know next to nothing of any part of the world beyond their own villages. Very few have ever ventured beyond the limits of the plateau. Elsewhere nobody seems to know of the existence of the villages of Dikenli or of its people and their way of life. Even the tax-collector goes there only every two or three years and has no contact with the villagers, only with Abdi Agha.

Deyirmenoluk, where Abdi Agha lives, is the largest of the villages of Dikenli. It stands on its eastern edge, at the foot of the purple rocks streaked with milky-white, green and silver veins.

Where the rocks begin a plane tree stands in all its majesty, its branches gnarled and bowed to the ground with age. If you venture within a hundred yards of it, or even fifty, nothing seems to stir. All round it reigns a deep silence, frightening stillness. Come within twenty-five yards, ten yards, and it is still as quiet. Only when you come close to the tree, with the rocks at your back, does the tumult suddenly startle you. The roar is at once enough to deafen you. Then it decreases, becomes quieter.

It comes from a spring known as the Mill Spring. It is not really a spring, but the people there call it that. The water bubbles up from the foot of a rock, scattering foam. Throw a piece of wood into the water and it tosses on the surface for a day, two days, even a week. But the actual spring is not really here. Coming from afar, from Akchadagh, the White Mountain, from among the pines, the water is scented with marjoram and thyme before it disappears under a rock, bubbling and boiling, to emerge later by the plane-tree, muttering like a madman.

From here to Akchadagh, the mountain-side is so rocky and steep that the whole Taurus seems no bigger than a plot of land for just one house. Giant pines and beeches rise to the sky from among the boulders, and there is hardly any animal life on the stony slopes.

Thistles generally grow in soil which is neither good nor bad but has been neglected. Later the peasants may root out the thistles and sow there. Such is indeed the practice on the highland valleys of the Taurus.

The tallest thistles grow about a yard high, with many twigs decked with spiny flowers, five-pointed like stars, set among tough, prickly thorns. There are hundreds of these flowers on each thistle.

The thistles do not just grow in groups of two or three. They sprout so thick, so close together that a snake would not be able to slip through them.

In spring the thistles are an anæmic, pale green. A light breeze can bend them to the earth. By midsummer the first blue veins appear on the stems. Then the branches and the whole stem slowly turn a pale blue. Later this blue grows steadily deeper, till a field, the whole boundless plain, becomes a sea of the finest blue. If a wind blows, towards sunset, the blue thistles ripple like the sea and rustle; just as the sea turns red at sunset, so does a field of thistles.

As autumn approaches the thistles dry up. The blue turns white and crackling sounds rise from them. Small milk-white snails, as big as buttons, cling to them in hundreds and thousands, covering them like milk-white beads.

Deyirmenoluk village is surrounded by a plain of thistles. There are no fields, no vineyards, no gardens. Only thistles.

II

The boy running through the thistles was panting. He had been running now for a long time without a stop. All at once he halted. Blood was oozing from where the thistles had scratched him. He could hardly stand. He was scared. Would he escape? Fearfully he looked over his shoulder. There was no one in sight. He felt more hopeful, turned to the right and ran for a while. Then he was so tired that he lay down to rest among the thistles. On his left he saw an ant-heap. The ants were big and the entrance to their nest was teeming with activity. For a while he forgot everything as he watched them. Then, pulling himself together, he rose suddenly from the ground and resumed his flight to the right. Soon he emerged from the thistles and sank to his knees. Seeing that his head still showed above the thistles, he crouched on his haunches. He began to rub his bleeding legs with earth. He could feel the sting as it touched them.

The rocks were only a little farther. With all his remaining strength he started to run towards them and soon reached the plane-tree below the tallest. At the foot of the tree he found a deep hollow like a well, filled with yellow, golden and red-veined leaves piled high, reaching half-way up the trunk. The dry leaves rustled as he threw himself down on them. On the tip of one bare branch of the tree a bird was perched, but it flew off, scared by the noise. The boy was tired and would have liked to spend the night there. But it occurred to him that this was impossible: the wilds were full of man-eating wolves and birds of prey. Some of the leaves still hanging from the tree floated down to join the others. One at a time they began to fall on his body.

He talked to himself, quite loud, as if someone were beside him. "I'll go," he said. "I'll go and find that village. No one knows about my going there. I won't turn back. I'll be a goatherd. I'll plough. Let my mother look for me. Let her search as long as she likes. Old Goat-beard will never see my face again. But if I cannot find that village, I'll die of hunger. I'll die, and that's the end of it."

The autumn sun was warm. It caressed the rocks, the plane-tree, the leaves. The soil was fresh in the sunlight. A few autumn flowers were already beginning to appear. The asphodel had a bitter scent and glistened with moisture. In autumn the mountains smell of asphodel.

Had he been there one hour or two? He wasn't sure. But the sun had sunk behind the mountain ridge. Some time later the boy stopped muttering to himself and suddenly remembered that he was being pursued. He became frantic. He had forgotten to watch the sun, which had set without his noticing it. Where must he go now, in which direction? A faint goat-track meandered among the rocks. He began to follow it. He ran without heeding the rocks, the bushes and the stones. His weariness had passed. He stopped, looked around for a moment, then ran again.

His feet pounded the soil. As he ran a tiny lizard on a rotten tree-stump caught his eye. The boy felt glad for some reason, but aware of being watched, the lizard disappeared beneath the tree.

The boy stumbled and stopped. He felt dizzy and black spots were dancing before his eyes. The earth seemed to spin round him like a top. His hands and legs were trembling. After looking back a moment he began to run again. Once a flight of partridges rose suddenly nearby and startled him. Any sound scared him and his heart was beating very fast. Hopelessly he glanced back again, drenched in sweat. His knees gave way beneath him and he sank to the ground on a small stony slope. He could smell his own acrid sweat, but mingled with the pleasant scent of flowers. Though he could hardly open his eyes, he raised his head heavily, fearfully, and looked below, where he could barely distinguish a mud roof. His joy was so great that his heart seemed to leap up into his mouth. Smoke curled slowly from the chimney, twisting this way and that, not black but a light purple. Behind him he heard a sound, as of footsteps, and he looked back fearfully. To the left the forest was like a black curtain of rain between sky and earth, threatening to engulf him. He started to talk, no longer muttering now but shouting aloud as he ran away from the forest:

9

"I'll go and tell him . . . I'll say to him . . . I've come to you to be a goatherd and I'll plough your land and sow your crops. I'll say to him that my name is Kara Mistik, Black Mistik. I'll say I have no mother, no father, no Abdi Agha. I'll look after your beasts, I'll say, and I'll plough your fields and be your child, just that. My name isn't Ince Memed, but Kara Mistik. Let my mother weep. Let that infidel Abdi Agha search for me. I'll be their child."

Then he began to sob. The dark forest was still there. As he sobbed he experienced a morbid pleasure from just lamenting at the top of his voice.

As he went down the slope he suddenly stopped weeping. His nose was running and he wiped it on his right sleeve, which became moist.

By the time he reached the courtyard of the house it was dark. Beyond, the shapes of other houses could be seen. He stopped for a moment to think. Was the village the right one? In front of the door sat a long-bearded man, struggling with a saddle which he was mending. When he raised his head the bearded man saw a shadow in the middle of the courtyard. The shadow moved one or two steps towards him and halted. The man paid no attention but busied himself with his work. When it became really too dark to see he stopped working and rose to his feet, looking to his left, where he had seen the shadow earlier. It was still there. He whistled and said: "What are you doing here?"

"I'll be your goatherd, Uncle," the shadow replied. "I'll plough your fields too. I'll do every kind of work for you, Uncle."

The bearded man seized the boy by the arm and dragged him into the house. "Come along, we'll talk about all that later."

A piercing north-east wind was blowing. Memed shivered as if it were going to blow him away.

The old man called to his wife who was inside: "Throw some wood on the fire. The child is shivering."

"Who's that?" asked the woman, surprised.

"One of Allah's guests," replied the old man.

"I've never yet seen a guest of that kind," the woman answered, smiling.

"Well, take a good look at him now."

The woman hastened to fetch an armful of wood which she threw into the hearth. Slowly the fire revived.

The boy crouched close to the wall, to the left of the hearth. She noticed that his head was big, his hair black, bleached here and there almost red by the sun and hanging straight over his forehead into his little face, which was thin and dry. He had huge brown eyes and skin tanned by the sun. He looked about eleven years old. His Turkish breeches had been torn by brushwood as far as the knees, leaving his legs bare. He was bare-footed, too, with blood clotted on his legs. Though the fire was burning bright, he could not stop shivering.

"Child," the woman said, "you're hungry. Wait, I'll bring you some soup."

"I would like it," he declared.

"It will warm you up."

"It may stop my shivering."

The woman began to fill a tin bowl with broth from a large copper pan that stood on the hearth by the fire. The boy's eyes were set on the steaming soup in the pan. She brought the soup, placed it before him and put a wooden spoon in his hand. "Lap it up, boy!"

"I will."

But the man added a warning: "Don't drink so fast, your mouth will burn afterwards."

"It won't burn," the boy replied, smiling. The old man smiled too, but the woman could make no sense of their smiles.

"The soup has put a stop to your shivering, my young lion."

"It's all over now," the boy said as he smiled. The woman smiled too.

The hearth was lined with fresh clay. The roof of the house was of earth too. The ceiling was made of brushwood which, with years of soot, had become a shiny black. The house was divided into two parts. The room beyond was the stable. Through the door came a warm, damp smell of fresh cow-dung, of straw and newly cut branches.

While they were talking the old man's son, daughter and daughter-in-law came in. The boy stared at them, bewildered.

"Why don't you wish a welcome to our guest?" the old man said to his son.

"Welcome, Brother," said the son, very earnestly. "What's new?"

"I'm glad I'm here," replied the boy with the same seriousness. "This is a good place to be." The daughter and daughter-in-law also wished the boy a welcome.

Suddenly, the log on the hearth caught fire and burst into flame.

The boy sat huddled up, not yet at his ease. The man came and sat beside him. The flames from the hearth cast strange shadows. Watching these, the man could understand what was going on in the boy's mind as he stared at the shadows that shifted constantly with the flickering of the flames. When the man turned his eyes away from the shadows, he was smiling. His face was narrow and thin, his beard white and full. His forehead, tanned by the sun, was the colour of copper; and his face shone like red copper in the flickering light of the flames.

As if it had suddenly occurred to him, the man remarked: "Well, guest, what's your name? Didn't they give you one?"

"They call me Ince Memed, Slim Memed," the boy replied. Then he regretted what he had said and bit his lip, lowering his head, ashamed. He had quite forgotten how, on the road, he had said to himself: "I'll say my name is Kara Mistik." He murmured to himself: "Well, it doesn't matter. What a strange idea, when I already have a name of my own. Why should I conceal my name? Who'll recognise me in this village?"

"Bring us our food and let's eat," the man told his daughter-in-law. "We're hungry."

The meal was set in the middle of the room and all the family, including Memed, sat in a circle. As they ate nobody uttered a word. After they had eaten in silence, another armful of wood was thrown on the fire. Right in the centre of the hearth the man set a log so that the flames surrounded it. He always enjoyed doing this. The flames soon encircled his log and it thrilled him to watch this. The woman leaned over and whispered in his ear: "Süleyman, where shall I put the boy's bed?"

"In the big horse's feeding trough," joked Süleyman with his usual warm laugh. "Where else should it be? He'll sleep where we sleep, of course! Who knows how far our guest has travelled to be with us?" He turned towards Memed, who was drowsy from the heat and seemed about to fall asleep.

"Well, guest, are you sleepy?" he asked, laughing.

Memed shook himself as he answered: "No, I'm not sleepy at all."

"Now, Slim Memed," said Süleyman, staring attentively into his eyes, "you've told us nothing. Where are you from, where are you going?"

Rubbing his eyes, which smarted from the smoke, Memed replied: "I've come from Deyirmenoluk. I'm going to that village."

"We know Deyirmenoluk, but what other village do you mean?" Süleyman inquired, somewhat puzzled.

"Dursun's village," answered Memed, not in the least perturbed.

"Which Dursun?" Süleyman insisted.

"He's with Abdi Agha," Memed said and stopped. His eyes seemed to be set on some distant place.

"Well?" questioned Süleyman.

"That's our Agha. Dursun works for him and ploughs his fields." His eyes shone. After a pause: "The other day he caught a young hawk! That's Dursun. Do you know him now, Uncle?"

"I know, I know. And what else?"

"Well, I'm going to his village. Dursun said to me, 'In our village,' he said, 'they don't beat children, they don't force them to plough. Thistles don't grow there either,' he said, 'in our village.' So I'm going there now."

"All right, what's the name of that village? Didn't Dursun tell you?"

Memed remained silent. He pondered for a long while, sucking his thumb, till suddenly he exclaimed: "No, Dursun didn't tell me the name."

"Strange," commented Süleyman.

"Yes, strange," repeated Memed. "We used to plough the fields together, Dursun and I. We would rest every once in a while, seated together on a big stone. 'Ah!' he would say, 'if only you could see our village. The soil is like gold. There's sunshine and pine-trees,' he would say. 'A man who sets out from there on the sea can go anywhere.' Dursun ran away from there. He told me not to tell anyone that he had run away. I didn't even tell my

13

mother." Then, leaning towards Süleyman, he added in a whisper: "You won't tell anyone either, will you, Uncle?"

"Don't be afraid," Süleyman replied. "I won't tell anyone."

The daughter-in-law went outside. Soon she came back with a full sack on her back. She put it down on the floor. When she opened it cotton-bolls poured out, cleaned and quite white. Each one was like a little white cloud. Immediately the whole house was full of the sharp smell of cotton.

"Let's see if you can tease cotton, Slim Memed," she said pleasantly. "Show us what you can do!"

"What's that! As if teasing cotton were work," replied Memed, taking a lapful of the cotton. His skilled hands soon began to work like a machine.

"Slim Memed," the son asked, "how are you going to set about finding that village?"

Memed pulled a wry face to show that the question didn't please him at all. "I'll look around for it," he sighed. "The sea is near that village. I'll search for it."

"Why Slim Memed, the sea's a good fifteen days' walk from here!"

"I'll search for it. I'd rather die than go back to Deyirmenoluk. I'll never go back again. I won't."

"What happened, Slim Memed?" interrupted Süleyman. "Tell us your secret. What has set you on the road?"

Memed's hands stopped. "Uncle Süleyman," he said, "wait, and I'll tell you everything. My father's dead. There's just my mother. No one else at all. I plough Abdi Agha's fields." At this point his eyes filled with tears and a lump seemed to form in his throat. But he checked himself. Otherwise it would all pour out. "For two years I've ploughed his fields. The thistles devour me. They bite me. Those thistles tear at your legs like a mad dog. That's the sort of field I ploughed. Every day Abdi Agha beat me, beat me to death. He beat me again yesterday morning. Until I ached all over. So I ran away from there. I'll go to that village. He won't find me there, Abdi Agha. I'll plough someone's land there. I'll be his goatherd. I'll be his son, if he wishes." He looked straight into Süleyman's eyes.

Memed's heart seemed about to burst. Another word and he would break down. So Süleyman changed the subject.

"Listen to me, Slim Memed, if it's like that you can stay here in my house."

Memed's face flushed. A wave of affection thrilled through him from top to toe.

"The sea is far. You won't find that village easily," said the son.

Meanwhile the cotton had all been teased. In the middle of the floor the insects that had fallen out of it were scurrying hither and thither, unable to escape, little black cotton beetles. By the hearth a bed was prepared for Memed. His eyes were full of sleep and he glanced longingly at the bed. Süleyman had understood Memed's need long ago.

"Tuck in," he said, pointing to the bed. Without a word, Memed crouched down and crawled in, pulling his knees up to his chin. His body ached all over, as if he had been pounded in a mortar.

"I'll be his son. Yes, I will," said Memed secretly to himself. "Let my mother look for me, and Abdi Agha too. Let them all search till the Day of Resurrection. I won't go back."

Two hours before sunrise, the hour when he always went off to the fields, Memed stirred, woke up, rose from his bed and went outside. Sleepily he relieved himself and was suddenly wide awake. He remembered the previous night and white-bearded Süleyman. "This is Süleyman's house," he said to himself. "What would I do if I went to that other village? I'll be Uncle Süleyman's son. I'll stay here. I won't go back."

The cold frosty air made him shiver. He crawled back into bed and pulled his knees up to his chin again. The bed was warm. To-day he knew he could sleep till sunrise. Thinking of this, he fell asleep again.

The sun rose on a frosty morning. The mother took the pan off the fire. The pleasant smell of hot soup filled the whole alcove of the hearth. The son had gone off to the fields long ago. Süleyman had returned to the saddle, resuming his work of the night before.

"Süleyman," called his wife, "the soup's getting cold."

"Is our guest up yet?"

"Leave the child. Poor thing, he must have been very tired yesterday. He's fast asleep."

"Yes, let's not wake him, poor mite. He's exhausted from yesterday."

"What made him run away?" she asked.

"They drove him too hard."

"It's a pity," she said. "And what a pretty child! Infidels, what did they want with such a small mite?"

"Let him stay here as long as he wishes."

Memed stretched himself and woke up. First he rubbed his eyes hard with his two fists, then looked towards the fire. The soup in the open pot was steaming. He turned his head towards the door. A knife-sharp sunbeam stretched through the doorway. He rose from his bed.

"Don't be afraid, Memed," Süleyman reassured him, seeing his fear. "It doesn't matter. Sleep!"

Memed turned to take the copper jug from the hearth and went outside. He washed his face with plenty of water, then went towards Süleyman and began to watch him working on the saddle.

"Come and drink your soup," called the woman again. "It's growing cold."

Süleyman rose, brushing his clothes with his hands, and winked at Memed. "Let's go and drink our soup."

The soup was a broth of milk and crushed wheat. The odours of milk and wheat mingled to produce a pleasant smell. They drank the soup with wooden spoons. Memed liked the soup. "I'll be your son," he repeated.

Süleyman was stuffing hay into the saddle which he had finished. The dry grass slipped easily through his experienced fingers. The autumn sun brought out the bright colours of everything. A fine golden dust fell from the hay as Süleyman worked it. The dust, in the sunlight, scattered in every direction.

"Did he drive you very hard, this Abdi Agha?" asked Süleyman.

Memed was not expecting such a question. He pulled himself together.

" He used to beat me cruelly and even make me plough the thistle fields barefoot. Then there was the frost. That was killing too. And always he'd beat me. Once for a whole month I was unable to get up and go to work. He beats everyone, but he beat me most. Mother said if it hadn't been for Yellow Hodja's amulet, I would have died."

"So it means you want to stay here?"

"What shall I do in that village? It's fifteen days' walk from here. There's the sea, but what of that? There are no thistles there, but there aren't any here either. I'm staying here. Nobody'll find me here, will they? Deyirmenoluk's far away from here, isn't it? They can't find me, can they?"

"You poor thing, Deyirmenoluk is just behind that mountain. Don't you know how you came here?"

Memed was dumbfounded, his eyes wide open. He began to perspire, the sweat streaming off him. All his hopes crashed to the ground. He was about to say something but gulped. In the sky the eagles were wheeling around. He stared at them, then nestled closer to Süleyman. "Perhaps I should go to that village and be that other man's son. If Abdi Agha finds me here, he'll kill me."

"Go to that other village, be that other man's son," replied Süleyman reproachfully.

"How wonderful it would be if I were your son," Memed said ingratiatingly, "but . . ."

"But what?"

"He might find me . . . God forbid! He would make mince-meat of me."

"What can we do?" Süleyman said, lifting his head from his work and staring at Memed. The boy's face was all wrinkled, like a leaf. His big eyes were dull. All the light had gone out of them. Seeing that Süleyman was looking at him, Memed crept a little closer and seized his hand. "Please," he murmured, his eyes full of unspoken desires.

"Don't be afraid."

Memed smiled, a smile of contentment tinged with fear. Süleyman had finished his job. He stood up. "Well, Slim Memed, I've got work to do in the house opposite and must go there. Do whatever you like. Go for a walk in the village."

Memed set off for the village alone. It was a cluster of twenty or twenty-five houses, all built of mud and rough stones set at random one on top of the other. The houses scarcely rose to the height of a man above the ground.

He wandered from one end of the village to the other. The children were playing *köküc*, an Anatolian game, on a manure heap. He saw only one dog, its tail between its legs, creeping fearfully along the foot of a wall. There were dung-heaps all over the village. Till nightfall he went from house to house. Nobody asked where he came from, where he was going. In his own village all the children would swarm round a stranger as soon as they saw him. This village was quite different. It puzzled him.

Returning to the house, he found Süleyman outside. "Well, Slim Memed, you haven't been home all day! What's new?"

"Nothing . . ."

After that Memed roamed about the village for a few more days. He made friends with a few of the boys. He played *köküc*. No one could beat him at it. But Memed didn't boast of his skill. Another boy would surely have boasted; he just shrugged his shoulders, as if to say it was child's play. That's why the other children didn't mind his winning.

Then the autumn rains of the Taurus began. Just as the autumn leaves fall, so do the Taurus rains, in great drops. It thundered. From the mountain above the village stones rolled down the slopes to the highland plain. The mountain was a forest, with huge trees that grew in close and tangled thickets.

One day Memed came to Süleyman and said: "Uncle Süleyman, how long will this last? I'm bored, eating your bread for nothing!"

"Wait a while, what's the hurry? We'll find work for you, my boy."

A few days later the rain stopped and the sun shone again on the wet stones and rocks, on trees and earth. The earth began to steam and the steam mixed with the smell of manure and drifted into the village. From time to time silvery clouds concealed the sun.

Memed was seated on a stone by the door of the house while Süleyman tried on him a pair of new sandals he had made of rawhide. The sandals were damp, with a purple down on the leather, so that you could see that they were made of the skin of a young bull. Memed was delighted with them.

Süleyman stood beside Memed and watched him as he tied them. The boy's hands were used to the tying of sandals, that was clear. He knew how to pull the laces tight and to knot them behind the leg.

"Young Memed, you're a master at tying sandals," said Süleyman.

"I can even sew them, Uncle Süleyman," replied Memed, raising his head and smiling. "But you've sewn these well." He rose to his feet and put all his weight on each foot in turn once or twice, then walked ten or fifteen steps away and returned. He looked again at the sandals in admiration. "They fit my feet perfectly."

They set off along the road together. Memed's eyes were constantly on his new sandals. Sometimes he walked fast, sometimes he stopped and examined his feet carefully, sometimes he stopped and stroked the down on the sandals.

Süleyman fully shared Memed's joy. "It looks as if you like them, Memed?"

"They fit me well. I love such sandals," Memed replied.

"If you'd gone to that village," said Süleyman, "no one there would have made such sandals for you."

"Don't they wear sandals in that village?" asked Memed, half serious, half teasing.

It wasn't quite clear whether Süleyman had understood the teasing or not. "Well, they wear shoes, not sandals."

"I see."

Walking steadily, they left the village. All of a sudden Memed brightened up. The fields stretched away to the foot of the other mountain. There were no thistles, but still the fields were not much good, full of stones. Memed stopped a moment and asked: "Where are we going, Uncle Süleyman?"

"Just for a walk."

Memed asked no more questions as they went ahead together. His new sandals became caked with mud, which he cursed under his breath.

The village lay far behind, out of sight except for one or two twists of smoke.

"Listen to me, Memed," said Süleyman. "This is where you will pasture the goats. You can go as far as the other side there, but don't cross the ridge of that red hill. Your village lies on the other side and they'll catch you and take you away if they see you."

"I won't go. It's well you told me."

As they returned, the clouds in the sky were quite white. The threshing floors, each one a deep green circle, were scattered among the stony fields. A few isolated snails could be seen clinging to the long grass.

"Tell me, Ince Memed, did that goat-bearded Abdi treat you very badly? "

Memed stopped. So did Süleyman. Memed glanced again at his new sandals.

"Let's sit here," suggested Süleyman.

"Yes," said Memed as he began to explain. "Listen, Uncle Süleyman. My father was dead and Abdi Agha took what little we had away from us. If my mother complained, he beat her cruelly and would beat me too. Once he tied me to a tree and left me there in the middle of the plain, far from the village. I stayed tied to the tree for two days, till Mother came and freed me. But for her the wolves would have torn me to pieces."

"So that's how it is, Memed?" sighed Süleyman as he rose to go. Memed also stood up. Süleyman repeated his advice: "Do as I tell you, Memed, and never go beyond that red-brown hill. Somebody might see you and report it to old Goat-beard, and then they would take you away from us."

"God forbid," exclaimed Memed.

Next morning Memed woke up very early and rose from his bed just as dawn was beginning to break. He went to Süleyman's bed. The old man was snoring, fast asleep. Memed poked him to rouse him.

"What's up? Is that you, Memed?" Süleyman was very drowsy.

"It's Memed," the boy said proudly. "It's time to go. I'll drive the goats."

Süleyman rose immediately. His eyes searched for his wife. She had been up and about for a while and was outside, milking the cow. He called to her: "Be quick and get Memed's food ready."

Washing the milk off her hands in a big pail, the woman replied: "It can wait. I'll milk the rest in the evening."

In no time she had prepared Memed's food-bag for the day and set before him a bowl of soup from the cauldron that was simmering over the fire. Memed gobbled it down, fastened the bag of food round his waist in the twinkling of an eye, and was off, herding the goats ahead of him. Snatching his old cap off his head, he threw it after the goats. "Get on there! This is fun!"

"Good luck to you," called Süleyman after him. Memed kept turning round and looking back at him until both he and the goats were out of Süleyman's sight.

"Well, well! What a child!" murmured Süleyman to himself.

"Troubled again," said his wife, as she came out to him. "What's worrying you now?"

"See what goat-bearded Abdi has done to this child," he sighed. "Still a babe and his heart broken. I used to know his father. He was a quiet, inoffensive man. But look at the state of the child! Sick of his life, he rushes off into the mountains, among the birds of prey and wolves!"

"Poor Süleyman, you take everything too much to heart. Come in and drink your soup."

It was evening and all the men had returned from the fields except Memed. The sun sank and he was still missing.

From next door Zeynep called to Memed's mother: "Deuneh! Deuneh! Hasn't Memed come yet?"

"He hasn't come, Sister," Deuneh moaned. "He hasn't come yet, my Memed. What shall I do now?"

Zeynep repeated her question to Deuneh perhaps ten times. Now she insisted: "Go and ask Abdi Agha," counselled Zeynep. "Perhaps he's gone to the Agha's house. Go and ask, Sister. All these things happening to you, poor Deuneh!"

"As if I didn't have enough troubles already! If Memed had reached the village he would have come home right away, without stopping anywhere. He wouldn't stay a moment at Abdi Agha's. But let me go and see . . ."

There was no moon in the sky. It was cloudy and even the stars could not be seen. Deuneh set off in the dark for Abdi Agha's house, feeling her way blindly in the narrow alley. From a hand-sized window a tiny light glimmered. She stopped, her heart beating wildly, and gulped once or twice. Her hands and feet trembled, her teeth chattered. Yet she managed to force some sort of sound out of her throat, a kind of death-rattle. "Abdi Agha! Abdi Agha! I kiss the soles of your feet, Abdi Agha! My Memed isn't home yet. Is he with you?"

From within a heavy voice answered: "Who's there? What do you want, woman, at this time of the night?"

"I beseech you, Abdi Agha," she repeated. "My Memed hasn't come home. Is he with you?"

"May God curse you! Is it you again, Deuneh?" the voice boomed.

"Yes, Agha."

"Come in. Let's see what you want."

She entered the house, bowed down with fear. Abdi Agha was squatting cross-legged on a divan by the fire. The velvet cap on his head hung down over his left ear. On the road, in the hills, in the village, it was always on his head, to show how pious a Moslem he was. He was wearing a silk-embroidered shirt and playing with the big amber beads of his rosary. A long sharp face, small and strangely blue-green eyes, pink cheeks—such was Abdi Agha.

"Now, what do you want? Speak!" he repeated.

Deuneh, her hands clasped beseechingly as she leaned forward, stood there all tense. "Agha—My Memed hasn't yet come home from the fields. I came to see if he was with you."

Abdi Agha stood up. "He hasn't returned, eh? The scoundrel! And my oxen?" He hurried to the door, his shirt-tails flapping in the draught. He bawled outside: "Dursun, Osman, Ali, where are you?"

"Here, Agha," answered three voices from three different directions.

"Come, quick!"

Three figures appeared out of the darkness. One of them, looking about forty, was Dursun, a great lump of a fellow. The other two were fifteen-year-old boys.

"Get off to the fields immediately and look for that young scoundrel Memed. Make sure that you find the oxen. Don't come back here before you have found them. Do you understand?"

"We were also wondering about him," said Dursun. "What can have happened to Memed? He hasn't come, we were saying. We'll go and look."

Deuneh began to sob.

"Shut up!" shouted Abdi Agha in disgust. "We'll see what troubles this scoundrel of yours has brought on us. If anything has happened to the oxen, I'll break every bone in his body. I'll grind his bones to powder."

Dursun, Osman and Ali disappeared in the darkness. Deuneh ran after them.

"Don't come, Sister," Dursun called back to her. "We'll find him. Perhaps the plough broke, or the yoke. He may be

23

afraid to come back. We'll bring him home. Go back, Sister Deuneh."

The woman returned to her hovel and the three men disappeared again in the darkness. Their steps could be heard dying away in the night. Their feet were accustomed to the road and they knew which way to go. First they came to a small stony field, then crossed an area of sharp rocks, beyond which they sat down to rest, all three in a row, close together, leaning against each other. For a long while they stayed quiet. It was very dark and there was no other sound but the chirping of insects. Dursun was the first to speak, not to anyone in particular, just into the night. "What can have happened to the boy? Where's he gone?"

"Who knows?" said Osman.

"Do you know what Memed said to me?" asked Ali. "He said, 'I'm going to that village. Let them kill me, I won't stay,' he said."

"He can't have run away. He would have never done such a stupid thing," said Dursun.

"If he has, all the better," Ali burst out.

"He's done the right thing," agreed Osman.

"Our life is worse than death," continued Ali.

"Why don't we too go off to the Chukurova?" exclaimed Osman.

"The Chukurova is near, with its soft earth," said Dursun. "In our village you work hard, but there you're your own master, with nobody to interfere, nobody to spy on you. If you take a look at the fields you would think that a cloud had sunk into the black earth, there's so much cotton. Gather it and you get threepence a pound. In one summer you can get five times what Abdi Agha gives in a year. There's a city there, Adana, all of clear glass. It sparkles day and night, just like the sun. You walk in the alleys between the houses, they call them streets, and it's all glass. It's as clean as can be. Trains come and go. On the sea, ships as big as villages go to the other end of the world. Everything shines like the sun, bathed in light. If you look at it just once, you can't take your eyes away. If it's money you want, it pours like a flood in the Chukurova. All you've got to do is work."

Osman suddenly interrupted him: "How big is the earth?"

"Huge," replied Dursun,

They rose to resume their search. Dursun was still talking about his village.

After the rocks they came through a patch of thistles that grew so thick that their legs were torn by them.

"The field that Memed was ploughing should be about here," shouted Osman, who was ahead of the other two.

"I don't know these parts—do you?" replied Dursun.

"It's here," called Ali from the right.

"Is this it?" asked Dursun doubtfully.

"Of course it's here. Can't you smell the newly-ploughed earth?"

Dursun stopped and took a deep breath. "You're right."

Osman was walking ahead and called back: "My feet are sinking into ploughed soil."

"Mine too," said Ali.

"Wait, I'm coming." They stopped till Dursun caught up with them.

"Now we must try and find the spot he was ploughing," he said.

"That's easy," answered Osman. "We'll find it."

"I'm cold," grumbled Ali. But Dursun interrupted his complaints: "Let's find him first."

"The furrows stop here," Osman shouted. "He didn't plough at all to-day."

Ali felt around with his foot, walking along the edge of the ploughed field several times. "Memed hasn't ploughed to-day. The furrows just stop like that."

"Has anything happened to him?" asked Dursun in a voice that expressed anxiety and surprise.

"Nothing can happen to him," replied Osman. "He's the devil's own brother."

"Uncle Dursun, you know him. Nothing much could harm him," repeated Ali.

"Allah grant it's true! Memed is a good boy, a poor orphan," said Dursun.

They stopped in the middle of the ploughed field. Osman began to collect sticks and branches and, while Ali talked with Dursun, lit a fire. They all three sat down beside it, to consider all that might have happened. Memed might, for instance, have fainted, or been attacked by a wolf. Or a thief might have come and stolen the oxen. There were other possibilities besides, and they considered them one by one. But there was no particular possibility that struck them as more probable than the others.

The flames of the fire flickered on Dursun's face as he smiled contentedly.

The fire burned and died down. A few embers still glowed like cats' eyes. They were all three bored and Ali began to sing a sorrowful folk-song. The tune went out into the night:

> "Sitting outside my door, harnessing the cart,
> I'm troubled to-day and my heart's desolate.
> Bring me holy books and I'll swear on them
> That I'll greet nobody, only you."

They shivered. Osman collected more branches to feed the fire. Dursun and Ali went off to gather brushwood which they stacked near the fire.

"What do we do now?" asked Osman.

"If we go back to the village empty-handed," answered Dursun, "Abdi Agha will be furious. Let's lie down here. In the morning we'll search again."

"We'll never find Memed. He's gone to that village, he has, wherever it may be. He spoke only of escaping to it."

Dursun smiled.

Leaving Ali to tend the fire, the other two curled up. Ali lay watching the flames. Once he lifted his head and looked away, searching the darkness, then, muttering to himself: "He's gone. Let him go. He's done well. He's gone to the city of glass, to that warm soft earth. He's done well. Let him go if he wants."

When Osman woke up, Ali left him to watch. Putting a lump of turf under his head, Ali said: "He's gone there, hasn't he, Osman? Memed has gone to the place that Dursun spoke of."

With the first light of dawn the three woke up. The eastern sky was beginning to blush, tinging the edges of clouds, which soon turned white. A breeze blew, chilly but pleasant, the dawn wind. Soon they could distinguish things in the half-light. Beyond the ploughed land an expanse of thistles spread to the horizon where the sun was rising. In the middle of the field the three rose clumsily to their feet. They stood in the morning light, with all the shadows spreading towards the west. They stretched their arms, then squatted to relieve themselves. Stretching again, they wandered across the field that Memed had ploughed.

"Look at the tracks," said Osman. "The oxen have passed here with the plough behind. Let's follow them."

They paused for a long talk. Here a pair of oxen had rested on the ground. The huge imprints of their bodies were still intact, like a mould. You could see that they had been lying there with the plough still yoked to them.

The newly risen sun was beginning to warm the earth. Leaving the thistles, the three men came to running water. Ali suddenly let out a cry. The other two turned to him and saw the oxen standing harnessed, the yoke round their necks, the plough behind them. One of them was violet-red, the other brick-red. The two were all skin and bone.

Osman's face had turned pale. "Something must have happened to the boy. If Memed had run away, he wouldn't have left the two oxen harnessed like that."

"Nothing's happened to him," retorted Ali. "It's his cunning. He's left them like that on purpose. He's gone to that village, Memed has."

"That village, that village . . ." shouted Osman angrily. "You too, you talk only of that village! Are you mad?"

"Don't start quarrelling," said Dursun, smiling.

They drove the oxen ahead of them. When they returned to the village the morning was well advanced. A slight mist was rising from the mountain on the other side of the valley.

A whole crowd of children and women, old and young, had gathered round Deuneh. When they saw the harnessed oxen approaching they all rose to their feet. No one spoke as they stared at the oxen.

Deuneh uttered a cry and rushed forward. "What's happened to my child, Dursun?"

"We just found the oxen harnessed like this in a glen."

"My child, my Memed," she cried, beating her breast. "My poor, innocent child."

"Sister, nothing has happened to him," Dursun tried to comfort her. "I'll look for him and find him."

But Deuneh was lost in her grief. Shaking convulsively, she

27

sank into the dust and lay there moaning. Her face, eyes and hair were soon white with dust, till her tears caked her grimy face.

The crowd stood still, staring at Deuneh and at the oxen. Two women came forward and raised her from the dust. Deuneh was almost unconscious. Her head hung like a corpse's on her left shoulder. Putting their arms through hers, they led her home.

When Deuneh had gone the crowd began to break up and move. Old Jennet was the first to speak. Her face was long, all wrinkled. They called her "horse-faced Jennet." She was very tall, with thin fingers like stalks. "Poor Deuneh, what's become of her son?"

Elif, a short woman, well known for her gloomy views, affirmed with conviction: "Memed has met his death. Otherwise he would have returned."

Her words ran through the crowd: "He's met his death."

Elif then added: "Perhaps his father's enemies have killed him."

"His father had no enemies," replied Jennet. "Ibrahim wouldn't have hurt an ant."

Wearing a white head-cloth or a many-coloured 'kerchief, a purple fez and a string of copper coins across the forehead, the women swayed, repeating everything in chorus: "Ibrahim wouldn't hurt an ant."

The crowd heaved. From every mouth rose the cry: "Poor Memed, the poor orphan! May that infidel be struck blind!"

Then a suggestion rippled through the crowd. It wasn't clear who first made it: "Deuneh should go and look where the eagles are hovering. They always hover over their prey."

"He's fallen into the spring."

The whole crowd then turned towards the woman who had just said this. All was still as the crowd seemed to freeze, then came to life again. "He's fallen into the spring."

The crowd began to shift towards the east. Barefooted children trotted ahead, behind them the barefooted women. The children were the first to enter the thistles, then came the women. The children's legs were streaming with blood, but they continued to run ahead. The women cursed the thistles: "May their roots rot . . ."

When they emerged from among the thistles they reached the rocks. Tired, their legs bleeding, the children hung behind. Now the women went ahead. By the time they reached the plane-tree all were exhausted. The great plane was rustling. Suddenly hearing the roar of water, they stopped. After resting a while they rushed towards the pool. The women, side by side, formed a circle. The water frothed and boiled up from under the big rock. To the left of the rock a wide pool had formed. Two or three leaves had fallen on to the surface of the bubbling water. They did not float away but whirled in the midst of the foam.

For a long time they all gazed at the pool without uttering a sound.

"If the child had fallen in here, by now he'd have come to the surface," said old Jennet.

The crowd stirred again. Heads nodded. "A body wouldn't stay down there. He'd have come up."

Tired, exhausted, hopeless, miserable, swaying this way and that, the crowd turned back. The children hung behind, playing, absorbed in their games. But now the crowd no longer moved as a single unit. They went one by one, each with head bowed.

That day Deuneh took to her bed and wept. She had a burning fever. The young girls of the village nursed her and after some days she rose from her sick-bed, her eyes all bloodshot. She tied a white cloth round her forehead as a sign of mourning.

A rumour soon began to spread through the village: "Deuneh refuses to eat or drink. She sits by the spring without moving an eyelid, staring at the water, waiting to see if her son's body will appear."

It was true. Every morning Deuneh rose at dawn, went to the spring and stared all day at the water. After ten days of this, utterly exhausted, she shut herself up in her house. Then another idea entered her mind. Again she rose at dawn, but now climbed on to the roof and stared all day at the sky. Whenever she saw a flight of eagles hovering afar, she set off at once in that direction. Sometimes the eagles were very far away, perhaps circling over Yaghmurtepe, a whole day's journey from the village, but Deuneh went there all the same.

One night there was a knock on Deuneh's door and someone called her: "Sister Deuneh, open! It's Dursun."

In hope and fear she opened the door. "Come in, Brother Dursun. Memed was fond of you."

Dursun sat down on Deuneh's bed. "Listen to me, Sister," he said, "my heart tells me that your son is alive. He must have taken it into his head to run off somewhere. I'll find him."

Deuneh threw herself down at his feet. "Have you any news of him?"

"No, Sister, but my heart tells me he isn't dead. I'll look for him. I'll find him."

"My only hope is in you, Brother," said Deuneh as he left the house. "If only I knew he was alive. I don't want anything else in the world."

IV

<hr/>

Summer came with all its scorching heat. The crops were being harvested. In the Chukurova they call this season the "yellow heat." In the foothills of the Taurus it is known as the "white heat." The white heat had indeed begun.

Memed was never treated as a hired goatherd but as the son of the house. Süleyman loved him like his own soul. But a strange mood had lately possessed the boy, usually so active and so full of joy. His lips were sealed, as if he were troubled. Before, he used to sing songs all day; now he sang no longer. It had been his habit to take the goats to the richest pastures, the greenest woods, and, when a goat stopped nibbling for a moment or seemed listless, Memed would notice immediately and find a way to encourage it. Now he let the goats go free to graze while he sat in the shade of a tree or a rock and day-dreamed, with his chin resting on his crook. From time to time, unable to bear the tension within, he talked to himself: "Little mother, my little mother, who is reaping your wheat now? Infidel Abdi Agha! Our wheat will dry up and wither. Who is reaping the wheat, little mother, now that I'm not there?"

He would stare up at the sky and the clouds, the fields, the ripening crops. "Stork's-eye field must be dry by now. Who'll harvest it? Dear mother, how will you harvest it all by yourself?"

At night sleep no longer came to him as easily. He would turn restlessly on his bed, all his thoughts concentrated on Stork's-eye field. "Its crops dry up so quickly. Nothing will be saved, not a seed, if they're late."

In the morning, when Memed rose to go to his work, his ribs would still be aching. He would herd the goats in front of him, allowing them to scatter, each one going its own different way. What did he care? He wasn't even watching. He would then remember Süleyman's smiling face, his eyes full of affection. This made Memed ashamed and he would stop dreaming, gather the goats together and herd them to better pastures. But Memed would soon be troubled again and sink to the ground. If the earth were hot he would not notice it. Looking around, he might see that it was already evening, with the sun about to set, but he would then herd the scattered goats together and, instead of returning to the village, drive them towards the red slope, its summit still lit by the last rays of the setting sun. Leaving the goats at the foot of the hill, he would climb to the top and discover a plain beyond, with the evening mists settling above the ground. This was the plain of the thistles. He couldn't see as far as Deyirmenoluk from the red hill. The village lay behind a ridge that concealed it like a curtain, a grey mound of earth. All the grass on the plain seemed ready to burn, it was so dry. Remembering his duties, Memed would scold himself. What had Süleyman said? "Don't cross the hill!" There was not a soul to be seen beyond the red hill, which made Memed all the more angry. He would rush back to the foot of the hill, and it would then be very late before at last he managed to herd all the scattered goats together, returning to the village only after dark. When Süleyman asked him why he had stayed so late, Memed would invent a lie: "I found good pasture and couldn't drive the goats away."

One day he rose very early and went as usual into the goatshed. The night had been hot and stifling. The goatshed exhaled a smell of rot. He drove the goats out of the shed and herded them off. Sometimes, long before dawn, a part of the eastern sky grows red. Soon the edges of the clouds are tinged with gold as the dawn breaks. Memed looked towards the east. To-day was just such a day.

Suddenly he felt light-hearted, as free as a bird. The breeze of the dawn began to blow in little waves, as if licking his face.

His heart was pounding as he drove the goats in the direction of the red hill. The herd trotted ahead in a cloud of dust. Reaching the foot of the hill, Memed brought the herd to a halt. He was confused. The goats scattered in all directions as he sat down on the ground, resting his chin on his crook. For a long while he pondered. Once he started moodily, wanting to drive the goats towards the hill. Then he changed his mind, sat down again and

was lost in thought. For a while his head rested on his hands as one
of the goats licked his neck and hands. Memed didn't stir. The
goat stopped and went off. The sunlight seemed to penetrate
everything; the mountains and the rocks, the trees and the plants
seemed about to melt and turn to light.

His hands fell away from his face. When he opened his eyes
they were flooded with light and he was dazzled. He couldn't bear
the light, but his eyes soon grew accustomed to it and he rose,
tired and listless. Slowly he herded the goats together, drove them
towards the hill, till they went over the ridge. Sheltering his eyes
with his hand, he gazed into the distance. It was as if the boughs of
the huge plane-tree had caught his eye. His heart missed a beat.
Behind the hill lay the plain and between the thistle-infested
plateau of Deyirmenoluk and this plain there rose a sharp grey
ridge. This time he drove the goats towards the foot of the ridge.
In front of him two small birds were flying low. Up in the sky he
saw only one bird. Apart from that, all was still. In the distance a
white cloud rose from the earth. All at once, below, at the foot of
the ridge, Memed noticed a small field. In the middle of the field
a tiny black figure bent down, then rose again. Now Memed drove
the goats in that direction. His manner was still listless, heavy,
tired. As he approached the field he recognised the reaper, old
"Beet-root" Hüsük. Hüsük hadn't yet noticed the goats or Memed,
but continued to swing his sickle while Memed let the goats wander freely till they came to the edge of the field. Then they rushed
into it from all sides with a great rustling and crunching. Hüsük
saw them at last and went mad with rage and angrily hurled his
sickle at them. In the wake of the sickle he rushed at the goats,
cursing with all his might. Memed stood still and watched him.
With a thousand and one difficulties, huffing and puffing, Hüsük
was herding the goats out of the cornfield when he saw the boy just
standing still and watching him. He realised that the boy must be
the goatherd, and it made him terribly angry. He left the goats,
picked up his sickle and went straight for the boy, cursing hard:
"You son of a whore who let you be fathered by a stallion! Your
goats run amok in the corn and you just stand there looking at
them. Let me get at you, you son of a worthless father and a whore
of a mother!"

Memed didn't stir as the old man, thinking he might not be

33

able to catch up with the boy if he tried to escape, picked up a handful of stones to throw at him. But Memed still made no effort to escape. Hüsük seized him by the arm and swung the back of the sickle at the boy's head, but his hand stopped in mid-air and he let the boy's arm fall. "Memed! Is it you, child? Everyone thinks you're dead." His breath nearly choked him and he sank to the ground. Sweat streamed off his red neck and face. Then all the goats rushed into the corn again. "Go and get those goats out of my field," Hüsük ordered.

It was only then that Memed, who had stood still as a statue, at last ran into the corn and drove the goats out of the field. Then he came and sat by Hüsük.

"Memed, boy, they've looked for you everywhere. They thought you were drowned. You've almost killed your mother. Haven't you worried about her?"

Memed hunched his shoulders, resting his chin on his crook, but said nothing.

"Those goats, whose are they?" asked Hüsük.

Memed remained silent.

"I'm talking to you, Memed. Whose goats are they?"

"Süleyman's, from Kesme village," murmured Memed, hardly opening his mouth.

"Süleyman's a good man," commented Hüsük. Then he added: "You young fool, if you intended to go you should have told your mother about it. You had had enough of Abdi's shameless treatment. All right, but tell your mother before you go, then go wherever you like."

At the mention of Abdi's name, Memed seized Hüsük's hand. "Whatever happens, Uncle Hüsük, don't tell anyone I'm Uncle Süleyman's goatherd. If Abdi hears, he'll come and fetch me. He'll beat me to death."

"No one will do you any harm. Can't a boy even tell his mother? Poor thing, she almost died of worry for you . . ."

Hüsük stopped reproaching Memed. He rose without looking at the boy and went back to reaping his corn. He worked fast. Memed could hear the rhythmical swish of his sickle.

Hüsük continued to reap without raising his head. Sometimes, when his back ached, he stood up, arms akimbo, and looked into the distance. Then he resumed his reaping. He seemed to have forgotten Memed, who remained on the edge of the field, motionless as he watched the reaper.

Day was drawing to its close. The shadows cast by the sun were lengthening. Memed glanced at the sun. It would soon be red. The grass of the meadow was now partly in the light, partly in shadow, with flashes of brightness moving over it in ripples.

Dragging his feet, Memed moved closer to Hüsük, who continued to reap with the same haste. He stopped in front of Hüsük, his heart pounding. Hearing the sound of Memed's feet, Hüsük raised his head. In the evening light his face was darkened by the sweat. Their eyes met. Tired, Hüsük looked deep into Memed's eyes, into his very soul. Memed lowered his eyes to the ground, took a couple of steps towards Hüsük and seized his hands. "If you love God and His Prophet, Uncle Hüsük, don't tell my mother or anyone else that you've seen me." He then let go of Hüsük's hands abruptly and ran off without once looking back.

By the time he reached the red hill the sun had set. He was drenched with sweat, both pleased and despondent, feeling a conflict in his heart. From the foot of the red hill he glanced back at the little field. He could just make out a slight movement in the middle of the field. Then he climbed the hill and went his way.

When Hüsük reached the village he smiled at all those whom he met, as if he had some important secret which he would keep to himself. He stopped in front of each one in turn and just smiled. No one could make out what had happened to the old man. He went to Deuneh's house and found her standing by the door. When she saw Hüsük looking at her and smiling, she didn't know what to think; he was a man who seldom smiled and never went to Deuneh's or any other house, only from his field to his home, from his home to his field. In any other villager his present behaviour would have attracted no attention. But when Hüsük had no work to do he would sit on a straw mat in front of his hut all by himself, without talking to anyone, carving finely-decorated wooden spoons, spindles, mugs and rosary-beads. Now he stopped before Deuneh's house, smiling all the while without taking his eyes off her, but saying nothing. Nor did Deuneh know what to say to him. After hovering about him for a while, she greeted him: "Welcome, Hüsük Agha, come and sit down."

He seemed not to hear her and went on smiling.

"Hüsük Agha, come and sit down," Deuneh repeated.

He stopped smiling. "Deuneh! Deuneh!" he murmured very slowly, just standing there.

She looked at him expectantly.

"Deuneh, I want a reward for good news."

Deuneh half smiled, though frightened. "Your good news is welcome, Hüsük Agha."

" I saw your son to-day, Deuneh," said Hüsük.

Deuneh was unable to utter a sound. Had she been struck at that moment, not a drop of blood would have been able to flow from her wound.

"Your son came up to me to-day. He's grown taller and gained weight."

"Your words are like honey, Hüsük Agha," she murmured. "May you be rewarded for the good tidings that you bear." Then, haltingly, "Is it true what you're saying, Hüsük Agha? Bless you for your words, your dear words. I thank you, Hüsük Agha."

Then Hüsük sat down and explained to Deuneh exactly how it all happened. Deuneh couldn't stand still but paced up and down as he spoke.

Soon the news was all over the village. Men and women, old and young, the whole village thronged around the door of Deuneh's house. The moonlight shone down on the mud roofs and the people swarming in front of her house.

A murmur that grew louder and louder rose from the crowd. All at once the uproar subsided. Not a sound could be heard. All heads turned to the south. A rider was approaching. The brass on the horse's harness glistened in the moonlight as the rider drew near. The crowd scattered and he rode into the middle of it before halting.

"Deuneh! Deuneh!" he bawled.

From the crowd a woman's voice answered weakly: "Yes, Abdi Agha?"

"Is it true what I've heard, Deuneh?"

Deuneh came and stood by the horse's head. "Hüsük saw him. He came and told me."

"Where's Hüsük?" Abdi Agha roared.

The crowd stirred. "He's not here."

"Isn't he there in the crowd?"

"If all hell broke loose he would never stir from his house."

"Go and fetch Hüsük," ordered the Agha.

Until Hüsük came not a murmur rose from the crowd. All remained silent as the grave.

When they brought him Hüsük was wearing only his white underpants and a shirt. He was struggling between two men who held his arms tightly. "What do you want with me at this time of night? What's the trouble? God curse you for a lot of cuckolds!"

"I called for you, Hüsük," said Abdi Agha.

Hüsük contained his anger somewhat. "You shameless bastards, why didn't you tell me the Agha wanted me?" He then turned towards Abdi. "Excuse me, Agha."

"So you've seen Deuneh's son, have you, Hüsük?"

"I explained it all to Deuneh."

"Now tell me."

As Hüsük began to explain the crowd pressed closer in a ring around them. Without forgetting any detail, Hüsük told how he had seen Memed, how he had almost struck him down at first with his sickle. Abdi Agha was in a rage.

"So Süleyman takes my men away from my own door to be his goatherds! I've had enough of his tricks already. So it's Süleyman from Kesme village, eh?"

"The same," replied Hüsük.

"I'll go and fetch him to-morrow," Abdi Agha roared at Deuneh. He rode off on his horse. The crowd murmured behind him.

The next day Abdi Agha took off at a gallop and drew rein only at Süleyman's door. "Süleyman! Süleyman!"

The old man was inside. He came out and, when he saw Abdi Agha, his face turned grey. Abdi Agha leaned down from the horse towards him. "Süleyman, have you no shame? How dare you take my men from my own door? Have you no pride? Does one take a man from Abdi's very door? Has such a thing ever happened before? If I didn't respect your white beard . . ."

"Get down from your horse at least, Agha! Dismount and come inside. I'll tell you everything."

"I wouldn't even enter your house," replied Abdi Agha. "Where's the boy? Tell me where I'll find him!"

"Don't take the trouble, Agha. I'll go and fetch him in a moment."

"Trouble, you fool! Show me where the boy is!"

"All right, Agha, let's go." Süleyman set off, walking ahead of the horse.

Until they reached the herd of goats neither of them uttered a word. They found Memed seated on a rock, deep in thought. When he saw them he rose and came towards them, not at all surprised to see Abdi Agha. His eyes met Süleyman's. Süleyman lowered his head, as if to signify that he was helpless. Abdi Agha spurred his horse a couple of paces towards Memed. "Go ahead, in front of me."

Without a word Memed stepped forward and began to walk. His head was sunk between his shoulders.

About midday, Memed in front and Abdi Agha behind, they came to the village. On the way Abdi Agha asked nothing and Memed said nothing. But Memed was always afraid that the Agha would drive the horse forward and trample him down. He knew his temper from experience. They came to Deuneh's door and stopped.

"Deuneh! Deuneh! Take your dog of a son." As Deuneh came out, the Agha turned the horse's head. With a cry Deuneh embraced her son.

Immediately all the villagers knew about it. Slowly the crowd collected in a ring, with Memed in the centre. They all asked Memed where he had been.

But Memed hung his head and wouldn't open his mouth. The crowd grew steadily.

V

Memed threw the last remaining sheaves on to the threshing-floor.
It had rained during the harvest and the long stalks were clinging
together. A coal-black dust rose from the stalks. Since early morning, without a break, Memed had been hurling the sheaves on to
the floor and was unrecognisable, his face black with sweat and
dirt. Only his teeth gleamed white. He threw down the last sheaf;
the pile now covered the middle of the floor.

Around the threshing-floor there remained a damp ring of faded
green. Breathless, Memed went and lay down in the sun. Columns
of ants were marching through the stubble. For a while he lay with
his face upturned, his eyes shaded by his hands.

He had been working for days. First he had reaped all alone.
The wheat of Stork's-eye field was full of thistles. Then, for the
threshing, he and his mother had worked to bind the sheaves. For
days he had now been driving the threshing-sledge until he was all
skin and bone, his face wrinkled, the skin drawn, his eyes sunk
in their sockets, his cheeks hollow.

A little farther off the horse was crunching noisily, almost too
weak to stand, its ribs sticking out. It was an old beast. In the
middle of its back it had a sore which never healed, exuding pus
and blood and coated with dust and chaff. Huge black flies
swarmed over the horse's eyes and sores.

It was high morning. Memed rolled over, on to his side, streaming with sweat. He wiped his face with his hand and shook off a
handful of sweat black with dirt.

The stubble in the fields glistened so bright in the sun that he
could not open his eyes without being dazzled. He was exhausted.
From where he lay he looked once or twice between the sheaves at
the horse.

Four or five storks walked around in a nearby field. He stared at them. Then he cut across the path of an advancing army of ants with his hand. The ants simply crawled over it. He made a desperate effort and sat up. But he rested his head on his right knee and was soon lost in his dreams again. With his hands on the ground he slowly pushed himself up. He could feel the ants crawling on his face and neck and brushed them off. The horse, standing near some dust-covered blackberry brambles, was licking one of its fore-legs. He went up to the horse and pulled it away.

The huge blue flowers of the thistles were open, swaying in the breeze.

With great difficulty he harnessed the horse to the sledge, but the tired animal could no longer drag the sledge over the swollen sheaves so as to crush them. Memed got down from the sledge and tried to lead the horse by hand over the sheaves, but the beast kept stumbling and falling on to the crushed sheaves. Memed felt a great pity for the horse, which was breathing so heavily that its chest and ribs rose and fell. Its flanks, back and rump were blackened with caked dirt and flecked with foam. Memed was likewise bathed in sweat that streamed from every pore of his body and made his eyes smart. His breath had the damp smell of mildewed wheat. After driving around the threshing floor for a while, the stalks were flattened out and at last it was now a little easier to drive round. Under the sledge the stalks crackled.

By noon the sheaves had been well crushed and were shining, no longer black. Now, from beneath the sledge, there rose a fine golden-yellow dust of chaff which tickled his nostrils with a smell of burning.

Far away a man was stacking his wheat. Beyond, a couple of others could be seen driving their sledge. But there was no other sign of life on the whole vast plain.

In the fields the stalks of the stubble were long. A harvesting machine cuts the stalks of the corn towards the bottom, leaving hardly any stubble in the field. When the wheat is harvested by hand, however, only the ears are taken and long stalks of stubble remain. Beyond the stubble the thistles could be seen spreading far and wide.

Memed's tongue and mouth were dry. In the heat the horse's head hung down almost to its hoofs as it plodded on wearily.

Memed, on the sledge, was lost in thought, looking neither to left nor to right. The storks had now ventured to the edge of the threshing-floor. Memed seemed to have fallen asleep. Sometimes the horse nuzzled its head among the sheaves and began to chew, but without much appetite, letting the stalks drop from its mouth. Memed took no notice of anything. The sun beat down on his head. Once he rose to his feet and looked searchingly in the direction of the village. There was no one in sight. He was disappointed: "That mother of mine . . ."

She should be bringing him food and water. He swallowed, but not a drop of saliva was left in his mouth. Then he slumped on to the sledge again. The horse stopped and pushed its head among the sheaves. Memed did not even notice. When at last he realised it, he pulled on the reins. "Gee, boy, gee up," he called.

Flies swarmed around. The horse slowly swung its tail, but the flies were not disturbed.

Angrily Memed stood up again and turned towards the village. Beyond the thistles a head could be seen. Soon he recognised his mother. In that moment his anger turned to joy.

She drew near, drenched in perspiration, doubled up as she hurried, the hand in which she bore his food reaching almost to the ground.

"How's it gone, child?" she asked. "Have you nearly finished?"

"I've finished hurling the sheaves."

"They're thick, aren't they?"

"Yes, but soft," replied Memed. He seized the water-jug from his mother's hand, raised it to his mouth and drank long and deep. The water trickling down from the jug wet his chin and his body all the way down to his legs.

"Come down," his mother said. "I'll drive for a while. Eat your bread."

Placing the reins in his mother's hands, he sat in the shade of the blackberry brambles, opened the bundle and found onion, salt and yoghourt. From the bag containing the yoghourt water was dripping. Tiny flies, like midges, were all over it. He filled a bowl with its contents.

After eating his fill he lay down with his head in the shade of the brambles, leaving his body from the waist down in the sun, and slept.

41

It was afternoon when he awoke. Rubbing his eyes, he rose to his feet and hurried to the threshing-floor.

"Mother, you're tired, aren't you? Very tired."

"Come up, my child," she said, bowing her head sadly.

Two days later they winnowed the wheat. The third day the chaff was swept away. On the fourth the red grains of wheat were piled up in the centre of the threshing-floor, but they couldn't fill the sacks and carry it all home. The heap lay in the middle of the floor, just as it was; Abdi Agha hadn't yet come to take his share. That night Memed and his mother watched over the heap, trying in vain to defend themselves from the gnats. The next day Abdi Agha again failed to come in the morning and at lunch-time there was still no sign of him. Towards the afternoon he appeared, leading three labourers mounted on horses with pack-saddles. His face was dark and threatening. Deuneh was afraid when she saw his mood. She had known him for many years. Her face, like dark wrinkled leather, became even more wrinkled.

Abdi Agha beckoned Deuneh to him. To the labourers he ordered: "Three quarters for us, one quarter for Deuneh."

Deuneh clung to the Agha's stirrup: "Don't do this, Agha, we'll die of hunger this winter! Don't! I kiss your feet, Agha!"

"Stop whining, woman! I'm giving you your due."

"My due is one third," moaned Deuneh.

The Agha bent down towards Deuneh, looked into her eyes and asked: "Who ploughed the field, Deuneh?"

"I ploughed it, Agha!"

"Didn't our labourers help you?"

"They did, Agha!"

"Tell your son he should never have gone to work as a goatherd for Süleyman."

Deuneh turned pale. The Agha spurred his horse and rode off. She could only call after him: "I beseech you, Agha, don't!"

The labourers began measuring the wheat. They put three measures for the Agha, one for Deuneh. The Agha's heap grew. Deuneh's remained pitifully small.

Looking at the two heaps, Deuneh cursed the Agha: "May it choke you, Inshallah, you old Goat's-beard! May all your money be spent on doctors and surgeons. May you be ill and not eat of it."

The labourers loaded the Agha's share on to the three horses.

Not one of them opened his mouth to say a word to Deuneh, each of them silent as a stone. Memed came and sat down by his mother. In the middle of the floor there was now a tiny pile of wheat where so much had been before. He looked first at the pile of wheat, then at his mother. He frowned guiltily.

"Now I know why he didn't beat you when he brought you back from Süleyman's. I understand. To deprive us of all our food, the infidel!"

Memed could not control himself. He began sobbing: "All because of me . . ."

With all her strength his mother pulled him towards her lap, held him to her bosom. "What are we to do?" she said. "All winter . . ." Then she began to weep. "If only your father were alive," she moaned.

VI

They had only one cow. This year the cow had calved, a bull-calf. If Memed had owned but an acre of land of his own next year there might have been another bull-calf from the cow. For that he would have waited, impatiently, watchfully. Already, as in a dream, he could see the bull-calf that might be born next year. Then there would be two calves growing together. A pair of fine young bulls, with rings through their nostrils, in the middle of a big meadow. Bulls don't come easily to the yoke. He would have to struggle with them. But at last they would be as meek as lambs. Is his field full of thistles? Let it be, let the thistles grow for a year, for two years. The third year he would burn the roots. As long as the field was his own!

The hair on the new-born calf was purplish-red. Later it would change, become yellow, a reddish-brown, or a violet-brown. The hair on its ears was soft as velvet. If anyone opened his hand wide to caress an ear with the palm, he would feel a pleasant thrill, it was so soft and cool.

Poor farmers always make room for a calf in their home, close by the fire, next to where they lay their own beds. They bed the calf in fresh grass mixed with flowers. The hut then smells of spring flowers, of grass, of calf-dung and of the young animal. The smell of a calf is like the smell of milk. When autumn comes the calf has grown and is driven out with the other oxen.

All through the spring Deuneh paid no attention to the calf. Had it not been for her troubles with her son, the calf would have been a cause for rejoicing in the home.

Memed's home was just a hovel, one room with a mud roof, its walls not even rising to a man's height above the ground. Every roof in the village leaked under the driving autumn rains, Memed's being the only one to resist them. Some time before his death his father had brought earth from Sarichahsak and covered the roof with it. Sarichahsak earth is something special, not the same black, sandy and dry earth that is usual in these parts, but yellow, red, purple, blue and green, full of quartz of all colours mixed together. Memed's roof thus sparkled in the sunlight with all the colours of the rainbow.

Throughout the summer mother and son worked in the fields as hard as they could, but to what purpose? In the autumn they returned to their house heavy with troubles and sorrow. It was then that they began to realise that they owned a calf. Till then the young beast had passed almost unnoticed. But now the calf was a young bull.

That evening Deuneh threw a big log on the fire. Outside, the black clouds were racing across the sky from south to north. A flash of lightning lit up the house. The flames on the hearth were dancing when Memed came home. His hands were chapped and red with cold. He knelt down by the fire and looked at the cow stretched out as she chewed her cud. The cow was quite content: she had straw, but was not eating. At the other end of the room more straw was stacked. Memed went to the cow and took the calf by the ear as it rested in the corner. The young bull became restive. Pulling its head away, it stumbled round to the other side of the cow. The boy smiled.

"While you were away," his mother said, "she gave birth to him in Alichli glen. In the middle of the night I found her among the bushes. She was licking its head. At first she wouldn't let me come near. Then I wrapped it in my apron and brought it home."

"It's growing."

They remained silent without looking at each other, their heads bowed as they stared at the embers.

"We'll never manage through the winter without giving it up. Already there's no flour left," Deuneh said.

Memed did not reply.

"Abdi Agha's angry with us. He'll pay us nothing for it. We'll never manage to live till summer."

Memed kept silent.

"There's no other way, my child. If only you hadn't run away! It's crippled us."

Slowly Memed lifted his head and looked at his mother. His eyes were full of tears: "He uses me as an excuse. If I hadn't run away, he'd have found some other excuse."

"Yes, child. That infidel was already your father's enemy."

They both turned towards the cow, a fat red-brown cow with speckles on her brow.

When winter came at last and the snow was already knee-deep, the sky at noon all dark with snow and clouds, Deuneh one day placed her soot-black copper pan on the hearth. The water in it had been boiling for some time when Jennet came in.

"Come and sit down with us," said Deuneh.

"Why would I sit down, Sister," sighed Jennet as she slipped down in a corner. "Since morning I've been going from house to house. I don't know what I'm doing, where I've been. I had heard you, too, have no wheat left, and that all your barley's used up. We finished ours a week ago. The bottom of our sacks has been bare for a long time. This year our crops were poor, Sister. If they'd only been like yours . . . The old man's been everywhere, to every house, asking for a loan. But no one can give us anything."

Seeing the water boiling on the hearth Jennet asked pointedly: "What do you expect to cook?"

A wan smile hovered grimly on Deuneh's lips: "I boiled some water, that's all!"

"Is there nothing left?" Jennet asked, aghast.

"All that we have is on the hearth," replied Deuneh.

"What'll you do?" Jennet felt pity for them.

"I don't know."

"Why don't you go and ask Mustulu again?"

"I might, but he, too, has nothing left. . . ."

The blizzard was roaring with all its might from the hills. For days it had been impossible to keep one's eyes open outside in the snow. Even the dogs avoided wandering in the alleys between the houses. All the villagers had covered their doors and chimneys and shut themselves in, no longer coming and going from house to house. But Deuneh had visited every house, begged at every door for the past week and more. "I'll die rather than beg from Abdi Agha," she repeated.

It was the same every winter. More than half the village came starving to Abdi Agha's door.

Deuneh couldn't bear it. For herself it didn't matter. But there was her son, who had been speechless for days. No colour was left in his face or lips, which were as thin as paper, his face and body lifeless, like a corpse.

If he sat down anywhere he would no longer stir till night. His head between his hands, he just stared ahead. All his life and energy, his hate, love, courage and anxiety were concentrated in his big eyes. Every now and then a tiny spark would light them up and then die, a sharp, piercing spark, to be feared like the spark that flickers briefly in the eye of a tiger ready to pounce and tear its prey. Where does this spark come from? Perhaps one is born with it. More likely it is born of torment, pain, anxiety. It had come to stay in Memed's eyes in the past year, though the light of wonder and pleasure had always glistened in his childish gaze before.

Across the sky the black clouds still rolled. Outside Abdi Agha's door a crowd stood shivering, all huddled together, their hand-woven clothes torn and threadbare. A single figure stood apart from the crowd, Deuneh. They were waiting for Abdi Agha, who would come out and speak to them. Abdi Agha appeared with his pointed beard, a ninety-nine-bead rosary in his hand, a camel's-hair cap on his head. "So you're hungry again?" he called out. Not a murmur rose from the crowd. Then Abdi Agha caught sight of Deuneh standing alone beyond the crowd.

"Deuneh," he roared, "you can go home! I'm not giving you a single grain. Go home, Deuneh! It's never happened before that a man has run off from my door to be a goatherd, a labourer in another village. That's what your damned son has done. Go home, I tell you . . ." Turning to the rest of the crowd he added: "Follow me." He took a bunch of keys from the pocket of his baggy trousers and held them in his hand. From his jacket pocket he produced a note-book.

Somehow plucking up courage, Deuneh called out from behind: "Agha, he's just a child. Don't let us starve."

The Agha stopped and turned on Deuneh. The crowd behind him stopped and turned too.

"A child should know that it's only a child. Up to now, so far as I know, no other child has run away to another village from Deyirmenoluk to be a goatherd, a labourer. Go home, Deuneh!" Then Abdi Agha opened the store-room door and the warm, dusty odour of wheat floated out. "Listen to me," he warned them, halting at the door. "None of you can give a single grain to Deuneh. Let her die of hunger. So far nobody has ever died of hunger in Deyirmenoluk. Let her die. If she has anything to sell, let her sell it. If you give her anything, if I hear you've helped her, I'll come to your houses and take back what I've given you. Don't say I didn't warn you."

"It isn't even enough for our own needs . . ." the crowd murmured to appease him. From the back of the crowd a rasping woman's voice exclaimed: "What business had Deuneh's son to run away . . . What is it to us? Let her die of hunger!"

Each one of them went home carrying a mixed supply of rye, wheat and barley on his back. The mill was at the far end of the village, just below the great plane-tree. The next day the entrance to the mill was blocked with sacks. The mill was busy for hours, and Ismail, the miller, rejoiced. As night fell the odour of fresh warm bread rose from each house. Durmush Ali was just sixty, the largest man in the village, as healthy as an old plane-tree with tiny eyes in a broad face. He had never worn shoes in all his life and the soles of his feet were covered with a thick black layer of wrinkled, worn skin. He no longer needed leather soles. His feet were enormous, and no shoes or sandals would be big enough for them. If he had wished, he might have worn sandals. When people asked him why he preferred to go bare-foot he said nothing, only swore at them.

One of the women was kneading dough, another was rolling loaves, a third baking them on the griddle. To the right of the woman who was baking, thick red loaves were piled up.

Ali ate one or two of the loaves with gusto. Then his eyes became blurred, as if with tears, and he turned to his wife: "Woman, to tell the truth, it sticks in my throat."

"Why, Ali?" she asked in amazement.

"The family of our Ibrahim. I cannot forget what that infidel Abdi has done to them," he said. "He drove Deuneh away yesterday and didn't give her a single grain."

"Shame on him! If only Ibrahim were alive . . ."

"Abdi warned us . . ."

"I heard."

"Are two creatures to go hungry before our eyes, in the very

48

middle of this great village!" Ali was furious. He roared at the top of his voice. His shouting could be heard at the far end of the village.

"Come on, woman," he said. "Make a good bundle of that bread! Put a measure of corn in a bag too. I'll take it to Ibrahim's family."

The woman dusted the flour off her skirt and rose from the kneading-board.

Bag and bundle in his hand, Ali rushed out of the house, like a tall tree with the wind whistling in its branches. He stopped before Deuneh's door.

"Deuneh! Deuneh!" he shouted. "Open your door."

Deuneh and her son were crouching by the hearth, where the fire had gone out. They remained motionless, like stones.

"Deuneh! Deuneh!" Ali shouted again several times.

It was a few moments before Deuneh recognised Ali's voice, and could pull herself together to rise. She reached the door and opened it listlessly. "Come in, Ali Agha."

"Why do you make me wait outside half the morning, woman?"

"Come inside, Agha," repeated Deuneh. Crouching, Ali came through the door. "Why isn't the fire burning?" he asked.

The spark was again in Memed's eyes. But when he saw Ali's good-natured laugh it disappeared.

"God is gracious," said Ali, showing his bundle.

"I see that He is," replied Deuneh.

"I'm cold, Deuneh! Look at the child, all huddled up. Light the fire, quick!"

Deuneh looked at the empty hearth. "Has it gone out? I hadn't noticed." She threw wood on the fire and kindled it.

"That infidel Abdi . . ."

As he heard Abdi's name the spark shone again in Memed's eyes and stayed there.

". . . May the hand of his killer be bright. He'll go straight to Heaven. Abdi's father wasn't like this. He used to look after his farmers."

After Ali, other villagers came and brought food to Deuneh. Abdi never knew of it. But what the villagers brought lasted only for about fifteen days. Mother and son then remained hungry the next two days. The third morning, without saying a word, Deuneh fetched the cow from her byre. She fastened a rope round her neck and drove her out. As the cow went through the door Memed called: "Mother!"

"My child," she replied. Pulling the cow, she set off and came to a stop by Abdi Agha's door. The calf pushed its head among the cow's teats and began to suckle. Deuneh stood motionless before the door. Dursun came out and, seeing Deuneh, told the Agha. Immediately Abdi came to the door. Deuneh couldn't raise her head. Her thin pointed chin was trembling and her lips, like a child's, pouted and quivered. A shiver ran through her body.

"Have you brought it to sell, Deuneh?" asked Abdi Agha, slapping the cow's rump with his hand.

"Yes, Agha," she replied, without raising her head.

Abdi turned to Dursun: "Take that cow from Sister Deuneh and lead it to our cow-shed!" He thrust his hand into his pocket, and pulled out a bunch of keys. "Have you brought a sack, Deuneh, my daughter?" he asked. His voice was gentle and paternal.

"Yes," said Deuneh.

VII

In soil where the oak grows, hardly any other trees are seen. Mountain and rock, valley and hill, all are covered only with oak-trees, stout and squat, their branches dwarfed, the longest branch no more than a yard long. The dark green leaves grow close together. The trees stand rooted in the ground with all their strength.

The soil for oaks is dry and white, like chalk. It looks as if it had sworn never to grow anything but oak.

Between Kadirli and Jiyjik the land is hilly. The soil of these little hills is clay, black, oily and fertile. It is here that the marshes of the Chukurova used to end. To the west the hills go as far as the marshes of Ahjasaz; to the east as far as the pine-woods of the Taurus. These hills are cultivated from top to bottom. The oaks grow scattered among fields, each one as tall as a cypress. A fresh green sprouts from the branches and the trunks are not gnarled as are those of stunted oaks, but smooth as the trunks of poplars, soft to the touch. The oaks stand among the crops like any other tree.

The thistles ripple like waves of green, purple-blue and white. To the east there is dry, stony land. Memed would plough in the midst of the thistles, which tore at his legs, while the frost tingled. He would thresh in the "white heat" that burned and scorched him. Struggle as he might with the earth, Abdi Agha took three-quarters of all he produced. From the other villagers he only took two-thirds. From that year on his spite had grown. At every opportunity he beat Memed or cursed him.

One grows up, develops, matures according to one's soil. Memed grew on barren soil. A thousand and one misfortunes prevented him from ever growing to his full height. His shoulders no longer developed, his arms and legs were like dry branches. Hollow cheeks, dark face, charred by the sun . . . His appearance was that

51

of an oak, short and gnarled. He was like a firmly rooted oak, strong and tough. Only one point, one tiny point, was still fresh. His lips were red as a child's, delicately curved. A smile always seemed to hover at the corner of his lips. Somehow it matched his hardness, his bitterness.

To-day Memed was happy. He went out into the morning sunlight, wandered in the sun, went inside again. He pushed a handkerchief into the pocket of his new jacket, which he had bought from the smugglers. He folded the handkerchief in different ways, kept on trying it: sometimes like an open leaf, then rolled up. His cap, too, was new. He put the cap on his head. Beneath it his long black locks hung over his forehead. Then he pushed them back and glanced again at the mirror. He was not satisfied. He pulled the black locks down over his forehead again and left them like that. His *shalvar*, loose Turkish trousers, were also new. He had bought these trousers two years ago, but had never yet tried them on and was now wearing them for the first time.

He put on his stockings, then took them off again. He had many stockings. His mother knitted good stockings and embroidered the best patterns. Watching her out of the corner of his eye, he went to the chest and opened it. The inside of the chest smelled of wild apple. Memed's eyes lighted up as he found a pair of embroidered stockings that lay tucked away in the corner. His hand trembled as he bent down to take them. The smell of wild apple spread everywhere. As his hand touched the stockings his trembling increased and a flood of warmth went through his heart, a pleasant warmth and softness. In the shadow of the chest the stockings were dark. He pulled them out and took them to the light, where the colours became bright.

If someone sings a folk-song at night, it does not sound as in the daytime. If a child sings it or a woman, it also sounds different, or if the singer is young or old, if it is sung in the mountain or in the plain, in the forest or on the sea. Sung in the morning, at midday, in the afternoon, in the evening, each time it is different.

These embroidered stockings were like a folk-song, knitted with all the fantasy of a song. The matching and mingling of different colours, yellow and red, blue and orange, all produced warmth and softness, a work of love and compassion.

Traditionally such stockings are an expression of love. Memed's trembling as his hands touched them, his thrill as he brought them to the light, were fully justified. On such stockings there is always a design of two birds, with their beaks touching as in a kiss. Then there are also two trees, with small trunks, each with a single big flower. The trees stand side by side, their flowers joined as in a kiss. Between the two patterns there flows a milky-white stream with red rocks on its banks. All these colours seem to dance like flames.

He pulled the stockings on to his legs and put on his sandals over them. The stockings reached to his knees, with their birds and flowers kissing, their white streams flowing.

Within him he felt a great desire to see Hatché. He walked straight towards her house. She was awaiting him by the door. As soon as she saw Memed her large bright eyes expressed her happiness. She was glad to see that he was wearing the stockings that she had made.

From there Memed walked ahead into the village. When he returned home he sat down on a stone, waiting there for his friend, who soon appeared from behind the house.

"Boys, don't dawdle too much," Memed's mother warned them. "Abdi Agha mustn't learn you've been to town. He would give you hell."

"He won't hear of it," Memed reassured her. His friend was Bald Ali's son, Mustafa, who was also eighteen. They had so often discussed what the town would be like that they had finally felt they had to go there and see it for themselves. Dursun's fairy-tale descriptions of the Chukurova had helped them reach this decision two years ago; ever since then, they had somehow been unable to arrange it. For one thing Mustafa was afraid of his father and Memed of his mother. Besides, both of them dreaded Abdi Agha.

Then, three days ago, they had confided their plan together to Memed's mother.

"How can you go off to town at your age? What will Abdi Agha say afterwards? If he ever hears of it he'll drive you out of the village for good."

Memed pleaded with his mother.

"No, you mustn't," she insisted. She said "no" but her heart was troubled for them.

"Let Abdi Agha drive us out if he wants," she said finally.

They didn't tell Mustafa's father. They only said they were going deer-stalking and would be on the mountains for a few days. They had always gone deer-stalking together. Memed was the best shot in the village, never missing his mark. Certainly if Ali had seen them in the village all dressed up and wearing their fine "lovers' stockings" he would never have believed they were going hunting. Mustafa left the gun he was carrying as an excuse at Memed's house.

That night they had planned and discussed their trip till dawn without allowing themselves a moment of sleep. They were ready to leave while it was still dark. When at last they left they almost ran in their excitement.

From the valley below a breeze was blowing, piercingly cold. For a long while they neither talked nor stopped to rest. When they came at last to the green fields, Memed halted and took a deep breath. "Over there is Saribogha. First we go there, then on to Deyirmenler and after that to Dikirli. Beyond Dikirli lies the town . . ."

They walked at a brisk pace, sometimes slowing down and smiling at each other, then hurrying on again.

They passed the burnt wooden bridge, the tunnel road and the bloody grave at Süleymanli. It was midday when they came to Torunlar. The air was warm. The red flowers of the pomegranates were in bloom. The earth was damp where they sat and rested. An old man came out from somewhere behind the pomegranate-tree; a tall man, but tired and his bare chest all sweaty, beneath the long white hairs that were as curly as those of his white beard. He lowered the saddle-bag from his back.

"Greetings, young men," he said. His voice was proud and resonant. He sat down and pulled a pouch from out of his bag. In the pouch there was white bread, a huge red onion and some mince-meat. He began to eat and called invitingly: "Help yourselves, young men."

"Good appetite to you," replied Memed and Mustafa in chorus.

"Won't you eat something?" he asked. Memed and Mustafa repeated their greeting.

The old man continued to insist. "We expect to eat in town," Memed explained.

"If that's so, all right," the old man smiled. "I understand. Town bread is better. But it's a long way yet to the town."

Nearby a brook was babbling as its waters foamed and gushed among the rocks.

"Follow this stream," the old man said with his mouth full. "It leads you straight there."

"Aren't you, too, going to the town?" asked Memed.

"Eh, my boy, I'm going to the town, but how can my feet keep up with yours?"

Memed was abashed.

The old man finished his meal. When he had tied up his pouch securely, he threw himself down by the stream and drank his fill. With the back of his hand he wiped his mouth and moustache, then came back and sat down. He pulled out a big tobacco-box and opened it. He rolled a cigarette, as thick as his finger, in some yellow paper, and began to strike his flint. It was some time before the tinder caught fire, with a pleasant smell. Only when he had lit his cigarette and settled his back against the pomegranate-tree did he ask: "Well, young men, where are you from?"

"From Deyirmenoluk," they replied.

"That's that goat-bearded infidel Abdi's village, isn't it? I hear the monster has become an Agha and works his villagers like slaves. They're all starving when winter comes. I'm told that without Abdi's permission no one can marry, no one can even leave his village. They say Abdi has killed men in the villages, beating them with his stick. He's become the lord of five villages, Sultan Abdi, answerable to nobody. Fancy old goat-bearded Abdi an Agha!" The old man burst out laughing. Then he stopped. "Is it true?" he asked, frowning.

The boys stared at each other. The tiny light came into Memed's eyes and stayed there.

Seeing that they were too embarrassed to answer, the old man said: "Well, young men, that old goat-beard's a dog, a brute and a cuckold, no fine hero but a coward, as timid as a rabbit. Just like a woman! It's too late now, my boys. If I'd known he'd turn into such a scoundrel I'd have allowed his soul to go to hell. But it's too late now." He began to laugh again. "So Abdi wants to be a sultan and to make slaves of five villages! Curse his mother! If I'd known you'd become such a scoundrel, Abdi . . ."

Memed and Mustafa stared at the old man, unable to believe their ears. Mustafa was almost smiling. "So you're Abdi's peasants? The days when Abdi came begging to me have gone by."

Mustafa laughed openly in disbelief, but Memed nudged him so that he should be less obviously incredulous. The old man noticed this and added: "Have you ever heard of Big Ahmet?"

"We've heard of him," answered Memed.

But the old man turned on Mustafa fiercely. "It's you I'm talking to. Have you heard?"

"Of course I've heard," Mustafa grinned impudently. "Who hasn't heard of him?"

"Going through Siyringich, two brigands jumped out and stripped Abdi. They took his wife too. I heard about it. Abdi came and begged me to help, so I went and got his woman back. I gave her to him. If I'd known he'd treat the poor so brutally . . ."

Big Ahmet was a legend in these mountains. Mothers would silence their squalling babes by warning them: "Big Ahmet's coming!" But Big Ahmet was greatly loved at the same time. He had been able to foster the two feelings together among the mountain people. Otherwise he would never have been able, as an outlaw, to survive a single year in the mountains. Brigands live by love and fear. When they inspire only love, it is a weakness. When they inspire only fear, they are hated and have no supporters.

In all of sixteen long years Big Ahmet had never suffered any injury. In sixteen years of brigandage he had killed only one man, the man who had tortured and raped his mother while Ahmet had been away from home doing his military service. When, returning to his village, Ahmet had heard of this, he had killed the man and gone off to be a brigand in the mountains.

He never held any travellers up and, in his district, no other brigand dared show his face. Ahmet would carefully choose the richest man in the Chukurova and send him a letter by one of his band saying: "I want so much money." Immediately the rich man, receiving the letter, sent whatever money was demanded. However much he asked of anyone during all his years of brigandage, Ahmet always obtained every penny of it. Other brigands went and tortured the rich or killed them, but most of them still got nothing much to show for it, returning empty-handed from the Chukurova with a posse of gendarmes at their heels.

Nor did Ahmet ever squander his money. How could he, on the mountain-top? In the regions he roamed he used to bring medicines to the sick, oxen to those who lacked them and flour to the poor.

When he came down to his village on the occasion of an amnesty, the peasants flocked from far and wide and stayed there for days, just to see him. After the amnesty Ahmet kept to his house, his farm and his pipe, unwilling to hurt even an ant. Only when he got very angry at some wrong-doing would he say: "Ah, for the good old days!" Then, almost ashamed, he would keep quiet till his anger passed and later would laugh at what he had said.

In the village the brigand Ahmet had long been forgotten. The villagers were accustomed to the presence of this white-bearded ancient who couldn't possibly be the Big Ahmet who had once ruled the whole Taurus for years. If a new brigand became famous in the mountains, "He's like Big Ahmet," they would say. If a brigand didn't look at a woman or stage hold-ups, "Like Big Ahmet," they would say. If he didn't kill men or oppress the people and was known only for good deeds, they would say: "Like Big Ahmet!"

The old man turned to Mustafa and asked: "What sort of a man is Big Ahmet? Have you heard?"

"My father used to say," Mustafa replied, "that in this country there never was a brigand like Big Ahmet, so brave and honest, such a father to the poor."

"Didn't he tell you what he looked like, his height, his face?"

"My father used to say that Big Ahmet was tall and dark, with heavy moustaches, solid like a mountain. In the middle of his forehead there was a big black mole. His eyes blazed very brightly. My father had even spoken to him."

The old man asked in a mocking voice: "Who was the man who saved that infidel Abdi's wife from the brigands and gave her back to him?"

"Who could it be but you? Didn't you say so?" replied Mustafa.

The old man shook his head sadly. "It wasn't I," he said.

Memed looked closely at the old man's face. Between the two eyebrows, among the white hairs, he saw a big green mole. It was green, not black. After that he couldn't take his eyes off the man.

"Didn't you just say it was you?" Mustafa insisted.

"No, no, it wasn't I who brought her back. The man who did it is dead," said the old man stretching himself and lying down on his back, with his saddle-bag as a pillow.

Mustafa nudged Memed. "Let's be off," he whispered.

Memed rose without answering. He still stared at the old man who, as they rose, opened his eyes.

"So you're going, are you?" he asked.

"May you live long," replied Memed with wonder in his voice. Mustafa echoed his words.

"Good-bye," answered the old man, raising his head from the saddle-bag to watch them. When they had gone he lowered his head again and closed his eyes. The brook babbled on.

Until they reached the pine-woods of Deveboynu the boys did not speak. Memed's face was bitter as poison. Alternately he felt some joy, then bitterness again, each time like the passing of a dark rain-cloud. He looked at Mustafa out of the corner of his eye several times. Mustafa was bewildered. When they came to the hill Memed sank down wearily on a stone and smiled. Mustafa knew this was his chance.

"Why are you smiling?" he asked.

Memed's smile spread over his face.

"What's up?" insisted Mustafa.

Memed was serious: "God knows, but this must have been Big Ahmet. I'm sure of it."

"Nonsense."

Memed became angry. "What do you mean? The man's exactly like Big Ahmet."

Mustafa scoffed: "That man's like any of us. Just like my own grandfather. What makes him like Big Ahmet?"

"Didn't you see the mole on his forehead? Right in the middle of his brow."

"No."

"In the middle of his forehead there was a big green mole."

"I didn't see it."

"His eyes blazed like kindling."

"I didn't notice it."

"I'm sure that man can be no other than Big Ahmet."

"If every such man were Big Ahmet, the world would be full of Big Ahmets. That man was just like you and me."

Still arguing, they walked downhill and suddenly discovered the plain. A stream meandered across it, shining in the sunlight. It was the first time they had ever seen such a long stream winding across a plain.

"We're nearly there," exclaimed Memed.

"How do you know?"

"In the Chukurova all the streams follow a winding course. I think this one must be the river Savrun, and those poplars the ones round the mill at Kadirli. Uncle Durmush Ali described it like that."

Mustafa thought Memed was angry with him for his earlier scoffing. Memed didn't anger easily, but once he was angry it was like all hell let loose, so Mustafa wanted to please him. "You must be right. You've remembered what Uncle Durmush Ali explained."

They came to Shabapli. An irrigation canal below Shabapli had overflowed its banks and flooded the lower road. They had to take off their shoes and wade through the waters.

On the farther side of Shabapli, near what is now Bolat, Mustafa's house, the red earth meets the white. This stretch was covered with wild bushes. After they had passed this scrub the first houses of the town appeared. Many of them were still thatched with reeds. Near these was a big tiled building and beyond it lay the whole town, like a toy city, with its roofs of shiny corrugated iron, its white-washed roof-terraces and its red tiles. Memed and Mustafa stared at this sight, their eyes wide with astonishment. How white it all was! How many houses there were! They couldn't take their eyes off it.

Crossing the Boklu stream they entered the town. The windows shone in the sunlight. Thousands of shiny panes, like crystal palaces, just as Dursun had said. A town for fairy kings, with palaces.

By the entrance of the town there was a cemetery on either side, with all its grave-stones aslant. The north side of each grave-stone was dark with moss. In the middle of the cemetery stood a massive mulberry-tree, old and leafless, almost naked, all withered on one side. It was the first time they had seen such a vast cemetery.

Until they reached the market-place their thoughts were still on the cemetery. It had filled them with uneasiness and fear. But the sight of the first shop made them forget the cemetery. It was only a little store roofed over with corrugated iron. On a table the shop-keeper had spread rows of bottles of multi-coloured sweets. In front of the display of bottles stood tins of lamp-oil and boxes full of sugar, salt, figs and grapes.

They stood side by side, staring at this shop. It wasn't at all like Abdi Agha's village store.

Stopping and staring again and again, they came at last t﹚ the centre of the market, but the sun was already sinking behind the hill. They stopped in front of a draper's shop with many attractive brightly-coloured prints, materials for trousers, caps strung on a cord, silks. The silks were draped from one corner of the shop window to the other. Inside, a short stout man was taking it easy and sleeping.

Then they stopped by a pavement of fair-sized stones taken from the bed of a stream, well set in the ground. "They even decorate the earth," thought Memed. A row of stunted old mul-berries ran along the right side of the market, planted close to-gether as in a forest. Beneath them was the smithy. A new smell reached their nostrils, a sharp smell of soap, salt, new cloth, rot and food.

Memed took Mustafa by the hand and pulled him beneath one of the mulberries. The tree was alive with sparrows, chirping so loudly that the whole market was filled with their noise.

"It's evening, Mustafa. What shall we do now?"

Mustafa stared vacantly into Memed's eyes, as if he were still in a dream.

"When people from our village come to town they sleep in the *han*," said Memed. "Uncle Durmush Ali told me so. Let's go to the *han*."

"Yes, the *han* is best."

"But where is it?"

The shutters of the shops were being pulled down noisily, with so much din that they were stunned. They walked away hand in hand. Two fat men, with watch-chains across their stomachs, passed by. But the boys couldn't pluck up courage to ask them the way to the *han*. Then they stopped in front of a shop. The sun had set and it was growing dark. They held hands like children. The shopkeeper took them for customers. "Come in, my Aghas. What do you want?" he asked in flattering tones.

They were ashamed to be called "Aghas" and left the shop hurriedly, though they had intended asking their way to the *han*.

Almost all the shops were closed and they wandered here and there for an hour without meeting anyone whom they trusted. They stopped and suddenly Memed looked pleased. In front of them a man was walking rapidly, wearing the hand-woven serge jacket of the mountain people. Memed forgot everything and ran after him.

" Brother!" he shouted, "stop!"

The man stopped, surprised at the other's haste. Memed was taken aback by the look on the man's face. He hadn't expected it.

"What is it?" said the man harshly.

"We're strangers."

"What do you want?"

Memed felt a sinking in his heart. "Where's the *han*? That's what we wanted to know," he said.

"Follow me," said the man, turning into a side street. He walked fast. Memed studied his gait. It was the gait of a man accustomed to steep slopes. When such men walk, they raise their feet high, then put them down again carefully, almost fearfully. It's the habit of mountaineers, but the men of the plain shuffle their feet along the ground.

The *han* was a tumble-down inn with huge worm-eaten doors.

"This is the *han*," said the man, going off at the same speed and as if he were still climbing up or down mountain slopes.

"We must go in and find the innkeeper," declared Memed.

They went inside. The courtyard was full of horses, donkeys, mules, carts. On the ground the manure of horses and donkeys lay knee-deep. It was damp, its stink smarting in one's nostrils. They felt almost sick from the pungent smell. In the middle a fair-sized lantern was hanging from a pole, much of its glass black with soot.

"Look at the lantern!" Memed said to Mustafa.

"Huge, isn't it?"

A small man with a receding chin was running hither and thither erratically. In a corner a dozen men or more from Marash, judging by the cloaks they wore, stood in a group, arguing at the top of their voices. One was angry, cursing all the time, cursing his Agha, his Pasha, the world, his destiny, his mother, his wives. He would stop for a while, then begin cursing again where he had left off.

One of the group began: "And if we don't manage to sell this cloth . . ."

"Curses on the cloth," interrupted the foul-mouthed one. Whatever they said, he would add a curse: "May they be cursed," or "May their whole tribe be cursed."

Memed and Mustafa approached the group without being noticed by those arguing. In the far corner sat an old man, completely indifferent to the crowd. He had a sweet, childlike face. Every now and then he smiled to himself.

Memed came up to him. "Uncle, where's the innkeeper?" he asked without the least timidity.

"What do you want with that cuckold?" asked the old man. Then he added: "The poor fellow's fallen into the stream."

"Poor man," said Mustafa. Memed nudged him. He had understood that the old man was joking.

"He fell down right on the top of his head," laughed the old man.

"What bad luck that was," said Mustafa, still not understanding.

"Don't pay any attention to him, Uncle," put in Memed. "We've come to spend the night at the *han*. Where's the keeper?"

Mustafa was confused.

Loud enough for the innkeeper to hear from where he was scurrying to and fro, the old man shouted: "There's that pimp who calls himself an innkeeper. Go and tell him your troubles."

The innkeeper heard and laughed. "Listen, if you're looking for a pimp, the real chief of all pimps is that white-beard by your side. His beard has grown white from his misdeeds!"

"Look," said the old man, "you pimp-in-chief, these young men want a bed."

Memed had approached the innkeeper who now explained: "You'll have to sleep in the same room as that white-bearded pimp. He'll show you the way."

"The scoundrel!" said the old man. "Come along, young men. I'll show you your beds."

Timidly they climbed a rickety staircase, thick with cobwebs. The steps creaked as though they would collapse beneath their weight. They entered a filthy room, with beds arranged in a row side by side.

"Is it the first time you've come to town?" inquired the old man.

"Yes," they replied.

"How is that? You both look about twenty. How is it you've never come down to town?"

"We didn't have a chance," replied Memed, ashamed.

"Which village are you from?"

"Deyirmenoluk," answered Memed.

"It's a mountain village, isn't it?"

"Yes."

"You haven't eaten yet," went on the old man. As he spoke they suddenly felt a gnawing hunger.

"My name's Corporal Hasan," said the old man.

"Mine's Memed. And this is Mustafa . . ."

Together they left the *han* and went into a grocer's shop where a swarm of flies hovered like a black cloud over the rusty tins of *halva*, molasses and raisins.

"Give these young lions whatever they want," said Corporal Hasan to the grocer. "As for me, I'll have some bread and *halva*."

"Give us some bread and *halva* too," said Memed.

They ate the *halva* with relish by the light of a spluttering lamp.

When they returned to the room in the *han* every bed except theirs was occupied. They went to bed without undressing. The room was thick with cigarette smoke, hanging in folds in the air. Through the smoke they could just make out a lantern on a filthy wall that was spotted with dead bugs. The men who were already in bed were talking noisily.

"So it's the first time you've slept in a *han?*" Corporal Hasan asked the youths as they tried to settle in their beds.

"Aye," replied Memed, then added: "This smoke and stink is enough to choke a fellow."

Memed and Mustafa finally stopped moving about in their beds.

"Well, did you like the town?" asked Corporal Hasan.

"It's very big," replied Memed. "Such huge houses. Like palaces. . . ."

Corporal Hasan laughed.

"You should see Marash! There they have a covered market full of coloured lights. Everything is shining bright, enough to dazzle you. In one corner the cloth-merchants, in another the saddlers, and then the coppersmiths. . . . How can I describe it? It's a paradise, Marash, a hundred times bigger than this."

Memed pondered his words without replying.

"Yes," went on Corporal Hasan. "Just like that. If only one could see Istanbul too!"

Memed stretched as if he were ready to burst. His face darkened as he frowned.

"Who's the Agha of this town?" he asked at last.

At first Corporal Hasan couldn't understand his question.

"What did you say?" he asked.

"I asked who is the Agha of this town," Memed repeated.

"My child," replied Corporal Hasan. "What Agha? How could this town have an Agha? There's no Agha here. Everyone's his own Agha. Here they call any rich man 'Agha.' There is no end of Aghas . . ."

Memed couldn't swallow this. "Who's the one Agha of this place?" he insisted. "What's his name? Who's the owner of all these shops and fields?"

At last Corporal Hasan understood. "Who's the Agha of your village? " he asked Memed.

"Abdi Agha."

"Do all the fields in your village belong to Abdi Agha?"

"Of course," answered Memed.

"And your village store?"

"It's his too."

"The cows and goats, sheep and oxen?"

"Almost all his."

Corporal Hasan stroked his beard thoughtfully.

"Listen to me, son. Here it's not as you know it. The fields in this town belong more or less to everybody. Of course there are some without land, but each one of these shops has its owner and some men are Aghas and own a lot of fields. The poorer people own less, and the very poor own nothing."

"Really?" asked Memed, almost shouting in his astonishment. "Am I lying?" demanded the corporal. "Of course it's true."

The old man explained about the landless at great length. Then spoke of Marash, the vineyards of Marash, the soil of Marash. He explained about an Agha named Hojaoglu who owned so much land that he kept his money in big jars. Memed listened in silence. Corporal Hasan had been a prisoner in the Caucasus. He told about that, then about Galata, Damascus, Beirut, Adana, Mersin, Konya and the great poet and mystic, Mevlana, who is buried in Konya in a huge mausoleum. Suddenly he stopped talking and pulled the quilt over his head. The roar of conversation had died down in the room. In one corner a man was leaning over his *saz* and began to strum on the strings of this long-necked Anatolian instrument. He sang softly, almost inaudibly, in a throaty voice as he played. In the light of the paraffin-lamp the man's face took on different shapes, sometimes long, sometimes short or broad. Memed listened to him for a long time, his mind quite vacant. Then the player hung his *saz* on a nail on the wall and pulled his quilt over his face.

Memed felt as if in an alien world. Sleep wouldn't come to him. His thoughts preoccupied him, flooding his head. He considered the greatness of the world. Deyirmenoluk village was but a spot in his mind's eye, Abdi Agha just an ant. It was probably the first time he had ever thought things out in a broader perspective. He thought with passion and yearning, yearning for vengeance. He had grown in his own eyes and began to consider himself a man. Turning from side to side in his bed, he murmured: "Abdi Agha's only human, so are we . . ."

Early in the morning Mustafa nudged him. Memed was sleeping soundly. Mustafa pulled the quilt off him and woke him up. Memed's eyes were swollen, his face all yellow. But his features revealed his satisfaction, his eyes the pleasure of new thoughts.

They gave the innkeeper his money. "Where's Corporal Hasan?" asked Memed. "We ought to say good-bye to him!"

"That pimp?" said the innkeeper. "He got up while it was still dark, loaded his pack and went off to peddle his goods in the villages. He might be back in ten days' time. Forget about him."

"If only we could have seen him again," sighed Memed as they left.

They walked to the market-place and stood staring in astonishment all around them. The sun was beating down, the crowd in the market-place was such as they had never seen. "They swarm like ants," Memed murmured to himself. The sherbet-sellers, with heavy brass ewers on their backs, clanged their metal cups and shouted: "Sherbet! Sherbet! Honey sherbet!" and "Drink only one cup! You'll want more!"

The brass ewers glittered in the sunlight and Memed couldn't take his eyes off them. To look at one more closely, he called: "Sherbet-seller, give me a drink. And one for my friend too!"

While the sherbet-seller bent forward to fill the cup, Memed timidly rubbed his hand over the shining brass. The sherbet-seller filled two cups and held them out. The sherbet was ice-cold and frothy. Neither of them could drink more than half of it. They didn't like it.

In one corner a man was sitting on a big stump, beating out a horse-shoe and singing to the rhythm of his work. This was the famous Blind Haji of the district. Memed was lost in admiration. Then a pleasant smell reached his nostrils, the smell of meatballs. Turning round, they noticed thick smoke drifting out of a tumbledown eating-house. The smell made their heads swim. Spontaneously they turned into the shop.

There they were greeted very politely: "Welcome, come in!" Surprised, they sat down and waited for their order for meatballs. The market of yesterday, the town of yesterday, the world of yesterday seemed completely different to Memed's eyes to-day. All the bonds restraining his feet and his heart were now broken. He felt free, unfettered, light as a bird.

They ate their meatballs timidly, as if all the people in the shop had stopped to gaze at them. By the time they emerged from the eating-house they were almost dizzy. They walked from one end of the market to the other. Memed turned to Mustafa and said: "There's no Agha here, it seems. Imagine a village without an Agha!"

They went into a shop that was all draped with textiles. Memed chose there a length of yellow silk, squeezing the silk in his fist and then releasing it so that it sprang out of his hand. They bought it and went out again.

Mustafa winked at Memed. "For Hatché, isn't it?"

"You've guessed it, Mustafa. Bright boy," Memed teased him.

They bought some *halva* from the same shop as the night before. Then, from the bakery, warm bread, still steaming. They wrapped the bread and *halva* together in a handkerchief, then sat on a white stone in the market-place and stared at the piles of golden oranges in the fruit-stalls. They rose, bought one orange each and peeled it.

It was almost lunch-time before they set off on the road back to the village. The sun beat straight down, casting shadows just under their feet, little round black circles of shadow.

Once they had left the town they turned back again and again to gaze at the view, till it was out of sight. White clouds were drifting over it. The silvery smoke rising from the chimneys hung in the air. The red tiles stood out against the dark blue.

They reached the village after midnight. In the east a bright star had risen. Mustafa left Memed in front of his house, so tired that he almost regretted havink gone to the town. But Memed was glowing with pleasure as he approached his door. Before entering he leaned his back against the wall and stood there a while. Should he go in or not? He decided not to go in, turned back and slipped away cautiously in the shadows of the brush fences. Breathless, he came to a halt in front of a house by a mulberry-tree, its branches spread out like a parasol. He stopped under the mulberry, then went and lay down in the shadows of the fence. Slowly his weariness passed.

There is a bird with long legs, finely shaped, a yellowish-grey like smoke, or rather almost green like trees seen through smoke, its neck so long that beak and body seem separate. It always stays near water. In Deyirmenoluk they call it the whistler, because of its call. It sings in a strange whistling manner, a long whistle which it then cuts short. It begins and stops, begins and stops. All the thrill of its singing lies in this sudden pause. Memed could imitate its call exactly. Several times from where he was lying he called like the whistler, his eye on the door. The door gave no sign of opening. He became impatient. He repeated his call again and again. Soon the door opened furtively. Memed's heart was beating as if ready to burst. A shadow left the door and stole silently towards him, then lay down beside him. Together they withdrew to the shadows beneath the fence.

Memed stretched out his hand gently: "Hatché . . ."

"Dearest, I've kept watching the road. I never took my eyes off it."

They felt each other's warmth. Their breath was like a hot wind. They clung closer to each other. Her head was swimming.

In the dark, the soft silk, cool as ice, flowed from Memed's hand to Hatché's.

For a while they embraced without speaking. She shivered and stretched her legs. There was a smell of fresh grass.

"Without you I would die. I couldn't live. You were away two whole days. I was so impatient."

"I couldn't wait either," whispered Memed.

"The town?"

"Wait. I've so much to tell you. Things are all different . . . I met a Corporal Hasan who has even seen Istanbul. He's from Marash. He told me all about Marash. This Corporal Hasan told me to take my bride and come to the Chukurova. That's what he said. Corporal Hasan said he would find a field for me, and oxen and a house. He told me to run away with my girl and go there."

"Corporal Hasan!" murmured Hatché.

"He's a good man whom you can trust. He'll do anything for us if we run away."

"Do you think we should?"

"Corporal Hasan has a long beard. If he's in the Chukurova, we have nothing to worry about. 'Well, my lad,' he said, 'get your girl and elope, come here.' 'All right,' I said, 'in ten days I'll come!' "

"Ten days!"

"He's better than a father. . . . He has a white beard, like flowing water."

"Let's go straight away," urged Hatché.

"In ten days . . ."

"I'm afraid."

"When Corporal Hasan will have returned to the Chukurova we'll go. But I'm worried about my mother. Abdi will kill her."

"Let her come too, since there's this Corporal Hasan."

"I'll beg her to. I'll tell her all about the corporal. Perhaps then she'll decide to join us."

"I'm afraid," said Hatché. "I'm afraid of Abdi. His nephew's always at our house, whispering with Mother all the time. Only yesterday . . ."

"Only ten days more. Let's agree to go on the eleventh day. You and I and Mother . . . That night we'll set off on the road for the Chukurova. We'll go to Corporal Hasan. He'll be surprised and glad to see us."

"Perhaps, but I'm afraid of my mother."

For a while they remained silent. No sound could be heard but their breathing. The night insects were humming. Memed's head was swimming, full of dazzling yellow lights.

Hatché was the daughter of Osman, a mild man, quiet, never interfering. But her mother was a real termagant. Whatever quarrel or disturbance there might be in the village, she was always at the heart of it. A tall, strong woman, she attended to all the business of the house and even ploughed the fields.

Memed and Hatché had spent their childhood together. Among the boys Memed built the best doll's house, and Hatché decorated it the best. Leaving the other children to their games, they would then go off by themselves and invent all kinds of new games.

When she was fifteen Hatché had made a habit of coming to Memed's house every day to learn how to knit stockings from his mother. Memed's mother showed her the best patterns, taught her the finest stitches. Sometimes, stroking the girl's hair, she would say: "If all goes well, you'll be my daughter-in-law, my beauty."

Hatché was nearly sixteen when Memed came back one day, tired from his ploughing, and met her as she returned from gathering mushrooms on the mountainside. A month had gone by since they had last seen each other. When they met that day at Alajagedik both were filled with joy and laughter. They sat side by side on a stone. Darkness soon fell and Hatché wanted to be going. Memed then seized her hand and made her sit down again. "Stay a bit!"

Hatché was trembling and burning all over. Memed took both Hatché's hands in his. "You're my girl, aren't you?" he asked. "You're mine . . ."

Hatché began to laugh.

"You're mine, aren't you?" he insisted.

Hatché pulled herself away from Memed. But he held her fast as she struggled. At last he managed to kiss her.

Hatché blushed scarlet, pushed him away violently and ran off. Memed caught up with her and held her. Then the girl became quiet as a lamb. Some of Memed's first excitement passed. "I'll come at midnight," he said. "I'll hide in the shadow of the big mulberry. I'll call like the whistler. Everyone will just think it's the whistler singing." Then he imitated the whistler, several times. "Like that," he added.

Hatché smiled. "It's really just like the whistler. No one will know the difference."

"We're engaged, aren't we? Nobody will know."

Hatché suddenly turned pale. "If someone saw us here," she cried as she ran off.

The days then went by as their passion grew till it was full-blown. Their love almost became a legend in the village. Every night, whatever happened, they would meet. If not, neither of them could sleep a wink. Hatché's mother once caught them and punished her daughter. It was no use. Every evening she bound her hand and foot, but in vain. She put lock after lock on the door; Hatché found a way round every obstacle. She knitted stockings and 'kerchiefs for Memed and invented songs over them, expressing her love, desire and jealousy in the colours of her embroidery and in the notes of her songs that are still sung throughout the Taurus. People who saw her stockings were thrilled, and those who hear or sing her songs still feel a thrill like the freshness of spring when everything is green.

That night, after seeing Hatché on his return from town, Memed didn't notice how or when he at last reached home. In the east the glittering star had paled and the sky was whitening.

"Mother!" he called from the door. Deuneh was not sleeping but worrying about her son. "My boy!" she exclaimed as she rose, opened the door and put her arms round him. "So you walked all night?"

"We walked."

As soon as he was inside Memed sank on to his bed. A great desire to sleep came over him. The yellow sparkling of brass flashed dizzily through his head.

Perhaps it is just hope, perhaps just desire. Desire is warm as a friend, as a loved one, surrounding you protectively. Memed's head, his heart, the marrow deep in his bones, all of him was gleaming bright. Beyond this bright light he could visualise red tiles silhouetted against the sky: the town. The bright sparkling yellow of the brass mingled with the deep purple smoke from the eating-house and the noise of Haji, the blacksmith, striking a horse-shoe on his anvil. The pavement was of polished river-stones that shone a dazzling white.

Deuneh sat down beside Memed. "How was the town, my child?"

He was thinking of the song Blind Haji sang as he hammered the shoe. His thoughts passed from the horse-shoe to the red-tiled houses. Half awake, half asleep, he smiled. He was thinking that soon they could run away. Corporal Hasan would not be back from the villages for another ten days. He worried about all this. Then he thought that it would take a good ten days to prepare their flight. Corporal Hasan, with his child-like, mischievous smile, his white beard that seemed to have been fixed artificially on to his face, would find them a new home, a plough, work. . . . Memed was relying on Corporal Hasan a great deal. But he knows the world, Memed felt, and has travelled everywhere. The town had no Agha. Hatché, his mother, he himself, the three of them would find different jobs. What they earned would be their own. Corporal Hasan would arrange it somehow. Memed had heard, though he didn't know where, that the Chukurova was fertile. This thought gave him pleasure and hope. Besides, there were no thistles in the soil of the Chukurova. Once settled there and a family man, he would return one day to his village and tell them about the Chukurova. Then the whole village would follow him down to the Chukurova. Abdi would remain alone in the village. He did not know how to sow or reap and would die of hunger.

"How was the town, my son?" repeated Deuneh.

Memed thought he answered his mother, but he went on dreaming, half awake. In front of the fruit stall he had seen a man in a clean white felt hat and wearing new trousers. Memed had noticed his long white fingers that counted the money rapidly as it slipped between them, silvery bright, when he paid for the oranges he had bought.

"My child, are you asleep?" insisted Deuneh.

Was he asleep? The sparkling brass, like the million rays of sunlight where the sun beat down on the Chukurova, flashed through his mind.

When he woke up in the morning it was broad daylight. His mother was sitting by his side, watching him. Suddenly he was shy before his mother. He pulled the quilt over his head. As a boy he had always done this when he was in a playful mood. His mother laughed and pulled the quilt back again.

"Be up with you, you big loafer! It's broad daylight. Get up and tell us about the town."

He opened his eyes, blinking. Outside the sun was shining. He glanced at it, then turned his dazzled eyes away. He rose from his bed, tired, exhausted. In spite of all his weariness and anxiety his heart was filled with light and joy. He himself did not know what it was that drove the anxiety out of his heart. His joy must have come from this light, but where was the source of the light that filled his heart?

He sat down at his mother's knee and told her about the town. She had heard about the town before, from her husband and from others, but no one had ever described it so beautifully. When he came to the yellow lights Memed was full of enthusiasm. The words flowed from his lips like a stream.

Memed finished telling about the town in a fever of excitement, but when he wanted to explain his plan to his mother he was tongue-tied. She was used to this and knew what it meant. She stroked his hair and looked into his eyes. Her son wanted to say something, something very important, but could not. He avoided his mother's eyes. To herself she said: "So there is something else. . . ." She looked at Memed. Memed was unable to move. "He can't tell it easily," she thought.

"Say what's under your tongue, my Memed," she burst out at last.

Memed was startled when he heard this. He went pale.

"Come on, say it," insisted his mother.

Memed's eyes evaded his mother's. "I was talking to Hatché last night. We've decided to run away."

"Have you taken leave of your senses?"

"We thought that if you stay in the village Abdi Agha will torture you. You must come with us to the Chukurova too. We'll settle in the town."

"Are you mad?" cried his mother in anger. "If I leave my village and my home, where do I go? And you, too, where will you take the girl?"

"Then what can we do? Suggest something."

"I've told you a hundred times, forget about Hatché. I've told you a hundred, a thousand times, forget her! She's engaged to Abdi Agha's nephew. It's impossible. Get the whole idea out of your head!"

"I can't forget her. I can't! Is Abdi Agha the Agha of everybody's heart? I'll take her and run away. I've only one fear, that he'll do harm to you. That's my only fear! Otherwise all would be well."

"I'm not going to abandon my home to go anywhere. Take Hatché and go. But you are alone, my son, and no good can come of it, with the powerful Agha of five villages against you. His nephew wants Hatché and it would be wiser to forget about it all. Isn't there any other girl for you?"

Now Memed was angry too, which happened rarely with his mother. "There's no other girl," he answered, "not in all the world." After that he was silent.

Two days later the whole village heard that Abdi Agha's nephew, who lived in another village, had sent to ask for Hatché in marriage. Abdi Agha was one of the spokesmen. At the first meeting, despite the girl's protests, Abdi Agha's nephew had been accepted. In the eyes of her parents it was an unexpected boon. Left to herself she would have preferred, in their opinion, any gipsy or strolling minstrel. Hatché could only weep distractedly. Within two more days the betrothal ring was on her finger and Abdi Agha had given her a gold coin.

After the engagement rumours began to spread. The women gossiped, the children repeated what they had heard, old and young were of the opinion that Memed would elope with Hatché and never leave her to Abdi Agha's nephew.

The whole village was anxious, wondering what Memed would do. One could only wait and see. But all this talk was repeated to Abdi Agha, who knew of every word spoken in the village and sent a man to summon Memed to his house.

73

When Memed stood silent before him with his arms folded, Abdi Agha flew into a rage. "You ungrateful scoundrel. You grew up at my door like a dog and now you are a threat to the morals of the village. I hear you've cast your eyes on my nephew's bride."

Memed stood motionless, his face pale. Only that pinpoint of light returned to his eyes and settled there.

"Listen!" roared Abdi Agha. "If you want to live and earn your bread in this village, you must do as I say. You're still a child and have no experience of the world. I can destroy my enemy's house so that only the wild fig-tree will grow there. Do you hear what I say, you wretch?" He grabbed Memed by the arm and repeated his threat.

Memed still held his tongue, which made Abdi all the more angry. "You good-for-nothing son of a pauper! Nobody's going to make eyes at my nephew's bride, or I'll tear him to pieces and throw his body to the dogs. Listen! You must never pass by her door again. Do you understand me?"

He seized Memed and shook him, but it would have been easier for him to obtain an answer from a stone than from this boy whose very silence offended him. Suddenly losing all self-control, Abdi Agha began to kick Memed.

Memed could hardly refrain from striking back and killing him. He ground his teeth, bit the flesh of his cheeks in his rage till his mouth was full of blood. Yellow lights flashed through his head.

"Get out of here! There's no point in trying to do good and to make a man of someone like you. Feed a raven and it turns against you and picks your eyes out. Get out, you son of a bitch!"

When he left the house Memed was half fainting, half stunned; he spat on the ground outside. His saliva was full of blood.

VIII

Houses, trees, rocks, stars, moon and earth, whatever there was in the world, all was lost, melted in the darkness. It was raining and a light wind was blowing, a cold wind. Every now and then the dogs howled in the darkness. Then a lone cock crowed lustily. Surely that cock, crowing at such an hour, would be killed in the early morning by its owner.

Far away, from the road on the other side of the mountain, a bell tinkled. The tinkling would stop, then begin again, sometimes at long intervals, a sure sign that the approaching travellers were tired.

For a long while Memed had been waiting, hidden under the fence by the great mulberry-tree, with its branches spreading like an umbrella. He was thinking, though in his present mood he could scarcely be said to think. He was cold, aware of many things without actually thinking. It was drizzling. Ever since night had fallen Memed had been soaking up the rain, letting it penetrate him. At times he shivered, then no longer felt the cold. Beyond the fence he heard a sound and listened. It seemed to be a cat jumping over the fence. He then thought of his mother. His body ached in places as though the flesh had been wounded. He felt the bitterness of poison in his heart. They would make his mother suffer for his own actions. A long way off the lightning flashed, lighting up the branches and trunk of the mulberry that was otherwise lost in the darkness. It seemed to light up the darkness in Memed's heart too.

At this hour the whole village, with its horses, donkeys, cows, goats, sheep, insects, hens, cats and dogs, was fast asleep. Its hatreds, grudges, loves and fears, cares and courage, all were smothered in a deep sleep. Only its dreams were stirring with life at this hour.

No matter how limited a man's field of vision, his imagination knows no bounds. A man who has never been outside his village of Deyirmenoluk can still create a whole imaginary world that may reach as far as the stars. Without travelling, a man can penetrate to the other end of the world. Even without much imagination the place where he dwells can become different in his dreams, a true paradise. Now, at this moment, in their sleep, dreams made everything appear wonderful to these poor distressed people of Deyirmenoluk.

Memed was also dreaming, in spite of his fears. Suddenly a light flashed through his mind. The rich sunlight of the Chukurova flooded it, spreading and growing more intense. Then this light disappeared and Memed began to worry. "If she doesn't come," he thought, "what shall I do?" Various plans of action offered themselves to his mind. "If she doesn't come, I know what I'll do," he said. His hand slipped down to the holster of his revolver, and all his cares vanished, all his fears were forgotten.

He was still thinking of his revolver when he heard a light tread and felt ashamed of what he had just been thinking. Hatché was there, standing by him. Had it been daylight and had she looked into Memed's face, she would have been surprised to see how pale it was and how he then slowly blushed.

"I've made you wait a long time," she apologised. "My mother just wouldn't go to sleep."

Holding hands, they slipped away furtively, walking so carefully that not even the crackling of a twig was heard beneath their feet, which hardly seemed to touch the ground.

Once they had left the village and seen that the last houses were behind them their fear decreased and they felt more free to breathe. Memed carried Hatché's bundle. She noticed that he was tired and insisted that she wanted to carry her own bundle, but he wouldn't give it to her.

The drizzling rain turned into a fierce downpour. To their right and their left, behind and in front of them, the lightning lit up the forest, bright as day. In these flashes they could see the water streaming down the trunks of the trees. Hatché began to sob.

"A fine time for crying," muttered Memed angrily.

They continued to walk until dawn began to appear in the east.

In the pouring rain, they had lost all sense of direction and were lost. Hatché constantly cursed the rain.

When it was already light they found a hollow rock and sought shelter beneath it. They stood there shivering, side by side, their wet clothes clinging to their bodies. Hatché's hair was dripping as if they were still walking under the rain.

"If the tinder isn't wet," said Memed, his teeth chattering, "we can light a fire and dry ourselves."

Hatché smiled happily.

"Don't laugh," said Memed. "We've been through such a downpour that we're not just wet, we're soaked to the bone."

With trembling hands he tried to open the pouch tied to his belt. All their hope, their salvation, lay there. They looked into the pouch. Then their eyes met and they smiled. The rain had not penetrated it.

"Do you know who made this pouch?" he asked.

"No," replied Hatché.

"When I ran away to the house of Uncle Süleyman, he made it. I've kept it ever since to remind me of his kindness."

He looked around anxiously. "There's nothing dry to wipe my hands on. The tinder will get wet if I touch it."

"For heaven's sake, don't touch the tinder with wet hands," Hatché exclaimed.

"See how I'll dry them!" he said proudly. He went to the back of the hollow. The rain hadn't reached that far. The earth there was like dry dust. He thrust his hands into it; they came out all coated with dust. Raising them in the air he turned to Hatché: "See?"

Hatché smiled.

"Off with you, Hatché. Go and collect brushwood and twigs," Memed ordered.

Hatché slipped out of the hollow into the rain and was soon back with a huge armful of brushwood. The branches were damp on the surface, but dry inside. They broke them up into tiny pieces and piled the wood in the middle of the hollow. Memed struck his flint. The tinder caught a spark, but not strong enough to set the twigs burning. For the brushwood to catch fire they needed a flame, however small. What could they do?

"Stay here," said Memed. "I'll go and find some resin-wood."

He was soon back with a piece of resinous pine-wood. He pulled out his big double-edged knife and split the wood in two. But the tinder wouldn't light the resin-wood either. The tiniest flame would have sufficed and, if they had only had a match, everything would have been easy. Memed had brought some matches, but they were all soggy now. "Hatché, can't you find a bit of dry cloth?"

Hatché's teeth were chattering. "I'll look in the bundle and see what I can find. Perhaps the rain hasn't penetrated everything."

Outside, the rain was still pouring, as if flowing from a hole in the sky.

Hatché opened her bundle, fumbled and searched everywhere. At last she found a 'kerchief screwed up inside a skirt. It was Memed's first gift to her, a 'kerchief with red spots. The women in the village all wore such 'kerchiefs round their heads.

"There's only this that's dry," she said, showing it to Memed.

Memed recognised the 'kerchief. "Only that?" he asked. He felt a pleasant thrill at seeing the 'kerchief again. "If I knew I was about to freeze here and die, I still wouldn't burn that," he burst out, a little angrily.

"Perhaps I can find a dry piece among my skirts," said Hatché. "Bring it all here."

Hatché brought the bundle to him. Memed fumbled in it.

"There isn't only one thing here that's still dry, but hundreds."

"Well, burn the lot and I'll go naked."

"If it goes on like this, you will," Memed assured her.

They tore out the lining of a fairly dry skirt. He struck the flint, placed the tinder inside the piece of cloth, began to blow on it, puffed and puffed. When he was tired he let Hatché continue. Then a flash of lightning struck the earth close to their refuge. The ground heaved slightly and the trees crackled. Hatché dropped what she was holding, but Memed bent down and picked it up. Puffing his cheeks he began to blow again till his cheeks ached. When a tiny flame at last caught the top of the cloth, he was glad, and immediately grasped the kindling-wood in his other hand. Sizzling, the resinous wood caught fire. He placed a few pieces of this kindling-wood together, then pushed them into the middle of the pile of brushwood and set the fire carefully. The rain continued to pour ever more fiercely. The sky was like black smoke, streaked again and again by flashes of lightning. For a few seconds each flash seemed to light up the whole earth, after which Memed's mind was a yellow blaze, remembering the brass ewers.

The fire grew. Memed piled more wood on to it. As the damp was driven out of the wood, it began to blaze, roaring with great dancing flames. They took off their clothes and hung them on a branch close by, then drew the branch closer to the fire. Hatché was ashamed and refused to take off her underclothes.

"Take those off," said Memed, "and your shivering will stop."

Hatché looked at him pleadingly. "They'll dry on me," she said.

"They can't dry on you," Memed exclaimed angrily. "By the time they've dried on you you'll be dead of cold."

Realising that Memed was angry, Hatché began to pull off her blouse and hung it on the brushwood, covering her breasts with her hands. Rounded and dark-skinned, her shoulders were shaking. Her neck was as slender as a swan's. Tiny locks of hair curled behind her ears, while her plaited black hair hung down her back to her waist. Her breasts swelled out between her fingers. The skin round the quince-yellow down was goose-fleshed from the cold. As the warmth began to penetrate her, these pimples disappeared and her skin became quite smooth, slightly pink.

Memed stared at Hatché. An uncontrollable desire began to rage within him. "Hatché . . . !"

She tingled as she understood the tone of his voice. "Memed," she said, "all hell must have been let loose in the village by now. They'll be searching high and low for us. I'm afraid they'll find us."

Memed could feel the same fear, but did not show it. "How can they find us in this forest?"

"I don't know, but I'm afraid."

For a long time they were silent. The rain seemed to pour less abundantly and the fire steadily gained strength. Even the nearby rocks were warm and the surface of the ground was soon dry. When Hatché was able to put on her dry blouse she took off her drawers. Memed saw her fresh, plump legs. His contained passion had become unbearable. "Hatché!" he called again, in the same way.

"I'm afraid, Memed."

Memed seized her wrist so tight that it hurt. She tried to release herself. With all his strength Memed embraced her and began to kiss her. Suddenly she no longer resisted. Memed carried her to the foot of the rock. Her full lips were half open, her eyes closed, her arms and legs limp. She kept on murmuring: "I'm frightened, don't, Memed."

The flames of the huge fire seemed to reach out towards them, licking the rocks.

It was some time before they again became conscious of their surroundings. Memed took Hatché by the hand and tried to raise her from where they had been lying. She half rose, then lay down again on her back. She no longer felt any fear. Her whole body was exhausted, crushed. Later she rose by herself. Her legs, her back, her hips, were smeared with dust.

IX

Her mother had risen before dawn. When she glanced at Hatché's bed, it seemed to be occupied, so she suspected nothing, but as morning came and Hatché still did not appear at the usual time, her heart suddenly missed a beat. She pulled back the quilt and her fears proved true. Hatché had placed a pillow lengthwise under the quilt, so that it lay there like her own body, proof enough that she had run away the night before; thanks to this trick, her absence had not been noticed earlier.

Thunderstruck, Hatché's mother stood there, the quilt in her hand. Only when her husband called her did she recover her presence of mind and drop it.

In the villages of the Taurus it is customary, if a daughter runs away, or a horse, an ox or a cock has been stolen, to stand before the door of one's house and rain curses on the whole village, on all those whose better fortune one envies. For hours one stands there and curses. The villagers pay no attention, do not even answer. After a time one's rage begins to subside and the event can then be seriously discussed.

"The girl's gone," she cried to her husband. "Now what do we do?"

With a clear sigh of relief, the husband replied: "Thanks be to God. My heart was never in this marriage with Abdi Agha's bald-headed nephew. I only agreed because there was no way out. Thank God!"

"Shut up. Don't let anyone hear you. If Abdi Agha gets the idea that we've helped her to elope he'll skin us alive."

Then, according to custom, she went to the door and began to wail. She had no desire to wail. She could not just curse anyone at random. She did not even scream, but rocked back and forth. "Oh, the troubles that come upon me!" she began, but her heart was not in it. "My daughter! My daughter! God grant that she may live in misery. She's destroyed my good name! Curse you, my daughter! May your eyes drop out of your head, my daughter!"

"Come indoors," called her husband severely. "The girl has done well. She's run away with her heart's desire, come what may. Shut your mouth, woman! Stop moaning. Go and tell Abdi Agha what's happened. But don't curse your daughter! Come inside!"

The woman did as her husband told her. She tied a black cloth round her head and went to Abdi Agha's house.

When Abdi Agha saw the woman, he called: "Where have you been, Sister? You never come to see me. Come and sit beside me."

The woman sat down and began to weep. Abdi Agha's heart missed a beat. "What's happened, Sister?" he asked anxiously. She hung her head and wept all the more.

"Speak up!" shouted Abdi Agha. "Speak up, you fool! Has anything happened to my daughter-in-law?"

"Agha . . ." she began.

"Say it."

"Agha! Agha!" she repeated and then stopped. Her words were drowned in sobs.

"May God curse you, woman. Don't torment a man."

The woman wiped her eyes. "She's run away. She placed a pillow in her bed beneath the quilt and ran away early last night."

"What!" roared Abdi Agha. "Did that have to happen too? Did Abdi Agha's daughter-in-law have to run away with a labourer?" Then he turned on the woman and gave her a savage kick. "I'll burn this village from end to end. I'll set fire to it and burn it." He stopped and reflected, then took the woman by the arm and leaned towards her. "Is it Deuneh's wretched son that's run off with her?" he whispered into her ear.

The woman wiped her tears with her head-cloth and nodded in affirmation.

Abdi Agha immediately called his men to summon all the villagers. This was a heavy blow to his esteem in the village and he had to do something about it. "He'll see," he kept saying, "that wretch, that vagabond, he'll see what I'll do to him. I'll break every bone in his body."

The whole village soon knew about the elopement and rejoiced over it, though none dared express his joy openly before Abdi Agha. Instead, in the presence of Abdi Agha's men the villagers pretended to be more concerned over it than the Agha himself and spoke only in whispers.

It was still raining relentlessly. Huddled together in the rain, the villagers formed little groups, with much coming and going from house to house and much gossip. They were all soaked to the skin, their wet clothes clinging to their bodies as if they had been rescued from drowning.

Suddenly, in a burst of noise, the men from the other village appeared, the bridegroom-to-be at their head. Each one had a shot-gun in his hand. The bridegroom was furious, cursing the whole village and threatening to destroy it by fire. He went straight to Memed's house. Deuneh was there, as if she knew nothing of what was going on outside. The bridegroom jumped from his horse, pushed his way inside, seized Deuneh by the hair and dragged her as far as Abdi Agha's door. Then Abdi Agha saw her and he could no longer control himself. With the heels of his boots he began to stamp on her. Not a sound escaped from Deuneh's lips as he trampled her in the mud. Even her eyes could no longer be seen for mud. When Abdi Agha left off, the bridegroom began to trample on her too, then stopped and wandered around the court-yard twirling his moustaches angrily, returning soon to kick her again. The blood oozing from the woman's mouth mingled with the mud, streaming over her clothes like red ribbons.

Abdi Agha was beside himself with rage. He roamed round and round the courtyard, heeding nobody. Those standing by just stared at him without uttering a word. Whenever an important de-cision had to be taken he had a habit of curling a wisp of his beard round his forefinger and pulling it. He was doing this now as he came to a halt in the middle of the yard; everyone was silent and looked towards him. He stopped pulling his beard and began to stroke it. "Listen! They must still be in the neighbourhood, either among the rocks or in the forest. We'll look for them, but not with all this crowd. Ten men are enough. If one of you finds him and I'm not there, don't kill him but bring him to me. I'll settle his account. I'll teach him to run off with Abdi Agha's daughter-in-law."

When Abdi Agha had finished speaking, Rustem, one of the

villagers, a bald man with a pock-marked face and a huge nose, made a suggestion: "It's been raining ever since last night, hasn't it?"

"Yes," came the reply from the crowd.

"Their tracks will show in the mud and, even if they don't, if they've gone among the rocks, we can find their trail. They're not far. We can certainly find them."

"Three of you can go down the road to the town," said Abdi Agha. "I've heard they may have run off to town." Then he turned to Rustem and asked: "Who can track them down?"

"There's Lame Ali."

There was a chorus of approval. All agreed that, if he felt like it, rain or no rain, on dry ground or on rocks, Lame Ali would be able to follow even the track of a bird.

"He can track down a bird," repeated Rustem, "if it has only grazed the earth with the tip of one wing."

"Fetch Lame Ali immediately, wherever he is," ordered Abdi Agha.

"Lame Ali's here," the answer came.

Lame Ali hobbled forward until he stood opposite the Agha: "Have no fear, Agha. If Memed's foot has only grazed the earth, I'll find him, unless he has wings and has flown off. Don't worry!"

The men from Lame Ali's village praised his achievements to the others and to the Agha. "Whenever there's a theft in our village, Lame Ali always finds the culprit."

"Lame Ali can even follow the scent of deer over the rocks and lead you to where they are feeding!"

Hüsük never mixed with crowds and rarely came to the village, but now stood in front of the Agha's house. He had known Lame Ali for many years. They had ploughed the fields side by side and Hüsük knew what a skilful tracker Lame Ali was. For miles around everyone knew it. Even Abdi Agha had heard of his skill. The villagers were praising Ali now because they enjoyed boasting of his legendary achievements.

Hüsük saw that Lame Ali had taken upon himself to track down Memed. Wherever Memed might be, whatever road or pass he had taken, whatever cave or hollow he had hidden in, Lame Ali would find him as surely as if he had placed him there with his own hand. Hüsük wanted to have a few words with Ali without attracting attention. Ali would not refuse his request; they had eaten bread and salt together all these years.

Ali was listening delightedly as the villagers sang his praises to Abdi Agha. Now and then he would interrupt them with modesty, though secretly bursting with pride: "Only with God's help and yours, Agha . . ." He was never interested in hearing men say that he was brave or good, without his peer in any of these villages, only in their agreeing that no man could follow a trail as well as he.

A man who needed Lame Ali's help would always, for two or three days, go round praising his achievements in such a manner that it would reach his ears, repeating everywhere that his equal was not to be found in all the region behind Adana. Once one was sure that Ali had heard this praise, one could approach him knowing that he would grant a request even if he were to die in his attempt to satisfy it.

Ali had left the crowd to look for the beginning of Memed's trail, near Hatché's house, when Hüsük caught up with him. "Wait, Ali! I have a couple of things to say to you."

Ali greeted him affectionately: "Brother Hüsük, I was longing to see you and hoped to come and see you one of these days. How are you? Let me finish this job and I'll spend the evening with you, Hüsük. It won't take me long to find the lad, it's an easy job."

"Come! Don't let anyone see us talking together. The Agha is suspicious of me."

Wondering, Lame Ali fell in behind Hüsük. The rain had stopped for a while but now began to fall again.

In front of the Agha's house they were saddling a horse for Lame Ali, who could track a man down on horseback, riding blindfold, and still follow his trail.

Hüsük slipped behind a house. As soon as Ali joined him he began in a voice full of reproach: "Come and sit beside me. Ali, how can you do such a thing? How can you hand over that poor child to Abdi? Don't destroy Memed, a poor orphan, Ibrahim's only son! Was there ever a man like Ibrahim? He loved you, too, and his bones would now rise up in their grave. I know you'll find Memed as sure as if you held him in your hands now. But Abdi will do terrible things to him and it will be as if you had done him the harm. Let me make a suggestion, Ali. Put them on the wrong track to-day. If he can live through to-day, Memed is safe. When

85

he was a boy he ran away to Süleyman's house in Kesme village. Everyone thought he was dead. Six months later, or was it a year, I saw him and brought his mother the news that he was alive. Now he'll again manage to hide somewhere. Come, Brother, put them on the wrong track. Who knows where the poor creatures are now, soaked through in this rain, and where they're hiding? Where could they possibly be in this storm? They must be shivering. Say something, Ali. Say that you refuse to take on this job!"

As Hüsük talked, Lame Ali changed colour. He had been proud a little while before, when he had declared before the whole village that he could track the runaways down and find them. As Hüsük talked, he kept silent, staring at the ground.

Ali said nothing and Hüsük began to speak all the more bitterly: " Brother Ali, the poor children must be huddled together, shivering under some tree. It's not rain but a whole river that's pouring down on them now. A river pouring endlessly. Ali, my brother, they're afraid, the poor children. Look what this rain is doing! If only it would stop and take pity on them! If a bird flashes past, they're frightened. If a mouse runs by or a lizard climbs a tree, they're scared. 'They'll find us,' they keep saying. They're lovers, Ali. One doesn't persecute lovers. Your hand will wither like a dry tree if you help persecute them. Put Abdi Agha's men on the wrong trail, Ali, and save these two lovers. A palace will then be waiting for you in paradise; at this very moment they're preparing it for you. Come, Ali! Give me your word!"

Hüsük stared into Ali's eyes as if to say: "If you don't do this, there's no more friendship between us." But Ali did not utter a word, either of acceptance or of refusal. Hüsük seized Ali's hand and began all over again:

"Let me tell you something, Ali! They have been in love since childhood. If Hatché failed one day to see Memed, she could no longer eat nor sleep and just sobbed her heart out. Don't you understand? Allah brought them together. When Memed ran away to Kesme village and I brought the news to his mother, the girl had been ill in bed, waiting for his return like a mad creature. That's how it is, Brother Ali. They forced the girl to accept Abdi's ugly nephew. So the two children ran away Think of the consequences. A bird takes shelter in a bush and the bush protects it. Memed has sought refuge in your heart, Ali; don't be the cause of his undoing.

If you do this you'll have Abdi for a friend, but the whole village will be against you. 'So long as Abdi is my friend,' you may well say. But it's not as easy as that, Ali, and you know it. That's all I have to say to you."

With hunched shoulders, his tired face distraught, Ali rose to his feet without saying a word to Hüsük.

Hüsük called after him: "You'll have the whole village against you!" Then catching up with him, he whispered in his ear: "Have you ever heard what happens to those who separate true lovers? If a man destroys the nest, his own nest is then destroyed, Ali! All the village rejoiced when we heard that the lovers had run away. You're now placing all your faith in a rotten tree. All the village will be against you. Look what they've already done to the boy's mother, still lying there in the mud!"

By this time the horse was harnessed and they called Ali. A youngster stood waiting, holding the reins respectfully. A long-haired black saddle-cloth was strapped on the horse's back. It was still raining steadily.

All the villagers were out, staring at Lame Ali, who could feel the burden of hundreds of eyes weighing on him. The pain that had been there since his birth revived in his lame leg, an unbearable pain. Whenever he was in a difficult situation, it began to torture him. The whole village, its stones and its earth, its people and its animals, seemed to be secretly cursing him.

Two tracks could be detected, side by side, under the mulberry-tree in front of Hatché's house. Ali followed these tracks, first circling round Hatché's house four or five times while all the village children followed him. Then he began to wander aimlessly through the village.

Two or three villagers stood beside Hüsük. "What did you say to him?" they asked.

"I said what I had to say," he boasted. "I don't think Ali will reject my advice." He was pleased to see him wandering idly through the village. This was unusual: if Ali ever found the beginning of a trail he would follow it rapidly to its very end, as easily as if he were unravelling a knitted stocking. His wandering like this was a good sign. Hüsük commented on it and his words passed from mouth to mouth: "It's a good sign, Ali's wandering like this."

"Who said so?"

"Hüsük said so."

"Lame Ali is still wandering around the village," said Hüsük. "God knows, perhaps he's taken pity on the lovers and will put them all on the wrong track. If only he would do it!"

"I know Lame Ali," answered another villager. "He would track down his own father, even if he knew that the old man would then be hanged. It's enough for him if there's a trail to follow. He can't help it. He's a good man, with a heart that will bleed for the lovers, but it's impossible for him not to follow their trail. When it comes to tracking, nothing else matters. Even if he knows that it means his own death, once you set him on a trail he'll follow it to the bitter end."

"All right," said Hüsük. "He's already gone round the house ten times and he's now been wandering round the village for hours, following their trail, let's say. But Memed didn't take the girl to go visiting every house in the village. A man who runs off with a girl doesn't stop even once to look back. Lame Ali's not the man to be confused by a trail, even in this rain. I warned him . . ."

The other villager considered Hüsük's words, and an expression of hope and joy appeared in his face. "Allah grant that Ali may change his ways. It really looks as if he has."

Meanwhile, Lame Ali came and went. In front of each door he dismounted to observe the ground carefully, examining every pebble, doing whatever might be necessary to detect a trail, but carefully avoiding the places where the real trail might be found. He knew that if he saw the trail again he would be forced to follow it to the bitter end. Pretending to follow it, he therefore went out of the village and even thought of running away. He stared at the forest for a long time. The trail led straight into the forest. It was as if he could already see the two lovers. His mind was utterly confused.

It was still drizzling when he turned his horse towards Hatché's house again, coming to a stop by the fence beside the mulberry-tree. On the ground he could distinguish the oblong imprint of a sandal. "Those sandals have been newly sewn," he remarked. "The hairs on the leather are still long. Surely that's the skin of a bull-calf that died last winter." He saw the two lovers in the forest again. Beneath the penetrating drizzle he was filled with a fever of excitement as if he were burning.

Seeing him so thoughtful, one of the villagers approached him. "What's the matter, Ali?" he inquired. "Will you stay here dreaming? Abdi Agha's getting impatient. He wants to know why you're wandering round the village and if this is how the much-praised Lame Ali follows a trail."

As they were talking, Abdi Agha rode up to them at full speed and stopped his horse beside them. "What's this?" he asked. "Congratulations, my tracker-in-chief, a fine trail you've followed! Ever since this morning you've been roaming around the village as though you were surveying the land. Now you'll probably go to sleep at the foot of this fence."

Lame Ali's eyes were grim. He turned suddenly towards Abdi Agha. "Agha," he said, "ask these villagers and let's see if Memed's wearing new sandals and whether his sandals were made from the skin of a bull-calf that died last winter."

The Agha turned to the villagers. "Is it true?" he asked.

"That's right," replied one of the villagers. "Ismail's young bull died last winter. You know Miller Ismail; it was his bull and Memed bought a piece of the skin from him."

"You were right," the Agha nodded to Lame Ali. "Now show us your skill, Ali."

Ali leaned forward and whipped his horse. With Abdi Agha and seven or eight riders behind him, he rode out of the village at full speed and stopped his horse only when he reached the rocks. The others halted too. The trail led towards the rocks. Ali was surprised. He had thought that the trail would lead towards the woods, but he now examined the tracks on the rocks. "They've gone by the rocks. Let's dismount and follow their trail on foot across the rocks," he said.

They left the horses to one of the men and fell in behind Ali. A small patch of earth appeared among the rocks. Three yellow flowers had blossomed there. The earth itself was black and shiny, the yellow flowers bright. One of the flowers lay on its side. Ali showed it to his companions. "Do you know why this one flower droops while the others are quite straight? Yesterday evening, or in the middle of the night, someone trod on it. See here, the edge of the sandal has left a mark."

They all bent down and stared, but not one of them could distinguish the mark left by the edge of the sandal.

Then Ali wandered about among the rocks, Abdi Agha never leaving his side. They came to the foot of a steep rock. "See," said Ali. "They turned back here."

They came back to the horses. The trail now led clearly towards the forest. Even the others could follow it. At the edge of the forest Ali halted. His face turned yellow, then grey as ash, then a deep red. The tracks now led towards the rocky heights in the middle of the forest. This was a blind man's course, that of a man who had no idea where he is going, leading now straight ahead, then turning off to one side and doubling back again. Ali felt anguish in his heart when he saw the tracks winding about and coming back to the same place time after time. "Let me lead Abdi to the heart of the forest," he thought, "so that these poor creatures may escape."

A turf of green grass was growing among the roots of a tree. The grass, fresh though it was, was flattened out on its roots, partly crushed. Beyond that, a broken branch had been crushed to the ground.

The rain was again beating down on them. Lame Ali pulled the saddle-cloth over himself. The others were silent.

"Time's passing, Ali," said Abdi Agha. "Have you lost the trail again?"

"No," replied Ali. "Let's go on." He rode on among the trees. This time he really lost the trail and turned to Abdi. "It's escaped me," he explained.

"Is this all your skill, Lame Ali?" Abdi taunted him.

The bridegroom was right behind them. In his clenched fist he carried his rifle.

Ali resented Abdi Agha's words. "Now I'll find the trail. They must be near. Here they were caught by the storm and circled around for a while. That's why I've missed their trail."

It was some time before he found it again. The trees grew so thick that the horses couldn't pass. They left them behind and went ahead on foot.

"Here they broke a branch," said Ali. Then he became excited: "We're getting near! They've taken an armful of brushwood from here, dry brushwood. The trail leads straight up to the rocks."

With the exception of Lame Ali and Abdi Agha they were all drenched. Abdi turned to the bridegroom. "Why didn't you bring a saddle-cloth?" he asked sternly.

The other was in no state to answer, his hand was trembling so that he almost dropped his rifle.

Lame Ali began to run towards the rocks, possessed with the fever of the chase. The others followed him.

"I've found them," he said. "They're beneath that huge rock. Go softly!"

"There? Say something, Ali!" shouted Abdi Agha from behind.

Ali was silent. Abdi caught up with him, breathing heavily. He stopped beside Ali and began to look around. The others followed and stood in a row.

"Here they lit a fire," Ali began to speak. "They spread out their clothes to dry on that bush. They didn't light the fire with matches but with tinder."

He went over to the dry ground to the rear of the hollow. He bent down to the ground, felt around for a long while. He could distinguish the outline of the girl's broad firm hips on the ground. A little above the hips the marks of her shoulder-blades were clear.

"Come here! Come here!" he called to those behind. "Come and see."

From all sides they bent down and stared at the ground. Abdi Agha looked inquiringly into Ali's face.

"It's done now," declared Ali.

Abdi Agha understood but insisted: "What's done, Ali?"

"Look, Agha, there's the place of the girl's hips. There, her shoulder-blades. There her head rested. Look at these lines. Here is where her hair spread out. It means, Agha . . ."

Abdi Agha's face changed. He remained silent, then slowly came to himself. "Where have they gone now, according to you?"

"They must be very near. We'll find them soon."

The sun was nearly setting. "We don't want to stay out all night, Ali," said Abdi Agha.

"They cannot have left here more than two hours ago. How far can you get in two hours in this forest? Besides, they must be starving. There isn't a single crumb where they've been warming themselves. If they had had any food, there would be some of it left on the ground."

The bridegroom was shivering. On all sides the rain was pouring off him and his teeth were chattering.

"Let's light a fire and warm ourselves," he suggested. "We're all dying of cold."

The others agreed.

"We'll go and look for them," shouted Abdi angrily. "You can stay here and warm yourselves. What a crowd of weak-hearted women!"

He set off with Ali. As they entered the forest Abdi Agha pulled out his revolver. Seeing how angry Abdi was, the bridegroom changed his mind about lighting a fire and followed them.

Slowly darkness fell. Ali had picked up the trail of the lovers; it was so clear that he might have followed it even in the darkness. At last they had tracked them down and were bound, come what may, to catch them. The tracks now seemed to be quite fresh. Behind a bush they heard a crackling and listened intently. It was dark now.

"Surround the bush," ordered Abdi.

"They're here," declared Ali.

Suddenly they heard a woman scream.

"Don't kill Memed," roared Abdi. "Seize him and bring him to me. With my own hands I'll do what's to be done to him, with my own hands!"

Memed was hiding behind the bush. His hand was on the butt of his revolver, which he held in the right-hand pocket of his trousers, feeling no fear at all.

"Don't be frightened!" he whispered to Hatché. "I won't give you up to them."

He stood up behind the bush. To those who were approaching him fearfully he called out: "Surrender! I surrender!"

"Stop," shouted Abdi. "Let me get at him."

The others drew back. Abdi and the bridegroom went ahead. Memed was standing erect behind the bush. As night had come he could be seen only as a slim shadow.

Only a moment before, Lame Ali had been exultant at having followed the trail successfully to the end, but he was now filled with a terrible sadness. He went and sat down on a tree-stump and buried his head in his hands, murmuring to himself: "I'll never do this work again. I'll never do it again, Memed."

"You scoundrel," screamed Abdi Agha. "You blackguard. Is

this what you would do to me? I'll take you back to the village. You can imagine the rest yourself . . ."

The click of a trigger was then heard. But the weapon failed to fire. Abdi turned round indignantly and bellowed: "Fool! Didn't I tell you not to do anything to him?"

Memed did not move. He was not excited. He felt no fear. He stood waiting as if turned to stone. His hand began to fumble in the right-hand pocket of his trousers. Slowly, he drew the revolver out, as calmly as if it were a package of cigarettes. He aimed straight at Abdi Agha. His hand was quite steady as he fired two shots.

"I'm wounded," cried Abdi Agha. As he fell to the ground Memed turned his weapon on the bridegroom and fired three shots at him. He, too, fell to the ground, exclaiming: "I'm wounded!"

Memed thrust the revolver back into his pocket. With the same calm he called out: "Hatché's here. If you hurt a hair of her head, I know what I'll do to you." Turning to Hatché he added: "Now go off home. I'll come later and fetch you. We'll take all our belongings and go to some place where they can never find us. Go straight home. They can't harm you."

They began to fire at Memed. This surprised him. When he was already far off, they continued firing into the darkness.

Towards midnight he came out of the forest. It was still drizzling.

X

There was a gentle, timid knocking at the door, stopping for a moment, then beginning again.

The woman woke her husband. "Get up," she said. "Someone's knocking."

After several fruitless attempts to rouse himself, the sleepy man laid his head on the pillow again. But the knocking at the door became more urgent.

"Get up, someone's knocking at the door."

Grumbling, the man rose from his bed. Swaying slightly, he went to the door. "Who's there?" he called out.

From outside a reply came: "I'm there." The voice was hoarse and the speaker cleared his throat.

"Who are you?"

"Let me in, please. You know me."

The man inside opened the door. "Come in, if that's how it is."

The visitor staggered into the house. The room was dark and the man called to his wife: "Light the lamp. We have a guest."

As soon as she had lit the lamp the woman came up close to her husband and the stranger. Rain was dripping off him, the clothes were clinging to his body. She stared at him in amazement, a glimmer of recognition in her eyes.

"I've a feeling I know him," she said at last. "But I can't recognise him."

"I don't recognise him either," the man added as he smiled, "but I'm sure I know him. I just can't figure it out." He placed his hand on the guest's shoulder and looked at him closer. "There's something familiar about him, but I can't make it out." Then, to his wife: "I can see that our guest is cold and wet. Light a fire."

Turning to the other, he added: "Let's see, who are you? I'm sure I know you. But I can't place you."

"Uncle," said the visitor, "I'm Slim Memed."

Süleyman called his wife, who was bringing wood from the other room. "Woman, see who has come!"

"Who is it?" asked the woman excitedly.

"It's our Memed. Praise God, what a fine fellow he's grown to be. I was talking about you only a few days ago, wondering what had become of you. It seems I had a feeling you were coming."

"Aye, lad," said the woman, "Uncle Süleyman's been talking of you endlessly all these last few days."

Süleyman had grown much older. The hairs of his eyebrows were longer, all tufted and white, hanging down over his eyes. His beard too was very long, like a wad of cotton-wool. It gave him a patriarchal look.

The woman brought a suit of dry underclothing and laid it before Memed. "Strip, lad, and put these on, or you'll catch your death of cold."

Memed went into a dark corner of the room and undressed. Then he came and sat by the fire in his shirt and drawers.

Süleyman looked at him questioningly.

"I've been longing to see you," replied Memed, "but what can I say? You know how it is . . ."

"Haven't you been to that village yet, Memed?" teased Süleyman.

Memed laughed bitterly. "We couldn't go." As he spoke something glowed in his head like a ball of yellow light.

"If I may ask," said Süleyman, "what sort of job are you up to at this hour of the night, Memed?"

"I'll explain," answered Memed. "I've come to you to find some way out of my troubles. I know nobody else in all the world who can help me."

"You're cold, child," interrupted the woman. "I'll warm up some soup for you."

As Memed took the hot bowl of soup in his hand, he remembered how, once before when he had been cold, he had drunk soup in this same corner, by the same hearth. Then he had been alone, afraid of everything. The forest had seemed to threaten him. Now he was brave and had made up his mind. His world was torn apart and he had tasted of freedom, but he didn't regret what he had done.

"You two can sit and talk," said the woman. "I'll go and lie down."

"Now tell me all about it, my Memed," urged Süleyman, once his wife was gone.

"I've killed Abdi and his nephew," he began, but Süleyman interrupted him with astonishment: "When?"

"To-day as night was falling."

"Is that the truth, Memed?" asked Süleyman incredulously. "You don't look as if you'd killed a man."

"Well, it's done. It was my fate." Then he explained to Süleyman all that had happened, in great detail. The cocks had begun crowing in the dawn. When he had finished, Süleyman said: "Good for you, boy. You've done well. Now let's hear what your plans are."

"I'm certainly not going to give myself up to the police. I'll take to the mountains."

"You can rest here to-day. We can still think about all that to-morrow."

"Won't they find me here?"

"No one will think of it. No one would expect you to come and hide in this village, under the very nose of the man you've shot."

"True," agreed Memed.

"If they look for you, it will be in more distant villages on the mountains."

Rows of embroidered bags stood against the wall. Süleyman called Memed. "Come, let's pull away those bags. We'll take precautions, just in case anything happens. I'll make your bed behind those bags."

After struggling for a time they moved the bags just far enough from the wall to hide a man. Then Süleyman made a bed behind the bags. "Get in and lie down," he said. "Lie there a month if you like. No one will ever suspect. Is the horse-blanket properly tucked round you? Lie down and sleep."

Without a word Memed tucked in and lay down. Süleyman bolted the entrance door carefully and went to bed. His wife was asleep. He woke her. "Listen to me. I've made Memed's bed behind the bags. Don't tell our son or his wife or anyone that Memed has come back."

"Of course I won't," she murmured as her head fell back on the pillow.

Memed thought of Hatché for a while. Then he remembered the scene of Abdi falling and writhing on the ground. Abdi had never expected that shot. The screams of the bridegroom tearing at the ground with his hands, biting the branches and the earth, his sudden collapse as he lay in a pool of his own blood, all this came back to Memed's mind. He had also noticed a man who, whilst everyone else was firing at him, had remained seated on a stump, his head in his hands, swaying back and forth, obviously in great anguish. Memed couldn't understand who this man might have been. But soon he forgot everything and his mind became clear as a new-born babe's. He slept as if nothing had happened.

When he awoke he felt light-hearted. What had been done was done. Süleyman called to him: "Listen! I was up early and wandered all through the village. The news that Abdi has been shot has reached us. Perhaps they'll search here. To-night you and I must go up the mountain and try to find the outlaws." Memed looked pleased as Süleyman continued: "Mad Durdu is some sort of relative of mine. I've treated him well and he'll take you under his protection, but don't stay with him more than three months. He's a mad dog and won't last long on the mountain. Sooner or later he'll get shot. Brigands like Durdu never last more than a year at most. Strike out on your own as soon as you can. Your couple of months with Durdu will give you enough experience to head your band. Don't stay with him too long; he's no brigand, just a plunderer, a thief. If it weren't for you, I wouldn't deign to speak to him. But in some ways Mad Durdu isn't so bad. He's been treated badly. One day he was invited back to his own village and they gave him food and drink and then betrayed him to the police. He escaped only by the skin of his teeth and has been in a rage ever since."

"Is Mad Durdu's band a big one?" asked Memed.

"All the wild ones from these parts have joined him, all those who have somehow escaped the gallows or the firing-squad. Listen, Memed, and I'll give you one or two bits of advice which you must

97

take to heart. You're still young, but you'll grow up. God knows whether you'll stay on the mountain for a long time or not. I've had lots of dealings with brigands and I've seen the downfall of most of them. Don't get too familiar with everyone as soon as you join Durdu's band. Each one of them will want to strike up a friendship with you and they'll all try to be pleasant and kindly. They'll take a great interest in you, they'll tell you all their troubles; people are like that. But you must keep to yourself and this will help you gain prestige in their eyes. You must behave with dignity. As a brigand you must be respected by your companions. Now don't go and say to yourself: I'll get to know them all the first day and be friends with them. If they find your weak spot they'll never leave you in peace to the end of your days, and nobody will respect you. As the days go by you'll get to know them better. Measure people not by their words but by their deeds. After that you can choose your own comrades. If you allow them to get a hold on you you're finished. There's no difference between the mountain and a prison. There are leaders in both places and those who follow are their slaves. The leaders live like men, the others like dogs. You must be a leader. But don't treat the others like slaves. Let this be the secret of your life. As soon as you get there, Durdu will give you a gun. You'll then obtain other weapons with time. I'll go now and find out where Durdu is hiding."

One of the villagers used to supply Durdu in his hideouts. Süleyman went to his house and learned exactly where the bandit was to be found.

Durdu was from the nearby village of Aksoyut and Süleyman had known him since his childhood. Durdu's father had gone to the wars and never returned. Because of their vague kinship, Süleyman had then helped him and his mother, and saved them from dying of hunger. Even as a child Durdu had been a wilful little brat. He had now been in the mountains for five years, burning whole villages and plundering right and left. All the villagers of those parts complained bitterly of him. No one could travel safely on the roads. If he caught anyone he would strip him naked of all his possessions, taking even his underclothing. Durdu heeded neither friendship nor relatives and Süleyman hesitated to entrust Memed to his care. Durdu was the kind of man who might suddenly decide to kill the lad for no good reason.

"I've learned where that mad dog is hiding," Süleyman told Memed. "It seems he's on Mount Duman. We must climb up Duman and then fire three shots. Mad Durdu's men will then come and fetch us. I don't trust him at all, but he is the only outlaw leader in these parts."

They went on their way after sunset, Süleyman in front, Memed following him. As they left the village Süleyman turned round. "Heh! Memed," he cried, "now that you're becoming a brigand, you won't come and destroy our house, will you?"

"I'll plunder your house first, as befits a member of Mad Durdu's band."

Süleyman laughed. "Now tell me the truth!"

"Do I ever lie to you?" asked Memed.

Süleyman's face changed. "Memed, my lad, if you had done an evil deed, if you'd killed any other man, I'd have taken you and handed you over to the police myself."

"You can be sure I haven't hurt any other man."

Süleyman stopped dead, seized Memed by the collar, and looked straight into his eyes. "Listen to me, son," he said. "If you ever kill an innocent man or one who has never done much harm, or if you kill for money, you won't escape me."

"After this I've had my fill of killing," replied Memed quite calmly.

Süleyman still held Memed by the collar and added: "But if you ever meet another Abdi Agha and don't kill him, you won't escape from my hands either. If you meet a hundred Abdi Aghas, kill all of them. . . ."

"It's a promise," said Memed, laughing. "If I find a hundred of them, I'll kill them all."

It had stopped raining only that morning. When they reached the mountain the soil was muddy, full of stones that slipped beneath their feet. The air had a tang of rotten timber, bitter flowers and grass. The stars in the sky seemed very big, each one of them surrounded by a halo of light. Every so often could be heard a bird that bleated like a kid. When Memed and his companion were a little higher they heard a dove coo. Its call sounded as if it were saying: "*Yusuufjuuuuuuk!* Little Yusuf!"

When they arrived beneath the very peak of Duman Süleyman said: "Take out your revolver, Memed, and fire three shots into the sky." Out of breath, he lay on the ground and groaned: "Old age! If only I could be young again!"

Memed fired three shots as he had been told. They echoed in the distance among the rocks, and were answered by a single shot.

"My knees!" Süleyman complained as he rose to his feet. "Now, my lad, let's walk in the direction of that shot."

Memed put his arm through Süleyman's. When another shot was fired close to them, they stopped.

"What's that, sons of dogs," shouted Süleyman. "Will you shoot *me?*"

"Who's that?" called a strong young voice.

"Come, man, come and lead us to Mad Durdu."

A man stepped out from behind a rock to their right. "Were you the ones who fired?" he asked.

"Yes," answered Süleyman. "Where's Mad Durdu? Lead us to Mad Durdu."

"Who are you?" The man sounded surprised.

"Tell Durdu it's Uncle Süleyman from Kesme village."

"Forgive me, Uncle Süleyman. I didn't recognise your voice," the man replied.

"Old age, my lad, changes even one's voice. Who are you, boy? I don't recognise you either."

"I'm Mustuk's son, Jabbar, from Karajaoren. I used to come to you with my father to order saddles. You used to make our saddles and sing us songs."

"Strange," answered Süleyman. "So you've become a brigand too? I hadn't heard about it."

"Well, that's how it is," said Jabbar, who then called out to Durdu: "It's Uncle Süleyman from Kesme village." His voice echoed among the rocks.

A fire was burning in front of a great cave. Seven or eight men were stretched out round it, cleaning their weapons. One rock, tall as a poplar, rose behind them and the huge fire cast strange and fearful shadows on it. Seeing the rock, the men, the weapons and the fire, Memed was filled with a sense of unreality.

One of the men by the fire rose to his feet. He was tall and his shadow, cast at full length on the rock, rose and fell as the flames flickered. The man came towards them.

"I think that's our Mad Durdu," Süleyman remarked.

"It is," answered Jabbar. "Durdu Agha . . ."

"Welcome, Uncle Süleyman," cried Durdu, his voice ringing like a bell. "What's this, in the middle of the night? Have you come to join us, Uncle Süleyman?" He took Süleyman's hand and kissed it.

"I've heard, young madman, that you have become lord of these mountains and do here as you will. . . ."

"So it is, Uncle Süleyman," answered Durdu. "I swear I don't let anyone pass on the roads along the valley. Soon people won't even be able to enter these lands. From here to Marash, whatever roads there are, I'll take toll on them. Then they'll know me in Aksoyut village! They'll know who Mad Durdu is!"

"You've begun to rant again," said Süleyman.

"If they trouble me any more I'll burn and plunder that Aksoyut village, raze it to the ground and plant wild figs in its place."

"That'll do, you madman!" Süleyman interrupted him.

"You seem to know nothing about my reputation," grumbled Durdu.

"I do, I do, you rascal. You've made brigandage a disgraceful profession."

"Only a few more years and I'll become rich. You'll see how a brigand should run his business."

" I'll die before that," answered Süleyman. "I'll never live to see your new kind of brigandage, though the report of your thieving already fills the world."

"You'll see!"

"If you go on like this you'll get killed like a mad dog," replied Süleyman angrily. "What I'll see will be your death. It's a pity, at your age. You know that I'm fond of you, mad as you are. . . ."

"You think I don't know you're fond of me! Ask my companions. Every day I tell them, if my bones are from God, my flesh is from Uncle Süleyman." And he turned round to ask his followers: "Isn't that true, friends?"

"Yes," they answered in chorus.

"I never wanted you to become a brigand. Must I tell you why you took to the mountain? Just to show off. It won't do, Durdu. It's sheer madness."

"At least sit down, Uncle Süleyman, and drink a cup of tea with us."

Süleyman crouched down with his hands on his knees. "Do you think you'll ever be young again? You've wasted your youth on these mountains." Then he smiled at Durdu. "You don't deny yourself any luxuries! Where did you find all that wormwood?"

The sweet-smelling wormwood was spread all round the great fire in a circle as big as a threshing floor and as soft as a thick mattress. The scent of the wormwood drifted into the night, soft and cloying.

"We find it, Uncle," Durdu said proudly. "These mountains are ours."

Süleyman burst out laughing: "So you have the title deeds to the wormwood field?"

Memed was watching intently. Each brigand was wearing a red fez, as is the custom in the mountains, where the red fez is the badge of brigandage. A brigand wearing a cap or hat, as men now do in the villages and cities, has never yet been seen. It is not known who first introduced the fez to the mountain or first used it there after the introduction of the hat in the rest of the country. Perhaps, when hats were introduced elsewhere, the brigands on the mountain felt no need to get rid of their fezes. After that, everyone who took to the mountains wore a fez too.

When Süleyman sat down all the bandits came and welcomed him, kissing his hand one by one. They looked at Memed curiously too. Memed remained behind Süleyman's back, sitting with his shoulders hunched, pitifully small.

" If you ask about this boy, his name's Slim Memed. He's committed a murder. I've brought him to you," said Süleyman as he introduced Memed. At this, Memed stared at the ground, looking even smaller.

Durdu looked first at Memed, then at Süleyman. "Does he want to join us?" he asked in astonishment.

"If you accept. . . . If not, then he'll go by himself!"

"Uncle Süleyman," replied Durdu, "you are respected among us. If you have brought him . . ." From his rucksack he produced a fez and threw it to Memed. Instinctively Memed caught it in the air. "Now, let's see you, my stout fellow. That's my old fez. It must do until we find you a better one." Then he turned to Süleyman and winked. "He's surprisingly young."

"He may be very young," Süleyman objected, "but he shot forty-year-old Abdi Agha. Men don't take to the mountains for stealing donkeys."

"Abdi Agha, was it?" asked Durdu aghast. "Abdi Agha, eh? Amazing!"

"Well, what do you think of it?" Süleyman asked.

Durdu stared at Memed with unbelieving eyes. "I suppose you haven't got a gun, Brother. It was a good thing to settle with Abdi Agha. Good for you! He's sucked the blood of five villages, like a leech. . . ." Then he turned to Jabbar: "Jabbar, that gun we captured in the last raid, dig it out from where we buried it and bring it here. Get some cartridges and bullets too." He just couldn't believe that this little mouthful of a boy had shot Abdi Agha. That was why he was still staring at Memed so curiously.

Suspecting as much, Süleyman added: "It wasn't only Abdi Agha. He killed his nephew too. Have you understood, Durdu?"

Durdu was even more surprised. "You mean to say his nephew as well?"

Memed sat huddled and shivering by the fire, seeming to have shrunk and to be even smaller than he was.

They filled slim glasses with hot tea and passed them to Süleyman and Memed.

Süleyman leaned towards Memed with fatherly affection. "Your life as an outlaw is beginning, Memed. Stand firm!"

They piled log upon log on the fire. Steadily the flames blazed higher. With the increasing warmth the wormwood's smell was more pleasant, more pungent. By the light of the fire the stars in the sky were now like tiny pinpoints.

"Have no fear, Uncle Süleyman," said Durdu. "While I'm about, not a hair of his head will be hurt."

Süleyman looked him over pityingly from head to foot. "You, Durdu, you're going straight to your death."

"Why, Uncle?" inquired Durdu with a laugh.

"A real brigand would never light such a fire on a mountain-top. Don't underestimate your enemy. It means that you are going straight to your death."

Durdu burst out laughing. "Why, Uncle, who is there on this wild mountain? Who would see us?"

"For a day they won't see. Maybe for two days they won't see. It's like the locusts in the proverb. . . ."

"They'll never see. And if they do, do you think the police can get the better of Mad Durdu? Ah, Uncle. You don't know Mad Durdu yet. He's the eagle of these mountains. Who would ever dare invade Mad Durdu's territory?"

"We'll see," answered Süleyman.

To change the subject Durdu turned to Memed. "Didn't your hand tremble at all when you shot Abdi Agha?"

"No, not in the least."

"Where did you aim?"

"At his chest. Right at the spot where his heart is. . . ." Memed suddenly felt indescribably lonely. Everything around him seemed to disappear. He would never learn to like Mad Durdu. Did the strange feeling within him come from this? The fire grew dim. The faces of the men cleaning their guns merged into the darkness. The shadows on the rock became huge, then faded away. The wind blew the flames down, towards the west. Suddenly he fixed his eyes on Süleyman. The old man seemed pleased. His white-bearded face changed continually in the firelight. Memed thought that Süleyman trusted him and his feeling of loneliness decreased a little. Then he was overcome by an irresistible desire to sleep and curled up immediately where he happened to be seated.

"Children," said Süleyman, "I'll lie down and get some sleep like our boy here."

"I've got a fine military cloak, Uncle," said Durdu. "Cover yourself with it."

"Bring it." Süleyman covered Memed with the cloak and tucked in beside him.

Then the other brigands lay down to sleep. One remained on watch, taking up his position on top of the rock.

When Memed awoke he felt like a stone, frozen stiff. Day had not yet broken, nor was there any sign of it. In the twilight he could see the brigands still asleep in a row by the edge of the fire, some of them snoring loudly. He peered around for the watchman, but couldn't find anyone. The loud snoring continued and he remembered how it is said that those who are not at peace with the world snore in their sleep. Memed felt fear now, for the first time in days. If a couple of men now took the camp by surprise, just two of them could easily shoot all these sleeping brigands and go away to boast of their victory.

Durdu was the first to awake and roused the others, including Süleyman.

Durdu rubbed his eyes and called: "Watchman!"

"Here, my Agha," answered Memed, coming down from the rock. "Everything's all right. I haven't seen anything," he reported.

"How is it that you're on watch, Slim Memed?" Durdu asked. "You've only just joined us. Wait a while. You'll have plenty of time for watching later. . . ."

"I wasn't sleepy, so I went and relieved my comrade. . . ."

"It's always like that. When a man first comes to the mountain, he can't sleep. One feels a strangeness in one's heart, a feeling of helplessness, as if one were alone in the world."

"Look at our madman! See how wise he has become!" mocked Süleyman.

"Whatever I do, Uncle Süleyman, you find fault with me. What's wrong now?"

It was growing slowly light. The sun had not appeared yet, but its rays had struck the peak of the mountain opposite, bathing it in light while all the slopes still lay in darkness. Slowly the light moved down into the valley until a little later the sun came up from behind the opposite ridge.

Without answering Durdu, Süleyman turned to Memed. "Good luck!" he said, as he kissed him on the forehead and walked off.

Durdu ran after Süleyman. "Uncle Süleyman!" he called. "Drink a cup of tea before you go. I swear I won't let you go till you've partaken of our tea."

"Thanks, my son, but I must be on my way."

Durdu seized him by his coat-sleeve. "I'm not allowing you to leave unless you drink a cup of tea. For once in a million years that you come to my mountain, would I let you go without even drinking a cup of tea?"

"There's no escape from this madman," Süleyman murmured to himself. "Let's go back."

"Light a good fire," Durdu ordered.

"But the smoke will show," remarked Süleyman.

"What can I do then? If I don't light a fire, what am I to do? Teach me," replied Durdu.

"I can't teach you anything, my son. You'll always manage everything your own way."

Mad Durdu pondered this and shook his head once or twice. Black locks of hair slipped from under his fez and curled over his forehead.

"You should never harm the poor," Süleyman continued, "even if you have your own way with wrong-doers and evil men. Don't trust too much in your own courage. Use your head! Otherwise you won't survive. This is the mountain, like an iron cage around you."

The tea was soon ready, steaming in the cold morning air. They offered the first of the slim glasses to Süleyman.

"Memed can be of use to you," said Süleyman to Durdu as he prepared to leave. "Treat my Memed well the first days. Don't bully him. Leave him to himself. He'll find his feet in a few days."

Süleyman then left them and began the descent, leaning on his stick as he went. His back was bent, but he climbed down the mountain fast enough, like a young man.

Tears rose to Memed's eyes as he watched him go. "Who knows when I'll see him again," he thought. "Perhaps never." His eyes were smarting. "What good men there are in this world," he said to himself.

The sun was quite high now and the earth was already warmer. Durdu called to Memed, who was seated by a rock: "Come, let's see, Slim Memed! Try that new gun. Have you ever fired a gun like that?"

"Once or twice . . ."

"Look, on that rock there's a white spot . . ."

"Yes?"

"Well, aim at it."

Memed raised the rifle to his shoulder, aimed and fired.

"You couldn't hit it, Memed," called Durdu.

"How's that?" Memed asked sulkily.

"Don't ask me," Durdu shrugged his shoulders. "You couldn't hit it, that's all."

Memed bit his lip. This time he rested the rifle well against his shoulder, took his aim more carefully and pulled the trigger.

"This time it's all right," said Durdu. "Right in the middle!"

A puff of smoke curled up from the white spot.

"Why didn't I hit it the first time?" murmured Memed, still puzzled.

"Come," queried Durdu, "Memed, do you hit the mark with every shot you fire?"

"I don't know," Memed smiled.

Durdu's long face contracted. Although young, it was wrinkled. He had a large mouth with thin lips and a long red scar reaching up to his scalp from his right cheek. His chin was sharp but energetic. He was always laughing, though there was bitterness in his laughter. "You've got something, my lad!"

Memed blushed like a shy boy, staring straight ahead.

Three separate whistles sounded suddenly from below. They listened attentively.

"The messenger is coming, Agha," called Jabbar.

Soon the messenger appeared, breathless. Without stopping to rest he reported: "Down there on the road from Chanakli five horsemen are travelling towards Akyol, all of them well dressed. They seem to be rich men."

"Be quick there," Durdu ordered. His men were already making ready. "Everyone must take plenty of ammunition. Mad Durdu will put out a few more hearth-fires." Then he turned towards Memed: "Look!" He aimed at the white spot. Smoke covered the rock and then cleared. "How's that, Slim Memed?" he boasted.

"Right in the middle . . ."

"Aye!" smiled Durdu. Then, with a wink, he added: "This is your first hunt, Memed. Stand firm."

Memed remained silent.

"Are you ready, comrades?" Durdu called out.

"All ready," they replied.

By the time they had descended to the road through the dense oak forest it was midday. They took cover along one side of the road, at intervals of fifty paces. One of them went ahead to reconnoitre.

Soon a man appeared in the middle of the track, driving a grey donkey ahead of him, its weak legs weaving in and out. He had a tangled, light-grey beard. His long moustache quite covered his mouth and its ends were stained yellow with tobacco, the yellowness visible from afar; his eyes were surrounded with wrinkles, his huge feet covered in dust and his patched shalvar trousers flapping as he went along jauntily, singing a song and almost dancing. Smilingly they listened to the song.

> "Mastic flows from the pines.
> Your lover, girl, is watching.
> The nipples of your bosom
> Smell of bitter oranges.
>
> Dear, my black-eyed girl, my dear,
> Comb your flowing locks, my girl,
> Does your father keep no watch
> On the pomegranates of your breasts?"

"Hands up," roared Durdu, "or I shoot!"

The song was cut short as the man stopped dead in his tracks. "I give in, Chief," he cried. "I give in. What's it all about?"

Mad Durdu jumped on to the road from his hiding-place and ordered: "Strip!"

The man stood there puzzled. "What shall I strip, Agha?"

"All your clothes."

The man laughed. "Don't joke with me, for heaven's sake. What would you do with my old clothes? Let me be going. I'm ready to drop, my feet are so sore. Let me be, kind Agha. . . ."

"I told you to strip," said Durdu, frowning.

The man wondered whether it was all a joke or to be taken seriously, and his heart thumped as he looked hesitantly into Durdu's eyes, smiling and cringing like a fawning dog.

"Hurry up," burst out Durdu harshly.

The man was still smiling incredulously. Durdu gave him a sharp kick on the shin. The man cried out with pain.

"Take them off, I tell you! Take them off!"

The man began to whine: "Pasha Effendi, I kiss your feet and your hands too. I have no other clothes. I'll be naked, stark naked. . . ." He placed his first finger in his mouth, sucked it, then took it out. "As naked as the day I was born. I've nothing else, Pasha Effendi. I kiss your hands and your feet! Don't take my clothes. You're a very great Pasha Effendi. What will you do with my old rags? I kiss your hands and your feet. . . ."

"You son of a dog, take them off, I tell you! Pasha Effendi, Pasha Effendi!"

The man continued to beseech Durdu and began to weep. "I've just come from five months of exile in the Chukurova. I've been working there."

"So you have money, have you?" cut in Durdu.

The man snivelled and wept like a child. "I'm dead after five months there. The insects of Chukurova have killed me. . . ."

"Where's your money?" insisted Durdu.

"At my age," continued the man, "I've worked in the rice-fields, in the mud. I almost died there, in the Chukurova. Now I'm going home. Don't do this, Effendi. Don't send me home to my wife and family naked."

"Take them off, take them off!" shouted Durdu, more and more angrily.

The man was writhing at Durdu's feet. Durdu drew his dagger, which sparkled in the sunlight as he brought the point down towards the man, who jumped and cried out: "Don't kill me. Let me see my family. I'll take off my clothes. They're yours!"

The men in hiding were all laughing, but Memed felt anger rise in him. That look of a hunting tiger came into his eyes. He loathed Durdu.

While the man fearfully fumbled about with his hands, taking off his coat and baggy trousers, Durdu urged him on: "That's it . . . Why did you make such a fuss, man?"

With trembling hands the man took off his clothes and put them down on the ground.

"Take off your drawers and your shirt too," roared Durdu, prodding him with the dagger again.

Shaking all over as he took off his shirt, the man cried: "Certainly, Agha. Don't kill me, Pasha! I'll take everything off." Then he looked at Durdu pleadingly.

"Get on, get on! Stop gazing into my eyes. Take your drawers off!"

With great reluctance the man took his drawers off too. His hands shook so much that they were like flying birds. Covering his groin with his hands, he set off running towards his donkey, which stood grazing by the side of the road. With his left hand he seized the reins and pulled. His legs were thin as matchsticks and all hairy, with the muscles standing out hard as bone. He was round-shouldered and his hollow belly was wrinkled like a sheepskin. The hairs on his chest were white. His skin was dirty, full of insect-bites that stood out in great red patches. Seeing the wayfarer's pitiful state, Memed felt even more bitter.

Suddenly the man they had set to watch the far end of the road ran towards them. "They're coming," he announced.

"The horsemen are coming," said Durdu.

The men in hiding were still laughing at the old man as he moved off slowly, one hand covering the front of his wrinkled body. He took five or ten steps, then turned round and looked longingly, fearfully, at his clothes.

"Come," Durdu called after him. "Come and get your things. Our prey has arrived. You've been lucky."

Despite his shrivelled and worn appearance, the man rushed up with unexpected speed and grabbed the heap of filthy rags that were his clothes. Then he turned and ran off again. His donkey trotted along ahead of him.

Memed's face was dark with anger and his hands were trembling. However many bullets there might be in his rifle, he wanted to fire them all into Durdu's head. Only with the greatest difficulty could he restrain himself from shooting.

This time Durdu roared out more harshly: "Hands up!"

All five horsemen halted their mounts simultaneously.

"One step forward and I shoot!" shouted Durdu. He then called to his men, who were still hidden: "I'm going to search them. At the slightest movement, all of you shoot from where you are."

Swaggering as if there were nothing unusual in all this, he moved towards the horsemen. "Get down from your horses!" he ordered.

Without a word they dismounted. Their harnesses were decorated with wrought silver. All the men were well dressed, two of them in city clothes, one of them a youth of seventeen.

Durdu called out again to his men: "I want three of you here!"

The seventeen-year-old boy began to scream: "Don't kill me! Please don't kill me! Take whatever you want, but don't kill me!"

"My young lion, you'll only be stripped stark naked and then you may go on your way."

The boy uttered a cry of joy: "You won't kill me then?" As he stripped off his clothes he asked gratefully: "So you won't kill me?" In the twinkling of an eye he stripped off his shirt, his vest, his drawers, everything, and brought them all to Durdu. "Take them," he said.

Without a word the others stripped too, remaining with only their drawers on.

"Take off your drawers too, my Aghas," said Durdu. "It's the drawers I really want!"

Again the men obeyed without a word. They took off their drawers, covered their groins with their hands and set off along the road.

Their horses, their clothes, all their belongings had been taken from them. Durdu and his men then headed for the mountain.

As they climbed Durdu turned to Memed. "You were in luck, my boy. This has been a good day for us. We took fifteen hundred pounds off them in money as well as their horses and clothes. The boy's clothes will fit you just right. They're still quite new. How that puppy cried! Like a baby!"

When they came to the foot of the dark cliff Durdu dismounted immediately, dressed Memed in the boy's clothes and inspected him admiringly. "That puppy's clothes fit you well, Memed. You look just like a nice young student!"

Memed felt humiliated and ill-at-ease in the strange garments. Suddenly he could not refrain from asking the question which, ever since they had left the road, had been on his mind, though he scarcely dared ask it: "We take everything from them, that I understand. But why must we take their drawers too? I don't understand why." After saying this he felt relieved and was less conscious of the strange clothes he was wearing.

Durdu laughed at his question. "We take their drawers so that our fame will spread around the countryside. Mad Durdu is the only brigand who takes drawers too. Let them know that they have been robbed by Mad Durdu. . . ."

XI

After the rains the heat set in, damp and clammy. They had placed the corpse of Abdi's nephew, Veli, on a blanket in the Agha's courtyard. Smeared with blood and mud, the wet clothes clinging to the body, glistening green flies buzzing around it, it lay there looking strange and lonely. The two hands, already waxen, hung sadly limp.

One of the shots had struck Abdi Agha in the shoulder and lodged itself under the shoulder-blade. The second had pierced his left leg without touching the bone. While they were still in the forest the village doctor had come and cauterised the wounds and bound them up, so that Abdi Agha had not lost much blood. Only the bullet under his shoulder-blade now troubled him, the inflammation congesting his lungs.

Abdi Agha had two sons, one fourteen years old, the other sixteen. His sons, his relatives, his servants and hirelings were all gathered round his bed waiting for him to speak. But he just lay there moaning and groaning. His wives sat weeping at the head of the bed.

Suddenly Abdi Agha opened his eyes. "How's my nephew? Is he all right?" he asked.

The woman answered him with a wail.

"So," he said.

"May your own head remain unharmed," said one of the villagers, offering his condolences.

Abdi's eyes flashed. "And that cursed one?" he asked again.

"He escaped us."

"And the girl, that whore?"

"We caught her and brought her here."

Abdi Agha closed his eyes and rested his head on the pillow with a groan. After a while he opened his eyes again. "You haven't beaten the girl, have you?" he asked.

"We haven't touched her."

"Good! Not a single bruise on her?"

Everyone knew that if Abdi Agha ever failed to beat a villager who had wronged him, something even more terrible was in store for the unfortunate man. To the end of his days he would have to pay the penalty for his crime. But if Abdi beat him, his crime was forgotten. Villagers who thought they had wronged Abdi Agha would come and sit in front of him and wait there until he had beaten them.

Again Abdi Agha closed his eyes. When he opened them, his yellow, thin face briefly expressed pleasure: "Are all the men here who went into the forest with me?" he asked.

"Lame Ali and Rustem are missing."

"Go and find them immediately," he ordered.

The courtyard was soon loud with the cries of weeping women. Veli's father, mother and fellow-villagers had arrived. The mother threw herself upon the corpse of her son and began kissing it in spite of all the clotted blood and mud. The father just stood there, one hand raised to his brow, as if his own blood had dried up in his veins. With the greatest difficulty they dragged the mother away. The father, still pale, slowly raised his head. He was a tall thin man, with a very long face and a broad forehead, wearing a collarless, embroidered jacket, shalvar trousers of striped cotton and sandals of rawhide. He stood there, his hands hanging loosely, his face distraught with grief and indescribably bitter. He could not even bring himself to look at his son's corpse.

Someone came and put an arm through his and led him towards Abdi Agha, who murmured, shaking his head: "It's fate."

The bereaved father could no longer restrain the flood of his bitterness. "Fate, fate . . . They don't call this fate, Abdi Agha! This is not fate. A cat, a dog, a bird, any living creature, if you keep on persecuting it, the first time it will be afraid, the second time too, but the third time it takes its life in its hands, becomes like a tiger and tears you apart. You shouldn't keep on at people as you do. They've escaped . . . God give them their deserts! Let them go . . ." Then he stopped, listless again, as if he had not spoken or moved at all since he entered the room, standing where he was like a stone.

"If I'd known he would do this," said Abdi Agha angrily, "if I'd only known! Wait and see what I'll bring down on their heads. That cursed boy and that little whore, they'll prefer death a thousand times. I'll make them seek it . . . Do you think I'll let them get away with this? Do you? I'll bind them to a pine-tree and set fire to it. We'll soon catch them. Have the men been out searching for him?" he asked.

"Since last night," someone answered.

"Has a man been sent to report to the authorities?"

"He was sent last night."

"Haven't the police come?"

"They'll be here by nightfall. The authorities have been notified and the police are probably waiting for the examining magistrate and the coroner."

"They can't do anything without the coroner," agreed Abdi Agha. "Let all those who were with me last night in the forest come here before the police arrive. Let them all be here without exception."

"Lame Ali and Rustem are outside," said one of the labourers.

"So they're all here?"

"Yes."

"Let them all gather round me here. No one else is to stay in the room."

The father of the dead boy, still listless, rose and left the room slowly without once looking at Abdi Agha. All the others followed him. In their stead those who had been in the forest came and sat expectantly in a circle round Abdi Agha. They knew that he would instruct them to testify to something or other. Whenever there was any government business they were not allowed to say anything for themselves. Abdi Agha would summon them before hand and make them rehearse and learn by heart whatever they would have to say. They would then go before the official and sing their pieces as loud and clear as nightingales. If, having done their turn, they were faced with other questions, they would only answer: "I don't know." Whatever they were then asked the only answer was: "That's all I know."

This time Abdi Agha looked in the face of each one of them in turn. They were all pale. Then he bowed his head in silence and concentrated his thoughts for a while. When he raised his head he scanned each face again with wild eyes.

"Listen to me, Brothers," he began in a weak voice. "First of all, lay your hands on your consciences. After that think a little. Now I'm going to ask you: If the dog that you've fed at your door turns upon you and kills your children, what do you do? I want the answer from you, with your hands on your consciences. Let your consciences speak." Again he stared at each one fixedly, watching the expressions on their faces. "Answer me! If it happened to you, what would you do?" His eyes flashed upon them like lightning. "What would you do? Speak!"

"What will be, will be," they murmured.

"What do you mean?" asked Abdi Agha, intimidating them by his stare.

"It's as you say, Agha. You know best."

Abdi Agha looked at them approvingly, as if they had just made a very important statement. "That's it, Brothers. My dog has bitten my child, tearing at my child and me. This mad dog has escaped and must now be caught. There's no escape for him. But his accomplice is here. Anyway, all these troubles have come upon us because of this girl and all the guilt is hers. It was she who killed the lad. With my own eyes I saw her shoot at Veli. Memed shot me, the girl shot Veli. Both of them had weapons in their hands. You all saw it. First of all he took aim and fired at me, then she aimed and fired at the lad." Abdi Agha shouted outside: "Boys, one of you come here." His elder son came in. "Bring me that weapon, my son."

From a cupboard set in the wall of the room the boy took out a new revolver and gave it to his father. Abdi Agha handed it to the man next to him. "Look at it, all of you," he said. "Is this the weapon you took from the girl? Is this the one that shot Veli? Look at it carefully."

The weapon passed from hand to hand and then came back to Abdi Agha.

"You've all seen it, haven't you?" asked Abdi Agha.

"We've seen it."

"This weapon was in her hand and was fired at Veli. She fired it. As Veli fell to the ground she dropped it and Haji picked it up.

Haji then caught hold of the girl too. You all saw this. It happened just as I've said, didn't it, Haji?"

Haji was a short man with grey eyes and a huge nose, aged before his time. His clothes were worn and patched, his face grimy, his tousled hair and beard had never seen scissors or razor. He looked as if he had been dragged through the mud.

"That's how it was, my beloved Agha, just like that. As the weapon fell to the ground, I picked it up. The girl had turned round and was running away. That is, she was holding the lad's hand. When I say lad, I mean that cursed Memed. She was holding his hand and they were both running away. I caught up with them and held Hatché and didn't let go. Hatché shot Veli before my own eyes." He shook his head, then wiped his eyes as if he had been crying. "My poor Veli Agha! Was there anyone like my Veli Agha? But it's like this, evil ones always attack the brave and the honest. Whoever saw a brave man hurt another brave man? My Veli Agha, my Veli Agha, struck down by the bullet of a worthless girl! That daughter of an infidel fired it before my very eyes. I saw her taking aim, that daughter of a scoundrel. Who knows where she learned to aim and fire?"

"Have you heard?" inquired Abdi Agha. "You all saw it, didn't you? You, Zekerya, didn't you see it too?"

"I saw it too," declared Zekerya.

"And you, Lame Ali?"

Lame Ali's indignation had long ago reached bursting-point. "I didn't see anything, Agha. Not the slightest thing. Because I followed this trail the villagers no longer look me in the face, neither in this village nor in my own. When I pass by even the children turn and run away, and my own wife now looks at me with disgust, refusing to speak to me. I didn't see anything at all, Agha, not even Memed when he shot at you." He rose to his feet and stalked angrily to the door, his whole body, even his gait, expressing his revolt.

Abdi Agha had never expected this from anyone. He was struck dumb, his mouth wide open with surprise. Then his head began to shake with agitation. He leaned forward as if to go after Ali. "Ali! Lame Ali! I forbid you to stay in your village. As soon as you get there, load your goods and go away wherever you like! If you stay in that house one more day, I'll send one of my men to demolish it over your head. Do you hear me, Ali?" he roared, then added to himself: "Shameless, ungrateful beggar . . ." Foaming at the mouth with rage, he demanded: "You others all saw it, didn't you?"

"We saw it," they all replied with one voice.

"Put your hands on your consciences, my villagers, my brothers. For a mere slip of a boy to rise up and kill me, the Agha of five great villages, his lord and master, all for a girl! If I had died, where would you all be? Think of that! Think of my being gone! For a girl who was about to become my daughter-in-law to run off with a scoundrel! Whoever heard of such a thing? Put your hands right on your consciences. A business where there is no conscience is no good at all. No good comes of it. No, we must act in accordance with our consciences!"

"It's for our Agha, isn't it? We'll put our hands on our consciences," declared Musa.

"Bravo, Musa!" exclaimed the Agha, approvingly.

"For our Agha," agreed Kadir, "we're ready to do anything."

"My thanks to you all," said the Agha. "This year I'll only expect a quarter of your crops from you. Besides, I give you all the cattle. All the animals that you're now tending shall be yours. Be off with you now! Put your hands on your consciences and learn by heart what you'll say to the authorities."

They left the Agha with smiling faces. Three-quarters of their crops and the cattle! It was an unheard of boon. They squatted down in a corner of the courtyard, fifty yards away from the dead man, and began to rehearse what they were to say.

"Well, sir, Haji . . . Why, this Haji here came and picked up the weapon on the ground. The girl was holding the lad's hand as they tried to escape. She let go the lad's hand and we came and caught her."

Haji interrupted them: "It wasn't like that. You'll say that Haji, that's me, came up as they were running away hand in hand. I put my arms round Hatché. Then, as I held her, that is as Haji held her, you'll say, the lad, Slim Memed, let go of the girl and ran off."

They all repeated what Haji had just said. "The girl was taking aim. Where did she learn that, the daughter of a scoundrel? She fired three bullets at Veli and all three hit him. What a daughter of a scoundrel! Then, as Veli fell lifeless to the ground, the weapon dropped to the ground from her hand. Haji came and picked it up."

"That's right," said Haji. "It was like that. Until they come, let's set to work and learn what we have to say."

Late in the afternoon the authorities arrived and dismounted by Abdi Agha's house. Two mounted policemen, armed with rifle and bayonet, rode ahead, then the doctor and the magistrate and, in the rear, the police sergeant. A flowered quilt had been thrown over the corpse in the courtyard, but one waxen arm remained bare.

The doctor was a young blue-eyed man with a complexion almost like a girl's. He examined the body with disgust, then covered it again with the quilt. "You can bury it," he said.

With solemn faces they all went into the house and sat down beside Abdi Agha. They were very tired. Three of them knew Abdi Agha from the town and the police sergeant was a close friend of his and made the most of every opportunity to express his condolences: "Don't fret, Agha. The murderer's as good as in my hands already. He'll get what he deserves. Don't worry about it. I've sent four men to track him down."

The sergeant had brought his typewriter with him. He took it out of his saddle-bag and placed it on the bread-board. Then they sent the men to fetch Hatché. They listened to her testimony as she recounted things just as they had happened; they noted all that she stated. After her the other witnesses were heard. Haji was the first. After he had explained all the preliminaries, he continued: "Whilst Memed was firing at Abdi Agha, I also saw the girl, I mean Hatché, had a weapon in her hand and was taking aim. She fired at Veli. When Veli called out 'Oh, I am wounded!' and fell to the ground, Hatché just stood still. The weapon fell from her hand and I went and picked it up out of the mud. Memed took the girl, I mean Hatché, by the arm and they ran off. I ran after them, overtook them and caught hold of them both. Memed escaped, but I didn't let go of the girl."

Hatché was horrified by Haji's testimony. What was he trying to say? She couldn't understand.

The magistrate turned to question her. "He says you shot Veli. What have you to say, Hatché?"

"No," answered Hatché. "How could I shoot a man like that?" It hadn't happened at all as Haji had said. What could it all mean?

Then they heard Zekerya's story. He told it exactly like Haji, not a word more nor a word less. As each of the witnesses gave the same testimony, Hatché realised that a plot had been compounded against her. A wave of fear swept over her and tears trickled down her cheeks.

The magistrate produced the weapon. "Is this the weapon that was in Hatché's hand?" he asked.

"Yes, that's the one," they all answered.

That night the authorities stayed as guests at Abdi Agha's house. Double mattresses were spread for them. Lambs were roasted in their honour under a covering of earth. Whenever the magistrate came to the mountain villages the meat was prepared for him in this way. Roasting under earth is undoubtedly the tastiest way of preparing meat.

Hatché was locked up in the next room. Unable to think of anything, she spent the whole night with her head on her knees, weeping silently. In the morning she was led out of the room by two policemen who marched her off to prison. She seemed to be unaware of what was happening to her and had no idea of where she was going or what they would do to her. As she walked her feet stumbled along the road. Only once before had she ever left her village. Then the man she loved and trusted had been by her side and she had known where they would go, what they would do. They had been pursuing together a dream of a field and a home of their own. Now her heart was chilled with fear and despair. When they left the village even her mother did not dare come to see her off, and none of her friends were there. This hurt her most and an unbearable anxiety overcame her. The future was dark and every step buried her deeper in this darkness. She could visualise the authorities only as something terrifying and the two policemen walking in front of her were like monsters in her eyes.

When they reached the town the next day Hatché was exhausted. All night she had been dragged along the road. But the town gave her a feeling of pleasure. It brought some tiny sense of security to her heart and her fears were somewhat diminished. She remembered how Memed had told her endlessly about the shining windows and the brass, the milk-white pebbles, the flowing river, the smell of *kebab*. There had been a room of glass on top of a house, like a stork's nest. Which house could it be? The window of one house now blazed in the sunlight as if the panes were of red glass. Suddenly her pleasure vanished. She remembered Memed: where was he now? If they caught Memed, they would kill him. "Poor lad, for my sake!" she thought.

The floor of the jail beneath the police station was of cement, but flooded ankle-deep with water. There was no real reason why the jail should be flooded or in such a state, but it stank like a public lavatory. It was dark, with only one small window that was securely closed.

They left her there to spend the night. Unable to sleep, she felt herself drawn deeper and deeper into an ocean of darkness. She had only one desire: that they open the door. She thought all her troubles would be over if only she saw the light again. But no light penetrated her cell from beneath the door or from anywhere else. Nevertheless she knew for certain when it was morning.

Suddenly the door opened. The light struck her, heavy as lead, so that she was stunned. Some time passed before she came to her senses. A policeman had seized her by the arm and was dragging her outside.

Quite a crowd had collected there. When Hatché appeared, all eyes stared at her. "There's the girl that killed her bridegroom!" The murmur of the crowd reached her ears and she realised that all these people had gathered to see her. She did not raise her eyes from the ground even once to look at the crowd. She passed through it, no longer frightened by the two policemen. She even felt that they could protect her.

She was brought before a very old judge, who began by verifying her identity and then asked: "They say you shot Veli, the son of Mustafa. Is it true?"

'I didn't kill Veli, I swear," Hatché answered simply. "How could I kill a man. I'm even afraid to touch a weapon!"

The judge knew villagers well. In the course of years he had listened to thousands of them. Immediately he understood that Hatché was innocent. But he had to imprison her because of the evidence against her.

The women's cell had been added to the prison at a later date. All the whitewash had flaked off its walls which were now covered with bloodstains. Mosquitoes in hundreds and thousands had been killed there after sucking the blood of the prisoners. The ceiling, the boards, the windows, the seats, had rotted and were still rot-

ting. The whole place stank of rot and urine. A can stood behind
the door. When the guard came he pointed to it and told her she
could use it, if need be, during the night.

Unwillingly Hatché broke off a piece of the bread which the
guard had brought her and forced it into her mouth. She chewed
and chewed, but could not swallow and after a while spat it out.

The next day and the following she could still eat nothing.
Her surroundings hurt and offended everything in her and she
could not get used to them. It was only the third day that her
mother appeared, her eyes red from weeping. She sat down in
front of the prison window and cried: "My girl, my girl, my lovely
girl! What's all this that's come upon you? Why did you shoot
that man!"

For the first time Hatché reacted and spoke angrily: "How
could I kill the man? Have I ever taken a weapon in my hands?
Don't you know?"

The mother was shaken. It had never occurred to her that her
daughter might be innocent.

"How should I know, my lovely henna-haired girl! Everyone
says that it was Hatché who shot Veli. How should I know? I'll go
to the public writer and ask him to draft me a petition. I'll say that
my daughter was afraid of weapons. Abdi Agha warned me not to
try to get any petitions filed. But without his knowing I'll go and
get a petition drafted. You've committed no crime. That infidel
Memed killed their boy. Now they're blaming it on you, but it's
that infidel Memed who has destroyed my home."

She pushed through the window the pouch full of food that she
had brought from the village. "I'll go to the public writer and get
him to write it all down. If the authorities read it, they'll understand you're not guilty. Even the Government are human beings.
They, too, can take pity. How can they lock you up, innocent as
you are?"

Her mother's coming had relieved Hatché's feelings to some
extent. For the first time she began to notice things. A newly-built
house with clean, bright-red tiles and, behind it, the dome of the
mosque with its milk-white minaret, straight and thin as a pencil;
beyond that, at the foot of the wall, the thick leaves of a fig-tree;
still farther, a huge dusty yard with people coming and going. All
these could be seen through the window. Memed had described

everything, but he had not told her of the scintillating beauty of the red tiles.

The guard came and opened the door. He was a very irritable man and spoke harshly: "You can go out and get some air."

Once at midday and once in the evening he opened the door and let her out. Till then she had never even noticed she was going out. Now she felt the pleasure of feeling the world anew.

The main gate of the prison faced the window of her cell. When they saw that she had become at last aware of her surroundings, one or two prisoners called out to her: "Hey, Sister! Don't worry! It's all in the day's work! You handled the wretch as he deserved. Bravo, Sister! Long live true love!"

Hatché did not answer. She went back to her cell and began to think about Memed.

Her mother had hurried to the public writer, Mad Fahri, who was always drunk. Years earlier he had been dismissed from his position as clerk of the court for accepting bribes. He had then become a public letter-writer and was now earning two or three times more than before. He had made a name for himself and everyone said: "He's more competent than a lawyer." He was drunk day and night, but could draft his petitions even when he was drunk.

Mad Fahri lay with his head on the dirty table where his typewriter stood. He was asleep, exuding a strong smell of raki. When he heard footsteps, he lifted his head, recognising the tread of a client who wanted a petition written. With the practice that only comes with years, Fahri knew the footsteps of those who would need a petition. As his table was under the eaves of a butcher's shop, there was always a crowd of people passing by. Mad Fahri never raised his head to look at any of his neighbour's customers. But when someone needing a petition approached, even if he were still at a fair distance, Fahri would raise his head immediately and, looking into the newcomer's eyes, would say, "Now tell us all about it."

To Hatché's mother he now said: "Now tell us all about it."

She sat down on the pavement and leaned her head against the wall. "Ah, Fahri Effendi, I have only one daughter, my lovely Hatché. Let me tell you, Fahri Effendi; they've taken her and locked her up in prison, and that's where she is now."

Fahri Effendi pulled the pencil out of his mouth. "Just tell me how that girl of yours managed to get herself locked up."

"Dear Fahri Effendi, listen and I'll tell you. We had promised our girl in marriage to Abdi Agha's nephew, Veli. Without our knowing it, that infidel, Slim Memed, Deuneh's orphan son, was also after her. The girl fell in love with him and one night they ran off together. You know Lame Ali, don't you? Everybody knows him. That infidel followed their trail and caught up with them when they were making love in the hollow beneath a rock. The lad pulled out his weapon and shot Abdi Agha and Veli. Then he ran off. They couldn't catch him. So, in his stead, they took my Hatché and brought her here. The police locked her up in prison, my rose of a girl, all because of that cursed Memed. They said my girl had killed Veli. The villagers all gave the same testimony. Only Lame Ali said he wouldn't give evidence, and Abdi Agha then drove him out of his village. How was I to know, Brother Fahri Effendi. I, too, believed that my girl had killed Veli. They couldn't all be lying, I said to myself. That infidel Abdi made them lie. A villager cannot do anything but what Abdi tells him to do. Ah, my stupid head! That I should have believed them, Brother Fahri Effendi! Then I came to my girl and asked her about it here. It was a different story. My girl told me: 'What do I know about using a weapon, Mother?' Then it struck me that my girl doesn't know how to use a weapon. More than that, she's afraid of all fire-arms, and there have never been any in our house. The father of my girl never liked them either. They all bore false witness against my poor girl, Fahri Effendi, my Agha, that's how the business now stands. My poor girl's afraid of weapons. She's frightened to death at the sight of one. You can write all that to the Government."

Fahri Effendi took a sheet of paper and placed it in his rattling old machine. Noisily he began to type. Without stopping once he wrote a petition five pages long. "Look, woman, I'll read it to you, so listen well. See how finely I've explained it all." Shifting his cigarette from one corner of his mouth to the other, Fahri Effendi quickly read off the petition. "How is it?" he asked.

"Thank you, you've made it sound so beautiful!" answered the mother.

"My good woman, I wouldn't have written that for anyone else

123

for less than fifteen liras. But you can give me ten. It's so finely written that I swear it'll bring tears to the eyes of a stone!"

With trembling hands, the mother untied her purse-strings and brought out the money. "Bless you, my friend! Please God it will move a stone."

As he twisted and turned the red ten-lira note in his hand, Fahri Effendi explained exactly where she was to take the petition and what she was to say. As she rose to leave she added: "Forgive me for not thinking of it, Brother Fahri Effendi. Next time I come I'll bring you some eggs and some butter."

Then she set forth according to his instructions and found where she was to deliver the petition. Confronted with one of the men who had arrested her daughter, she was afraid at first, but soon plucked up courage.

"Let me be your slave, Agha," she pleaded. "But why did you carry off my girl and lock her up in prison? My girl doesn't know how to use a weapon, let alone kill a man. My girl's terrified of any weapon. Whenever she saw one as a child she would come crying to me and try to hide herself in my arms. I've brought you a petition. Read it and give me back my daughter, Brother. Let me kiss the soles of your feet. My girl's not guilty of anything. She fell in love and ran off with that infidel Memed. Any girl can elope. Please set my girl free. I kiss the soles of your feet, Brother . . ."

"Stop trying to be so clever. Leave the petition here and be off," said the magistrate harshly. "The court will give a just decision." He returned to his papers and began writing again.

By the time the mother reached the prison it was afternoon. Hatché had been on the alert, waiting for her since morning.

"I got Fahri Effendi to write such a fine petition that it'll move a stone. Just wait till the Government reads it! They'll set you free immediately. They'll realise that you're innocent and they'll let you go. I got him to write in the petition how you're afraid of weapons. You know how, as a child, you used to run away at the sight of a gun and hide in my arms. Well, I made him write that too. He expressed it so beautifully, did Fahri Effendi, it sounded like twenty liras. But he only took ten liras from me. Let him have them! Isn't it all for my girl? Let all my money go and my life too."

"If only it turns out all right," said Hatché. Then she looked into her mother's eyes and bowed her head. "Mother, bring me some news from Memed next time you come. . . ."

"Hasn't that accursed boy caused us enough trouble?" the mother answered angrily.

Hatché raised her eyes from the ground and looked at her pleadingly. "Mother, darling Mother! See how I'm rotting in this hole. But for Memed I would die. Do you want to kill your daughter? Bring me some news, please . . ."

"I hope they'll tear him to pieces," said the mother. "I hope I'll bring you news of his death . . ." But as she was saying it the girl burst into tears.

At that the mother was silent. For a long time the girl wept without uttering a word.

"The sun's setting, Hatché. I must be going."

"Mother!" Hatché pleaded.

The woman stopped. Her eyes had filled with tears. "All right," şhe said in a hoarse voice. "For the sake of my rose, I'll try to get some news. They've beaten Memed's mother. Perhaps she'll die, poor thing, poor little Deuneh. Keep well, my child," she called as she walked off. "Don't be afraid. Fahri Effendi said it all beautifully in the petition."

She put great trust in the petition that she had just filed.

XII

It was very dark and the whole forest was murmuring, stretched across the night like a black wall. Far away, somewhere near the peak of the mountain, a fire flickered. They walked with their arms stretched out ahead of them, groping among the trees. The night was full of the moist scent of pine, heather, moss, wormwood and sweat. In the sky one or two stars were twinkling.

For months they had now been raiding countless homes, holding up travellers, fighting the police who no longer pursued any other robber gangs but Mad Durdu's. Durdu was only teasing them, playing with them. Memed had soon proved his usefulness and earned the respect of his companions and of Durdu. He had made himself indispensable to the band.

Durdu's voice came through the darkness: "Let's stop here. We're done for, dead. For two days we've been on the run without any rest. A pretty state of affairs!" His voice was harsh and stubborn.

Memed came up to him. "Quiet! Speak softly, Agha!"

"What does it matter?" answered Durdu angrily. Had it been another he would not have taken it so much to heart. For a newcomer like Memed to give him lessons in brigandage!

"Even if your enemy is an ant . . ." began Memed.

"And if so?" prompted Durdu.

Memed ignored the mockery in Durdu's voice. "What I mean is—don't despise your enemy!"

Durdu could control himself no longer and gave vent to his feelings. "I see, Süleyman didn't bring you to us as a comrade, but to be our chief-of-staff. Mind your own business!"

Jabbar, to Memed's left, said breathlessly: "Memed is right, Agha. If we stay in the forest, we'll be surrounded. They're on our heels, following us without pause. If they encircle us they'll shoot us down, by God, like partridges. You can be sure that Sergeant Asim is just looking for such a chance."

"Like partridges," agreed Memed.

"It isn't that we have only a few policemen after us, but the villagers too, and rival bands besides. We can't cope with them all."

"And we have no reserves of ammunition," added Memed.

"We're not going a step farther," said Durdu stubbornly. His voice echoed through the forest. "For two days we've been running away like dogs!"

One of the brigands was known to his companions as Sergeant Rejep. Nobody knew where he came from or how many years he had been a brigand; in fact, nobody knew anything about him or even dared to ask about his past. If anyone did he lost his temper and was ready to kill. After that he would refuse to associate with the inquisitive one and, if he met him, even to speak to him, as if he were a lifelong foe. Sergeant Rejep was over fifty. The only thing known about him was that he had once belonged to Big Ahmet's band. When this band had been amnestied the others had all come down from the mountains and surrendered to the Government; but he had not accepted the amnesty. For two years he had then wandered alone on the mountains. When brigands appeared there again he had joined them. There was not a band he had not joined and left. All of them knew him, esteemed and liked him. But he would never stay with any band very long. To-day if he felt like it he would join Durdu's band; to-morrow he might go off and join Durdu's mortal enemy, Yozju. Sergeant Rejep never gossiped with anyone or about anyone. He was welcome everywhere among the outlaws and none ever asked why he had come, why he went. It was felt that his presence in a band brought good luck. He was a pastmaster in the tricks of brigandage. In a fray his hands worked like a machine-gun.

Now in the darkness his deep and easily recognisable voice was heard. "Durdu, the boys are right. Let's get out of the forest and stick to the rocks."

"Sergeant Rejep," roared back Durdu, "we're not going a single step farther."

"Durdu Agha," pleaded Jabbar, "if they can't do anything else they'll surround us and set fire to the forest. . . ."

"Not a step!" insisted Durdu.

"Please, Agha!" begged Jabbar.

"I've made up my mind."

"It'll mean the end of us," Jabbar muttered.

"Am I the leader of this band?" demanded Durdu.

"Of course you're our leader," agreed Jabbar. Memed and the others echoed Jabbar's words.

"Agha, don't be angry if I say something," Memed pleaded.

"Go on then, Chief-of-Staff," said Durdu, laughing.

"Let's go at least to some hollow that's thickly wooded and rocky and where we'll find cover."

"We're not moving a step from here," replied Durdu. He sat down where he had been standing. The others sat down too, not one of them breaking the silence. One or two of them had lit cigarettes which twinkled like stars in the darkness. Not a sound was uttered. Jabbar rose to his feet and stretched. He set off uphill by himself. Memed followed him.

Jabbar and Memed stopped to relieve themselves side by side against a tree. When they had finished they turned round and saw a tiny light. Surprised, they stopped in their tracks. Durdu had set fire to some pine branches. In the light of the fire he swayed like a shadow.

"He's really looking for his death," said Memed.

"It isn't so much Sergeant Asim I fear, but the villagers that are after us. They're the ones whose drawers we have stolen!"

"Since I've joined you we've stripped at least five hundred people of their drawers," commented Memed.

"If only we had given all those clothes to the poor of the villages," continued Jabbar, "perhaps we would now be safe from the villagers. That's why for two days we've been unable to shake them off. We have no allies outside. If ever we fall into the hands of the villagers of Aksoyut they'll wipe us all out. There's no crime Durdu hasn't committed, nothing he's left untouched in Aksoyut. Tyranny, torture, insults, he thinks of everything to hurt and humiliate."

"Listen," interrupted Memed, "it's always wrong to drive people to desperation. You may kill or rob them, but you must avoid keeping always after them. For a man to return to his home and his village without his drawers, stark naked, is worse than death. That's what one shouldn't do; one should never humiliate people. They're sensitive about certain things and you should never hurt them there. I know that from my own experience under Abdi Agha. You should respect this in people and never despise them."

On the way back they suddenly found themselves up to their knees in a little stream. The waters were scented with mint and its perfume was everywhere in the starry night. "If only we could persuade Durdu to take shelter here," Memed suggested.

"He wouldn't move an inch if you threatened to kill him. He's obstinate."

Durdu's fire was burning high, the flames filling a space as big as a threshing-floor and rising to the sky. Great logs crackled as they burned. Durdu was walking up and down by the fire, laughing. "Just look at it! Would anyone else light such a fire?"

"It would be better if it weren't lit!" grumbled Jabbar.

"Shut up, Jabbar!" said Durdu angrily.

They spent the night there, huddled round the fire. Not one of them could sleep except Durdu. They were all afraid of being attacked and killed in their sleep.

Three of them, Sergeant Rejep, Horali and Memed, stayed on watch while the others lay down for a while, trying to sleep but turning restlessly where they lay. Jabbar was the first to rise. He sat down cross-legged by the fire. One by one the others followed his example. Durdu was still sleeping profoundly and peacefully while his men sat round the fire staring into the flames.

The skirmish began with a sudden volley as the day was breaking. On all·sides the air was suddenly thick with bullets. They had been expecting it at any moment since the previous evening. Now they scattered away from the fire to find cover.

Memed was able to throw himself down behind a tree-stump as a bullet whizzed past his ear. He realised he was close behind Sergeant Asim, whose rear was unprotected. Memed raised his rifle, but he felt sick inside, lowered the gun and fired elsewhere instead. Laughing, he shouted: "Sergeant, you haven't taken good cover. Careful, or one of those shots will hit you!"

Bullets were being fired all round the sergeant; one of them soon struck his cap and knocked it off. "Wait till I catch you!" he threatened.

"They call me Slim Memed, Sergeant. The only thing you'll ever catch is your own death. You're a family man. Get out of here, Sergeant, and go back to your police station!"

A bullet grazed the hand with which the sergeant was holding the butt of his gun. Blood trickled to the ground from his wound.

"Get back to your job, Sergeant. Leave us in peace. Don't let your death be on our hands. You've been after us too long."

The sergeant was exposed on all sides. It occurred to him that the man who had shot away his cap and grazed his hand might have killed him long ago. Who was this Slim Memed? If Mad Durdu had caught him like this he would have been a dead man by now. Slim Memed? Sergeant Asim did not recollect ever having heard the name. There were many Memeds around, but Slim Memed?

"Man, I'll teach you a few Slim Memed tricks that you don't know yet," he cried.

The shots continued in a steady stream in the dawn light. Durdu was striding around in the open, disdaining any cover and still firing, stopping every once in a while to curse the sergeant: "Sergeant! Don't get the idea that Mad Durdu's run away from you! I'll send you back to your captain without your drawers! Just let me get hold of you."

But the police and the villagers had surrounded them, and Durdu now realised that he was in a trap. He crawled over to Memed's side. Memed was the most trustworthy member of his gang. If their pursuers came any closer and drew the noose around them a little tighter, they would be able to shoot Durdu's band one by one. Perhaps for the first time in his life, Durdu was worried. But the men who had encircled him were still afraid of him and dared not draw any closer. They were puzzled because Durdu had accepted to fight them here in the open; they suspected some trick or ambush and refused to move forward any farther.

"We're in a tight spot," said Durdu. The sweat was pouring down his face and he was breathless. "Not one of us will escape."

Suddenly a cry was heard: "I'm wounded!"

"There goes the first," said Durdu. "Sergeant Rejep's done

for! I'm not afraid of any of them. They say there's one man among them from Dortyol, a policeman. Then there's Black Mustan from my own village. If it weren't for those two, I'd manage to get away. They're shooting so fast and furious that even a flea would find it difficult to escape."

"My rifle's red-hot," said Memed. "It's beginning to burn my hand. What should I do?"

"You've fired too often, my boy. Otherwise it's a fine gun. Hold your fire for a while and rub the metal with earth until it cools off, or else you won't be able to load it any longer. The metal will expand and the gun get jammed."

"Damn it!" Memed was annoyed.

"Listen to me," said Durdu in a low voice, "we're surrounded. Don't bother about me. I know a few tricks. Whatever happens, I'll manage to escape and, if I die, what of it? But I'm thinking about you. Because of me, because of my madness, how will you all escape? That's what worries me. They'll say Mad Durdu ran off and left his friends in trouble."

"As far as I can see there's no way out," said Memed. "Let's wait till nightfall."

Two bullets buried themselves in the ground just in front of Durdu, raising a cloud of dust. "There's no way out. We must wait till nightfall," repeated Memed.

Durdu pointed to where the two bullets had fallen. "Those are Black Mustan's bullets. He must have spotted us."

"Durdu Agha, is Sergeant Rejep dead?" asked Memed. "If only we could get to him . . ."

"Wait! That fellow will be the death of us."

A great cloud of dust rose in front of them. They had no idea how many shots had been fired at them. "Didn't I tell you?" muttered Durdu. "I know Black Mustan well enough. Curse him!"

"If we don't move to other cover at once . . ."

Crawling on their bellies they managed to get behind a fairly thick tree-trunk. Memed was still worried about Sergeant Rejep. "There's not a sound from the sergeant. If we could only reach him . . ."

A hail of bullets fell around them, splitting the branches of the trees, lopping them off. They crawled ahead, through the enemy's fire, and reached Sergeant Rejep, who was lying on his right side in a pool of blood. He smiled and gritted his teeth when he saw them.

"Lads," he said, raising his head with difficulty. "Look after yourselves. There are at least a hundred and fifty of them. Leave me where I am. It's my fate. . . ."

They examined his wound. The bullet had pierced his neck and come out again above the shoulder-blade without damaging the bone, but the flesh was torn where it had emerged.

"I've got something to say to you," said Sergeant Rejep. "That Jabbar, mark my words, is a fine sturdy lad. He could face a whole army. If it hadn't been for him I would have been lost. When he saw I'd been hit he drew their fire on to himself by firing at them so relentlessly that it shook them."

Tearing the sergeant's shirt, they bound the wound.

"Break out of the circle . . ." murmured the sergeant, almost losing consciousness.

"We can't, Sergeant," said Memed. "If we try to, they'll know that we're desperate and will mow us down. But they're afraid of us now. Either we hold out till nightfall or we die here."

Sergeant Rejep's face was distorted with pain and it was with difficulty that he kept himself from crying out as he spoke. "You know, I think you've got it right, Memed. If one of you moves to escape it'll be the death of all of you. Collect all the men and make them swear that they won't budge an inch. As I see it, it's death to try to escape now. Stand firm. I'm sure they daren't attack. If they were going to they would have done it long ago. They're afraid of an ambush."

"Come, Durdu Agha, let's stay where we are," said Memed.

"Zala's boy is the only one to worry about," said Sergeant Rejep. "He's a coward. Keep an eye on him. He may try to run for it."

"Let's gather the men together," agreed Durdu. "Horali and Jabbar must go on firing to keep them busy." He whistled his command to assemble. The men could make no sense of this at such a moment, when bullets were raining on them.

"How can we assemble in all this mess?" grumbled Zala's boy to his neighbour before answering Durdu's command. "There's no way out, that's sure."

Horali came first, then Yusuf and Güdükoghlu.

"Where's Zala's boy?" said Durdu suspiciously.

"He's coming," said Horali. "He's been cringing on the ground and hasn't fired a single shot. Trembling like a leaf. . . ."

"Strange," replied Durdu. "I always thought he was one of the tough boys of our band."

Zala's boy came crawling towards them, his hands smeared with blood.

"Now then, you two, keep on firing," Durdu told Horali and Jabbar. "We've business to discuss."

The momentary lull in the firing while they assembled had confirmed Sergeant Asim's suspicions. It wasn't the first time he had come up against Durdu and he still found it difficult to figure out what the man was up to. Durdu might do the maddest thing or the wisest. As for this decision of his to face an attack in the open, was he simply being a fool and courting death, or was it an ambush? Durdu was the sort of man to escape through the eye of a needle. Surely he wouldn't let himself be caught so easily, but would play some trick on his pursuers. Asim could not decide what to do. If he retreated, his reputation would not be worth much. If he stood firm, if all this were an ambush, he and his men might all be wiped out. What was the meaning of the shots that had carried off his cap and grazed his hand? Were they a warning? The man who had fired them might have killed him long ago if he had wished.

Asim could not bring himself to retreat after having for once at last managed to surround Durdu. Would the bandit ever allow himself to be surrounded again?

"Men," he called out, "stand firm, all of you. We'll see what that madman is up to. We've got him surrounded, in the palm of our hands. He allowed it to happen deliberately. He might easily have escaped long ago to the cliffs of Mordagh . . ."

"I know his tricks," the corporal muttered. "He's stayed here of his own free will. But he didn't dream up an ambush for us, he trusts his own luck too much. Let's draw the noose tight and you'll see we'll get our hands on him."

"He's been an outlaw for years," replied Sergeant Asim. "Such a rascal doesn't easily accept an encounter in the open. But here in this clearing . . . There's surely something cooking! Let's be on our guard!"

133

"No, Sergeant," insisted the corporal. "He's just trusting his luck. Let's draw the noose tight and finish the job."

"We'll stay here," the sergeant decided sharply.

When Horali and Jabbar began firing again the sergeant was even more disturbed.

"Friends," said Durdu, "there's no slinking off one by one. We'll have to stick together. Whatever comes, even if they ram their rifles down our throats, there's no moving. Agreed?"

They all agreed.

"Then let's find a good spot."

"Shall I look around," asked Memed.

"Go ahead."

Suddenly Memed shouted: "Down! Down!" He threw himself to the ground. The others also lay low. The bullets whizzed above their heads.

"They've spotted us," said Durdu. "They won't give us any peace here."

They didn't dare to move from where they were, in spite of the bullets that rained around them.

Zala's boy was still trembling. "Memed's been hit," he said with an expression of horror.

"Is it true?" called Durdu.

Memed realised that they were speaking about him. Turning, he asked: "What's the matter?"

Zala's boy answered, his teeth chattering: "You're covered with blood. You've been hit."

"I didn't feel any pain," said Memed. He raised his hand to his head and then looked at his hand. It was bathed in blood. His heart began to beat more rapidly. He felt himself here and there, but could find no wound.

Pale with anxiety, Durdu came up to him and began to look for the wound. "There's a slight scratch on your head."

"Don't worry," replied Memed. "After all, it's the first one." He stood up, plunged into the woods and ran through the enemy fire as if it did not exist. After a while they heard him cry: "Come over here!"

The police gave them no peace as they ran into the wood, where they found a hollow full of dead branches.

"A good cover," said Durdu. "Pull the branches out."

Suddenly all hell was let loose on them. The leaves fell from the trees and the branches splintered. Without waiting to clear the wood out of the hollow, they took cover there and returned the enemy's fire. Both sides now kept on shooting for a good half-hour, then seemed to agree to hold their fire for a while. Durdu was no longer afraid. If they had intended to attack they would have done so by now. Even if they tightened the noose round him it would soon be night and his men could keep going till dark. Above all he was anxious not to have to run away from the sergeant.

Horali and Jabbar had also sought refuge in the hollow.

"What about Sergeant Rejep?" Jabbar asked. His question caused some disturbance.

"Don't argue about it," interjected Memed. "I'll go and fetch him." They were quiet again.

With great difficulty Memed crawled out of the hollow. He was tired, so tired that he could hardly breathe. He stretched his aching limbs behind a tree-trunk. Suddenly the firing began again. There was no way of moving from his cover. The shots peppered the whole length of the tree-trunk behind which he hid. Still he made a leap for it and felt at once a terrible pain.

"I've been hit," he said to himself. He was afraid. He felt down his right side, then his left, examining the place that hurt. There was no wound.

When he reached Sergeant Rejep there was blood all over him and his hands and feet were bleeding.

"What's up, my lad?" cried Sergeant Rejep. "You're bleeding all over."

Memed smiled, but his face and eyes were so clotted with blood that his smile could scarcely be discerned. "Come on, Sergeant Rejep. I've come to fetch you."

"Get along with you, boy," replied the sergeant. "Look after yourself and I'll look after myself. The scoundrels have surrounded us. We've fallen into this trap because of that mad dog. Not one of you will escape now. Sergeant Asim has been clever this time. Let me stay here. Listen, Memed, you're a good boy. If ever you escape, don't stay with that madman."

"Come on, Sergeant, get up and let's be off. If we die, we die together. If we live . . ."

"Memed, if only I could get away from here."

"Your wound's a light one. You'll get away."

The sergeant was in no state to walk. Memed took the huge, heavy man on his back. After he had carried him for a while he set him down.

The sergeant understood that he was too heavy for Memed. "My boy, it won't do like that. Let me lean on you. It'll be better."

"All right," agreed Memed.

As they went they left a great trail of blood behind them. Again their assailants began to fire. They lay down, clinging to the earth, the enemy's volleys raining down all round them. "Now they're really having fun. They've just come to their senses, the devils," exclaimed Sergeant Rejep.

With great difficulty they reached the hollow and saw that two more men had been wounded, Zala's boy and Horali. Zala's boy was trembling all over and weeping hysterically.

The enemy was obviously closing in on them. The firing was becoming more accurate and deadly. Durdu's fellow-villager, Black Mustan, began to taunt him: "Durdu, Aksoyut will soon have a chance to test your courage. You know your Uncle Mustan well. Don't be proud, my boy. . . ."

Durdu was too angry to answer. For a long while he continued firing.

"Mad Durdu, my boy," Black Mustan called again, "have you swallowed your tongue?"

At last Durdu could bear it no more and rose to his feet. "Uncle Mustan, I know you well and you know me too. If I don't make a cap for your head out of your wife's panties, then my name is no longer Mad Durdu. I'll be damned if I don't."

Memed suddenly grabbed Durdu so that he fell on him. On the other side Black Mustan and four others had taken aim. The five guns fired as one, but Durdu was no longer there.

"You're crazy! If you play the fool like that once more, the first bullet to hit you will be mine. All this is your own fault."

Durdu laughed at Sergeant Rejep's outburst. "If you're in a state to fire, why don't you fire at the enemy rather than at me?"

Rejep pointed to Memed. "You can thank your stars for this chap. If it hadn't been for him, we'd all be lost by now."

Memed felt a great hunger. He looked at Durdu, who gave him

a friendly glance and smiled when he saw the clotted blood on Memed's hands, face and hair, remembering the day the boy had arrived, how he had made himself so small behind Süleyman. "Man really is a puzzle!" Durdu said to himself. "This little fellow who became a brigand only yesterday has shown himself a better man, more of a leader, than many a brigand who has been at it fifty years!"

On the other side a voice called out: "Surrender!"

Durdu raised his gun. "I've had enough of you, Black Mustan," he cried. "This one is for you!"

Black Mustan fell to the ground, bellowing like a calf. "Was I wrong, Sergeant?" Durdu asked Rejep.

"You did well. And now what, for heaven's sake—have you decided to stay here and die?"

"We've sworn to. We won't leave this hollow. Isn't that what we all agreed?"

"They've begun firing a machine-gun, just sweeping the terrain. There's no hope of escape. It's death or surrender."

"Is it death or surrender?" asked Memed, in astonishment and fear. The familiar sparkle of brass flickered in his memory and was gone.

"If you know any other way, Memed, tell us," exclaimed Rejep.

"If you don't know, how should I, Sergeant?"

The sergeant pondered a while. His wound smarted no longer, but had begun to throb, leaving him no respite to reflect. With his head bent forward the sergeant wrinkled his face and chewed his lip endlessly. When he raised his head he looked at each one of the others in turn before speaking. "I've got a suggestion. If it works, we're saved."

"What is it?" they all cried.

"Just three hand-grenades," he explained. "Is there one of you plucky enough to go and toss three hand-grenades at that machine-gun?"

"We've all got enough courage for that," said Jabbar as he reloaded his gun. "Sergeant Asim will mow us down whatever we do, so it's six of one and half a dozen of the other. . . ."

"Is there no hope?" asked Memed.

"The only hope is what I've said," answered the sergeant.

"Well, I'll do it," said Memed, as a point of steely light came

137

back into his eyes and stayed there. Again the sparkling of brass flashed through his memory and was gone. He felt a pleasure mixed with pain.

"Now, now, no hurry!" laughed Durdu. "Give me a couple more hand-grenades." He took them from Jabbar, sprang out of the hollow and ran as fast as he could. Bullets whistled all round him. He threw himself behind a rock so suddenly that the men behind him were surprised. They thought he had been hit.

Crocuses were growing beneath the rock, yellow and fresh. The rock was quite big and round. Durdu examined it, pushed it out of its place and started rolling it before him to protect himself. Bullets peppered the white rock. There were shouts. He realised that the rock would soon be of no use. Fifty yards ahead there was a hollow tree-trunk. He lunged to reach it, hurled himself forward and fell there. A smell of earth and rotten leaves reached his nostrils. He saw a purple flower, but could not remember its name. It has a peculiar perfume and generally grows among rocks, not just any-where. A cloud drifted gently across a mountain peak, its edges tipped with light, all golden.

The rattling of the machine-gun near him brought him back to his senses. Before him was a small mound, behind it another one, a little higher than the first. The machine-gun must be between the two mounds. He would have to skirt the first to reach the second, which was crowned with a thick clump of trees.

He rose to his feet and walked easily, swinging his arms, as if he were on a long tramp. Those watching him were breathless with surprise.

In the twinkling of an eye he had pulled out the pins and hurled the grenades at the machine-gun. First one, then another, then a third. The ground shook with a great roar. Everything was hidden in smoke.

When Durdu ran back to his companions, the sun was setting. He did not speak, did not look at anyone. His eyes were fixed and hard. Now the bullets came only at intervals. He rose to his feet, stretched his limbs, and called out: "Sergeant Asim, I wish you the best! Just take that rattle away and repair it, then come back. I'll be waiting for you."

Not a sound came in reply.

Durdu turned to Sergeant Rejep. "You know the country well, Sergeant. Is there any kind of a village around here?"

"No."

"Must we go all the way up the mountain? We'll be in a fine state if we do!"

"There's no place to stop till we get there," replied Sergeant Rejep. "Even with my wound and at my age I'm still ready to walk there."

By dawn they had reached the cliffs, but not one of them looked any longer like a human being. Horali had kept on cursing someone or something, it was not quite clear who or what, and was still cursing. Although he gritted his teeth with all his strength Sergeant Rejep could not bear the pain and had begun to groan.

Wounded, exhausted, Durdu sat down on a rock. Very slowly he rolled a cigarette and lit it. After several puffs he turned to Memed. "Brother, do you know what I would like above all else in the world?"

"No."

"That Black Mustan I killed, I'd like to take his head and stick it on a pole right in the middle of our village. What business had he to come after me? what did he want?"

"I'm just dying of hunger," called Jabbar from farther off. "We must find some food."

"If you can find any," said Durdu, "I'll congratulate you."

"Listen," shouted Jabbar. "I can hear dogs barking in the distance. But there's no village around here. What do you think that barking of dogs means?"

"Jabbar," moaned Sergeant Rejep, "I've seen plenty of asses in my life, but I've never seen a bigger one than you."

"How's that, Sergeant?"

"I just haven't," replied the sergeant.

"I'm in the sergeant's bad books."

"Do you mean to say you don't know where that barking comes from?"

"How should I know, Sergeant? I didn't whelp them."

"That barking comes from the tents of the nomads. They're camping somewhere around here. Do you understand now?"

"Yes," answered Jabbar.

"Well, it took time."

"I'll go with Memed as far as their tents and ask for food. Are you coming, Memed?" Jabbar suggested.

"Do as you like," said Durdu. "We'll light a fire and warm ourselves while we wait."

"Let's go, Jabbar," said Memed. "But we don't look very trustworthy. They'll take us for gipsies."

"Don't worry, Brother. When we've washed our faces it'll be all right."

They went down from the rocks to the plain without speaking, not even exchanging a glance, as if they had committed a crime. Jabbar suddenly stretched out his hand and took hold of Memed's little finger. Memed slowly raised his head and their eyes met.

"Jabbar, he's no good, the man we're following."

"Yes, but we must stick together. We owe him a lot."

The sun was quite high by the time they reached the tents. Five or six huge dogs rushed out to greet them.

"Hold back your dogs!" shouted Jabbar.

A few children came out of the tents and ran inside again. "The bandits! The bandits are coming!" they screamed to their mother .

At this the women came out, followed by their menfolk.

"Peace be with you!" Memed greeted them.

The nomads stared in astonishment at so young a bandit. Beside Memed, Jabbar was a big, strong, fine-looking man.

"Come inside, Aghas," said a bearded nomad, showing them into a fairly big tent.

Bending as they entered, they followed. Inside, Memed stopped open-mouthed, in wonder at the beauty of the tent. All eyes, he did not even hear the nomad's greetings. At the back of the tent were embroidered bags of dazzling colour. How could so much light penetrate the tent? One bag in particular, in this orgy of light and colour, caught Memed's eye. For a long time he could not take his eyes off it. There were tiny love-birds embroidered on it, perhaps a thousand of them, their beaks touching. Green, blue, yellow, red and purple birds. His eyes filled with tears.

The tent-pole was carved with a pattern representing deer in flight, worked in mother-of-pearl.

Jabbar prodded Memed. "What are you dreaming about? Wake up!"

Smiling, Memed pulled himself together. "Up to now I've never seen the inside of a tent. It's like paradise. How beautiful it is!"

" Whose tent is this?" Jabbar asked.

A white-bearded, red-faced old man sitting opposite them answered with a pleasant smile: "It's mine. They call me Kerimoghlu."

"I've heard of you," said Jabbar. "You're the chief of the Black-haired tribe, aren't you?"

"That is so."

The smell of fresh, steaming, newly boiled milk filled the air.

The Agha looked at Jabbar and Jabbar at the Agha. Then the Agha turned to his wife. "These young men must be hungry. Be quick, woman!" he said reproachfully.

"The milk is on the boil," answered the wife. "Let it finish boiling and then . . ."

Memed smiled. "My nose . . ." he began.

"What's wrong with your nose?" asked Jabbar.

"My nose caught the smell of milk at once. It never fails me!"

"Neither does mine. When you're hungry, all noses are like that."

Kerimoghlu's red face became redder as he asked shyly: "You'll be coming from some fight, boys?"

"Sergeant Asim encircled us but we escaped, thank God," replied Jabbar.

"He's a coward. He could have shot us all down, one by one, like partridges," added Memed.

"He couldn't have missed us, but he just wasted his ammunition."

The woman brought the meal and set it in the middle of the tent. Kerimoghlu made room, smiling. It was the first time Memed had felt himself a stranger anywhere. More exactly, he felt a strangeness within himself. His eye wandered to his rifle. Then he glanced at his clothes. His whole chest was covered with cartridge-belts. At his side hung a huge dagger and some hand-grenades. On his head he wore a dirty, crumpled purple fez, Mad Durdu's old one. "So I've become a brigand, eh?" he thought. "And from now on, all my life I'll be a brigand!"

First milk was served, steaming, bluish-white beneath the

wrinkled skin of cream. Then they were offered molasses and fried meat. Their mouths watered as they looked at each other, laughing like children. Kerimoghlu understood. His old face smiled, too, and his fine white teeth glistened.

"Come, my lads, don't stand on ceremony."

The two picked up their spoons. First of all they had their fill of milk. In their first hunger all the bread on the table was consumed and fresh bread was brought; when the milk was drunk, fresh milk came too. They ate ravenously and had soon finished.

"Many thanks, Agha," they said.

"That's all right, lads," said the Agha, who continued eating very slowly.

Then he rose from the table, wiping his moustaches with the back of his hand. "Do you smoke?" he inquired. "Will you have a cigarette?"

"Neither of us smokes," replied Jabbar.

Kerimoghlu put his cigarette to his mouth and struck his flint. A pleasant, fragrant smell of tobacco spread through the room.

"I'd like to say something, but don't take it wrongly. Don't think . . ."

"Speak, Agha," interrupted Memed. "Say whatever comes to your mind."

Kerimoghlu flushed with confusion. "What I wanted to say is that you have no mother, no home on this mountain. You've just come from a fight and there's blood all over you. Perhaps you're wounded too. Strip off your clothes, boys. The girls will wash them straight away and they'll dry quickly. If you're in a hurry, they can be dried over the fire. Meanwhile you can put on some of mine. Don't think that Kerimoghlu will rob you. Nobody ever comes to harm in Kerimoghlu's tent. He would die rather than do harm to a guest. You can be sure of that."

"We know that, Kerimoghlu, Agha," said Jabbar. "How could you imagine such a thing!" Memed agreed.

"Don't say that, lad. Every man has sucked raw milk and can do harm as easily as good."

A girl with darkened eyelids and reddened cheeks placed before each of them a set of underclothes which smelled of soap.

"I'll just go out while you change," said Kerimoghlu.

"Well, Jabbar," said Memed, "what good people there are in this world!"

"There are cruel and wicked people, too, in this world, Memed!"

"Look at this Kerimoghlu," went on Memed. "How courteous he is to his guests."

From outside Kerimoghlu called: "Have you changed, lads? May I come in?"

"We've changed," replied Memed.

"Let's have a look at your wound," said Kerimoghlu to Memed.

"There's no need, really," answered Memed. "The bullet grazed my head. It's just a tiny scratch."

Then Kerimoghlu asked Jabbar: "Is there nothing wrong with you?"

"Thank God, no," he answered.

Kerimoghlu went out and soon returned with a plate and some linen. He made a poultice with his own hands and began to bind Memed's wound. "In two days there'll be no sign of it. We've all been wounded in our youth. Everything passes." He bound Memed's head more skilfully than a surgeon.

"Thank you, Agha," said Memed gratefully.

"It's only a slight wound, but it's infected. The poultice will draw out the poison. Don't be afraid."

Kerimoghlu had a childlike manner. When he was about to ask a question he would blush and smile in confusion before bringing himself to speak, as he now did again. "My boy," he said to Memed, "if it isn't rude to ask, are you really a brigand?"

Jabbar laughed. "Agha, our Memed only plays at being a brigand."

Memed smiled. "Don't I look like a brigand to you, Agha?"

"Don't be offended, my boy. I didn't want to belittle you, but you're very young. You don't look more than sixteen. That's why I asked."

"I'm eighteen," replied Memed proudly.

"I was only surprised. Why did you go off to be a brigand at your age?"

"He stole a donkey from his Agha and sold it," Jabbar explained. "Then he was afraid his Agha would beat him, so he came to us. What could we do? We took him in. Let there be a donkey-thief among us too. One more or less . . ."

The Agha understood that Jabbar was making fun of him and was hurt. It was clear from his face that he regretted having asked the question.

Seeing that Kerimoghlu was offended, Jabbar asked him: "Agha, have you ever heard of a man from Deyirmenoluk named Abdi Agha?"

"I know him well. I heard he'd been shot recently. But he isn't dead. His nephew died."

"This is the man who shot him," said Jabbar.

Kerimoghlu looked at Memed for a long time. "Strange, you don't look the kind of boy who would shoot a man. Strange!"

"Agha," Memed said to Kerimoghlu, "do you think you could make a little more of that ointment for us? Some of our friends are wounded. We could take it back to them."

"There's some ready," answered Kerimoghlu. "I'll prepare the bandages too."

"May you never fall on evil days!"

Kerimoghlu wrapped the ointment in a fairly large piece of linen and gave them the lint for the poultice.

As they set off on the road Kerimoghlu said: "I was puzzled about you, Memed. You don't look in the least like a brigand. But what can you do? Who knows how cruel the man was. That's human nature, you never know what's inside a man."

"Good health to you," they both called to their host as they parted.

Baring his glistening teeth as he smiled, Kerimoghlu answered: "Good luck! Come back some day and we'll have a chat."

Each of them now carried two heavy bags in his hands. Keri-moghlu had filled them with bread, cheese and butter. Jabbar and Memed agreed that their host had been very generous.

"Jabbar," Memed suddenly remembered aghast, "we didn't give him back his clothes!"

"It doesn't matter," answered Jabbar. "We didn't steal them, we just forgot."

"That won't do. Let's go and give them back."

"Kerimoghlu was right," laughed Jabbar. "You're not like a brigand at all."

"What can I do? We're not all born brigands."

They turned back hurriedly. Kerimoghlu seemed surprised as he met them at the entrance of his tent. "What's up?" he asked. "Why have you come back so soon?"

"We forgot we were wearing your clothes. We've brought them back," replied Memed.

"I was afraid something might have happened," said Kerimoghlu. "You can keep the clothes as a present."

"Do you really want us to keep them?" asked Memed.

"Of course. If you take them off I'll be offended."

Night was falling when at last they reached the cliffs. Far off, on the very summit of the cliffs, a light sparkled.

"That light must be our camp-fire," said Jabbar.

"Do you think so?" said Memed doubtfully.

"Naturally! Who would light such a big fire? Durdu's doing it to spite Sergeant Asim."

"I haven't the strength to move. Blow the warning whistle!"

Jabbar placed two fingers in his mouth and whistled loud and long.

"Jabbar, I swear your whistle can be heard a day's journey from here!"

A shot was fired from near the camp-fire, followed by a whole volley.

"Is anything wrong?" asked Memed.

"Mad Durdu is celebrating. When he's in that mood he fires all the time."

But nobody came in answer to their whistling and this vexed both Memed and Jabbar.

By the time they reached the fire they were soaked in sweat and worn out. Durdu and all their companions rose to their feet to greet them. Durdu pulled out his gun.

"Glory be!" he cried, firing off several rounds. "We were dying of hunger. A little longer and you wouldn't have found us alive. See how Sergeant Rejep is still groaning. It's not his wound. It's hunger, by God!"

The flames of the huge fire bent and twisted as they mingled and rose to the full height of a man. The loud crackling of burning wood filled the air with a pleasant odour. Fresh moist branches

145

twist in the flame for a long while before they split down the middl
and are lost in the flames.

Memed's first care was to go to Sergeant Rejep. "How are you
feeling, Sergeant?" he asked.

"My wound hurts," groaned the sergeant. "It's burning. I'l
never get over it. I'm dying . . ."

Then Memed went over to Horali. "How are you, Brothe
Horali?"

Horali's reply was a torrent of abuse and obscenities; he curse
Abdi Agha's mother and his wife, his own life as a brigand and hi
wounds, Abdi's village and trees and stones and rocks, his ow
wounds, Abdi Agha's wife all over again, finally exclaiming: "Hav
you heard the news? Abdi isn't even dead, the scoundrel! But don'
worry, we'll attend to him. At least that whining baby of a nephev
of his is dead!"

"I've brought you some ointment for poultices. Kerimoghl
gave it to us. He made it himself. He's wise and experienced and i
should heal your wounds within a couple of days."

Horali cursed the ointment too, in a new outburst of obscenities

"It'll make you feel better, Brother Horali."

"Let's hope so," Horali relented.

"Your Kerimoghlu seems to be pretty sure of himself!" sai
Sergeant Rejep, sitting up. "If his ointment heals my wound
within a month, I'll be glad."

Memed cleaned their wounds, put on the poultices and the
went and sat down by the fire.

"Memed," called Durdu. "What's Jabbar saying about you
He says that you saw the inside of Kerimoghlu's tent and jus
stood there open-mouthed."

"It was like a place in paradise," said Memed.

"Kerimoghlu is one of the richest nomad chiefs," said Jabba
"If the inside of his tent weren't as it is, whose would be?"

"Did you already know him?" asked Durdu.

"I had heard of him. He has a fortune . . ."

"What kind people there are in this world!" interrupte
Memed. "He thought of everything. He bound my wound and le
us eat our fill. Then he had our linen laundered and gave each of u
a change of clothing."

"He's a very great Agha," added Jabbar.

146

"Why haven't we yet heard of such a famous and rich Agha?" asked Durdu.

"He is the Agha of the nomads. They pitch their tents and go off again," explained Jabbar.

"His tent-pole is wrought of pure mother-of-pearl, I hear," said Durdu in astonishment. "That means he's a mighty rich fellow."

"He must be," returned Memed. "His tent's so big that it has ten or fifteen such poles. A girl brought us food. There were perhaps fifty gold coins round her neck. He's both a rich and a good man. A pleasant man, with a smiling face."

Durdu was staring into the flames. He did not speak or ask any more questions. He was wrapped in thought. It was Durdu's custom, before he came to any decision, to fix his eyes on something, it did not matter what, a man, a tree, a cloud, a flower, a bird, a gun, the fire, and remain like that for hours, without moving. Seeing him so quiet, the others stopped talking too.

In a harsh voice Durdu gave his orders for the night. "To-night Horali, Sergeant Rejep and I will keep the watch. The rest can sleep."

No one dared speak. If anyone, no matter how dear to him, dared contradict him, Durdu would shoot. So they went off without uttering a sound and all curled up at the foot of the rock. If not as audibly as before, Horali continued to curse every now and then. Sergeant Rejep stopped groaning.

Some men seem to have been gifted from birth with an ability to make friends. Sergeant Rejep was one of them. Does anything special make them more pleasant than others? Was Sergeant Rejep, for instance, a good talker or particularly cheerful? Always smiling and joking, or especially kind to others? Not particularly; his quality was something secret.

When they first met Rejep had said to Durdu: "Listen, if you were one of those clever bastards, I wouldn't stay in your band more than two months; those conceited fellows get things confused and soon fall into an ambush and are lost. Do you understand me?"

"Yes," Durdu had replied.

After that Sergeant Rejep never discussed the matter again. He had never protested, whatever Mad Durdu had done. Once or twice, quite unnecessarily, Rejep had been wounded, but had still said nothing to Durdu.

Nobody knew anything much about Rejep's past. His speech suggested that he came from around Antep, but even this was uncertain. He had obviously lived there for quite a while and often spoke of that part of the country.

There were many other rumours about his life. For instance, it was said that one night Sergeant Rejep had woken up suddenly and exclaimed: "Wife, give me my rifle and prepare me some food. I'm going." His wife had brought him his rifle and set it beside him and prepared him some food. He had then greased the weapon carefully, strapped on his cartridge-belts and said: "Wife, give me my old fur cap. I'm taking to the mountain. Forgive me all my shortcomings and don't bear me any grudge." His wife had been surprised. "Are you crazy, man?" she had said. "Waking up like that in the middle of the night and taking to the mountain? Who ever heard of such a thing?" Sergeant Rejep had then answered: "That's how I feel, woman, I'm going." Without saying another word he had walked out of the house and never returned.

Others said that Sergeant Rejep had lost his temper with his son-in-law because the latter had insulted him while cursing his own wife. One day, while passing by his son-in-law's door, the Sergeant Rejep had heard the young man say: "You no-good daughter of a no-good father." The father-in-law had then taken to the mountain because he had not the heart to avenge his own honour by killing his son-in-law.

Others again said that Sergeant Rejep had been very rich but had never been willing to pay any state or road taxes and, whenever the tax-collector came, would pretend to be ill and take to his bed. So he had one day taken to the mountain rather than pay. Some also said it was because he had killed his mother-in-law. Everybody invented something, but no one knew for certain which story was true and which was false. It was not even clear whether he had committed a crime or not. Whatever his reason for taking to the mountain, Sergeant Rejep would get at least thirty years if he were arrested now. He had been in so many raids, so many skirmishes, so many hold-ups and killings.

Day broke and the sun rose, but Durdu slept until late, though it was not his custom to let sunlight fall upon his sleeping body.

Midday came and still he was not awake. Jabbar was suspicious. "There's surely something at the back of his mind," he thought. "Durdu never sleeps as late as this. He's planning some new raid. Before any dangerous raids it's his custom to sleep longer, perhaps once a year or every two years. What's he planning now, I wonder?" He was curious.

Sergeant Rejep was cheerful, singing songs in an old cracked voice. "Listen, boys," he said suddenly. "Wake that madman! Let's have a bite of food."

"I'm not interfering," answered Memed.

"Nor am I," added Jabbar.

Güdükoghlu went and leaned over Durdu. "Durdu Pasha," he said. "Wake up. Durdu Pasha." Güdükoghlu always addressed Durdu as "Pasha." It flattered Durdu's vanity. Güdükoghlu had various duties in their band and playing the clown to put Durdu in a good mood was an important one.

"Wake up, Pasha. It's past midday, Pasha."

Durdu rose slowly, rubbing his eyes with his great fists. "We'll eat straight away. Then we'll be going."

"What about the wounded?" asked Jabbar. "Sergeant Rejep and Horali are in a poor state."

"Can you walk with us?" asked Durdu, turning to Rejep.

"I'll walk," replied Sergeant Rejep. "It doesn't hurt much now."

Horali agreed to walk too, but began to curse his wound again.

They sat down in a wide circle to eat.

The shadows were beginning to turn from north to east as they descended the cliffs. The barking of dogs from the nomad tents greeted their approach.

"Where are we going?" Memed asked. Durdu remained ominously silent. Memed did not insist.

When Durdu turned in the direction of the barking dogs, Memed and Jabbar realised what was afoot.

"I don't like what's on Durdu's mind," Jabbar whispered in Memed's ear.

"Nor do I," replied Memed.

"If he plays some dirty trick on Kerimoghlu, what do we do?"

Memed was silent. They were perplexed. Durdu was clearly

149

bent on some evil. His face was so full of contained ferocity that anything might set off an explosion.

Slowing down, Durdu asked Jabbar: "How many tents were there besides Kerimoghlu's?"

"Three," answered Jabbar. Durdu began to walk faster.

When they came to the tents they were again met by the dogs, with the children and the women behind them. Last of all came a few men, Kerimoghlu leading them and greeting the brigands as they approached. Flocks of white sheep were all round the camp, milk-white against the black felt of the tents. The sheep and lambs were bleating, the huge sheep-dogs prowled and swaggered about them, the camels were resting on the ground, foam dribbling from their mouths.

"Welcome, my guests, welcome," Kerimoghlu called cheerfully, shaking each man's hand.

"We're glad to see you again," replied Memed, smiling. But the smile remained frozen on his face. He was paralysed by a growing suspicion. What was Durdu up to? Then he introduced Durdu to Kerimoghlu: "He's the leader of our band."

Kerimoghlu was an experienced man. He glanced at Durdu from under low brows and was clearly perplexed. Durdu walked on without looking around, his face sulky and his head erect.

"What's his name?" Kerimoghlu asked Memed.

"Durdu."

"Is he the one who strips his victims even of their drawers?"

"Yes," Memed answered with a sigh. The smile froze on Kerimoghlu's florid face. His eyes clouded.

When they entered the tent Durdu was dazzled, though not as much as Memed had been. On the wall hung a finely-worked gun. With a greedy look Durdu said to Kerimoghlu as they sat down: "Bring that gun and let's have a look at it, Agha. Let's see an Agha's gun!"

Kerimoghlu sensed his envy. There was a stab of pain in his heart as he became aware of impending disaster. He did not like Durdu's face and eyes. "Would you like your meal now," he said, handing the gun to him, "or will you eat in the evening?"

Durdu's eyes flashed. "I neither eat the bread nor drink the coffee of the man I've come to rob. If I do, I can no longer rob him."

He rose to his feet, ready for violence. The others rose too.

"Eat and then rob," countered Kerimoghlu. "Those who come to Kerimoghlu's tent never leave without eating their fill." His voice was shaking and a slight flush spread from his cheeks to his nose and forehead. Beads of sweat appeared on his brow. "Listen, Durdu Agha! These mountains are full of brigands. Up to now not one of them has dared rob Kerimoghlu's tent. If you've come to rob it, go ahead!"

Memed and Jabbar stood aghast, stunned by what they were witnessing, overcome with shame.

"I'm not like other brigands," answered Durdu.

Kerimoghlu stood as silent and unshaken as his tent-pole.

"Bring out your money, Agha," ordered Durdu.

Sergeant Rejep and Horali had stood up with the others, but now sat down again, watching. For some reason Sergeant Rejep's eyes were smiling.

Seeing that Kerimoghlu did not move, Durdu came slowly up to him and suddenly brought down the butt of the rifle with all his strength on his shoulder. Kerimoghlu fell to the ground. Durdu seized him by the arm and pulled him up. At the back of the tent the women and children were shrieking with fear.

"Listen, Agha, you rule over the tents of the Black-haired tribe, not over me. On these mountains, Mad Durdu's word is law!"

"Go with the Agha," he ordered Güdükoghlu, "and bring whatever money he has. Collect the women's gold coins as well!"

This was also one of Güdükoghlu's duties. Whenever they went on a raid he did the torturing and extracted the money, having become an expert at such work. Once he had searched a house not a piastre remained there. He knew how to drain it dry.

It was always a great moment for Güdükoghlu. While the rest of the brigands stood ready to shoot, he seized the Agha's arm and twisted it. "Come, Kerimoghlu. Show me where your money's hidden or I'll shoot you."

"Kerimoghlu," shouted Durdu, "it's either your life or all your money!"

All the women and children had gathered in front of the tent. When Durdu saw them blocking the entrance he came out and shouted: "Off with you, back to your tents! It'll be your turn later."

Kerimoghlu's eyes sought Memed and Jabbar, who were standing behind him. Memed was ashamed and avoided his gaze. Then Kerimoghlu looked at Jabbar, too, as if to say: "Is this how you thank me?" A tear formed in the corner of each eye as he turned and went off ahead of Güdükoghlu. They passed into the back of the tent where he said to one of the weeping women who were huddled like a flock of terrified sheep: "Open the chest. Whatever money we have, bring it out and hand it to him. Whatever gold coins, bracelets and rings you're wearing, take them off and give them to him too." Kerimoghlu had understood that Durdu would not leave them a single coin. Whatever they possessed would have to be given up.

Güdükoghlu came back with a thick wad of paper money and a bag of gold coins which he handed over to Durdu. Meanwhile Kerimoghlu had collected all the women's necklaces, rings, bracelets and head-pieces of gold coins and handed them over too.

"Is that all?" asked Durdu.

"I've cleaned the place out," answered Güdükoghlu without any hesitation. On all other raids, when Durdu had asked Güdükoghlu if that were all, he generally answered: "There's some more, Pasha," and would go off and bring back more gold or paper money. He might thus comb a house ten or twenty times before he had brought out, little by little, whatever money had remained concealed in odd corners and purses. Only then would he report that nothing was left. Besides, Güdükoghlu knew, just by looking at a man, whether there was anything left or not. He was never mistaken in this respect.

"You're a wise man, Kerimoghlu," said Durdu. "You've handed over all your money and jewellery. I've never met a wiser man than you among those I have robbed."

Kerimoghlu stood there like a stone, his face pale, his lips trembling, as Durdu began to shout in a sharp, overbearing voice: "Mad Durdu has one custom. Do you know about it, Kerimoghlu?" he asked. "Other brigands don't have it, but other brigands, of course, don't dare rob Kerimoghlu."

Kerimoghlu remained silent.

"It is Mad Durdu's custom to strip the men he has robbed even of their drawers. Off with your clothes, Kerimoghlu!" he shouted.

Kerimoghlu made no movement.

"It's you I'm talking to. Off with your clothes."

Kerimoghlu still remained motionless.

Durdu could no longer contain his anger. He walked around Kerimoghlu and suddenly gave him a sharp blow under the ear. Then he struck him again and again on the chest with the butt of the rifle. Kerimoghlu swayed and was on the point of falling, but Durdu seized him by the arm and began striking him again savagely. "Take them off."

"Don't do this to me, Durdu," Kerimoghlu pleaded in an agonised tone. "No man has ever yet raided Kerimoghlu's tent. This will not go unpunished!"

Infuriated, Durdu let go of Kerimoghlu's arm and began to kick him. Kerimoghlu fell to the ground, crying: "Don't! Don't! This will not go unpunished." His threat only increased Durdu's fury. Durdu began to trample the prostrate man beneath his feet. "I know that this will not go unpunished. That's why I'm stripping you even of your drawers. At least it'll be said I took the drawers off the great Kerimoghlu's legs. Do you understand?"

Hearing the commotion, some of the women who had been weeping in the back of the tent now came through to the front. One woman threw herself on Kerimoghlu to protect him. Her screams filled the tent. Güdükoghlu seized the shrieking woman, dragged her off Kerimoghlu and flung her aside.

"If you don't strip stark naked," shouted Durdu, "and if you don't do it yourself, I'll kill you."

The women's wailing grew louder.

"Don't do this to me! Don't do this in front of all my family," moaned Kerimoghlu.

Kerimoghlu's eyes met those of Memed, who was biting his lips and trembling all over. As Kerimoghlu stared pleadingly, Memed felt something explode within him. He turned to Jabbar, and they exchanged glances. A needle-point of light came to rest in Memed's eyes again. Jabbar was also biting the lining of his cheeks with indignation. When he was angry he would suck in his cheeks and chew the flesh until it bled.

"Don't do this to me, Durdu Agha," Kerimoghlu kept repeating. "Don't!"

"Strip!" bellowed Durdu, "or else . . ." He raised the barrel of his rifle threateningly in the direction of Kerimoghlu's mouth. "Strip!"

Just then, in a flash, Memed rushed out of the tent shouting: "Don't move, Durdu, or I'll fire. Forgive me, but I'll fire. What you're doing . . ."

Jabbar's mocking voice was heard: "Leave the man in peace, Durdu Agha, or I'll fire too. You and I have been friends a long time. Don't let your death be on our hands now."

"Don't let your death be on our hands," repeated Memed.

Durdu had never expected this. "So that's how it is?" he shouted. Then he raised his gun and fired two shots outside.

It was already dark.

"That's not how to shoot, Durdu Agha," called Memed. "Look!" Two bullets whizzed past Durdu's ears. "Let the man go. You've done enough. This is wanton cruelty. Leave him and go."

"So that's how it is, Slim Memed."

"Unless you want to die," answered Memed, "leave the man and get out of the tent."

Once more Durdu kicked the prostrate man at his feet. "Come on, friends, let's be going."

Outside he saw the shadow of Memed, who lay in a hollow. "You'll pay for this, Memed. You too, Jabbar."

Sergeant Rejep was the last to leave the tent. "I liked what you did, boys," he said. "May I stay with you too?"

"Stay, Sergeant, stay!" they cried.

"You too, Sergeant?" asked Durdu.

"Yes, Durdu Agha," he replied.

"Then you'll pay for it too, Sergeant."

Durdu was about fifty yards away when he suddenly threw himself down on the ground and called to his companions: "Let's get to work! It's a life and death struggle from now on."

He fired a volley at Memed and Jabbar. But they had known what to expect of Durdu and were careful to remain under cover.

"Go your own way, Durdu Agha," called Memed. "Don't be childish!"

"It's you or I . . ." shouted Durdu.

"Off with you, man," said Sergeant Rejep. "Stop pestering the boys. You'll have enough trouble on your own head as it is. By now all the tents of the Black-haired tribe will have heard of this and the whole tribe will be combing the mountains for you. Off with you!"

The firing stopped.

"They're going," said Jabbar. "Curse them! They're off to divide up the loot from Kerimoghlu."

"Let them go," said Sergeant Rejep. "The Black-haired tribe will make them pay for it a hundredfold. If this man's really Kerimoghlu, the Agha of the Black-haired tribe, the mountain will soon be teeming with men hunting high and low for them."

"Now what can we go and say to Kerimoghlu? How can we look him straight in the face?"

"He was good to us and we repaid him with evil," said Jabbar. "What can we say to him? That we're proud of what we've done? That this is what we call being a man? Forget it! Let's be off without seeing him again!"

"What can I say to Kerimoghlu?" repeated Memed.

He came out of the hollow where they had been concealed and set off towards the tents. A great noise of weeping and wailing came from Kerimoghlu's tent. Memed opened the flap of the tent. One or two women were holding Kerimoghlu's bleeding head over a basin and washing his wounds.

Memed called: "Kerimoghlu Agha." All heads turned towards the entrance. Memed felt like running off without saying a word, but he couldn't.

"Agha," he stammered, "forgive us. We didn't know it would be like that." Then he turned and began to run.

"Don't go," Kerimoghlu called after him. "Don't go without eating your supper, my son."

Memed came up to Jabbar. "Come along, let's be going. I can't stay here any longer. My heart bleeds for the poor man."

"What can you do?" said Jabbar, rising to his feet. "It's done now."

"We should have killed Durdu," Memed sighed.

"It isn't easy to kill that brute," said Jabbar. "If it were, would I have let him get away like that?"

"What would have happened if we'd shot him?" asked Memed.

"He wouldn't have been hit. I've never seen a man like that."

"There's something strange about him," agreed Sergeant Rejep.

155

"Whatever he's done, he always gets away with it. If another brigand had done it, he would never have survived it more than a day. There's something strange about him and we've done well to leave him. But he's no coward. He's ready to face death any minute."

"That's just what scared me," admitted Memed. "That's why I couldn't shoot at him."

"Anyway, there's something strange about the man," Jabbar concluded, then remained silent.

XIII

Iraz had been left a widow when she was only twenty, with a nine-months-old baby in her arms. She had loved her husband dearly.

"After Huseyin," she had sworn before his dead body, "there can be no other man for me."

She had kept her word and never remarried.

A few days after her husband's death she had left their child to the care of a woman relative and gone to work, ploughing the land her husband had left her. A month later she had ploughed the field and finished the sowing.

When summer came she then harvested the field all by herself. She was young and strong and the work did not hurt her.

Later she would take the boy in her arms and wander through the village playing with him. "Won't my baby grow up because his uncles neglect him? Just look how my Riza's growing!" she would say to spite his uncles, the eldest of whom wanted to marry her. "I'm not marrying," Iraz would reply to his offers of marriage, "I'm not taking any other man into Huseyin's bed. If I live till Doomsday I'll never marry again."

"Iraz," people would insist, "this is Huseyin's brother, not just a stranger. He's the child's uncle. He'll look after him like a father."

But Iraz remained obdurate.

Her brother-in-law bore her a grudge for having rejected his offer and soon obtained possession of the field she had inherited from Huseyin, though he had no right to it. When their father had died the three brothers had divided in equal shares the fields they had inherited. This field had been the share of her husband,

Huseyin, but there was nothing Iraz could now do. She was a young woman, ignorant of the ways of the law and of those that lead to the Government.

Deprived of her field, Iraz still stood firm. "Will my baby's uncles' dirty tricks prevent him from growing up? Won't my Riza be able to grow up if we no longer own a field?"

In the summer she toiled in the fields of others, in the winter she worked as a servant in the homes of the rich. She managed to scrape through and her child grew to be a bonny boy. But on her lips there was always a lament, like a lullaby, a bitter song: "Won't my orphan grow up?"

He grew, but why were they always in such poverty, without even a field of their own? He grew, hearing the reasons for their poverty every day from his mother and the other villagers. The bitter song was graven deep in his mind, a song born of a mother's pain, trouble and courage: "Won't my little one grow up?"

When Riza was almost twenty-one, he was tall and slender, like a healthy plant. No boy in Sakar village could ride a horse, throw a javelin, hit the mark, dance in a ring as Riza could. But mother and son were both unhappy. In their hearts they nourished incurable woes. To have to work for others, to be mere labourers when you have once owned your own field!

Compared with that of other villages the land around Sakar is very fertile and plentiful, a vast plain with a huge rock called Adaja, right in the middle. When the whole plain had been sown and all the fields were turning green, the rock of Adaja stood out white against the green.

One of the largest fields at the foot of Adaja was the one that had belonged to Riza's father. For years his uncle had ploughed it now. Riza dreamed of its rich fertile soil and hatred grew and hardened in his heart. Wherever he went, wherever he drove the plough, his mind's eye was set on the foot of the Adaja rock.

Every day his mother would moan: "Ah, my son! The Adaja field . . . Your father used to keep us in fine style, thanks to that field. May they be struck blind!"

Riza would lower his head and remain as if in a trance. In his nostrils he could sense the smell of rich, shining earth. His longing for the earth consumed him.

"That infidel uncle of yours," his mother would say. "May he get his deserts!"

Riza's hatred grew until there came a time when he could no longer conceal it. He had never been like this before. He would now wake up early in the morning and set out in the direction of Adaja. Reaching the field at the foot of the rock he would sit on a stone and day-dream. The crops were ripe and the earth swarmed with insects. As the sun rose the earth would begin to steam. The longing to own such steaming soil is the most violent of all longings. Riza would thrust his hand into the soft warm soil and let the earth slip through his fingers. "This soil is mine," he would say, a quiver running through his body. "Mine! But another man has sown and harvested it for twenty years."

He would be tired when he rose at last to return home.

"Where have you been since dawn?" his mother would ask. He would remain silent, his face dark and scowling.

This went on for two months. The crops were knee-high and had turned from yellowish-green to a deep dark green.

"Mother," Riza said one day, his mind made up, "this field is ours."

"It's ours, child, whose else would it be?"

"I'm going to apply to the Government," declared Riza.

"How I've waited for this day!"

"I've asked the elders. While he was still alive my father divided up with my uncles the fields inherited from my grandfather. As a consequence, what was ours remains ours and has come to me from my grandfather."

"Yes, child," agreed his mother, "what's ours is ours."

As this was a matter of inheritance, the case did not last long. The rich soft earth at the foot of Adaja passed back to Riza. After so many long, crushing years, young Riza welcomed the field as if he were welcoming his bride into his home. It was summer when the field was handed over to him. The earth was hot and scorched. The crops had already been harvested and the stubble blazed bright in the sun.

Riza found a pair of oxen to turn over the summer earth. He harnessed a plough behind the oxen and the soil then crumbled beneath the plough as he worked fast to have the field ready to receive the seed and then yield thirty-fold or forty-fold what had been sown.

The ploughing for the summer crop is always done at two different times, two hours before dawn and again in the afternoon, when the west wind has risen. The ploughing that begins at dawn continues until the sun is too hot for the oxen to plough. Then they are left to rest in the shade of a tree. In the late afternoon, when the little clouds like sails rise over the Mediterranean, the oxen are harnessed again and the ploughing continues until night-fall, sometimes even until midnight if the moon is bright.

There was a moon when Riza started ploughing his field. He planned to work without a pause until the day grew too warm, then again from the late afternoon till midnight. He would not notice the heat or his own weariness. He could easily forget everything and go on ploughing until morning. The soft ploughed earth would seem more beautiful in the moonlight. At night, in the stillness, the crunch of the plough as it cut through the earth would sound sweeter to his ears.

Iraz was proud that she had raised such a fine lad and that they had now taken the field back from those good-for-nothing uncles. She would wander around the village in a turmoil of joy. If she were asked about her son she would answer: "He is ploughing his field."

It was the fourteenth of the month and the moon was full. All the fields, especially the one Riza was ploughing, gleamed like silver in the moonlight. A fresh wind was blowing. The hoofs of Riza's oxen sank into the ground as they slowly dragged the plough behind them.

Riza was tired and sleepy. He left the oxen and, pillowing his head on a mound of earth, fell asleep.

The next morning, as on every other day, one of the neigh-bourhood's children, fourteen-year-old Durmush, brought Riza his food. The day was already hot and the field was shimmering as the boy looked for Riza at the foot of the trees. Riza would always greet him cheerfully and, without yet taking the food, place his own hands under the boy's arms and lift him high in the air. The boy was now puzzled. He looked all round at the foot of the trees, but found no sign of Riza. Then he saw the young man lying curled up in the middle of the field and no sign of the oxen. When the boy came near where Riza lay, he was so shocked that the food dropped from his hand. He turned and began to run off, screaming all the way.

The boy entered the village breathless and exhausted. He was screaming, but his voice came out as a faint whistle. He threw himself down on the ground in front of the houses. The women gathered around him and pulled his tongue out, thinking he had been frightened into a fit. They made him drink cold water and poured water on his head. After a while the child recovered his senses: "Riza Agha is lying all covered with blood, in a pool of blood on the ground," he said. "Blood was trickling from his mouth. When I saw him like that I came running here all the way."

The women understood what had happened. They bowed their heads and were silent. The news spread instantly through the whole village. Iraz heard it too.

Iraz went ahead of them, tearing her hair and sobbing, with all the villagers behind her. They came to the field. Riza's head had slipped from the mound where it had rested and was hanging at an angle when they found him.

"My orphan boy, my ill-starred son!" cried Iraz as she threw herself upon the corpse.

Riza was curled up with his knees close to his chest. The hollow in the ground in front of him was full of blood that had already clotted with insects and flies all over it. The sun was shining bright, with the sharp smell of blood rising like steam from a boiling cauldron. There was mist in the air and a swarm of bright-green flies on the dead body, glistening as they moved. In spite of the heat the blood had not yet foamed, but was hard as brick, though it seemed to be bubbling.

"My orphan boy! My ill-starred son!"

Women, boys and men stood in a circle round the dead body. Most of the women were weeping.

"Who killed my Riza?" Iraz was beating her breast and struggling piteously to contain her emotion. The other women tried to raise her from the corpse but she could not be dragged away. "Me too," she kept saying. "Bury me alive with my Riza." She lay on her son's dead body till nightfall. News of the murder reached the town. The police, the magistrate and the coroner came. The police dragged the woman, her eyes bloodshot and her face congested from weeping, away from the body and pulled her to her feet, but she sank to the ground and remained motionless as if dead. For a long while she refused to move or to utter a sound.

Later they brought her before the magistrate.

"Woman, who could have killed your son?" he asked. "Whom do you suspect?"

The woman raised her face. With vacant eyes she stared at the magistrate's face.

"Who killed your son? Whom do you suspect?" repeated the magistrate.

"Those infidels," she said. "Who else but those infidels would kill him? His uncles killed the boy, because of the field."

Having inquired closely into the matter of the field, the magistrate took notes on the spot and the crowd broke up as they left the field.

The dead body with the green flies swarming on it, the empty yoke and the plough waiting for the oxen, the mother with eyes tearless from too much weeping, these remained in the desolate solitude of the plain. The rich earth shone in the middle of it as dark as a piece of embroidery.

They arrested Riza's cousin Ali as a suspect and brought him to the police station. According to Ali's testimony, however, he had not been in the village that day; with the aid of local witnesses he proved that he had been at a wedding in a neighbouring village, four hours from Sakar. But Iraz and all the villagers knew that Ali was the one who had killed Riza, because of the field.

Iraz was astounded and the villagers could not believe their eyes when, two days later, Ali swaggered into the village ostentatiously swinging his arms. Iraz lost all control of herself, seized an axe that she had in her home and ran towards Ali's house. She had only one thought: to kill the man who had killed her son. When Ali's family saw Iraz descending upon them with the axe in her hand, they shut their door and bolted it. Finding the door shut, Iraz began to break in with the axe. But Ali was not there. If he had been inside to protect them, they would not have closed the door. His mother, two girls and a baby were inside, and the door was on the point of giving. Iraz swung the axe with all her strength to break it down and kill all those who had sought refuge inside. The villagers hastened to see what the row was about and gathered by the house. But they could not approach Iraz, nor did it occur to them to approach her. Let her avenge her son!

Every now and then a man called: "Don't, Mother! Those inside aren't responsible. Ali isn't in the house. Forget about it."

"Ali isn't here; leave us, Iraz," called the mother from inside.

Somehow Ali managed to slip through the crowd and to catch hold of Iraz from behind. He seized the axe from her hand; with all his strength he threw the exhausted woman aside and began to trample on her. The villagers rushed to her assistance and dragged her from beneath his feet.

That night Iraz set fire to Ali's house. While the villagers were trying to put out the fire, Ali jumped on to a horse and set off for the police station. There he filed a complaint about the events of the morning and about her setting fire to their home, declaring that the house was still burning.

It was morning when Ali returned to the village with the police. When they saw this, the villagers gathered round Ali. "Don't do this, Ali," they said. "The poor thing is broken-hearted from the loss of her fine lad. Don't rub salt into her wound. Don't send her to rot in prison. In any case, the villagers have put out the fire."

Ali refused to listen to them and the police arrested Iraz and took her off to prison.

"Yes, I broke down their door," Iraz told the police, "and if I could have entered the house I would have struck them all down with my axe. But I couldn't. Is it too much if I kill those who killed my only son? Yes, I set fire to their home in the night so that they would all burn to death inside. But those accursed villagers gave the alarm and put out the fire. Do you think it's too high a price for my Riza? My orphan boy was worth a whole country. Do you know at what cost I raised him? Do you think it's too high a price?"

To the magistrate at the time of her arrest and later during the trial she always gave the same testimony. Though they arrested and imprisoned her, she never changed her story and only repeated: "My boy was worth a whole village, a whole country. Is it too much? Is it too high a price?"

They had put her into the one-roomed women's section of the prison. She had never expected this. To avenge the death of her fine tall son she had set fire to a house. It was hard to bear this new wrong after the death of her son. She entered the prison with her head low, groping her way around like a blind person. She could see nothing and did not even notice whether she were alone in this room or with another prisoner. She sat down silently in one corner and remained there like a stone that has been dropped into a well.

Normally Iraz wore her hair tied up in a clean white 'kerchief. Her large light-brown eyes would shine brightly and her slanting eyebrows would give a strange beauty to her broad, sun-tanned face with its small pointed chin and a lock of black hair curled down over her broad forehead. But she was now in a dreadful condition. Her face was almost black and the whites of her eyes were blood-shot from crying. Her chin seemed withered and her lips were bloodless, their skin dry and cracked from thirst. Only her 'kerchief was still white and spotless.

"My fine lad!" she kept repeating. "He was worth a whole country. Was it too high a price? If I burn a whole village to ashes, would it be too much?"

Hatché had been pleased to see this woman come here as a companion in this lonely prison. For herself she felt pleased, but she was sorry for her. Who knew what had befallen the poor creature? She could not rejoice at another's misery. She wanted to ask the woman many questions that were on the tip of her tongue, but somehow she could not bring herself to speak. It is not easy to ask anything of someone who is so exhausted, engaged in such a life-and-death struggle. Hatché just stared at the woman.

In the evening Hatché set her soup on the brazier in the yard outside and began to cook it. When it was ready she brought it in, smelling of onion and rancid butter as it steamed gently. After the soup had cooled a little, she approached Iraz timidly: "Aunt, you must be hungry by now. I've prepared some soup. Come, drink it."

Iraz's eyes were quite vacant. She stared blindly at Hatché as if she had not heard her.

"Aunt," repeated Hatché, "drink a little of this soup. You must be very hungry by now."

Iraz acted as if she simply were not there, not even blinking. Even in the eyes of the blind there is an anxiety to see, a desire, a struggle. Here there was nothing. In deaf ears, too, there is a straining, a reaching out to hear. Here not even that. But Hatché was not to be discouraged and kept on urging her.

Slowly the woman raised her vacant eyes and fixed them on Hatché. Hatché could not sustain her gaze. She mumbled something confusedly, left the bowl there in front of the woman and slipped out, holding her breath.

Until the guard came to shut the door of the cell Hatché stayed in the yard. She was afraid to go into the cell and see her companion's condition. When the door was closed on her she prepared her bed and slipped in immediately, trembling fear, with without casting a glance at Iraz. For a time she lay curled up in her bed. Darkness fell, but she did not light the lamp as was her custom every night. She could not bear to see that face in its life-and-death struggle. Although she was afraid of the dark, it now seemed welcome to her, stretching like a curtain between them.

That night Hatché was unable to sleep. As the first light filtered in between the window-boards she rose from her bed. Iraz was still there like a vague shadow in her corner, motionless as ever. Only her white 'kerchief stood out like the brightness of a window against the dirty wall.

At midday Iraz was still in the same position. Evening came and she still had not moved. That second night Hatché spent fearfully, like the first, half awake, half asleep.

In the morning when the light appeared again, she opened her inflamed eyes and went over to Iraz. There was something compelling in her manner.

"Aunt!" she said. "I beseech you, don't stay like that!" She took the woman's hands in hers. "Don't, please!"

The woman turned her big, wide-open eyes on her, eyes that were black, lustreless. There was no white left in them; they were all black.

Hatché did not give up. "Tell me your troubles, Aunt," she said. "I beseech you. Does anyone without troubles ever come here? What business would a person without troubles have here? Isn't that true?"

"What's that, my girl?" moaned Iraz.

Hatché was so pleased to hear Iraz speak at last and say something that it was as if a big load had been lifted from her back.

"Why do you behave like this?" she asked. "You haven't opened your mouth since you came. You haven't even eaten anything!"

"My son was worth a whole country. My son was the pride of the village. Was it too high a price?" she said and fell silent.

"When I saw you I forgot my own troubles," said Hatché. "Tell me your troubles and unburden yourself."

"If I burn the house and break down the door of those who killed my son, is it too much? If I kill them one by one, is it too much?"

"Oh, my poor aunt! May they all be struck blind!"

"He was the pride of the village," moaned Iraz. "Is it too much if I kill them all?"

Hatché showed her sympathy.

"And now they've brought me here and locked me up, while my son's murderer struts around the village swinging his arms. If this doesn't kill me, nothing will!"

"My poor aunt!" said Hatché. "You're dying of hunger. You haven't eaten anything since you came here. I'll go and prepare you some soup."

To-day she decided to make the soup with plenty of butter. A month after her arrival she had begun to launder the clothes of some of the richer prisoners and had now saved a little money. A little girl used to bring food and other things for the prisoners from the market. Hatché called the girl and put fifty piastres into her hand. "Go and get me some butter," she said. She was filled with joy. The woman had spoken at last and someone who speaks does not die so easily of her grief. But it is a terrible end for anyone who does not speak and remains buried within themselves. That was why Hatché was pleased.

All the gay tunes she knew were now singing in her head. She filled the brazier with charcoal and began to fan it. Soon the coals glowed red as Hatché fanned them and puffed over them. She filled the little tinned copper pot with water and put it on the brazier. The soup was soon ready, so soon that even Hatché was surprised.

When Hatché had spoken of soup Iraz had felt a crushing pain.

Her bowels and stomach seemed to have frozen into a solid mass. She had not eaten a single mouthful since the day her son had been killed. From outside the smell of melted fat and fried onion now reached her nostrils. She heard the sizzling of the boiling fat as it poured into the soup...

Hatché brought in the pot of soup and placed it before Iraz. "Please, Aunt," she begged, placing a wooden spoon in her hand.

Iraz seemed to have forgotten how to use a spoon. It rested in her hand ready to fall to the ground.

Hatché was afraid she might not drink the soup. "Come on," she repeated. "Come on, please!"

Iraz slowly dipped the spoon into the soup.

When she had finished drinking it Hatché spoke again. "Aunt, there's water in the ewer. Wash your face. It'll make you feel better."

Iraz did as Hatché told her and went and washed her face.

"Thank you, my lovely girl. May God grant you all your wishes."

"If only He would," Hatché repeated several times. She sat down and told Iraz all her misfortunes. "Yes," she said, "this is how it happened, Aunt. I don't want anything in the world if only I can have news of my Memed. I've been here a full nine months, but no one has come to see me. Even my mother came only once. The first days I lay hungry in this hole. After that I began to do the prisoners' laundry. Oh, if only I could have some news! If I could only know if he is dead or alive. Let them hang me if they like. I don't care. If only I could have some news of my Memed."

As the days passed Iraz grew less weary and confused. She learned from the other prisoners that she should never have declared before the judge that she had broken the door with an axe with the intent of killing all those inside, or that she had set fire to the house to burn Ali's relatives. She might have killed ten people, they told her, but if there were no proof, if nobody had witnessed it or knew about it, the authorities could not have held her as a murderess. At first Iraz simply could not understand this injustice. Slowly she began to learn. In all the evidence that she gave later in court, she denied everything.

"Ah'" she would then say, "If I were free I would show the authorities who killed my Riza."

Hatché tried to console her. "God willing, you will soon be free, Aunt. You'll get out of here and hand over your son's murderer to the police. Think of me! At my age I shall be left to rot here. Everybody comes and bears witness against me!"

As the days passed Iraz and Hatché became like mother and daughter. They shared everything, including their troubles. Hatché knew Riza's height, his black eyes, his slim fingers, his dancing, his childhood, what he had done as a child, with what trouble Iraz had brought him up, the whole story of the field and the final tragedy, down to the last detail, as if she had lived through and seen it all herself. It was the same with Iraz. She, too, knew everything about Memed, from the day he and Hatché had first played as children together.

All day and all evening, until midnight, Iraz and Hatché knitted stockings till they were almost blind with weariness. The stockings they knitted became famous in the town. "The stockings of the girl who killed her fiancé and of the woman whose boy was killed." The saddest of designs went into the stockings. Hatché and Iraz did not copy any known designs, but created pattern after pattern of their own, in colours more bitter than poison. The town had never seen such striking and beautiful stockings.

Anyone going to prison for the first time is confused on entering so different a world. One feels lost in an endless forest, far away, as if all ties with the earth, with home and family, friends and loved ones, with everything, have been broken. It is also like sinking into a deep and desolate emptiness. Then there is another feeling experienced by a new prisoner: everything becomes like an enemy, the stones, the walls, the little bit of sky that can be seen, the windows with their iron bars. Above all, if a prisoner has no money he is lost.

So it was not for nothing that Hatché and Iraz blinded themselves day and night knitting stockings. They did not touch the money they earned and for many months their food consisted only of what the prison gave them. Sooner or later Memed would come, they thought. Maybe to-morrow, maybe in a month. Surely one day he would be caught and brought here too. Then he would need money. It was for this that they now toiled.

"My girl," Iraz would say, "Memed won't have as much trouble here as we. We are here to look after him."

"Yes, we are here, Auntie," Hatché would reply proudly.

"Our Memed has money here. We'll earn more before he comes and then we'll put all the money in his hands and he won't find himself destitute like the other prisoners. He won't have to turn to strangers for help."

At night they would retire to bed exhausted, with aching eyes, and still talk and share their troubles for hours on end, discussing everything that might possibly happen to Memed and all the most impossible things too. What did they not invent? Finally Hatché would become angry with her mother. "That mother of mine," she would begin. "What sort of a mother is she? I didn't ask much. Only for news of my Memed. She went off and never came back."

"Who knows," Iraz would reply, "what's happened to your poor mother?" Iraz would always defend Hatché's mother.

That night, as on every other night, they had gone to bed at midnight. Their bedding was wet from the damp air. The night insects were humming.

"Aunt Iraz," said Hatché.

"Yes?"

That's how they began every night.

"It's damp here."

"What can we do, my girl?" answered Iraz.

"That mother of mine. . . ."

"Who knows what troubles have come upon her?"

Without wasting further thought on her mother, Hatché skipped to another subject. "We'll have a tiny little house in the Chukurova on the soil of Yuregir," she said. "Memed will work for someone else to begin with, then we'll have a little field of our own. That's what Memed used to tell me."

"You're young. It'll all come to you," Iraz comforted her.

"He wanted to take me to the little restaurant in the town."

"He'll still take you there."

And so their conversation would continue, till at last Hatché would be lost in thought. She forgot that she was in prison and that Memed was an outlaw. Iraz forgot her troubles too.

"Yuregir earth," Hatché continued to muse, "Yuregir earth is warm. It's sunny there and the crops rise so thick that a tiger couldn't crash through them. Our field is thirty acres. . . ."

"Yes, my girl, thirty acres."

"We've sown half with wheat and half with barley."

"And half an acre of onions in the middle of the wheat," went on Iraz.

"I've plastered the inside of the house with green earth."

"Green earth and red earth too."

"We own a cow, a red cow with big eyes, and a suckling calf."

At this Iraz was quiet and uttered no reply. But Hatché continued: "Our house is yours. Memed is your son and I am your daughter."

"You're my daughter," repeated Iraz.

"In front of our house is a willow-tree with its branches reaching down to the ground."

"We'll put a fence all round our garden and we'll have lots of flowers."

Hatché came to herself, as if roused from a deep sleep. "When will they arrest Memed and bring him here, I wonder?" she asked Iraz. "What do you think, my aunt?"

"If not to-morrow, then in a month or so . . ."

"Well, we're ready, aren't we, my aunt?" insisted Hatché.

"Yes, we're ready," Iraz replied proudly. "We have enough money for him."

After that they would fall asleep.

Friday was market-day in the town. On Fridays Hatché would stare out of the window, watching the roads. If her mother were to come, it would be on a Friday. This particular Friday Hatché woke up very early, before sunrise. "If only she'd come to-day," she said; but she said this every Friday.

Towards midday a tall woman with a double saddle-bag over her shoulder came timidly towards the prison.

"Aunt Iraz," Hatché called in a shrill and excited voice.

"What is it, girl?" answered Iraz from inside, hurrying towards her.

"My mother!"

Iraz looked out along the road. They stood there side by side, staring at the tired, bare-footed woman who was limping towards them, the ends of her black scarf between her teeth as she hung her head and at last stopped at the gate of the prison. Small, thin and nervous, the guard called out: "What do you want, woman?"

"My daughter's inside. I've come to see her."

"Mother!" called Hatché.

The woman slowly raised her head and looked at the guard. "Brother Effendi, that's my daughter," she said.

"You may go and talk to her."

She put down her bag at the foot of the wall, then squatted there, with her back against the wall. "Oh, my bones are aching!" she moaned.

Hatché stood there quite still, staring at her mother. The woman's feet were covered with wounds that were caked with dust from the road. Her hair was white with dust and a muddy sweat ran down her neck. Her eyebrows and lashes were concealed by the dust. A torn and dirty skirt hung round her legs. Seeing her in such a state, Hatché's anger against her suddenly passed. She was filled with pity and there were tears in her eyes. She could feel a lump in her throat but simply could not come closer to her mother.

Hatché's mother saw her daughter standing there, staring at her with her eyes full of tears. She, too, could feel a lump in her throat. "Come, my ill-starred child," she suddenly burst out. "Come to your mother."

Unable to restrain herself she began to weep quietly. Hatché approached, kissed her hand and sat down beside her, followed by Iraz.

"Welcome, Sister," said Iraz.

Hatché introduced Iraz to her mother. "This is my Aunt Iraz," she said. "We sleep in the same cell."

"What are your troubles, Sister?" asked the mother in surprise.

"They killed her son Riza," said Hatché.

"Oh!" exclaimed the mother. "May they be struck blind, Sister!"

For a while the three women were silent. Then the mother raised her head and began to talk. "My daughter, my dark-eyed girl, forgive your mother. What hasn't that infidel Abdi done to me because I took that petition to the Government! Only I know what I have suffered at his hands. He's forbidden me to come to town again, my rose-girl. If not, would I have left my rose-girl

171

alone here in the town, locked up between four walls? I'd have
come straight away to my beautiful girl."

For some reason suddenly she stopped talking. For the first
time since she had come her face lit up. Drawing close to the other
two women, she began to speak in a low voice: "Wait a moment,
my beautiful girl, I was almost forgetting. I've news for you.
Memed has become a brigand, an outlaw!"

At the sound of Memed's name Hatché's face became pale.
Her heart began to beat as if it would burst.

"Memed went and joined Durdu's band after shooting Abdi
and Veli. And now these brigands have been up to all sorts of tricks.
They don't let anyone go on the roads and have stopped all traffic,
killing anyone who resists them. They strip men naked, even of
their drawers . . ."

"Memed wouldn't do things like that! Memed would never
kill a man," objected Hatché in anger.

"I don't know, my girl," answered her mother. "That's what
they all say. Memed's name comes right after Durdu's. His fame
has spread all over the country. What do I know, my girl? I only
tell you what I've heard. When that infidel Abdi heard about
Memed becoming a brigand, for a whole month he placed four or
five guards round his house every night, but was still afraid and
never slept a wink all night, wandering about the house till morning. Then Sergeant Asim came to his house and said he had been
after Memed. He declared he had never seen a brigand like
Memed in the mountains. If it hadn't been for him, he said, he
would have put Durdu's band to rout. At this Abdi Agha took to
his heels and left the village. Some say he is staying in the town,
others that he has gone to a village in the Chukurova. Some even
say that he's gone and taken refuge with the great Government in
Ankara. So, with Abdi Agha no longer in the village, I said to
myself, let me go and see my rose-girl, that's how it is."

While she was explaining all this her face was calm and smiling.
Suddenly it turned pale, as if she were choking.

Iraz and Hatché were pleased that Memed had become a
brigand. They exchanged eloquent glances, but, when they saw
Hatché's mother turn pale, they were frightened. "Mother,
Mother, what is it?" whispered Hatché.

"Don't ask, my girl, but I have bad news for you. Let's hope it's false. I heard it as I was coming. My tongue won't bring it out, my girl. I heard yesterday morning that Durdu and Memed had quarrelled because of a nomad Agha. Durdu had shot at Memed and his two companions. That's what I heard, my girl. Memed had protected the nomad Agha, so Durdu shot at him. A horseman passed through our village, a mounted nomad loaded with arms, on his way to help the nomad Agha, he said. His horse was covered with foam and he said that Memed had been wounded."

At first Hatché remained motionless. Then she threw herself into Iraz's arms. "Did this have to happen to me as well, Auntie?" she sobbed. Suddenly she was quiet.

"I'm going," said her mother. "God be with you, my girl. I'll let you know the truth as soon as I can. There's some butter in the bag I brought you, and eggs and bread. I'll come again next Friday if that infidel hasn't come back to the village. Don't lose the bag. Good health!" she called, as she set forth.

"I shouldn't have told her that. I shouldn't," she said to herself as she walked down the road.

Hatché had begun to sob again. "How could that infidel Durdu have killed my Memed? Does a man do that to his companion? How could he?"

Iraz tried to console her. "Every day they bring news of the death of a brigand, but don't believe it. You'll get used to it."

But Hatché was not listening. "I can't live," she sobbed. "I can't live without my Memed."

Iraz lost her temper. "How do you know the lad is dead, child? One doesn't mourn a man who is still alive. In my youth I heard of Big Ahmet's death at least twenty times. But Big Ahmet's still alive to-day."

"Aunt Iraz, this is different," said Hatché. "He's still such a young brigand! I can't live any more. I'll die."

"Don't you know, you stupid girl," continued Iraz, "that sometimes the brigands themselves spread false rumours about their own deaths? Listen! When that goat-beard heard that Memed had become a brigand, he fled from the village. Perhaps Memed's spread this news to fool him. When old goat-beard returns to the village, Memed will come and kill him. Perhaps it's all a trick."

"Memed doesn't do things like that, Aunt Iraz. I can't live after this; I'll die!"

She began to tremble, as if shaken with malaria. Iraz took her in her arms, carried her to the bed and laid her down.

"Wait a while, you stupid girl. How many things can happen before a day is done? Don't believe everything like that."

Two days later Hatché rose from her bed, pale as a corpse. She had bound a black 'kerchief round her head. Her face was waxen and still. Every day her condition deteriorated and she became increasingly pale and weak. Unable to sleep, she sat all night, resting her head on her knees and clasping her arms around her legs.

Nor could Iraz sleep. They no longer chattered at night. Only every once in a while would Iraz say: "You'll see, my crazy girl, you'll see. Good news of Memed will soon reach us."

But Hatché paid no attention to her.

XIV

"Let's sleep here for a couple of hours," suggested Ali.

"We haven't far to go, Ali," objected Hasan. "By noon we'll reach my village. You can then spend the night in our home and be on your way again to-morrow morning."

Ali was a tall man, with a long pock-marked face, so thin that he looked as if a puff of wind could blow him over.

"It's midnight," he said, "and there isn't a soul in sight. Come, let's sleep here till morning. It will be dawn in a couple of hours at most."

"I'm not stopping a minute," answered Hasan. "It's four years since I've seen my home."

"I haven't seen mine either, but . . ."

"Well?" asked Hasan.

"I'm tired."

"Listen, there's running water nearby. Go and wash your face. It'll make you feel better."

"Cold water's just what one needs when one is tired," agreed Ali.

"The water of our village," said Hasan. "Is there anything like it? It's like ice. It bubbles out from under the ground, white as milk. In the old days there used to be a great plane-tree right over the spring. I've seen it there myself. One day it rained, the sky was dark with rain. . . . Suddenly a ball of green light burst in the sky and struck the plane-tree. We went and looked. The tree had disappeared, burned to ashes. I swear, I saw it with my own eyes. Now you can't even see where the plane-tree stood."

"For three years, three long years, I've sweated and struggled in the Chukurova," said Ali. "But in the end I've earned a tidy sum, Brother."

Perhaps a hundred times, in the same phrases, the same words, Ali had explained all about the Chukurova, how he had earned the money at the cost of countless pains, and what he would now do with the money. On the road, whenever a lull occurred in their conversation, they would walk in silence for a while before beginning to explain again all that they had already explained. Again and again, Hasan had talked about his village, his boy, the plane-tree burned to ashes, the Chukurova and the man for whom he had worked in the Chukurova.

"First," continued Ali, "I'll give two hundred liras to the father so that I can bring the girl home. With the rest I'll buy a pair of oxen and order a quilted coat lined with cotton for my mother. She feels the cold, poor thing! Then I'll pull down the roof of the house and build a new one. You should see our house when the rains begin. It leaks like a sieve. . . ."

"Repair the roof, Brother. It's bad when a roof leaks. It's unbearable."

"It nearly killed me, that life in the Chukurova. It's so hot you get roasted in that land of infidels. Never again, I swear! The malaria's in my blood. This winter I'll get well again."

"I've got malaria too," said Hasan.

"I bore it all to bring a woman into the house and a pair of oxen and a warm coat for my mother. How else could one bear it?"

"It's unbearable," agreed Hasan, then interrupted Ali's train of thought: "Brother, if we walk like this by to-morrow noon we'll reach the pastures of my village."

"Over there . . ." continued Ali.

"Yes, yonder, in the middle of the plain . . ."

"I know, there's a big tree . . ."

"A tree with murmuring branches."

"Then you pass the tree . . ."

"To the left of the tree you come to a cemetery overgrown with grass."

"This time you didn't mention the tree in the cemetery," Ali reminded him.

"The day I left the village," Hasan corrected himself, "someone, I don't know who, had planted a tree as thick as your wrist, with drooping branches, in the middle of the cemetery."

"What a poor lonely tree," said Ali.

"That's how it was."

"If it hasn't withered away . . ."

"It'll be enormous by now," said the other. "But as we go past the cemetery someone will see us."

"Not just someone," Ali corrected him, "but Korje's son, Bekir."

"Bekir will see us," repeated Hasan, "because he always comes and sits on the stone rim of the fountain. He gazes at the shining water and ponders."

"It's his habit, isn't it?" asked Ali.

"Yes, that's his habit . . ."

"Bekir will then go and bring the news of your return to your home."

"Come, let's sit down here for a while," suggested Hasan.

Hasan was small, weak and withered. His huge teeth stuck out between his parted lips. His eyelashes were strangely white, as if covered with dust. He wore blue cotton *shalvar* trousers that were new, the cotton still smelling of the factory. His cap was also new, set at a tilt on his head. His red flowered waistcoat fitted him perfectly. He had bought a pair of town shoes too, but had not had the heart to wear them on the road and now wore his old rawhide sandals over the thick stockings he had originally brought from his village. They were still in good condition, embroidered woollen stockings.

"Am I tired!" he exclaimed, as they sat down.

"So am I."

"Get up!" said Hasan after a while. "That's enough rest for a traveller. What does the proverb say?"

"A traveller's place is on the road," said Ali.

"My boy's almost six now. When I left the village he was two."

"He'll come to meet you too, and he'll say 'Father.' And then we'll come to the house."

"All the village will gather at our house. 'Now then, Hasan Effendi,' they'll say, 'what did you earn in the Chukurova?' 'Nothing,' I'll say. 'What can a man earn in the Chukurova? I went and came back, that's all,' I'll say."

"Next day I'll get up early," said Ali. "I'll drink the soup your wife has cooked, full of milk-curds. Then I'll be off . . ."

"After you've gone I'll take the boy with me and go to the next village because I also want to buy a fine pair of oxen, with great curved horns. Then I'll go and pick all the stones, one by one, out of that stony field by the river . . ."

"And you'll plough the field two or three times, as they do in the Chukurova, so that the earth becomes as smooth as flour. After that you'll sow."

"Then there'll be such a crop!" Hasan went on. "Each ear loaded down to the ground, heavy as a tiger's paw."

"My mother's coat . . . I'll go to the tailor at Goksun and get him to make it."

Hasan leaned towards Ali. He could feel his breath on his own face. "How long is it since you left your village?"

"Three years."

"As soon as you get there you must go and fetch your bride home, that's the first thing to do."

"She's waited a long time for me, poor thing. It's six years now since we exchanged rings. As soon as I arrive I'll put the money in her father's hand and, the second day . . ."

"You'll do well, Brother," approved Hasan.

"In one day I'll forget all the hardships I suffered in the Chukurova!"

They stopped talking as they climbed a slope. When they came to the top of the hill a broad plain spread out beneath their eyes. Far off, in the middle of the plain, thick smoke was curling up.

Suddenly, hearing a sound by the side of the road, they halted. Then came the click of a trigger and a voice: "Don't move!"

"We're in for it," said Hasan. "Let's run. If they shoot, they shoot. It's better than being robbed. If we don't get hit we'll soon reach our village."

"Come on," said Ali.

They started to run. Shots were fired after them. Screaming, they threw themselves down on the ground.

The voice which had said "Don't move," now shouted: "Don't stir from where you are. We're coming."

Ali and Hasan were too scared to move.

Memed, Jabbar and Sergeant Rejep came running up to them and stood by their heads.

"Get up," ordered Memed.

They rose slowly, more dead than alive.

"Where are you coming from like this?" asked Memed.

"From the Chukurova, Brother," answered Hasan.

"In that case you've earned a lot of money," laughed Jabbar.

"If you hadn't come along we'd have died of hunger. Hand over your money."

"Kill me," said Hasan. "After these four terrible years . . ."

"Hand it over," repeated Jabbar.

"Kill me, Agha," insisted Hasan.

"My bride's been waiting six years for me. I'd rather you killed me."

"Yes, six whole years!" said Hasan.

Jabbar slipped his hand under Hasan's arm and produced from inside his clothing a purse full of money, all soaked in sweat. He opened it and found there a cloth, waterproofed with bees-wax, wrapped round the wad of notes.

"See how much there is!" shouted Jabbar. "How well it's hidden!"

"Put your gun into my mouth and shoot me," begged Hasan. "I can't go home to my family empty-handed."

"Six whole years!" repeated Ali. "I can't go back. Kill me!"

"Four whole years I've been drinking the poisonous waters of the Chukurova. The malaria's now in my blood," went on Hasan.

"I kiss your hands and your feet, but kill me," pleaded Ali.

"Kill me," said Hasan.

Memed's eyes filled with tears. "Jabbar, give him back his money," he said in a kind voice. "Here, take it!"

Hasan could no longer believe his eyes or his ears. Still afraid, he stretched out a trembling hand, not knowing what to say.

"God grant you a long life," he blurted out at last, then began to weep.

"A long life," Ali repeated.

"Now listen," said Memed. "Don't go across the Chanakli plain. Mad Durdu's band is in control there. He'll strip you even of your drawers. Good luck to you. God willing, you'll soon be with your bride, Brother." His voice was hoarse. He wanted to say more but could not bring the words out.

Hasan was sobbing like a child. "Thanks, Brother," he said, as he started to walk off. "May you be prosperous! May God save you from these mountains and bring you back to your loved ones."

Slowly they departed, turning back to offer thanks again, then starting again; as they went on their way, Hasan was still weeping.

"That's enough, man," said Ali. "What's all this weeping?"

"What good people there are in the world! Look at this brigand. If it hadn't been for him, that giant would have taken all our money."

"No," said Ali, "they wouldn't have taken it."

"If we don't cross the Chanakli plain," went on Hasan, "it'll take us at least two days to reach our village."

"What shall we do then?" asked Ali.

"If they were to give me the whole of the Chanakli plain and our journey were otherwise to last two months and not two days, I would still refuse to cross it."

"In that case, let's sit down and have a good rest. We won't go along the road but keep off it and only follow it from a distance."

They sat down.

Memed watched them for a while. "After we'd taken their money, they'd have been almost glad if we'd killed them," he said.

"How that tall fellow begged us to shoot him!" added Jabbar.

"Who knows with what hopes they toiled?"

"His bride has been waiting six years for him!"

"If they'd gone by Chanakli Durdu would certainly have stripped them."

"Durdu's very existence is a crime," exclaimed Jabbar.

The sergeant had kept out of all this. He couldn't hold his bandaged neck straight. Now he stretched and relaxed.

"I feel strange, boys," he said. "There's a coldness in my heart, a shivering. If I die . . ." he added, then regretted what he had said and was silent.

"No harm can come to a man from such a little wound," said Memed.

"Rest your head and sleep a little," advised Jabbar.

The sergeant closed his eyes to sleep.

After a while Memed leaned towards Jabbar as if to tell him a great secret. "From now on you and I are brothers, Jabbar," he declared. "Do you agree, Brother?"

Jabbar was pleased. "Of course, Brother," he replied.

"I'm torn with anxiety," said Memed. "My heart is burning."

"Tell me all about it and we'll try to find a remedy together."

"It's months now since I wounded Abdi Agha and I've heard he isn't dead. But what's happened to Hatché and my mother? I'm torn with anxiety. Following Durdu from one robbery to another, from one skirmish to another, I never found time to inquire after them . . ."

"We'll go to the village and find out, Brother," answered Jabbar. "There's nothing to worry about."

"That infidel hasn't died. I'm sure he's wrought his vengeance on Hatché. There's something inside me, I can't explain it, like a pain or a wound in my heart. It says, 'Go, Memed, don't wait.'"

"As soon as the sergeant's wound is better, we'll go to the village."

"My heart says, 'Don't wait,' Brother Jabbar," repeated Memed.

XV

For two days they had been hiding by day and travelling only by night. They had reached the tip of the pine-clad cliffs and were now resting, afraid lest Durdu be lying in ambush for them.

"He can't forgive us," said Jabbar. "He'll never sleep till he's done us some harm. I know what goes on in his heart. I've been with him four years. He would rather die than abandon our trail. If he can't wreak his vengeance on us, he'll die. I wish now we hadn't . . ."

"Are you frightened, Jabbar?" asked Memed.

"No, but . . ."

"But what?"

"I'm only saying that he'll never abandon our trail."

"Let him come! He'll see what's waiting for him."

"He's a wily one. He'll come when we least expect it; he'll set an ambush and we'll fall into it. If not, if he came upon us openly like a man, God would be either with us or with him."

Sergeant Rejep was staring dreamily at the dying day as the setting sun touched the top of a pine-tree with crimson. He lowered his head slowly. The rays of the setting sun lit up his face and the multi-coloured bandage on his wounded neck.

"If God were with us," he murmured, then was lost in contemplation of the pine-tree again.

"Are you angry with me, Brother Memed?" asked Jabbar.

"No, why should I be angry, Brother? Perhaps there's some truth in what you say. I'm sure he won't leave our trail."

"I only wanted to say that we must be watchful, just in case . . ."

"You're right," agreed Memed.

"Listen," said Sergeant Rejep suddenly, "do you know what I like about these mountains?"

"No," said Memed, smiling.

"The trees, when the sun is setting and the light falling along them. That's what I like!"

"I understand," answered Memed.

The sun set and it was night. In the sky there was only a half-moon which would soon set. The moonlight made the shadows of the trees stretch far along the ground, all intermingled, indistinguishable.

"Shall we go ahead?" asked Jabbar.

"Let's go," said Memed, rising to his feet.

"Stop, boys, wait for me," called Sergeant Rejep, as he went towards the foot of the rock. After a while he turned and came back. "As the darkness fell, I saw a strange greenness there at the foot of the rock, like a green spark . . . I went and looked, it was only moss. . . ."

Jabbar laughed.

"So, Sergeant Rejep," said Memed, smiling, "there in the darkness you saw the moss as a green spark."

Quite seriously Sergeant Rejep answered: "It surprised me. Look, there it is."

"Have you finished looking at your green flame?" asked Memed. "If so, let's be going."

"I would have liked to look at it a little longer, but we have a job to do."

"Yes, a job," agreed Memed.

They began to climb down from the cliffs. They had been travelling two whole days up there, not walking but literally crawling. Their last food had been eaten that morning and they were now hungry. There were no soles left to their shoes; the rocks, like emery-stone, had worn them away, leaving only the leather of the upper part intact. Their hands were wounded too, from clinging to rocks that cut into the flesh and made them bleed.

"We're at it again," said Sergeant Rejep. "We've begun crawling again. Why are you so afraid of that mad ruffian? Let's go down. Is it an ambush he's going to set for us? Let him try!"

"Don't be angry, Sergeant Rejep," said Memed. "We're going down."

"The pain in my hands is as bad as the one from the bullet

wound in my neck. How can I fire a rifle with these hands? And then you tell me not to be angry!"

"It'll pass, Sergeant. When we get to the village, I'll ask them to prepare some ointment for your hands."

"You've grown worse than an old woman," said Jabbar.

"If you only dare speak like that again, Jabbar," cried the sergeant angrily, "by God, I'll nail you to that tree. Do you understand?"

"Shut up, Jabbar," Memed warned him.

Jabbar roared with laughter. This infuriated Sergeant Rejep even more. "That fellow's not a man," the sergeant exclaimed. "He's the son of a bitch!"

"Soon we'll be coming down on the plain, Sergeant, my lion," said Memed, trying to calm him.

"Tell that son of a bitch to stop laughing or else, I swear, I'll nail him to a tree."

Jabbar came up to the sergeant, seized his hand and kissed it. "There, we've made it up. What more do you want?" he said, laughing.

Sergeant Rejep was reconciled. "I don't make peace with sons of bitches," he muttered nevertheless.

Memed tried to change the subject. "Sergeant, is your gun loaded?"

"Of course!" he replied sharply.

"Good."

"I'll empty it into the head of that infidel Abdi," the sergeant boasted. "I'll blow his head to smithereens! That oppressor of the poor!"

"We'll fire together," said Memed. "My heart will never find peace if I don't kill him with my own hands."

Overwhelmed by the hatred he felt, he thought of what it meant to kill a man, to finish him, destroy him utterly. He realised suddenly that this was wholly in his power. The scene of the shots fired in the forest rose again before his eyes. He saw Veli dying, kicking and struggling in the earth and mud. That was not killing a man; as he had fired he had not realised he was taking a man's life and this had made it all seem easy and possible. Now he was bent on killing a man in cold blood, on destroying something that felt love and anger and other emotions. Memed was suddenly obsessed with the idea that he had no right to do this. He had learned to think things out for himself in their full length and breadth and depth, perhaps under the influence of Sergeant Hasan in the town, perhaps because his own love had taught him to think. Who knows? Supposing he refrained from killing Abdi? This frightened him and he tried to drive the thought away, but it kept gnawing at him. "Let's get to the village," he said to himself, "and then . . ."

Memed's thoughts were interrupted by a cry from Sergeant Rejep: "Help! I'm falling!"

The sergeant had tried to reach with one leg across a ravine from the rock where he stood to another; unable to make it, he was now unable to draw back; he grasped the roots of a tree and just hung there. Jabbar and Memed came to his rescue.

"For God's sake, Memed, tell me how far we must still go to reach the plain," burst out Sergeant Rejep, disgruntled.

"We're almost there," answered Memed.

The moon was sinking behind the ridge opposite them when they came out on to the plain.

"Here we are!" exclaimed Sergeant Rejep. "We've managed to reach the plain without falling off a rock and breaking our necks. Now let that mad bastard set any ambush he likes! Let's rest here a while. The palms of my hands are so sore . . ."

The hands, knees and feet of the others were sore too, all cut by the sharp edges of the rocks over which they had been climbing and crawling for days.

Memed was lost in thought and his two companions were also silent. He was thinking: "Abdi has deserved his death." He remembered how Abdi had taken away their cow that winter when they had almost starved to death; he saw himself again ploughing Abdi's thistle fields in the knife-sharp frost, his own feet and legs torn by the thorns. In the cold the wounds inflicted by the thorns could burn as if he were being branded, eating into his very heart. Like a bitter poison his wretched childhood all came back to him. "Abdi has deserved his death," he concluded. "If only we can reach the village!"

Jabbar nudged him. "Dreaming again?"

"It's nothing," said Memed, ashamed.

"Let's be up and on our way. If we leave it till morning we'll never be able to do anything," said Jabbar.

Memed, My Hawk

"You're right," said Memed.

They set forth again and soon came to the thistle fields.

"Curse it!" cried Sergeant Rejep. "These thistles make you home-sick for the rocks. They nip at a man's legs like mad dogs!"

"This is the thistle field where I used to plough," said Memed, his voice breaking.

"Curse it!" repeated Sergeant Rejep endlessly.

"You can't plough through such thistles," said Jabbar. "It's not a thistle field, it's a forest."

Sergeant Rejep continued to curse. They rested a while, wiping away with their hands the blood that oozed from their legs. Memed now felt pleasure in repeating the curses he had uttered when he was still a boy. He had learned most of these curses from Dursun. Where would Dursun be now?

The thistles rustled as they trod them down. In the stillness of the night the sharp metallic sound of the crushed thistles could be heard from far off.

"If it were only the thistles," grumbled Jabbar. "But the stones in this ground are like another plague!"

"Now we've come to where I once ploughed. Just here."

Far off, to the south, a cock could be heard crowing for a long while without stopping. Then they reached a valley, the loose stones rolling from under their feet as they went downhill. The thistles here were even worse.

"We've now reached the village," said Memed. "Let's go down to the water and wash our hands and faces. To-morrow I'll make you each a pair of new sandals."

They followed Memed down to the stream, took off their shoes and bathed their feet. Sergeant Rejep was still cursing.

"Sergeant Rejep," said Jabbar, "that's enough, man! We're out of the thistle fields now."

"I've never come across such damned thistles!"

"This is our spring," said Memed. He remembered how, when he had run away to Süleyman's house, his mother had come here every day for weeks and stared into the spring, expecting to see his dead body rise from under the rocks. He wondered for the thousandth time what might have been his mother's fate. "Eh, Jabbar, what can they have done to my mother?"

"They can't do much to her."

186

Sergeant Rejep stopped cursing and listened. "I can hear something!"

"It's the noise of the spring. Down by the mill, Earless Ismail's mill."

"Before going into the village, let's go there and ask for news. It would be wiser. For the love of God, that's enough cursing, Sergeant," Jabbar protested as the sergeant continued to pour forth a torrent of invective.

"Perhaps it would be better if we went to the mill," agreed Memed.

"To my way of thinking, it's always better not to go swaggering into a village without first making some inquiries."

"That's right," exclaimed Sergeant Rejep. "This clown Jabbar has some sense after all. In brigandage you may well find an enemy in every mountain, every wolf, every ant. You must act as if you expect an ambush behind every rock. You're still green, my son Memed, but forethought can take the place of experience. Just think out every smallest detail beforehand."

They rose to their feet. They could see a light, twinkling like a spark, not so very far from them.

"That light is Earless Ismail's mill," said Memed.

As they approached the mill they heard the howling of dogs beyond.

"The village must be where those dogs are barking," said Jabbar.

"Yes," answered Memed as they reached the door of the mill and halted.

"Who's there?" called Earless Ismail from within.

"Slim Memed, Ibrahim's son," answered Memed.

At first no sound came from within. "What would Memed want here?" Ismail then called. "It's a lie. We've heard that Durdu killed him."

The smell of flour spread through the night.

"I'm not dead, Uncle Ismail," shouted Memed. "Don't you recognise my voice?"

"I do. I'm coming. I'll open the door in a moment."

The door opened with a great noise and a shaky beam of orange light fell on their faces. Ismail stared at Memed. "So, Slim Memed, you couldn't kill that infidel and save the village from his clutches."

Memed smiled.

They went inside. The smell of flour was even stronger.

Ismail's long wrinkled neck, his thin pointed face, his beard and his old greasy cap were all white with flour.

He saw their bleeding hands and feet, and asked anxiously: "How did you get into such a mess?"

"We had a fight with Durdu and for two days we've now been out on the rocks," answered Memed, smiling.

"Yesterday a nomad rider passed through the village on his way to fight Durdu and told us that Durdu had killed you. All the village grieved. The villagers are very fond of you, you know, Memed." He patted Memed's back, then gently stroked his face. "Eh, Memed, I really can't believe my own eyes. What are all these weapons you're carrying? How can you carry so many cartridges? It's strange to see you with all those cartridge-belts. I can still remember you ploughing the Sarija plain. When I then see you as you are now, I can't believe my own eyes."

"Well, that's how it is . . ."

"You're hungry. Let me go and prepare some food for you. The fire's burning . . ."

Memed was surprised to see how Ismail's back was now bent. He had known him still young and remembered him as he had seen him in his own childhood. Anxiously Memed asked: "What news of my mother and Hatché? Is Abdi in his house?"

Ismail stopped short, neither moving nor answering. He had been expecting this question and dreaded having to answer it. He looked about him in distress and heard Memed repeat his query: "My mother . . . ?"

"They're all right," he stammered. "Wait, I'll tell you all about that infidel. Oh, but I was forgetting! Let me bathe your hands and feet in salt water . . ." He hurried out of the room.

Memed had long been uneasy about the fate of his mother and Hatché. His misgivings now increased.

Ismail returned with a basin of water. "Bathe your hands and feet in this. Salt water will be good for your wounds."

"Have you seen my mother lately?" Memed asked again.

"They're all right, I've told you . . . Let me tell you about that infidel. When he heard you'd joined the brigands, he just locked himself up. Every night he put five, six, ten men on watch. Then he disappeared. You should have seen how he had changed! That's what fear does to a man. Now that he's heard you're dead, he may be back in the village."

Memed was very tense, anxious to get to the village. "Come," he said, " we must be in the village before morning."

Jabbar and Sergeant Rejep rose to their feet without a word.

"Your food will soon be hot," said Ismail, downcast. "Can't you wait a while? That salt water is good for you. You can bathe your hands and feet again later."

But Memed left the mill, followed by his two companions. After going only a few yards they were again among the thistles and Sergeant Rejep began cursing anew. In the sky the last stars were glistening like drops of water.

Sergeant Rejep stopped to relieve himself and then turned to the east. "The morning star hasn't risen yet. It's my star. There's plenty of time till daybreak."

The others walked in silence. Their hands and feet ached less. A fox crossed their path and vanished ahead of them. If they had not been so close to the village Sergeant Rejep would have shot it there and then. The fox ran with its bushy tail sweeping over the thistles, its fur like frosted glass in the starlight.

As they approached the first houses a few big dogs rushed at them. Memed stopped and called "Kuchu! Kuchu!" The dogs recognised his voice and lay fawning at his feet.

The village was deserted. This seemed odd to Memed, who had never seen it at this hour. They walked straight to Memed's house and knocked softly on the door. There was no sound. They knocked again and waited. Memed could bear it no longer. He went to the little window and called gently: "Mother! Mother!" No sound of life came from within. He pressed his ear against the wooden window-frame, straining to listen, but heard only the rustle of insects eating at the wood. His anxiety grew, but the last glimmer of hope had not died in his heart. He turned to his companions and whispered: "She's not at home."

He pondered. Who was his mother's closest friend in the village? She liked Durmush Ali's family most.

By now Durmush Ali was seventy-five years old. Recently his back had begun to bend, though he was still as strong in other respects as a man of fifty.

In the shadows in front of Durmush Ali's house Memed could distinguish a black form, a huge dog. When it heard their footsteps the dog raised its head, then slowly laid it down again on its paws.

Memed leaned wearily against the door. "Uncle Durmush Ali! Hey, Uncle!" he called.

Excited voices began to be heard within. Memed could distinguish Durmush Ali's deep voice repeating: "My God, that's our Memed. It's his voice. It must be Memed!"

The door opened and Durmush Ali appeared in the doorway, in his shirt and drawers, holding a lighted torch of resin-wood. His milk-white beard flowed down to his waist. He was so huge that it seemed as if the house could not hold him and he was overflowing outside.

"Why, Memed," he said, smiling, "only the other day we heard bad news of you from one of the nomads. I'm pleased to see that you're alive. Girls!" he called inside, "it's Memed! Light the fire and spread the mattresses." He stepped back from the door. "Come in, boys," he said. They all entered the house.

Durmush Ali placed his burning torch in the hollow of the chimney above the fire and sat down. "Well, Memed, tell us how you are. All the village was mourning for you when they heard you'd been shot. If Hatché hears it she'll die of grief. Do you get any news from her? And your poor mother! I buried her as if you were here. I placed her in her grave with my own hands."

Memed's face was dark with emotion.

"Memed, what's the matter with you? Don't tell me you didn't know," cried Durmush Ali anxiously.

Jabbar's eyes were brimful of tears. Even Sergeant Rejep moved away, took the ammunition out of his gun and began to reload it nervously.

"What's happened to Hatché?" asked Memed, barely able to control himself.

"Oh, my poor stupid head!" cried Durmush Ali, beating his hands against his temples. "How could I talk to you like that? How was I to know you hadn't heard all this months ago?"

Durmush Ali's wife had been crouching down beside the hearth, staring into the fire without moving, not even opening her mouth to bid welcome to Memed. Now she burst out in anger: "You always do things like that! If you had only let the boy eat first and waited to break the news to him later! Why do you have to make such a mess of things?"

"How was I to know?" cried Durmush Ali. "It happened months ago. How was I to know he hadn't heard?" He seemed to be almost ready to weep. "Forgive me, boy, it's old age. . ."

Durmush Ali's sons, grandchildren, daughters-in-law, all his household formed a circle round them as they sat together by the fire. They all stared at the purple fez on Memed's head, the cartridge-belts on his chest, the dagger, pistol and hand-grenades on his hip, the field-glasses round his neck. They seemed surprised and incredulous, perhaps somewhat amused, as if Memed were only playing at being a brigand with the two other huge outlaws.

"What's happened to Hatché?" Memed asked again.

Instead of answering, Durmush Ali hung his head and gazed at the flames in the fireplace.

"Aunt Hürü!" said Memed, turning to Durmush Ali's wife, whose cheeks were sunken, framed in the hennaed white hair that escaped from beneath her 'kerchief. "Tell me, what's happened to Hatché?"

"What shall I say to you, Memed, about Hatché?" Hürü's face flushed and paled in turn.

"Someone will tell him sooner or later," put in Sergeant Rejep. "What's happened to her?"

The old woman turned her head and looked at Durmush Ali as if she would kill him. "What shall I say? Who knows how long the poor boy has been on the road? If only he'd eaten before you broke the news to him like that!" She rose, came towards Memed and sat down heavily beside him. "Listen, my child, I'll tell you how it all happened. Abdi was wounded. If only that bullet had gone right into his heart and not come out! When he recovered he collected all the false evidence he could. Lame Ali, the ill-omened infidel who had tracked you down, refused to bear false witness. Old Goatbeard then drove Lame Ali out of his village. Lame Ali loaded up all his possessions and went off somewhere else with all his family."

Then she told Memed who the false witnesses had been, how Hatché had remained for a long time all alone in a cell in the prison in town, and how it was now rumoured that they would soon hang her.

A needlepoint of light had settled in Memed's eyes. Jabbar noticed it. Whenever this light came into Memed's eyes his whole face changed and he looked, with his tense face, like a tiger all ready to pounce on its prey.

Memed rose slowly to his feet. "Come, Brothers," he said. "Let's go and settle our accounts with Abdi Agha." He turned to Durmush Ali's wife and clasped her hands. "Tell me, they killed my mother, didn't they?"

Hürü's eyes were full of tears. She couldn't speak.

"Is that what happened?" Memed insisted.

She remained silent until Memed released her hand. "Let's be going, friends," he said.

They went out into the darkness. Memed checked his gun and loaded it to the full.

"Check your rifles. If they're not fully loaded, load them now and have your grenades ready too."

Sergeant Rejep had been deeply disturbed by what old Hürü had said. While she was speaking he had kept looking at Memed, turning his head this way and that without uttering a word. Now he grasped Memed's arm as he was hastening away and stopped him. "Listen, we'll kill the whole family; we won't leave a single one alive."

"You know this kind of business better than I do, Sergeant." Memed pulled his arm free and walked ahead.

None of them really knew how and when they reached Abdi Agha's door.

"You can call," Memed said to the sergeant. "Say that we've brought a very important message."

The sergeant knocked on the door three times.

"Who's there?" called a woman's voice from inside.

"Open the door, sister!" answered the sergeant. "I've brought a message. I must go back straight away."

Muttering, the woman came and opened the door. "Wait a moment. Let me light a torch."

Leaving Sergeant Rejep in the doorway, she went inside and struck a match. When the light was on the three of them walked straight in. The woman was speechless. Her bewildered eyes dwelt on Memed briefly before she uttered a scream. Immediately Sergeant Rejep seized her and placed his hand on her mouth till she stopped trying to scream.

"Is Abdi Agha here?" Memed asked her gruffly.

"No," she answered. "He doesn't come here any more, may he be struck dead!"

By that time the whole household was awake. They all stood staring in terror at the brigands, Abdi Agha's two wives, his two sons and some women guests from another village.

"Let them go ahead of you while you search the house," Memed ordered the sergeant. "The minute you see Abdi, shoot him!"

"I'll fire all five of my bullets into his head!" He prodded Abdi's wife with the butt of his gun. "Get a light and go ahead of me."

Without a sound she lit another torch and went ahead of the sergeant into the other rooms.

Memed stood in the middle of the room, overcome by his anger. His slim body seemed to have acquired gigantic proportions. His expression was terrifying and all the women of the house were weeping while the two boys trembled like leaves in the wind.

The sergeant soon returned and reported gloomily: "I've searched every nook and cranny. He isn't here."

"He went off to the Chukurova a month ago," said the woman. "He knew you would come and could no longer sleep, so he went off without saying where."

"Sergeant," said Memed as he pointed at the children, "take these two boys outside and do your job."

The two women threw themselves at Memed's feet. "Don't, Memed, I beseech you, what have these little ones done? Find that infidel and kill him, but what wrong have our poor innocents done?"

The sergeant had seized the boys and was already dragging them outside as they struggled and fought. Jabbar caught hold of one of them by the wrist and flung him to the ground. The boy screamed with all his might.

One of the women remained silent. She just lay at Memed's feet, pale as a sheet, while the other begged endlessly: "Memed,

Memed, what have my children done to you? What wrong have they done?"

With all his strength the sergeant flung the other boy to the ground and placed his foot to hold him there. He pointed his gun at the boy's head and turned to Memed. "Is it necessary to take them outside? What are you waiting for? Shall I finish the job?"

The woman who had been lying at Memed's feet jumped up with the speed of a hawk and threw herself at Jabbar, who was dragging one of the boys to the door. With one hand Jabbar pulled the dagger that hung at his waist and plunged it into the woman, who fell to the floor with a cry.

Seeing the sergeant's gun pointed at the boy the other woman begged: "Memed, Memed, don't kill my child. You're right, Memed, but what has my poor innocent done to you?"

Memed's expression changed rapidly as the needlepoint of light died in his eyes. He saw that the sergeant was about to press the trigger. There was no time to say anything. With his foot he kicked the barrel of the rifle pointed at the child's head. The bullet buried itself in the wall.

"Leave the child," he ordered Jabbar.

The woman started kissing both Memed's hands. "Go, my Memed, go and find that infidel and kill him. You have good reasons to do so, my son. If I waste a single tear on him, let my name no longer be Zeynep. Find him and kill him. You're in the right, my child."

Memed did not utter a word. Slowly, as if every bone in his body were hurting, he went outside.

Sergeant Rejep was cursing violently. He seized Memed's arm and squeezed it as if he were going to break it. "What kind of brigand do you think you'll make, with your soft heart? You can't even take your revenge. Abdi and his men will soon be setting an ambush for you in some valley to kill you. Isn't one enemy as deadly as Durdu enough for you?"

"Listen, Sergeant," interrupted Jabbar, "don't talk nonsense. We may have an enemy in Durdu, but we also have a whole tribe of friends, the Black-haired tribe. Should we kill these poor brats instead of Abdi?"

Sergeant Rejep was silent.

The sound of all this shouting and weeping had attracted all the neighbours round Abdi Agha's house in their shirts and under-clothes. The word passed from ear to ear that Memed was still alive.

"Memed would never die before killing that infidel, Abdi."

"But he didn't kill the children."

"Memed's heart is as vast as the ocean."

Memed and his two companions broke through the crowd, out of the courtyard and into the night. The crowd watched them go, so still that its breathing could be heard.

Memed then spoke for the first time. His voice was sad. "The villagers have now heard the news and won't leave us in peace. Let's go!"

"My wound is inflamed," objected Sergeant Rejep. "It's very painful. If we leave the village, where can we go? In any case, we're dying of hunger."

"We'll come back later," answered Memed.

They walked towards the fields. A great hubbub rose behind them, accompanied by the loud barking of dogs.

Taking a deep breath, the sergeant said: "Let's sit down. I'm dead tired. My wound gives me no peace."

"When you get wounded," taunted Jabbar, "you're worse than an old woman."

The sergeant leapt to his feet in anger. "You puppy," he snarled, "if you open your mouth once more, I'll finish you off here and now."

Jabbar laughed.

"Don't, Jabbar," said Memed. "You'll only stir up trouble for us."

"That son of a bitch will be the cause of some accident. I swear he will," growled the sergeant.

"Don't mind him, Sergeant Rejep. It's his way of joking."

"Well, I don't like it. I have enough troubles without his jokes."

"Jabbar, no more joking," said Memed.

Jabbar came up, put his arms round the sergeant and kissed him. "Forgive me. There'll be no more jokes."

"That bastard must surely have a hair of the devil on him as a talisman," said Sergeant Rejep, relenting.

"Never again, no more jokes!"

They sat down and waited for the turmoil in the village to

cease and for all the villagers to go back to their homes. Each of them pursued his own thoughts in silence. Slowly the noise died down and the dogs stopped barking. But the silence was too much for Jabbar, who couldn't contain himself: "Sergeant Rejep . . ." he began.

"What do you want?"

"If Memed hadn't interfered, would you have killed that child?"

"I would not only have killed him, I'd have taken his very soul. What of it?"

"Nothing. I just asked."

Sergeant Rejep ground his teeth. "Jabbar, the whore of your village was surely your mother. And your father must have been a pimp."

"Enough, Jabbar, shut up," Memed interposed.

"There, I've shut up."

The uproar had now died down in the village, which was again buried in silence and darkness.

"Let's go," said Memed. "We must reach Uncle Durmush Ali's house before daybreak."

"For the love of God, Memed," said Sergeant Rejep, "let's get there quickly."

The village was now as silent and deserted as when they had first entered it. Only Durmush Ali stood waiting for them in his doorway.

"I haven't slept," he said. "I've been waiting for you for some time."

"Well, here we are, Brother," said Sergeant Rejep.

"I've a hen cooked for you. You must be hungry."

"That was a good guess, Brother!" replied Sergeant Rejep.

Durmush Ali noticed now that all Sergeant Rejep's cartridge-belts and the strap of his gun were decorated with silver, worked by a master-jeweller, and that his long hanging moustaches were carefully dyed with henna.

As soon as they were seated a shy young girl served the food, smiling secretly at Memed. The rice was piping hot and the roasted hen was served separately.

"This rice-pilaff is just what my wound needs, a steaming pilaff that smells of fresh butter."

"Yes, Sergeant," said Jabbar, "you're no real brigand, you should have been a civil servant."

"Shut up!" the sergeant exclaimed angrily.

"Leave him alone," Memed said to Jabbar.

"But I didn't say anything," cried Jabbar.

Durmush Ali had been trying to bring himself to say something to Memed but was still unable to express himself. Either some other conversation began, or he himself changed his mind. "Uncle Durmush Ali, what is it you want to say? All morning you've been holding something back."

"It was clear from childhood that you would grow up to be a good man, Memed. You did well not to kill those poor children."

Durmush Ali's words infuriated Sergeant Rejep. "Man, you can't understand such things. Do you know what revenge means? Have you ever felt the need for it?"

Durmush Ali bent his head. "No," he replied.

"If I had been Memed, I wouldn't have left a creature alive in that house. I'd have killed the lot and razed the house to the ground. Do you understand, man?"

"I understand," said Durmush Ali, looking at Memed.

Throughout the meal Memed sat with his head bent over his food, thoughtful and silent.

"Uncle Durmush Ali," he said when he had finished, "many thanks for your hospitality."

The sergeant and Jabbar echoed Memed's thanks.

"Uncle Durmush Ali," continued Memed, "there's something I want to ask you."

"Ask, my boy."

"Where did Lame Ali go? To which village, do you know?"

"They say he went to Chahsak village, two days' journey from here."

"How can we find out if he's there or not?"

"Lame Ali's sister is married there, but she came to Deyirmenoluk two days ago. I'll ask her."

Memed turned to Jabbar and Sergeant Rejep. "We must find Lame Ali. If he's at Chahsak village we'll go there."

"All right," said Jabbar.

The sergeant objected. "My wound is bothering me again . . ."

"You can wait for us here, Sergeant," said Memed. "Uncle Durmush Ali will look after you."

"I'll look after you, Brother, and hide you too."

"Me? I'm not leaving you. Do you understand. Even if I die, I'm still not leaving you. But I've a suggestion to make. Let's send a man to bring Lame Ali here."

Durmush Ali's old wife had been sitting silent in a corner. Now she cut in: "That heathen who tracked down Memed? He'll never come. He'll go and hide himself in the mountains. Do you think that infidel would ever dare come here?"

"Do you really want to see Lame Ali, my boy?" asked Durmush Ali, looking into Memed's eyes.

"Yes," said Memed.

"Would you trust me enough to stay two days in our barn?"

"Two weeks," answered Memed without hesitation.

"Then I'll send a messenger on horseback to tell Lame Ali that I want to see him. He'll be told there's a job for him. They say Lame Ali has given up that kind of work and has sworn, after that business with you, never to follow a trail again. But Lame Ali will come for me, trail or no trail. You won't do any harm to him, will you, Memed?"

Durmush Ali's wife interrupted them. "Get him under your dagger, Memed, and kill him! Haven't all these troubles come upon my Memed only because of that infidel? Who else but Lame Ali could have found my Memed in that forest? Let Durmush Ali send someone to bring him here and you can then hack him to pieces right in front of my door. I'll call all the villagers here to watch you do the job."

"Stop talking nonsense, woman," said Durmush Ali. "Lame Ali didn't intend doing any harm to Memed. When he's following a trail he forgets everything else. His eyes no longer see the world nor can he know good from evil. Didn't you see his face when he came from the forest? It was all pale and bloodless, like that of a corpse. When everyone else testified, he refused to bear witness against Hatché, even though Abdi Agha drove him out of the village and made him homeless. He had to go off and leave his home and his land. Don't do him any harm, Memed! He's not a bad man."

"Maybe he's a good man, maybe he's a bad man," said the old

woman. "But he's the one who brought all these troubles on your head and you should kill him, Memed. If the messenger Durmush Ali sends doesn't bring him, go and find him yourself in his serpent's nest. What's the use of that great knife that you carry in your belt? Stick it into his belly!"

Durmush Ali was quite angry by now. "Listen, woman, if you love God's religion, keep your nose out of this whole business."

"Don't try to talk the boy into anything! Let him do as he wishes." she replied.

"Yes," said Durmush Ali. "Let him do as he wishes and kill the poor fellow! Everyone knows that Lame Ali is mad when it comes to following a trail. But he never thought he'd bring all this on Memed's head and, even if he had thought it over, he would still have followed the trail. It's his kind of madness."

"I only want one thing," she answered, "to see his bloody corpse!"

"You won't do anything to the poor fellow, Memed, will you?" Durmush Ali begged.

"I'll ask him to follow a trail," answered Memed slowly.

"Make him do anything you want," said the woman, "but kill him afterwards. It's that infidel who got you into all this trouble, with poor Hatché rotting now in prison because of him."

Durmush Ali whispered into Memed's ear: "Is it *his* trail?"

Memed's eyes gave an affirmative answer.

"I like to hear that, Memed. I'll go and get a messenger out of bed and send him off at once. Lame Ali will come right away. Now they can make your beds in the stable and you can rest here a couple of days." He called to his wife: "Woman! Instead of standing there gabbling, go and make the beds in the stable for our guests. I'm going to find a messenger!"

"Go," she replied. "You can go all the way to hell!"

She was a little wisp of a woman, with white hair and grey eyes. All her teeth had fallen out so that her mouth was like the wrinkled opening of a purse. She came up to Memed, making all sorts of signs, giving the impression that she had some great secret to tell him. "Come close, come close!" So Memed leaned towards her.

"Don't believe these worthless people, don't trust them. Don't trust your Uncle Durmush Ali. They're all in league with that in-

fidel Abdi Agha. Perhaps they'll put you in the stable now and then
go off and warn the police behind your back. Don't trust them.
That's why I'll go and wait by the mill for a couple of days. If the
police come I'll let you know and you'll be able to slip out and
escape. Yes, my Memed, if there's one soul in this village who
doesn't wish you any harm, I'm the one. You're all that's left of my
Deuneh. And your father, what a good man he was! Now I'll make
your bed in the stable. Will you go to sleep at once?"

"I'm dead tired, Mother Hürü," he answered. "For three days
we haven't slept!"

"May my eyes drop out!" exclaimed Hürü as she called to the
women: "Daughters of an infidel! The boys are dying for lack of
sleep and we didn't know it! Take the beds to the old cowshed.
Spread them on the straw."

The sergeant was again moaning.

"What's the matter?" asked Memed.

"Look at my neck. See how it's swollen!"

"We'll prepare some medicine for it," answered Memed.

"Mother Hürü will make you a poultice for it that will cure it in
no time," added the old woman.

The bedding was hurriedly carried to the shed and the guests
followed. A small torch had been fixed on to the centre post of the
shed, glowing feebly. The shed was half full of straw and its dust
at first made them sneeze. On one side bitter-smelling dried dung
was stacked for fuel. The ceiling was full of cobwebs in which bits
of straw were dangling, thousands of bits of straw. The women
went out and shut the door. The first pink rays of light crept in
through the tiny window. It was almost dawn.

Jabbar stood by his bed, yawning his head off, his eyes shut.
Sergeant Rejep came and threw himself on the bed. "I'm burning,
lads. But we shouldn't all sleep. One of us should keep watch."

"You can sleep," said Memed. "I'll keep watch."

Memed was grieving. Jabbar lay down and fell asleep at once,
while Sergeant Rejep lay moaning. Memed took his gun and went
and sat on top of the stacked straw, his head on his knees.

Towards midday Hürü brought them some food. The sergeant
was still groaning. When Hürü saw this she exclaimed: "Tcha! I'd
forgotten."

"What have you forgotten, Mother Hürü?" asked Memed.

"That poultice for your friend's wound," she replied as she went off to prepare it.

They had finished their meal when Hürü returned carrying a steaming bowl.

"My father used to make this poultice. If anyone was hurt it would heal the wound immediately." She began to untie Sergeant Rejep's bandages quickly, with deft hands. The bandages adhered to the wound and were not easy to unwind. "My poor man," she cried, "your wound has begun to fester!"

Sergeant Rejep clenched his teeth and groaned as Hürü covered the wound with the poultice and bound it up with clean rags.

"Health to your hands, Sister," sighed Sergeant Rejep. "Health to your beautiful hands. I feel easier now." After that he lay down again to rest.

"Now you lie down, Brother," Jabbar said to Memed. "I'll keep watch."

"And I'll go off to the mill," said Hürü, "I'll see to it that they don't play any infidel tricks on you. If I see any policemen from there, I'll send you word. No one shall do any harm to my Memed in this house, to the son of my dear Deuneh."

Memed lay down but still could not sleep, though he had not slept for days. The shock of his mother's death and of Hatché's imprisonment had been too much for him. He felt oppressed by all these sorrows, suffocating and burning all over, unable to escape from his dark thoughts and suddenly frightened of himself, of people, of his friends, of everything.

It was midnight when Jabbar roused him from his thoughts. "I feel sleepy. You can take over now."

Memed took his gun and went and sat again on top of the heap of straw. Drawing his knees up to his chest, he rested his head on them and was soon lost in his thoughts.

Towards morning he had dozed off. But when the door of the shed opened he pointed his rifle immediately.

"What's that, Memed? Would you shoot me?" asked Durmush Ali, smiling. "The messenger has brought Lame Ali. They're in the house. Wake your friends and come over. I've explained the business to Lame Ali. He's very much afraid, almost dead of fear. And what hasn't our mad woman done to him? She leapt at him and spat in his face. 'If Memed doesn't kill you, I'll do it,' she said.

At that all his courage left him. 'Did you bring me here to kill me?' he asked, trembling all over. He'll die of fear."

When he heard that Lame Ali had come, Memed seemed pleased. Jabbar was also awake and they decided not to wake the sergeant: then they thought he might be offended and woke him too.

"Get up," said Jabbar. "The famous Lame Ali has come."

Sergeant Rejep was unable to raise his head. "Lame Ali?" he asked in bewilderment.

"Lame Ali, who follows trails . . ." Jabbar repeated.

Sergeant Rejep began cursing again. "So he's come, has he?" he groaned. "Oh, my poor neck!"

"What's the matter, Sergeant Rejep? Don't groan like that, man!"

"Get up," said Memed. "We'll go and see him."

"Wait," said the sergeant. He brushed the chaff off his clothes, put all his silver ornaments in place, twirled his moustaches, pulled out a silver comb and straightened his hair carefully. But he could not bring himself to look at his feet. The soles of his shoes were completely gone. He brushed the dust off his fez with his sleeve.

"Come on, Sergeant," said Jabbar impatiently. "Our shoes are a bit poor, but what can we do?"

"Yes, what can we do?" agreed the sergeant.

As they entered the house Lame Ali, who was seated by the fire, tried to rise to his feet then sat down again, his face ashen.

"I've sent for Brother Ali," said Durmush Ali.

"Good!" answered Memed.

Grinding his teeth, Sergeant Rejep stared into Lame Ali's eyes. "Are you the dog who tracked our Memed down? Have you no fear of God, man? Have you no shame?"

Lame Ali stared into the embers of the hearth without moving.

"Be quiet, Sergeant," said Memed. "I'll talk with Ali Agha."

"Let's see you talk, then!" replied the sergeant angrily. "Go ahead and talk with this worthless dog!"

Memed went over to Lame Ali and sat down beside him. "Ali Agha, I have a job for you. Will you come outside with me a moment?"

Lame Ali remained frozen to his seat. "Memed, I never

thought it would turn out that way. Don't kill me. I have a wife and family. Don't!"

"Don't be afraid. I have something secret to discuss with you outside!"

"Don't kill me!" Lame Ali moaned. "Please don't kill me. I did it, I admit, but don't kill me!"

"Get to your feet and I'll say something to you in this corner."

Lame Ali's face was bloodless. He was trembling. "Please don't kill me! Don't make my children orphans. Let me kiss the soles of your feet, brother Memed. I did it, but don't kill me!"

"That's enough, you lame dog," cut in the sergeant angrily. "Get up!" He drew the dagger hanging from his belt.

"Sergeant, don't do him any harm," said Memed.

"We'll do him no harm," said the sergeant, shaking his head in disgust. "What's it to us? Take your stinking Lame Ali, stick him in your button-hole and wear him as a flower." Reluctantly he put the knife back in its scabbard.

"Don't be afraid, Ali Agha," said Memed. "I've no intention of harming you. If I were going to shoot you, I'd have shot you where you were sitting. I want to discuss something with you."

"Don't bring trouble on my wife and family," moaned Lame Ali, as he rose to his feet. Dragging his lame foot, he went and stood in the darkest corner of the room.

Memed followed him. "Listen, Lame Ali," he said. "You brought all these troubles on me, but you also showed courage when you tried to make up for it. All that business is now dead and buried, but we have other worries. You're going to follow a trail for me!"

"By God," cried Lame Ali, "after all the trouble I had with you I swore never to follow another trail. Kill me! I can't do it. I'm not going to have blood on my hands again."

"If you don't follow it, then I'll kill you."

Lame Ali was cowed. "Don't do this to me! For God's sake, don't!"

"You'll follow it, so don't waste time pleading!"

"Whose trail is it?" asked Lame Ali naïvely.

"Abdi Agha's trail. You'll find him. Whether he's hiding in a serpent's hole or under the wings of a bird, you'll find him. If you don't find him, we'll . . ."

"Brother, is that what you wanted me to do? So it's Abdi you want? I'll find him for you even if he's in hell. He must be in town or in the village of Avshar or perhaps at Saribahche. In any case he's in one of these three places. Come with me to the Chukurova and I'll lead you where he's hiding as sure as if I'd put him there myself, the infidel. He wrecked my home because I wouldn't bear false witness. He has left all my family starving in Chahsak village among strangers. Tear that infidel to pieces! I'll do everything in my power to find him. I'll even become a brigand and take to the mountains with you if necessary."

"It will be enough to find him. Now let's go and sit by the fire. We'll talk over the details later. Don't talk to anyone about what we've said. Durmush Ali is the only one who knows and he won't tell anyone either."

"I don't care if the whole world hears. What that infidel has done to the villagers, to you, to Hatché and then to me, it all weighs on my heart like a mountain. Let the world hear! I might even take a gun and join you. Why should I worry now?"

Memed went and sat down by the fire. Lame Ali was smiling.

"You look happy, Lame Ali," Durmush Ali teased him. "Are you on a new trail?"

"No, Memed has forgiven me and that's why I am happy."

Sergeant Rejep, Jabbar and Memed then returned to the cowshed, accompanied by Lame Ali. Later they rose from their straw beds and were on the road before it was day.

"Good health, Mother Hürü! Uncle Durmush Ali, good health to you all," said Memed as they left.

The village was slowly waking up. Smoke had begun to rise from one or two chimneys.

"Memed! Memed!" called Hürü angrily. "If you don't destroy that infidel Lame Ali, I'll never forgive you. Deuneh's bones will never rest unless you kill him. Did you hear what I've said?"

"May your road be easy, boy," called Durmush Ali. "Pay no attention to this mad woman's words." Then he turned to Lame Ali. "Don't take offence, Ali. Women don't improve with age."

When they left the village Lame Ali licked his lips and exclaimed: "So I'm going to see that infidel's death with my own eyes!" Whenever he was pleased Ali licked his lips. "Listen, Brother Memed," he continued. "I've done you a lot of harm but now I want to do you a good turn and, after we've cleaned up this business with Abdi Agha, I want to go on helping you. You're a good boy. If anyone else had been in your place he would have killed me long ago. But you understood that I'm not guilty. Look, if I had lied and testified against Hatché, then my guilt would have been great."

Sergeant Rejep had not participated in the conversation for a long time. Now he asked Lame Ali: "You're good at following a trail?"

"I used to be. Then I swore not to track down another man in my life; now I only track down the deer with those who go out hunting. It's my only livelihood and my only pleasure."

"So!" exclaimed Jabbar.

Until they came to the hanging rock they all remained silent. The dew had fallen on the road. Here the earth was red and gave out a peculiar odour, like that of the Chukurova.

Sergeant Rejep was groaning again and cursing. "My knees are breaking and I can't hold up my head."

"Don't talk like that, Sergeant Rejep," said Jabbar to encourage him. "What's come over you?"

But the sergeant kept on moaning.

"The wound's very inflamed," said Lame Ali. "We must do something about it. It's getting more and more infected. Let's go down to a village. Yellow Ummet's house is somewhere near here. We can go there if you like, he's a good man."

"No," said Sergeant Rejep. "Just because of a wound I can't stay under a roof and abandon that infidel's trail." He was really angry. "Memed, Jabbar, come here! For this job you'll let me be your leader. Whatever I say you'll follow my orders. Agreed?"

"Agreed, Sergeant," said Memed.

"Whatever comes, agreed," said Jabbar. "Let's see what you'll do."

"Whoever goes against my orders, I'll shoot him. Nothing shall stop me."

"All right," said Jabbar. "Now tell us what you plan to do. We'll all follow your instructions."

"Don't meddle in this!" The sergeant then turned to Lame Ali: "You're good at following a trail. You've promised to find where this infidel Abdi is hiding."

"I've promised. Even if I hadn't promised I'd have wanted to kill him myself. I want to eat him raw."

"Tell me, where do you think he is now?"

"I don't know where he is right now. Either in town or in the village of Avshar. Perhaps he's gone down as far as Yuregir. If he fears you might be looking for him he'll be sure to have gone down to the Yuregir plain. Brigands can't go down to Yuregir. They can't find any cover in the plain."

"Well, what do we do if he's gone down to Yuregir?" asked Sergeant Rejep.

"I'll keep watch and the minute he leaves Yuregir I'll send you word. I won't let him out of my sight."

"What should we do now, in that case?"

"Stay in Yellow Ummet's house. I'll go down to the Chukurova and find Abdi's lair. Then I'll come and tell you. Come on, let's go to Yellow Ummet's. He's a distant relative of mine and doesn't love that infidel either."

It was late in the afternoon when they came to Yellow Ummet's house. It stood all alone on a woody knoll.

"This is our Slim Memed," said Lame Ali, introducing him to Ummet.

"Brother, was I glad to hear that you'd taken to the mountains. I've been wanting to meet you for a long time."

Lame Ali left them in the courtyard of the house and sped away immediately. Yellow Ummet called after him: "Have a cup of coffee before you go, Brother Ali."

Without turning round and as if muttering to himself, Lame Ali replied: "I've got some business to attend to, Brother Ummet, urgent business." He was almost running, in spite of his lame leg that made him walk with a heaving gait.

That night a gentle wind was blowing. The moon was clear as a lump of ice, its light pouring down in patches through the trees.

"Even if he's hiding under the wings of a bird I'll find him," Lame Ali said to himself as he went. He relived the destruction of his home, the house for which he had worked through the years, so cleanly built and well furnished; Abdi Agha's men had destroyed it in an hour, leaving but a ruin. His resentment increased as he recapitulated his woes.

When he reached the town it was early morning. The streetsweeper, Refugee Murat, was sweeping the market-place, raising a cloud of dust and shivering in the cold morning air. Greeting him, Ali walked on to Tevfik's coffee-house. It had only just opened and he ordered himself tea, which they brought him in a steaming cup. Scarcely able to contain his excitement, he waited in the coffee-house until the shops opened.

As the first rays of the sun fell on the white stones of the pavement he came to Uncle Mustafa's. Uncle Mustafa, a pleasant white-bearded man from Marash, had not yet opened his shop. Ali leaned his back against the door, sat down and waited. A mangy dog, its nose snuffling the ground, passed in front of him. Blind Haji's smithy was just opposite. Soon Blind Haji came, entered his workshop and began to strike the horse-shoes, singing as he worked. The dung at the foot of the wall opposite was beginning to steam. With the light of day the steam gradually disappeared. Then Mustafa Effendi showed up. He laughed as he came down the street and saw Lame Ali at his shop door. "What's up, Ali?" he exclaimed. "Have you traced a thief to my shop?"

Lame Ali stretched himself and rose. "That's it," he answered. Mustafa Effendi opened his shop and they went inside.

"Well, Ali, where have you been all this time, Brother?" said Mustafa Effendi. "I haven't seen you for a long while."

"Don't ask," replied Ali. "I've had nothing but troubles."

"I've heard about them. Abdi hasn't behaved at all decently. He may very well pray five times a day, but his actions remain evil. What he did to you no man should even do to a dog."

"I've heard that Abdi is here in town," said Ali. "In that case I'd better not show myself. It would only bring trouble on my own head."

"Don't be afraid," answered Mustafa Effendi. "He's busy with his own troubles. You know that lad who became a brigand? A bold lad, by all accounts. Abdi's trying to find some hole where he can hide in safety from that boy. He can't even stay in town. Yesterday he came and bought cigarettes and matches from me and stuffed them into his saddle-bag. Then he galloped off at full speed towards Aktozlu village. He'll possibly have settled somewhere in that village. A villain can only fall prey to an even greater villain and you must still be patient for a while. He behaved disgracefully in your case, but see how he's now running for his life from a mere child!"

"Whose house would he be staying at in Aktozlu village?" Ali asked, trying not to appear too eager.

"Whose house would it be but that of the Headman Huseyin? They're related."

To make quite sure that Abdi was in Aktozlu, Lame Ali said: "He doesn't like Aktozlu. When he comes down to the Chukurova, Abdi Agha always stays at his cousin's in the village of Saribahche."

"What are you saying, Ali?" cried Mustafa Effendi. "The man's turned yellow as amber, all the blood's gone out of him. Would he trust his life to such a spineless fellow as his cousin? He's a crafty one, that Abdi! We heard a few days ago that this brigand lad had already raided Abdi's house and was going to kill his children, then took pity on them and changed his mind. A squad of police have now gone to search for the brigand lad. Isn't his name Slim Memed? Abdi knows all this, so do you think he'll stir from Aktozlu village? Headman Huseyin's a brave man. Only over his dead body would anyone be able to do harm to a guest in his house. Oh, he's a crafty one, that Abdi! Would he ever go to Saribahche village? If you go this minute to Aktozlu, I swear you'll find him by Huseyin's fireplace, as if you'd put him there with your own hand."

"You have to pay in the long run," commented Lame Ali. "What he did to me, may God do to him! May he long grovel miserably at other people's doors! May he sweat in mortal fear all his days!"

"You can rest content," said Mustafa Effendi. "He'll get what he deserves."

Although Lame Ali had learned the exact whereabouts of Abdi Agha, he was still far from content. "I must be careful not to bring Memed down into the Chukurova on a wild-goose chase," he thought. "He might get into trouble for nothing." He bought himself some *halva* from Mustafa Effendi and some bread from the bakery opposite, then set off towards Aktozlu village.

An hour's journey outside the town one reaches the swamps of Aghdjasaz. The sedge grows thick here like a forest. As the shining crystal-clear waters of the Savrun river flow through the sedge-covered marshes, they become dirty and carry with them some of the mud of Aghdjasaz. Aktozlu is on the banks of this swamp and all its villagers are plagued by malaria.

Coming to the reed-bed of Yalnizdut, Ali became confused as to which way he should go. He noticed the trail of a jackal and could not keep himself from following it, though it drew him deeper and deeper into the swamp. He was both pleased at his skill and angry with himself. "This jackal's mad!" he muttered to himself, but he could not abandon the trail and, cursing the jackal, followed its tracks until they brought him on to dry land. "There's something in this scoundrel of a jackal," he exclaimed. "Truly, all jackals are wise . . ."

On the morning of the second day he reached Aktozlu village. All the huts in the village had thatched brush walls and the reeds of the roof were fresh and green. In all swamp villages the roofs are always new, as the villagers only have to go to the swamp close by to cut the reeds. But in villages that are far from the swamps the reeds of the roofs are thin and dry and have turned to silver in the sun.

The village was deserted as Ali walked down its dirt path. At the door of a tiny hut with sagging brush walls a woman thrust her head out and drew it in again.

"Sister!" Lame Ali called after her. "Sister, where is Huseyin Agha's house?"

The woman appeared again and pointed to a long hut roofed partly with reeds and partly with corrugated iron. Hardly able to breathe from excitement, Ali limped towards the house. Its big door was open and he stood for a moment before it, till a tall man came out and asked: "What do you want, Brother?"

"I'm one of Abdi Agha's villagers. I have a message for him."

"Come in," said the man.

They went through the long house from one end to the other and came to a room that was spread with bright woven rugs. Abdi Agha was seated by the fireplace, bending towards the roaring fire in the hearth and gently telling his beads as he swayed, almost dozing off.

"Agha, there's a man here from your village," said the tall man.

Slowly, absent-mindedly, the Agha raised his head and fixed his eyes on Ali, who stood there as if about to collapse on his lame side. At first the Agha did not recognise him. Narrowing his eyes he stared again, then turned pale and tried to say something but remained silent. What he had begun to say was not clear. When Ali walked over to him, Abdi Agha's eyes opened wider and the beads in his hand dropped to the ground. "Come over here, my son, Ali," he managed to say. "Have you brought news from the village?"

Ali sat down beside him near the fire.

"Speak up, what is it?" said the Agha.

Ali cast a couple of glances at the tall man standing there. Abdi understood and said to the man: "We have private business to discuss, Osman. Leave us alone for a while."

The tall man went out of the room and closed the door.

Abdi tried to be as friendly as possible. "What news, my Ali?" he asked. Then his face changed and betrayed his fears. "Or are you here now to track me down too?"

Ali looked wretched, as if about to weep. "Agha, there's no end to the worries that I've had since I followed that trail for you. I've lost my home, everything, and now it will be my life too. Memed came and caught me in Chahsak village and took me to Deyirmenoluk village. He was saying: 'I'll catch Abdi Agha, too, and kill both of you together.' One night he even broke into your house. This gave me a chance to escape and I fled to Hüsük's house. Hüsük unfastened my hands which were tied behind my back and I then said to him: 'Go and see what's happening in my Agha's house.' Hüsük went there and came back: 'The Agha isn't there,' he told me. 'Memed has locked the door from inside and nobody can get in. The women and children are shrieking.' Aye, Agha, the village was a scene of destruction as I fled and the screaming could be heard right down the valley. So I came to you for help." Lame Ali began to weep. "My wife and family are still in Chahsak village, Agha. Is it any fault of mine? How can I go there again? Give me some advice, Agha. I'm thinking of you too. What will happen to you here in the Chukurova? It doesn't matter about us. It's about you that I'm worried to death. You are a great Agha, the Agha of five villages, and everywhere, in all the mountain villages, it's being said that you've run away from a boy the size of your little finger, to hide yourself in the Chukurova. My own honour is of no importance, Agha, but I weep for yours."

Abdi Agha's face had slowly changed from pale to scarlet. There were tears in his eyes. "Ali, my son, I did you wrong. Bring your household from Chahsak back to Deyirmenoluk. I'll sign a paper for you and my men there will give you oxen and seeds. Forgive me, Ali, my son. Go and bring your household back to Deyirmenoluk."

"How can I go back and settle in Deyirmenoluk again? " cried Ali. "That worthless son of a scoundrel will kill me!"

"Don't be afraid of him," said Abdi Agha. "I'll see to it that he does not live long in the mountains. He's quarrelled with Durdu and now I've sent word to Durdu; soon I'll set Chichekli's band on his trail too. As long as I live I'll see to it that they hunt him down like a partridge. Fear nothing!" He put his hand in his pocket, pulled out a wad of paper money and took ten green bank-notes from it. "Take these, Ali, my son. This money's for you. Listen to me now. Go straight to the village and tell them at my house to send three of the flocks of sheep down to the Chukurova. Don't let that cursed one get wind of your presence there. You can enter the village at night if you like. Then send one of my labourers to your house in Chahsak and let him bring your household back. After that come back quickly with news of my children. What has that cursed one done to them? I'm worried. Have a meal here before you go on your way."

Lame Ali began to weep again. "Don't, Agha! Don't send me up there again. I managed to escape from that devil once. He'll kill me."

Abdi Agha became angry. "Do as I tell you! Be off with you! Perhaps by now the police have caught him. What does he know about brigandage?"

"I'll go, Agha. You're right."

They served Ali a meal which he ate hurriedly before setting forth. Without stopping to rest he reached Yellow Ummet's house in a day and a half. It was midnight when he whistled softly at the door. Ummet recognised the signal and came out.

"Welcome, Brother. Speak softly. It's full of police inside. They set out after our friends. Now they've come back and are fast asleep. How angry Sergeant Asim was! As for your friends, they're having a good time in the hay-loft. I slaughtered a lamb for them. That Memed of yours seems to be a fine strong lad. He doesn't gossip and he keeps his nose out of other people's business. He obviously has worries of his own on his mind. You can see it in his eyes. You'll see, he'll be the most famous brigand on these mountains. Come, I'll take you to him."

They walked over to the hay-loft. Yellow Ummet took two stones from the ground and struck them against each other three times. Someone opened the door a little.

"Here I am," said Lame Ali.

"Welcome," replied Memed. He withdrew to let them in and then closed the door behind them. "Your friend Ummet is a fine fellow. Anyone else would have handed us over. We might have been fighting it out with the police long ago. I'm glad you've come."

"Brother," said Ali exultantly, "I've found Abdi Agha. He was sitting there by Huseyin Agha's fireplace in Aktozlu village."

Memed was so pleased that he lost his usual composure and struck a match to light a torch, an unusually rash thing for him to do under such circumstances.

Jabbar and Sergeant Rejep were sleeping side by side in a corner. Quietly Memed went over and shook Jabbar, who started with fear in his sleep and seized the gun that lay beside him. Memed grasped the gun.

"It's all right, Jabbar. It's only Memed!"

"What's the matter? Has anything happened?"

"Ali's back," replied Memed.

"Has he found him? Is everything in order?"

"Yes."

"Then let's get going at once. But what shall we do about Sergeant Rejep? He's in a bad way and can't move his neck at all. He's afraid he's going to die. Should we leave him here?"

"He won't stay," said Memed. "He'll only make trouble if we try to argue with him."

"Then there's nothing to do but to wake him," said Jabbar, shaking the sergeant, who only turned over sleepily. "Get up, Sergeant," he whispered.

"I can't," moaned the sergeant. "I'm dying. Can't you see I'm dying?"

"Get up, Sergeant, get up, man. We must be off at once," insisted Jabbar as he tried to pull him out of the bed.

"Don't do this to me," wailed the sergeant. "I'm dying, I tell you. I'm dying."

"Get up, for heaven's sake, my brave Sergeant! Aren't you our chief? Is this how you planned to lead us?"

"Poor fellow," said Memed. "It's the first time in days that he's slept."

"What can we do?" asked Jabbar. "Shall we leave him here?"

"We can't," said Memed. He took the sergeant by the wrists and pulled him up. "Sergeant! Sergeant!" he repeated several times into his ear, "Abdi Agha's in Aktozlu village. Ali has just come back from there and he's seen him."

Sergeant Rejep opened his eyes. "What?" he asked.

"We've found out where Abdi's hiding. In Aktozlu."

"Did Lame Ali find him?"

"Yes," replied Memed.

"If he hadn't found him, I had decided I would kill Ali. He's had a narrow escape," said the sergeant as he rose to his feet. He grimaced as if he had just swallowed some poison, but he was trying hard not to show how much his neck hurt. "Boys, before we set off, put some more ointment on this wound of mine. Sergeant Rejep is about to do the most useful thing he's ever done in his life. He'll kill that infidel Abdi. Just for this whatever sins I've committed will be forgiven me."

"Wait," said Lame Ali. "Let me tend to the wound." He sat down beside the sergeant.

"Ali, Ali," moaned the sergeant. "It's a good thing you found him, otherwise you'd have been a dead duck. I'd have killed you."

"Well, we've found him, this enemy of all honest men. Give him his deserts."

"You'll see!"

Ali finished spreading the ointment over the wound and then bandaged it carefully.

"Let's be off," said Sergeant Rejep. "Hurry! Every minute we let that infidel live is too much."

They set forth at once, neglecting even to take leave of Ummet.

"Thank God we've seen this day," muttered Jabbar.

"Thank God!" echoed Memed. He was walking ahead at a brisk pace, his heart bursting with impatience.

"Abdi Agha gave me ten liras," said Lame Ali, regaling them with the tales he had invented.

By the time they reached Yalnizdut they were starving. In their eagerness they had not stopped anywhere on their way. All day they had remained in hiding, going ahead down the valleys and through the marshes only by night.

"Don't worry," said Lame Ali. "I'll find you something to eat right away. Wait there in that hollow."

He entered the village of Yalnizdut. Half an hour's walk from there, by the fortress of Anavarza, the village of Aktozlu could be seen.

Some time later Ali returned with a bag full of bread and one of yoghourt. "I stole the yoghourt," he announced. "It was hanging on a door-post and I took it as if from my own house."

When they had eaten each one rolled a cigarette. It was clear from his anguished expression that Sergeant Rejep's wound was plaguing him unbearably.

"I'm the chief," he kept repeating as he gritted his teeth and wrinkled his face with pain. "If you don't follow my orders, I won't answer for the consequences. I've done so many evil things in my day, now let me do one good deed. You'll all do exactly as I say, agreed?"

"Agreed!" they answered.

"Let's wait here until dark. Under cover of night we'll then go and hide in the marshes around the village. I don't want any meddling. I know every step and stone around here," he insisted. "That place, over there, is the island of Djeyhan. Behind the fortress of Anavarza lies the low ridge of the Hadjis. They're sure to send at least a squadron of police after us. It'll be hard to escape, but nobody knows these parts as I do. I know every nook and cranny. Take care to follow my orders exactly. Brother Cholak once rejected my advice and lost his whole band. He himself was shot. Remember, the Chukurova is Sergeant Rejep's territory!"

The hollow where they had taken cover was a dried-up floodbed. The floods had driven milk-white pebbles, pine-cones, reeds and oleander roots among the bushes. Later floods had stopped here and, unable to uproot the bushes, deposited their flotsam and passed on, spreading over the neighbouring fields.

Evening came. The sun was sinking, making the level plain

shine like a huge, burnished brass tray, lighting up the clouds and finally seeming to settle on the other end of the plain.

"Ah!" exclaimed Sergeant Rejep. "It's a long time since I've seen the sun set over the Chukurova! It hangs on the edge of the plain for a long while and turns red, red as blood. Then it suddenly sinks. Stop and let me watch it. I'm going to die anyway."

Jabbar laughed.

"What are you laughing at, you pup?" cried the sergeant angrily.

"At Lame Ali," said Jabbar prudently.

The sergeant was silent.

The sun sank and darkness fell. The sergeant rested his hands on his hips and stood there like a statue, staring out towards the west. "I'm going to die, but at least I've seen the sun set over the Chukurova once more. . . ."

They passed Yalnizdut and its fields and came to another swamp. When they emerged from it the huts of Aktozlu village appeared. Only one or two lights gleamed feebly in the whole village. Beyond, all was wrapped in darkness. They were very tired as they sat down and leaned their backs against the bushes. Ali was about to light a cigarette when he was interrupted by a furious remark from the sergeant: "You cuckold! Put that match back in your pocket or I'll shoot you."

Lame Ali complied without a word.

Then the sergeant spoke in a low, harsh voice: "For the last time I tell you, if anyone disregards my orders I'll shoot him without a qualm. Am I your leader or not?"

"You are, Sergeant," they all replied.

The sergeant leaned forward and remained in deep thought for half an hour, then raised his head and asked Memed: "After we've done the job, will Lame Ali still be useful to you?"

"He will," replied Memed.

"A man like Lame Ali is useful in every brigand outfit," agreed Sergeant Rejep, then fell silent again and remained so for a long while. Jabbar could no longer control his impatience.

"What's the matter, Sergeant? Have you gone to sleep?"

This enraged the sergeant. "You son of a whore," he muttered between his teeth, "do you think it's easy to kidnap a man and carry him off from a big village in the middle of the plain like this?

I'm not asleep. I'm working out a plan." He was soon lost in thought again. Some time later he raised his head as if waking up. He fixed his eyes on each shadowy figure in turn, but could not distinguish their features in the starlight. "Boys," he began. His voice was warm, with a motherly affection. "This will be my last job. My wound can never heal and will be my undoing, I know it. But I'm thinking of you, Memed. You're a good courageous boy. In all these years, among the men of five villages, you were the only one to stand up and resist tyranny. If I survive I'll protect you like the apple of my eye. But I'm going to die." He turned to Lame Ali: "You're a wise man, Ali, and in addition you're not yet an outlaw. You can be a great help to Memed."

"I'll do anything for Memed. Can I ever forget the destruction of my house and how I was driven away from my village? It all weighs on my heart like a mill-stone."

"Now, let's get down to our business," said the sergeant. "Towards midnight we'll go to Huseyin Agha's house. We'll force them to open the door, shoot Abdi inside and make off quickly. But Lame Ali must not be with us."

"It must be midnight by now, Sergeant," said Memed. "Let's be off! All right?"

The sergeant rose to his feet. He straightened his cartridge-belts, loaded his weapons and checked his grenades. Then he searched through his pockets. "Ali," he said, "give me your matches, and don't stay here. Go at once, wherever you have to go."

Ali handed over the matches. "May your holy cause be blessed," he said as he turned and walked off.

"Thanks, Ali. We'll be seeing you again," Memed called softly after him.

A fresh north-easterly wind was whistling through the eaves of the reed huts as they entered the village. They stopped as soon as they found the only house roofed in part with corrugated iron.

"Knock at the door, Memed," said the sergeant. "Jabbar, stand ready and take cover behind that mound. Shoot whoever approaches the house from the outside!"

Memed picked up a stone and began to knock on the door. The corrugated iron roof glistened like ice in the starlight. The blows he struck on the door shattered the silence of the sleeping village.

A man's voice soon called from inside: "Who's there, at this hour of the night?"

"One of Abdi Agha's villagers, Brother. Open the door! I've brought a message."

"Come back in the morning," replied the voice from inside.

A dog began barking at the other end of the village.

"It's an urgent message. I must see the Agha at once," called the sergeant. "Open the door, Brother!"

The man opened the door, but closed it again immediately and bolted it.

"This damned wound! If it hadn't been for my wound I would have pushed my way into the house. Never mind, I'll make them open the door soon enough." At the top of his voice he shouted: "I'm the bandit chief, Sergeant Rejep. If you haven't yet heard of me, now's your chance to find out all about me. Hand over to me that infidel, Abdi Agha. If you don't, you know what to expect."

Memed called out too: "I'm Slim Memed, here to avenge my mother and my sweetheart, to avenge the villagers, too, and all the poor! Cast him out. We won't move from here until you have handed Abdi over to us."

"Abdi Agha isn't here," called the voice from inside. "Go about your business elsewhere. He isn't here."

"I'm Sergeant Rejep, chief of this band of brigands. I'm not going away without that infidel Abdi. Memed! Put one of your hand-grenades under the door. Let's blow the door up!"

"My wife and family are all here," shouted the man inside. "Abdi's not in the house."

"Then why don't you open the door?" asked Sergeant Rejep.

"I can't open it."

"Memed," shouted Sergeant Rejep, "take out the pin and place the grenade by the door."

"Ready, Sergeant. Shall I let it rip?"

"What are you waiting for?" roared the sergeant.

There came the sound of a weapon from inside.

"Lie down, Memed, lie down! That infidel's about to shoot."

A volley of shots poured from the house.

"Be quick with that grenade, Memed," shouted Sergeant Rejep.

"Don't do any harm to my wife and family," said the man from inside. "Let us all come out first, then you can do whatever you like. Abdi Agha, don't fire yet! Let us get out first and then you can have it your own way."

The firing stopped and the door was opened. Sleepy children and trembling women in their underclothes hurled themselves out of the house, running off as fast as they could. Last of all, a very old man and two youths left the house.

"Abdi's inside," said the old man. "Go and settle your accounts with him."

No sooner had he spoken than the firing began again. Abdi's shots came fast and furious.

Hearing the sound of a skirmish, the villagers had all been awakened and now came in crowds towards Huseyin Agha's house. "It's the brigands," said one of them, after which they all rushed back to their homes and soon there was no longer a soul in sight.

"Memed," called the sergeant, "cover the door and fire as fast as you can."

"What's the use?" said Memed. "The fellow's inside. He can shoot all three of us."

"Let him shoot!" mocked the sergeant. "I'll make short shrift of him. You can fire through the doorway. Do whatever I tell you to do and don't answer back! Don't stop firing into the open doorway." Then he shouted at the top of his voice: "So, Abdi, instead of throwing yourself at my feet you want to fire at me? Do you still want to hide in the house and shoot me? I'll show you."

The sergeant went round to the windward side of the house while Memed kept firing into the doorway and wondering what the sergeant was up to.

Abdi Agha also kept firing without respite. Jabbar meanwhile lay motionless, watching the whole village. Abdi Agha's shots were well aimed and Memed, had he not found cover by the side of the door, would have been wounded long ago.

There was not a soul in sight and the village was now as deserted as when they had first entered it.

Memed was still firing into the open doorway. What would be the end of all this? The sergeant had not yet reappeared and Memed soon wearied of firing to no good purpose. But as soon as he ceased fire the sergeant cried out from behind the house: "Don't hold your fire, you son of a whore! Keep firing as I told you!"

Though unconvinced, Memed obeyed. But a voice called from behind the mulberry-trees: "Go on shooting till it's morning! You'll never force Abdi out of the house."

"Who are you?" asked Memed.

"I'm Huseyin Agha. No other brigand but Reshit the Kurd ever dared come down to the Chukurova, and the Chukurova then swallowed him up. In the morning they'll pick you up like ripe pears on the ground, in this open plain. If I were in your shoes, I'd give it up and go back where I came from!"

Sergeant Rejep interrupted them, hoarse with anger. "Jabbar, shut that devil's mouth. Fire, man!"

Jabbar fired a volley towards the mulberry-trees.

Suddenly the house was enveloped in red flames, the fire bursting out everywhere at once. The whole place was soon burning.

"Huseyin Agha, you great cuckold!" shouted Sergeant Rejep exultantly. "They may have been able to hunt down Reshit the Kurd, but they can't get me. I'm Sergeant Rejep, the wolf of the Chukurova. I'll kill Abdi to-night or burn the whole village."

The man under the mulberry-tree began to shout and suddenly the whole village was in an uproar.

"Memed," called Sergeant Rejep, "cease fire! As soon as that infidel starts to suffocate, he'll be scurrying out through the door."

Memed stopped firing through the open doorway.

The north-easterly wind fanned the flames. They rose, tall as poplar trees, twisting this way and that. Soon the adjoining house caught fire too. In less than twenty minutes ten houses were ablaze.

Jabbar and Memed had taken cover and were waiting. Sergeant Rejep was still running in a circle round the house and shouting: "Come out, Abdi, come out! You'll roast in there. Come out and throw yourself at Memed's feet. Perhaps he'll still spare you your life."

No answer came from within, but every once in a while a bullet whizzed past Sergeant Rejep's ear. The flames rose even higher, scattering sparks into the sky, bending and twisting as they fitfully lit up the darkness. From the purple rocks of Anavarza to the marshes along the banks of the River Jeyhan, the whole countryside could be seen clearly in flashes of light.

Villagers were running hither and thither in their white underclothes, trying to save their possessions from the burning houses as the fire spread.

"Come out, Abdi," the sergeant kept shouting. "You'll roast like a *kebab* in there. Come out!" Then he turned to Memed. "There's no other way out of the house except that door, Memed. Don't worry! He'll come out now. Shoot him the minute he appears!"

An old woman came out from beneath the mulberry-trees and dashed into the burning house, so suddenly that Sergeant Rejep couldn't say a word. She was soon out again, carrying a mattress in her arms. Panting, she deposited the mattress behind the mulberry-trees. Then she returned and brought out an oak chest, some saucepans, rugs, bowls, quilts, and, last of all, a huge quilt rolled up in her arms. Then the flames enveloped the doorway, and it was no longer possible to enter the house.

Memed and Jabbar in their retreats, Sergeant Rejep circling round the house, all waited impatiently. But Abdi still failed to appear. The roof caved in and they continued to wait as the walls of the house collapsed inwards. There could no longer be any survivor in those smouldering ruins.

The north-easterly wind was now blowing high, the flames leaping from one hut to another till almost all the village was on fire. It was now bright as day, as if the Chukurova sun, like a glowing ember, were beating down on the plain. The long shadows of the mulberry-trees and willows fell on to the damp soil and mingled with the shadows of the scurrying villagers. The wind now seemed to be all flames, as if the fire were endlessly pouring into the village from some place afar.

"He's escaped us," cried Memed anxiously.

"There wasn't a hole for him to escape," said Sergeant Rejep. "I kept circling round the house so that he couldn't break out. He's been burned to ashes. He preferred that to falling into our hands."

"Perhaps," said Jabbar doubtfully.

"He may be dead," sighed Memed, "but I wanted to see his dead body with my own eyes. And I'm sorry now to see a whole great village burning because of that infidel. . . ."

"Let it burn," said Sergeant Rejep. "Let the whole Chukurova burn, soil, stones and all!"

"What will happen to these poor villagers?" Memed wondered.

"They didn't own much anyway," said the sergeant. "If they've lost their homes, they're still not much worse off than before. They're as poor as they've always been."

"Well, Sergeant," asked Memed, "are we going to wait here for ever? They'll already have heard of this in town. There'll be plenty of trouble in the morning."

Sergeant Rejep laughed noisily. "They'll send a telegram to Ankara to say that a village has been destroyed by fire. Yes, there'll be plenty of trouble, so we had better take to the rocks of Anavarza. If they catch us on the plain we're done for."

The three of them sighed as they gazed at the smouldering ruins of the house. Then they turned their backs on the burning village and went their way.

Once out of the village they looked back. The whole village was a ball of fire, a leaping wave of flame.

"Not a single house left," said Memed. "All because of that north-easterly. It wouldn't have happened but for the wind. I'd have died rather than let this happen."

"Not a single house!" said Jabbar. "The whole village has been destroyed!"

"When we left the village all the men and women and children stood there as if turned to stone, without uttering a word. They didn't even curse us or stone us, but just stood like statues and stared at us. I would rather have died than see this."

The sergeant preferred to change the subject. "Well, it's happened and you've seen it. Now my neck's aching like all hell and I'm going to die."

He moaned as he sat down on the ground, took his face between his hands and remained silent and motionless for a while.

Memed and Jabbar stood waiting beside him. Suddenly the sergeant stretched himself out on the ground and began to writhe in torment. Jabbar tried to hold him in his arms but could not control the huge man whose spasms were like the movements of a steel spring.

A tumult reached them from the village, the noise of a crowd. The morning star had appeared, just above the horizon where the sun would soon be rising. The great sparkling star seemed to be whirling like a Catherine-wheel.

The noise of the crowd was no longer so distant. One voice could now be heard affirming repeatedly: "They went this way. They've only just gone!"

"Which way?" another voice asked.

Memed leaned over the sergeant. "That sounded like Sergeant Asim's voice."

"It's he," cried Jabbar excitedly. "Let's be off. Sergeant, we'll soon be surrounded. Get up!"

He lifted the writhing sergeant on to his shoulders and they made off as quickly as they could into the darkness, away from the burning village.

They heard Sergeant Asim shout: "Keep to the road through the marshes, the Anavarza road!"

"We're done for," exclaimed Jabbar.

"If only I were sure of the death of that infidel I wouldn't mind anything," said Memed. "If only my heart could believe that he really died there, roasted in that fire."

"The sergeant's stopped writhing," said Jabbar.

"Don't put him down," said Memed. "I wonder what's happened."

"Nothing's happened," moaned the sergeant. "The worst is over. Put me down."

Jabbar lowered the sergeant from his back.

"Where are we going?" asked the sergeant.

"Sergeant Asim's after us," answered Jabbar.

"Get me to my feet," the sergeant murmured.

Jabbar held him by the arms and raised him to his feet. Swaying a little, the sergeant examined the place where they had stopped.

"Listen! We're near the marshes. If only we could take shelter on Anavarza we'd be saved. But it's impossible. They'll catch us on the road there." He listened intently: "They're very near. Can you hear their voices? We may yet escape by the skin of our teeth through the marshes, though all the villagers in the neighbourhood will be out combing the reed-beds as soon as it's daylight. But there's no other way."

Memed agreed.

"Behind the marshes lies the Jeyhan River," continued the sergeant. "We can throw ourselves into its waters and trust to the current. We may be able to make it. Ah, well! At least we've killed that infidel . . ."

"Yes, we've burned him," said Memed.

"I've my doubts," said Jabbar. "He may well have escaped . . ."

This infuriated the sergeant. "A plague on you, Jabbar! You'd be glad if he escaped! Tell us how he might have slipped away. Memed was at the door and I was circling round the house. How could he possibly have escaped? Tell me, how?"

"He was roasted to death," said Memed. "If I should die now, I no longer care."

"That's what I want to hear," cried the sergeant.

Jabbar remained silent.

There was a great rustling, a sound of many footsteps in the night, of feet dragged through the bushes, plants and earth, beating against the night like a giant wave of the sea. The crowd was silent as it pursued them.

"They're near us," said Jabbar.

"To the reeds," ordered the sergeant. "Hold my hand and follow me."

They began to run towards the reed-beds. The sound of feet behind them became louder and more rapid. The night was flowing towards them like a flood of shuffling sounds. The mountains, the stones, bushes and trees, were all bearing down on them, it seemed, as they fled.

They cursed the plain. How far could it still spread? The hills were small, mere mounds. If the rocks of Anavarza could only be reached, they would be safe. Beyond the reed-beds, they knew, the River Jeyhan rushes impetuously, later slowing down to be almost still. Its banks are of black, slippery earth, marshes that are the home of long-legged night herons.

The stink of the swamp enveloped them as they entered the reed-beds. It is frightening to penetrate these marshes which in places have never yet been visited by man.

The rustling grew louder, sweeping over the plain like the wind, rushing ahead like a fire.

"This way, boys," Sergeant Rejep moaned breathlessly. "Only a few more yards to go."

Suddenly a volley was fired ahead of them.

"Lie down," said the sergeant, throwing himself to the ground. "They're firing into the marshes. Don't utter a sound. Let's crawl through the reeds. Take the ammunition out of your guns, boys. If a single shot is accidentally fired, we're as good as dead. Those villagers are ready to tear us to pieces . . ."

The firing continued unceasingly, lighting up the darkness in flashes. Then it died down.

"They're not here," said a discouraged voice. "If they were, they'd have fired back."

"The villagers are coming," said another voice. "They'll know."

The crowd of villagers caught up with the police, men, women and children, mingling with them as a hubbub rose on all sides: "To the Anavarza! They've surely fled to Anavarza! A brigand would be mad to try to hide among the reeds. He'd be lost there!"

A great roar filled the night. Angry and vengeful, the crowd could not keep still, swarming everywhere, on the edge of the reed-beds and over the fields. "To Anavarza! To Anavarza!" they cried. A sound of shuffling filled the plain as the crowd swept on towards Anavarza.

"Don't stir," whispered Sergeant Rejep. "The crowd has served our purpose. They've completely misled the police. For heaven's sake, don't stir!"

Sergeant Rejep's breath was like fire on Memed's ear and neck.

Some fifteen yards away the police hesitated. The three crouched under the bushes, their hearts beating painfully. The sound of shots at the foot of Anavarza increased and this seemed to convince the police, who made off now in that direction.

Sergeant Rejep heaved a profound sigh. "Thank God! They'd have torn us to pieces if we'd fallen into their hands, those villagers. Now let's go right into the heart of the reed-beds."

They stood up, and Sergeant Rejep went a couple of steps ahead but stopped at once.

"What's the matter, Sergeant?" asked Memed.

The sergeant only moaned.

"Tell us what to do, Sergeant," said Memed anxiously.

"Go in, under cover!" the sergeant managed to gasp.

Memed took hold of him by one arm, Jabbar by the other. The

sergeant's legs were as lifeless as a corpse's, dragging on the ground as they continued to pull him along until dawn. An orange light then fell over the swamps, with the deep green of the reeds melting into it as a blue mist rose slowly to the sky.

The thorny blackberry bushes tore at their legs, reminding Memed of the thistle fields as a blinding yellow light suddenly flashed through his mind and was gone.

At last they laid the sergeant on a thick bed of moss. He was swollen all over, his neck indistinguishable from his shoulders. Once or twice he opened his mouth to speak but could no longer utter a sound. With his hand he pointed to Anavarza, then stared insistently at the ground. Tears welled into his eyes and he closed them. Suddenly, he stretched and sat up, then collapsed.

"Poor Sergeant!" murmured Memed. "I never thought he was going to die."

"He knew he was dying. He was saying so all the time."

"I wonder if he died at peace with the world."

"Nobody knew what he was, where he came from, why he ever became a brigand. Who knows if he died at peace?"

"He wanted Abdi's death more than I did. What could it mean to him? Abdi was my enemy, yet the sergeant almost tore you to pieces when you suggested that he had escaped from the fire."

"Take out your dagger and let's dig a grave for our mysterious sergeant," suggested Jabbar.

Memed took out his dagger, drove it into the ground and began to dig. "He was a strange man."

Within an hour they had easily dug a wide grave in the wet earth of the reed-bed, as wide as the sergeant's chest. They then cut some thick branches and thornless brush, laid the sergeant in the grave fully clothed and propped the branches above him to prevent the earth from falling on the body. Over these branches they spread the brush and then filled the grave with earth.

It was difficult to find a tree in the swamp. Finally they saw a mulberry-tree, as thick as a man's wrist. They uprooted it and planted it at the head of the sergeant's grave.

"This is surely the first grave in these marshes," said Memed.

"Who would ever come and bury his dead in the darkness of the reeds?" agreed Jabbar.

Soon the sun rose and the fresh earth of the sergeant's grave began to steam and glisten in the heat and light. With daylight the sound of shouting at the foot of Anavarza increased.

"What were the sergeant's last instructions?" asked Jabbar.

"He pointed to the rocks of Anavarza."

"We'll have to go towards the River Jeyhan. It's no longer possible to cut through the reed-beds to Anavarza."

"We must follow the sergeant's orders," Memed insisted. "He knew this country well. How pleased he was with the burning of this village, wasn't he, Jabbar? If the whole of the Chukurova had been burned to ashes, he would have been even more pleased. But he was naturally kind. Perhaps he had met with a lot of trouble in the Chukurova. Who knows?"

"Ever since I've known him," Jabbar mused, "he always cursed the Chukurova. No one could even mention the Chukurova when he was around. Sometimes, lost in thought, he would absentmindedly sing this song:

'Burning, burning, the Chukurova's a blazing fire,
A ravening wolf its every mosquito.
If you should die my heart will ever weep;
Rise, Brother, let's be going home!'

"When he'd finished, he wouldn't open his mouth to speak to anyone for a long time, but would wander all by himself, deeply troubled. Then his mood would pass. Who knows what the poor fellow had suffered? And this is the end. He lies here in the reed-beds of Anavarza. Lately, he hadn't cursed the Chukurova any more, nor had he sung his song. I've heard from other brigands that he would refuse to accompany them if they went down into the Chukurova. Until they returned, the sergeant would wait for them all alone up there. This was his destiny: to be buried in the earth of the Chukurova!"

"Perhaps it's all as he wanted it to be," said Memed.

"Let's be going, Memed. The swamps will soon be full of men and dogs searching for us."

Memed turned once more to look at the sergeant's grave. "Rest in peace, Sergeant, farewell," he said as they walked away. Two heavy tears had formed in the corners of his eyes.

It was not easy to make any headway among the reeds, so thick that a tiger would not have been able to force his way through them. Jabbar had taken the sergeant's gun and his silver-worked cartridge-belts. All this load, as well as the solid wall of reeds, was wearing him out, but Memed seemed stronger and more agile than ever. If he could not break through a clump of reeds he would mow it down with his dagger and Jabbar then followed him.

The midday heat was unbearable, never disturbed by any sound except the rustling of the reeds as they forced their way through the tangled brush. They were now two hours' journey from Anavarza, but could still see only the sky and the summit of its rocks. By the time they reached the middle of the reed-bed the sun was already setting behind Anavarza's summit.

"Let's wait here and come out of the reeds when it's dark," suggested Memed.

"I'm dead tired," said Jabbar as he lay down and stretched out. Immediately Memed lay down beside him.

They were quite close to the rocks and could hear hundreds of footsteps, if not thousands, as the crowd came down from the heights. Memed stood up and looked. "I can't see anything. The villagers are still looking for us. Let them go on searching. We're almost saved."

Jabbar sat up. "Now that they've failed to find us either on the rocks or among the reeds, they'll hold all the roads to Azabli, Sumbas and the town. They'll lie in ambush and wait for us."

"In that case we'll wait here a few days," replied Memed.

"We can go up to the mountains above Kozan," suggested Jabbar.

"Do you know the road?" asked Memed.

"I don't know the road, but I know the mountains. Once we get to the top of Anavarza we can see everything."

"Come on then, let's go before it's too dark."

"I can no longer hear the crowd."

"Perhaps they've set an ambush for us by the edge of the reed-beds."

"No," answered Jabbar. "They would never think of that!"

"Let's go, then."

Night was falling as they reached the summit of Anavarza. They could now see the lights of the villages of the plain with patches of darkness between them and the River Jeyhan as it twisted and meandered like a shining black ribbon. The village of Aktozlu was still smouldering beneath a heavy cloud of smoke.

Memed pointed towards the east and asked: "What's that?"

"It must be the village of Bozkuyu," answered Jabbar.

"Why don't we go that way? It's quite near."

"I'm afraid they might be holding the roads there too."

"Let's go that way," persisted Memed. "If we meet the police we'll give them hell. There we're no longer in the plains." Then he turned to Jabbar, whose face he could just make out in the darkness. "What's on your mind, Brother Jabbar? Is that infidel dead?"

"I don't think so. If he had been inside the house and hadn't yet escaped, he would have made a dash for it when the house caught fire. At least he would have screamed."

"Perhaps he was suddenly choked by the smoke," suggested Memed.

"He was firing from inside right up to the end. If he'd been choked to death he couldn't have done that."

"Perhaps he was caught under one of the blazing walls that collapsed or under the roof . . ."

"If only it were as you say, then we wouldn't have had all that trouble in vain."

They began to climb the hill. They were starving.

XVI

Old men used to talk of the old-time Chukurova. In the days of Memed's brigandage, Big Ismail, then more than ninety years old, spoke repeatedly of those times. He had moss-green eyes, a sparse beard and a pointed chin, like all the Turcomans. His broad shoulders were still as strong as in his youth, his eyes as sharp as a hawk's. He had not yet given up hunting and would sing sad Turcoman songs too, or tell about tribal feuds. At the end of every tale he would proudly show the wounds he himself had earned in such feuds.

The sedentary life of the village often weighed on him unbearably, seeming too restricted. He still wanted to live the old Turcoman way of life and preserve every detail of it intact.

Some days he would be brimful with memories of it and become like a drunken man. Mounting the wild red foal he had reared with his own hand, he would gallop off to the mountains, to their scents of pine, thyme and marjoram.

Like a wind blowing from the homeland of the old Turcomans, Big Ismail would tell of migrations, exile, and the long struggle against the Ottomans; of the fine old rifles decorated with little mirrors, the beating of the huge wooden mortars in the tents, all the tents resplendent with green and red, a wondrous sight as the tribe moved slowly from the mountains to the Chukurova plain.

"Up to fifty years ago," Big Ismail would begin—and once he had begun he never stopped, as if he were reciting a love story or a song—"the Chukurova was nothing but swamps and bullrush beds with only a few tiny fields at the foot of the hills, not a soul living in the whole wide plain except the nomads. When the bare trees and the earth would deck themselves out for the spring, the Turcoman migration would begin in all its majesty, a riot of red and

green. We would set forth over the mountains and pitch our tents
for the summer on the highlands of Binbogha. When winter set in
we would come down again to the Chukurova plain. In those days
the plain was so thick with reeds and brush that a tiger could not
penetrate it; throughout all twelve months of the year, the grass
was knee-deep in the flat fields. Herds of bright-eyed, timid
gazelles grazed there. We rode valiant and swift horses to hunt
them, the quality of a steed being proven in this hunt. The reeds
and bulrushes used to grow as tall as poplars in the Chukurova,
along the shores of the lakes. From end to end the Chukurova was
covered with narcissus in spring. Day and night the winds were
laden with the scent of the flowers as the silvery sea-waves beat
upon the Chukurova's far shores, foaming white. The tribes would
pitch their tents all over the plain, the smoke of their settlements
curling up to the sky. The Osmaniye-Toprakkale plain, along the
upper reaches of the River Jeyhan, towards the mountains, was
occupied by the Tejirli tribe on the seaward side. Below that,
around Jeyhanbekir and Mustafabey, it was the traditional camping site of the Jerit tribe; between Anavarza and the Castle of
Hemiteh, the Bozdoghan tribe; between Anavarza and Kozan,
the Lek Kurds; between the River Sumbas and the Taurus, the
Sumbasli tribe. Between what is now Ekshiler village and Kadirli,
the Tatarli tribe would pitch their tents. Sometimes the tribes
would change places. The Bozdoghan tribe would then settle on
the traditional lands of the Jerit and the Jerit on those of the Bozdoghan. The most powerful tribe was the Avshar; they could settle
wherever they liked in the Chukurova, and no one dared protest."

"I remember," Big Ismail would continue, "the great struggle
against the Ottomans, after which the Ottomans were victorious.
They captured our Kozanoghlu and carried him off. Then they
exiled the Avshars to Bozok and scattered the whole tribe."

At this point Big Ismail's eyes would fill with tears and with
trembling lips he would sing the famous dirge for Kozanoghlu in
his thick, powerful voice:

> "I fled up the snow-capped Kozan Mount,
> Dragging myself, crawling on my knees.
> Alas, my wounds were festering
> As I searched in vain for a healer.

"Can it be? Can it be true?
Does a son shoot his own father?
Ah, ye soldiers of the Sultan,
This world will not forever be as now.

"What matter if the pole of the Black tent be broken
And its top brought level with the ground?
How can you flee, brave Kozanoghlu,
When only five hundred riders have come after you?"

Big Ismail would then resume his account of the history of the tribes: "Then the Ottomans settled the tribes by force in the Chukurova and distributed fields to them and drew up deeds of possession. They stationed soldiers on the mountain roads so that we might no longer migrate to the summer pastures in the highlands. The nomads died like flies in the Chukurova, some from malaria, some from the heat, or from epidemics that broke out among them. But the nomads had no intention of settling down for good and would burn the roots of the vines and the saplings that the Ottomans had given them, planting them for spite like that. That is why there are no trees in any of the villages now. Finally the Ottomans realised that the tribes would die out completely and allowed them to return to their summer pastures. Much later, the tribes grew accustomed to the idea of settling down and began to build villages in place of their encampments and to raise crops of wheat. After that the tribes finally broke up and their customs changed. Everything was suddenly different. People became mean. What the Ottomans had foreseen had come to pass."

Once Big Ismail was launched on the subject of the tribes he could go on for days, tirelessly, driven by a nostalgic yearning for the old unfettered way of life. His every speech began: "I am a man who has actually seen Dadaloghlu, the great poet of the revolt against the Ottomans." He was very proud of this.

In 1917, 1918, 1919 and 1920, the last years of the First World War saw the defeat of the Ottomans, when the Chukurova was suddenly full of deserters and brigands, the whole Taurus range becoming impracticable because of them.

The French Occupation Forces then came to the Chukurova and the brigands, the deserters, the irregulars, the thieves, those who were good-for-nothing and the honest men, the young and the old, all the people of the Chukurova joined in the fight to throw the enemy out of the plain. They drove the French out and the whole country was thus liberated. A new government was set up and a new era began.

Towards the end of the nineteenth century, years after the Turcoman rebellion, conditions had slowly forced the people to accept being bound to the soil. The value of land had steadily increased and the Turcomans, who had so long rebelled and fought against settlement, then left the highlands altogether to cling to their newly-found land. Every year the fresh Chukurova soil gave back forty-fold, fifty-fold what they had sown, which seemed incredible. In the years after 1900, the swamps of the Chukurova were slowly drained, and the reed-beds burned down and turned into fields, so that almost half the land was already under cultivation.

After the First World War, the new Government tried to put an end to feudal land tenure, abolishing what remained of the unbounded power of the feudal landlords. In any case the feudal system was breaking up by itself. A class of newly enriched was coming to the fore, most of them seeking to gain possession of as much of the fertile soil as possible. They succeeded by all sorts of means in wresting the land from the poor, in the course of a great struggle between the people and the newly rich. The landholdings of the rich steadily increased when they also began to make use of the brigands as a means of pressure on the poor who were fighting to defend their rights in a life-and-death struggle for the land. Nearly every Agha supplied some band of brigands on the mountains and protected them from the Government. An Agha who had no brigands at his beck and call would then organise a new band of them, till the Taurus Mountains were overflowing with such bands. But the conflicting interests of the Aghas in the plains began to lead to fights among their brigand supporters in the mountains. The brigands on the mountains were continually fighting among themselves and oppressing the poor, while the estates of the Aghas grew steadily on the plain.

Ali Safa Bey was the son of an old-time Agha who had lost his fortune, but had still managed to send his son to the Imperial School at Adana, then to the Law Faculty in Istanbul. For some reason or other Ali Safa Bey had left the law school half-way through his studies and begun to practise as a lawyer in the town. Later he had given up his practice to try his hand at many different jobs, till he suddenly came to his senses and realised the value of land. Thanks to a lot of legal quibbles he managed to obtain from the villagers the return of the lands which his father had once been forced by poverty to sell. This success whetted his appetite and he began to have recourse to all sorts of other tricks to obtain new lands. His appetite became truly insatiable.

The villagers were no longer as they had been at the time of the rebellion or immediately after it. They now understood that the soil was worth its weight in gold and they clung to it. The struggles between Ali Safa Bey and the villagers thus lasted for years, but Ali Safa Bey showed the cunning of a fox and always found new ways of wresting land from them. He might thus start by stirring up trouble between two or three villages and, by supporting one side, obtaining control of the lands of the other. This was his easiest device and proved very practical, but could not be used very long. The quarrelling villagers soon understood who was their real enemy, but by that time at least half the lands of that area had passed out of their hands. Ali Safa Bey had thus added the lands of two or three villages to his own farms and was still busy with new tricks which the villagers generally understood too late. By the end of each year, Ali Safa Bey's holdings had again increased.

Things reached such a pitch that Ali Safa Bey's reputation began to impede him in his intrigues. Not a single farmer was beguiled any longer by his tricks and he had to change his tactics radically.

In those days there were brigands in the mountains, deserters, robbers, murderers, rebels. Ali Safa Bey sought to profit by their presence and therefore came to terms with one or two brigand chiefs. He also sent some of his own men into the mountains to unleash the brigands upon the villagers. At last Ali Safa Bey met with no opposition. Not a single villager dared stir any more. In one night a recalcitrant villager's house would be destroyed, his wife kidnapped, he himself tortured to death. Everybody knew that it was all Ali Safa Bey's doing, but not a hair of his head was ever hurt. The police remained content to pursue and shoot only the brigands.

Other Aghas of course followed Ali Safa Bey's example and the soil of the Chukurova soon ran red with blood. Brigand bands on the mountains split up to follow the orders of two, three, four or five masters, fighting among themselves. In a single night several old bands might disappear and several new ones be formed.

Only a few brigands, Gizik Duran, Reshit the Kurd and Jotdelek, remained independent and refused to be enticed by the promises of the Aghas. While the names of many sanguinary murderers in the Taurus Mountains have been forgotten, these few are remembered in songs and epics which are passed on from mouth to mouth by the people.

While the brigands in the pay of the Aghas were thus fighting among themselves and the peasants in the Chukurova were toiling as serfs in fields which had been forcibly wrested from them, Memed first took to the mountains. Ali Safa Bey's twenty thousand acres had meanwhile grown to thirty thousand in one year and then increased steadily in the following years: thirty-five thousand, forty thousand, forty-five thousand, fifty thousand. All the landless villagers had become his serfs, toiling in fields that had once been their own.

Ali Safa Bey was a tall man, with thick black brows and a strangely dark complexion. He always wore shining boots which he constantly flicked with his silver-mounted riding-crop.

One Tuesday news reached him that the ammunition supplies of Kalayji's band had run out. It would take another week for more ammunition to arrive from Syria. Ali Safa Bey was anxious. He was pacing up and down ceaselessly in his big house as he pondered, his thoughts moving in a vicious circle. He must still be patient for a few more years to gain possession of the land of Vayvay village. Then he would send telegrams to Ankara and complain that the brigands were masters of the mountains, asking the Government what it was planning and why it still took no action. One or two more years, and then he would show that brigand Kalayji with whom he had to deal!

Ali Safa Bey's wife, seated on the divan, watched her husband with admiration as he stalked up and down, flicking his shining boots with his riding-crop. When in an angry mood he always unburdened himself, confiding his secrets and plans to his wife.

"Woman, do you know what I'll do?" he asked.

"Tell me!"

That was how he always began. "Do you know what I'll do? By God, these bandits have made my life a misery. Every blessed day they need ammunition. Every blessed day new complaints are filed with the police. The villagers got together yesterday and went to the governor to complain that they were weary of these brigands endangering their property, their lives, their honour. They were about to send a telegram to Ankara, but I prevented them. 'Don't give our town a bad reputation in the eyes of the Government,' I pleaded. We must still be patient for a year or two. Do you think I'm happy about these brigands? Wait till I get possession of the land of Vayvay village; then what do you think I'll do, woman?"

She nodded, and remained silent.

"I'll gather the villagers about me and send one telegram after another to Ankara. I'll say that a rebellion has broken out, that the brigands are in control of the mountains, that they have formed an insurgent government of their own. Then the Government will send a regiment or a mounted brigade here, and that'll do the trick, capturing all of them. Our Government was once able to quash the great Kurdish rebellion; you'll see how they'll deal with a couple of petty brigands! I've arranged with the operator at the post office: not a single telegram about the brigands will be despatched to Ankara to give our town a bad reputation. But as soon as Vayvay village passes into my hands in a couple of years' time, I know what I'll do about these brigands . . ."

He was silent, lost in thought as he paced up and down, his head in the air.

Not two years but many years later Ali Safa actually sent telegram after telegram to Ankara. But he also ordered the brigands whom he kept in the mountains to raid the town just as the soldiers sent by the Government as a result of his complaints were arriving, and that was how he managed to rid himself of brigands who had become but a thorn in his side.

Ali Safa Bey was now roused from his musings by one of his servants: "There's a man with his head all bandaged who wants to see you. He has a long beard."

"Let him in," answered Ali Safa.

The man with the bandaged head entered the room, dragged himself moaning to the divan and flopped down. "Greetings, Brother Ali Safa Bey."

"Greetings."

"Ali Safa Bey, your father was my best friend and I now seek your protection," he said, repeating his pleas again and again. "Abdi seeks your protection. Save me from this calamity. That brigand Memed set fire to a huge village before my very eyes. Save me! I kiss your feet but save me from this calamity."

Ali Safa smiled. "Why all this fuss? Relax a while and we'll talk it over later."

"Why all this fuss, you ask!" exclaimed Abdi Agha. "If I weren't worried, who would be? The fellow hangs over me like the sword of Azrael. Because of me he set fire to a fine village, Aktozlu. I kiss your feet, Ali Safa Bey, but save me from that monster's hands! There's no sleep nor rest for me any longer."

"Abdi Agha," said Ali Safa Bey, half mocking, half serious, "I've heard that this Memed of yours is just a slip of a boy."

"It's a lie, it's a lie," cried Abdi Agha, leaping to his feet. "He's grown as tall as a poplar now. I saw him with my own eyes when he was setting fire to the house. As large as both of us! Could a slip of a boy do all these things? He's as big as a giant, curse him!"

"Don't worry, Agha," Ali Safa Bey soothed him. "We'll find some way out. Now drink your coffee!"

With a trembling hand Abdi Agha took the coffee that the servant had brought. Its pleasant odour rose to his nostrils as he began to drink, sipping noisily, while Ali Safa Bey's wife sat down beside him on the divan.

"I congratulate you on your escape, Agha," she said soothingly. "We were all very shocked to hear of the dreadful things that happened to you. But Ali Safa Bey will get the better of this infidel. Don't fret!"

Since the burning of the village Abdi Agha had behaved very strangely. He would talk on and on, endlessly telling his misfortunes to anyone he could find, whether they listened or not. Most of his listeners pitied him and cursed Slim Memed. The governor, the chief of police, the governor's secretary and clerk, townspeople, villagers, all felt sorry for Abdi Agha. It was impossible not to feel pity as he explained, weeping, all that he had suffered. Every time he set out to recite the events of that fateful night his face would assume such a woeful, miserable expression that the whole story could be read on it before he even uttered a word.

"We were all so sorry for you," the woman repeated. "The governor's wife came to us yesterday and said that her husband was furious about it. She assured us that they'll do everything to catch that bandit. Can one allow a big village to be burned down like that? The governor's wife was anxious to see you and asked us what kind of a hero could escape so miraculously from the fire. Let Ali Safa Bey finish this business with Vayvay village and then he won't leave a single brigand alive on the mountains. All of us were grieving for you, Abdi Agha."

Ali Safa Bey was pacing from one end of the room to the other, flicking at his shiny boots with his crop.

"Ah, my daughter!" Abdi Agha began, his lips trembling, his face taut. "The things that have happened to me! Never has a human being suffered such woes. Veli was my nephew, tall and slim as a sapling, engaged to marry Hatché. Then this villain kidnapped Hatché. Let him elope with her, why should we care? If two hearts beat as one, it's no good to interfere. Were there no other girls for my Veli? He only had to raise his hand. I am the Agha of five villages, as were my father and my grandfather before me. But that villain Memed kidnapped my nephew's bride and I said 'Let them come and stay in the village again instead of living among strangers.' All my villagers are as children to me, you know, but if you feed a crow it'll pick your eyes out, they say, and I didn't believe it. Pity is the cause of many woes, they say, but I didn't believe it. What a mistake I made! I should have let them stay away from the village, living in misery among strangers. I forgave that serpent, my mortal enemy, and even brought him back to the village. Then he killed my nephew and wounded me. I almost died. I'm repaid with evil for all the good I did . . ."

"Poor Abdi Agha," exclaimed the woman. "It's no use being kind to such people. Our Safa Bey never does any good to anyone!"

"We shouldn't," agreed Abdi. "But it's too late now. After he had shot me, that ungrateful, miserable wretch who had bitten the hand that fed him ran off and joined the brigands. Let him go, I said. God will punish him. Let him become a brigand, a smuggler, whatever he likes. One day news then reached me that he has sworn to kill me and is about to raid our village with his band. Yes, my daughter! He's sworn to drink my blood like sherbet! What would he want from an old man like me, with already one foot in the grave? I saw that the wretch was about to raid the village to kill me, so I fled, abandoning my own house and home and seeking shelter in the house of Huseyin Agha of Aktozlu village, a relative of ours. If only I hadn't sought shelter there! Because of me the whole village has now been burned to ashes."

"If only you had come to us," said the woman. "All this would never have happened!"

"How could I know, my daughter? It never entered my mind that the wretch would do such a thing. A whole village burnt to ashes! The poor people left naked in the open! It breaks a man's heart to think of the children, left there with no food or clothes! They'll starve this winter. Most of the livestock was burned to death too. When I saw those poor villagers with their hungry children I forgot about my own troubles and sent Lame Ali back to my village to bring them some wheat. My heart always bleeds for the poor, and now I'm afraid that infidel may set fire to our village too. It's becoming a habit and he's quite capable of it. When that beast got wind of where I was hiding, my daughter, he and his band in the middle of the night came and asked for me. I understood immediately what was happening. The very night before, I had seen it all in a dream. My heart missed a beat, but Huseyin Agha didn't hand me over to them. Then Memed fired a continuous shower of shots into the doorway, calling to Huseyin Agha: 'Bring your wife and family outside.' So Huseyin Agha took his wife and family outside in the middle of the night. What could the poor fellow do? He said I ought to surrender, but I didn't. I defended myself, firing from inside. Then they set fire to the house and it all went up in flames while three of them stood at the door, firing into the house. I couldn't leave by the doorway and could find no other escape as I rushed about in the fire and the smoke. Once or twice I was on the point of making a dash for it, but changed my mind, preferring to roast alive rather than fall into their hands. The flames were already surrounding me and I couldn't even see the door, enveloped as I was in a dark cloud of smoke that choked me.

I gave up all hope of escape. Death, I said, death . . . My children, my villagers! If I am no longer there to look after them, the villagers of my five villages will die of hunger, the poor people. Then, let me tell you, my clothes caught fire. In my desperation I threw myself on the ground and rolled there. But a voice reached my ears: 'Abdi Agha! Abdi Agha!' It was Huseyin Agha's wife searching for me. 'I'm here, Sister,' I called. 'Come,' she said. 'Come beneath this iron roof. Let me hide you in this quilt.' She rolled the quilt round me, a big quilt. How big am I, anyway? She took me under her arm and dashed out. That infidel still thinks I was burned alive and if it hadn't been for Huseyin Agha's wife, it would have happened. They'd have shot me if they'd seen me, but it never entered their minds that I could escape that way."

The woman's eyes were filled with tears. "It's a good thing they didn't suspect it, Agha," she said, "otherwise they would have killed you."

"After that they waited until Huseyin Agha's house was a pile of ashes. Then they wandered around the village and set fire to all the other houses, one by one. Huseyin Agha's house doesn't matter so much. They burnt it because of me, but Huseyin is a rich man. In a few days he'll build himself a new house. But why did these wretches, these infidels, have to wreak their vengeance on the other houses, those of poor people, leaving them homeless and naked when winter is coming on? What had the poor villagers done to you? My heart bleeds for those poor people!"

"This winter," said the woman, "they'll all shiver with cold, homeless, without food. But wait till this Vayvay village business is settled and Ali Safa Bey won't leave a single brigand alive on the mountains. He'll send telegram after telegram to Ankara, to Ismet Pasha. The infantry will come, not just policemen, and catch the brigands one by one and hang them. So they want to go around burning villages now? Abdi Agha, don't ask what we have endured at their hands all these years! Ali Safa Bey's earnings all go to the brigands, for their food and ammunition, but once this Vayvay business is settled . . ."

Ali Safa Bey was still pacing the room absent-mindedly. Hearing his wife he gave a start and seized her arm. "What were you saying to the Agha?" he asked angrily.

"It doesn't matter, Ali Safa Bey, I'm not a stranger," said Abdi Agha. "Your father was more than a brother to me."

"Yes," said the woman uneasily, "if I'd considered Abdi Agha as a stranger, would I have said such things to him?"

Ali Safa Bey looked at his wife as much as to say: "You've let the cat out of the bag." Then he said sharply: "Be off with you, to your room. I have private business to discuss with the Agha."

The woman rose guiltily and left the room.

Smiling, Ali Safa Bey sat down beside Abdi Agha and placed his hand on his knee. "I've been thinking a lot, Agha. This Memed cannot be beaten and swallowed whole like that. You're right to be afraid. A man who sets fire to a big village without fear of the Government or the villagers is to be feared. The police and villagers have now been out on the mountains for a week without finding him, though at least fifty men from Aktozlu village are on his trail, with the best shots from fifteen villages accompanying them. It won't be easy to get rid of such a man."

Abdi Agha's face kept changing colour, first red, then white. He seized Ali Safa Bey's hand. "You must do something to save me. The next thing you know, he may come down to the Chukurova and burn all the villages."

"It's difficult, Abdi Agha, but I'll try to deal with it," replied Ali Safa Bey. "However, there's something I must ask you to do for me too . . ."

"Anything you wish, Ali Safa Bey," said Abdi Agha, standing up in his excitement. "Ask for my life, son of my dear brother! I would gladly give it for you!"

Ali Safa Bey grasped his hand and made him sit down again. "Thank you, Agha. I knew you loved me. Please don't believe that I'm asking anything in return for this business. If that's what you think, then I'll say nothing now. I'll only attend to this Memed business without wanting anything in return for that."

"Of course not," exclaimed Abdi Agha, breathless with excitement. "I swear I don't believe you want anything in return, son of my dear brother, Ali Safa Bey!"

Ali Safa Bey sat quietly thinking for a while, then raised his head and looked into Abdi Agha's eyes. "You know, Agha, I too have all kinds of troubles. Thank goodness, these last years my

worries have been fewer but this business of the land at Vayvay
village robs me of my sleep."

"I know," replied Abdi Agha eagerly. "All the land of Vayvay
village used to belong to your father, who supplied the seed and
owned the crops. When he died, you were at school and the villagers of Vayvay came and settled there. The title-deeds you pos-
sess, haven't I told you before, comprise all the lands of Vayvay
village. I know this and so do all the people of my five villages and
of Aktozlu. Everyone knows it. Don't worry about it, Uncle Abdi
can take care of everything. In six months the fields of Vayvay will
be yours."

"Agha," repeated Ali Safa Bey, "be sure not to think I wanted
anything in return."

"Oh no," the Agha cried, shaking his head.

"Leave it to me. You'll see how well I can settle that kind of
business."

"The ammunition will be here from Syria in a week."

"And then?"

"I'll supply it to Kalayji's band."

"Abdi will do anything for you," said the Agha as he rose.

Ali Safa asked his guest to stay, but Abdi Agha realised that
there was no point in it. "Let's not be seen together too much," he
said. "Just in case . . ."

XVII

They travelled all night at top speed without halting. When dawn began to break they had reached the rocks of Akchacham, speaking not at all as they went. After climbing the rocks they were breathless and sat down and stared down at the Chukurova plain, all veiled in mists beneath the rising sun. Slowly the mists rose and the villages, the roads, the hills and the meandering shiny river appeared.

By the middle of the morning no trace of the mists was left. The plain lay before them with each tree and stone standing out and glittering in the sun. The fields, sown or fallow, black, red or grey, seemed to be almost within reach.

"Look, Memed," Jabbar was the first to break the silence. "Last night we were there."

Without turning Memed replied: "Yes, we were."

Jabbar was perplexed by Memed's listlessness. He tried to remain quiet but somehow could not refrain from talking. "Look at the foot of Anavarza! Those black spots are the marshes. Aktozlu village is still wreathed in smoke curling up into the sky. Can you see it?"

Memed hung his head. "I can see it," he mumbled.

Finally Jabbar burst out: "What are you thinking, Memed? Why are you so gloomy?"

"Did we burn him, that infidel? That's what I'm thinking, and about the people of Aktozlu. They didn't deserve it. I'm wondering what to do."

"Put it out of your mind," said Jabbar. "What's done is done."

"I suppose it is . . ."

"Let's get to Yellow Ummet's and stay there overnight. Tomorrow we'll go back to our mountains."

Memed's eyes were sparkling. "Do you know what else I was thinking, Jabbar?"

"No."

"I'll go to the Dikenli plateau. I'll gather all the elders of the five villages round me and tell them: 'There's no Abdi Agha any more. The oxen you have are yours. There'll be no more share-cropping for any Agha. The fields are yours too and you're free to sow as much as you like. As long as I'm on the mountain every-thing will be all right, but if I get shot you must look out for your-selves!' Then I'll take the villagers with me and make them set fire to the thistle fields. No one will ever plough the fields again with-out burning the thistles first."

With tears in his eyes Jabbar replied: "That's good! A village without an Agha. What each one earns will be his own . . ."

"Yes," smiled Memed.

"We'll keep armed watch over the land."

"There's one more thing we must do."

"What?" asked Jabbar, excitedly, wondering.

"I don't know, Brother. But certainly we must do something."

"What must we do?"

"Those poor people of Aktozlu did not deserve it. We must do something. They lost their homes because of us."

"I know, but what can we do?"

Jabbar stretched and stood up, his long legs and broad shoul-ders taut as steel wire. Memed also stretched and rose to his feet. His face was sun-tanned and he was so thin that he seemed to con-sist only of skin and bones, though there was no trace of weariness in him, only health, dignity and agility in his gait, his speech, his every movement. He had changed a great deal since he had become a brigand.

As he now rose, a yellow flash of light sparkled through his head again, growing stronger all the while. "Jabbar," he said, licking his lips in pleasant anticipation, "what each one earns will be his own. We'll be the watchmen. Each one will be master of his own land."

They came down the eastern slope of the cliffs, Memed ahead of Jabbar, following the narrow goat-track.

"Perhaps the police are after us," said Jabbar.

"Of course! That's why we'll go into the forest."

"That's a good idea!"

"Since I've thought of this matter of the fields, I don't want to die at all."

"To die?" Jabbar's voice quivered.

"To die," answered Memed. The image of Sergeant Rejep rose before his eyes. "That Sergeant Rejep," he continued, "I never understood what sort of man he was. Even while he was dying he wanted to help us. But he was pleased to see the village burn. I just couldn't understand him. He could be friendly with almost everyone. Yet he was everyone's enemy. When we set fire to the village he was pleased, but if we'd done the villagers a good turn he would probably have been just as pleased."

Jabbar was sniffing the tang of the pine-trees, sucking a sliver of pine-wood that he chewed endlessly. "I think so too," he said.

"I feel strange, as if my heart were ready to burst. My head's swimming. I don't know whether to laugh or cry. This business of the land, what will the villagers say of it, I wonder?"

"Who knows?"

A gentle breeze was blowing, bearing the smell of mountain springs and of mint.

They walked through the woods and over the rocks, and it was sunset by the time they reached the heights above Ummet's house.

"Once it's dark we'll go down to Ummet's," Memed suggested.

They sat down and rested for a while. The sun set and a dark curtain sank over the misty Chukurova. The sky was suddenly crowded with stars. One star in the east glittered like a mass of sparks. Every now and then a shooting star fell, disappearing behind a mountain ridge. When it was quite dark they rose and came at last to Yellow Ummet's house. In a low voice Memed called: "Brother Ummet!"

No sound came at first from within, then the door opened and Ummet appeared. He was speechless when he saw Memed and Jabbar.

"Greetings, Brother Ummet, what's new?" said Memed.

"Sh!" whispered Ummet. "Follow me. I'll lead you to the mountain. It's full here."

"We're dying of hunger," said Jabbar.

"Wait a while." Ummet went inside. Ten minutes later he came out again. "Now let's be off."

They followed Ummet up the slope of the mountain, leaping

from rock to rock as they made their way through the dark forest for over an hour.

Ummet was breathless when he stopped. "Curse you, Memed," he began. "What sort of nonsense is this? You've set fire to a whole village down in the Chukurova. How can you do such things? Even the great brigand, Gizik Duran, never dared anything of the kind. Why did you do it?"

"What's happening around here?" asked Jabbar. "Tell us, Ummet."

Ummet paused to recover his breath. "Nothing! What could there be? Armed men from nine or ten villages, perhaps a thousand all told, and a whole squadron of police, combing the mountainside for two days. They've looked for you in every squirrel's nest. If you fall into their hands they'll pound you into minced meat. A great village of the Chukurova! It's never happened before!" Ummet fell silent.

"Well, we did it." Memed's voice was muted.

Ummet had not heard all the details and felt it wiser to change the subject. "You did it . . ." he said and was silent again, unable to think of anything else to say. Then like lightning what was really on his mind shot out. "And that infidel, were you able to kill him?"

"He was burned to death in Huseyin Agha's house," answered Jabbar.

Ummet seemed relieved. "There's a hollow here like a cave," he explained. "No one ever comes this way. Stay here until they call the manhunt off. If you want to know about Lame Ali, he's in Deyirmenoluk. To-morrow I'll bring you food. Don't think of stirring from this place."

They came to the hollow. "Here, get inside. If your pursuers come here, don't think of escaping towards the Chukurova. That would be your undoing. Go up towards the peak. After the peak, you'll reach a stream, the Keshish. Good luck."

Ummet left them and they sat down at the mouth of the hollow, eating their food hurriedly.

"I'll go in and sleep," said Jabbar. "If you get very tired, wake me."

Memed did not reply. A yellow light was flashing through his mind, like a bright and sparkling stream flowing and twisting with a merry murmur. Everyone's field is his own. Whether Abdi is dead or alive, what does it matter? The thistle fields are blazing, the flames sweeping across the plain like a stream rushing downhill. The whirlwind, rolling a ball of fire ahead of it, rushes hither and thither in the darkness, a ball of fire that rolls over the plain for ten or fifteen days, perhaps a month. Then the fire dies out at last and all the plain of thistles is black as coal. Songs rise from the plain of thistles, from every corner a merry tune. The farmers are plough-ing, but without the thistles tearing at their legs, their toil made easier now. In Deyirmenoluk there will certainly be celebrations, a great feast. In a gay mood Durmush Ali dances his strange dance on one leg, the other leg raised high above his head as everyone laughs. If Sergeant Rejep could only hear this he would be over-joyed. But that can never be. He is now lying among the reeds of Anavarza.

Then something like fear seized Memed. More than a thousand villagers. Unbelievable! What would a thousand armed villagers want on these mountains? No one had ever seen anything like it. A village had been destroyed. What does it matter to him and Jabbar? And a squadron of police! Well, let them come! The fear in his heart vanished as easily as it had come. Now he felt ready to face fifteen hundred or two thousand armed men. He had more than three hundred rounds of ammunition, not one of which, he well knew, would be fired in vain.

Until morning he thought of all this and of Hatché, who was always present in his mind. The thought of her in prison tortured his heart. He wondered how so many misfortunes could beset one person all at once. It was not his habit to curse, but he now cursed angrily.

The sun had risen a quarter of its way when Jabbar awoke. "Why didn't you wake me, Memed?" he asked, his eyes dazzled by the light.

"I wasn't sleepy."

"Let's have a bite. Then you can sleep."

"All right."

Jabbar brought the bag and opened it. They still had some cheese and fresh onions. They wrapped their cheese and onion in thin layers of bread. Slowly they began to eat. A spring was bubbling from under a nearby rock; after eating they lay down on the ground to drink.

"I'll lie here in the sun," said Memed. He fell asleep as soon as his head touched the ground, like a child, innocently and peacefully. When the sun reached the peak of the mountain he awoke in a sweat. He stretched and washed his face in the spring. It refreshed him.

"Would Ummet play a trick on us?" asked Jabbar.

"He can't, but let's get away from here. Let's go to Deyirmenoluk."

"But if we fall upon an ambush?"

"Brigands don't fall upon an ambush. Brigands lay them!"

"I think we'd better wait for Ummet," said Jabbar.

"Let's wait then. We can't go without a word with him."

An hour later they heard a crackling sound among the bushes. They threw themselves behind the rocks. The sound grew louder and Ummet soon appeared from behind a pine-tree. When he saw that they had taken cover, he smiled and Memed smiled back.

"They've given up hope," said Ummet. "They're going back. I told them that brigands who raised hell yesterday in the plains of Anavarza can't be up on Akarja mountain to-day."

"You spoke well, Brother Ummet," said Jabbar.

Ummet graspedMemed's hand. "I love you like my own soul, Brother. May all my family serve you."

"We burned him, burned him alive," boasted Jabbar.

Ummet did not reply.

"Brother Ummet," asked Memed, "if everybody owned the land they cultivated, how would it be?"

"Fine!"

"If the oxen on each man's plough were his own?" Memed continued.

"There could be nothing better in the world."

"If we burn the thistle fields thoroughly and then plough, how would that be, Brother Ummet?"

"Very good."

Jabbar took the bag of bread which Ummet had brought and bound it to his belt.

"Good health to you, Ummet," they said.

"If you get into a tight corner, come to me. I'll look after you like a brother. I've taken a liking to you, Memed."

"Thanks!"

They set forth, Memed going ahead. Suddenly he halted. Jabbar caught up with him and halted too. With his left hand Memed squeezed the hand with which Jabbar was holding his rifle. They looked into each other's eyes.

"Brother," exclaimed Memed, "I'm so pleased about this business . . . !"

"So am I."

XVIII

The village of Karadut is situated on the banks of the River Jeyhan. Before the village, the river spreads out in the plain, much broader, like a lake, almost stagnant. In this part of the country the Jeyhan changes its bed every ten or fifteen years, striking out to left or right. Wherever it goes it deposits abundant silt, and that is why the Chukurova is more fertile here than in other places. The soil around Karadut village is worth a fortune.

The last farm Ali Safa Bey had wrested from its owners was on the borders of Karadut. More than half the land of the farm had already come to him when the Armenians had been driven out. The rest he had obtained from the villagers of Karadut by force or by guile. The struggle between Ali Safa Bey and the villagers of Karadut had been going on for years. There had even been some shooting. How Ali Safa Bey had obtained possession of the fertile lands of Karadut would make a long story, revealing Ali Safa Bey's boundless cunning, greed and guile in becoming owner of even a small piece of land.

Yellow Bekir was from Karadut, the only man there who knew how to read and write. He had already been known for his intelligence when he had gone to school in the town. Brave, intrepid and honest, never uttering a lie, he was tall and slim, with a smiling face, clean and frank as a child's. Bekir was an obstacle in Ali Safa Bey's path. If it had not been for him, Ali Safa would long ago have swallowed up all the fields of Karadut village among his own land-holdings. But Bekir stood up against him like a mountain, protecting his own fields and those of the other villagers. He was different and the other villagers were all devoted to him and did exactly as he told them. For years Ali Safa had not been able to do Bekir any harm, and his lawsuits against the villagers of Karadut dragged on inconclusively.

The brigand chief Kalayji Osman was Bekir Effendi's cousin, a good-for-nothing vagabond who was also Ali Safa's man and brought him all the news from the village. The villagers hated Osman who had finally gone to work on Ali Safa's farms, stealing the villagers' cattle, setting fire to their crops, causing all kinds of damage. The villagers were desperate, but there was nothing they could do about it. On the one hand they respected Bekir Effendi; on the other they feared Ali Safa Bey. Besides, they preferred not to get involved in a life-and-death struggle with Kalayji Osman.

On the day of Bekir Effendi's wedding the drums were beating and the pipes blowing for all they were worth. The whole village was in a stir, with everyone dancing and singing. Every house in the village was decked as if the wedding were taking place there. The village's own dear Bekir Effendi was getting married.

On the last night of the wedding celebrations, in front of the wedding house, three shots were suddenly fired, causing a panic. Bekir Effendi had been killed and it was Kalayji who had fired and then slipped off under cover of darkness and taken to the mountains. The bride's hands were red with henna, the marriage not yet consummated.

For Kalayji to shoot Bekir Effendi on his wedding night was something that nobody would have expected. The villagers were unanimous in condemning and cursing the man who had killed their beloved Bekir Effendi.

None knew Kalayji's real motive. Some said that Ali Safa Bey had put him up to it and given him money to kill Bekir Effendi. Others said that Kalayji was in love with the girl and couldn't bear to see Bekir Effendi marry her. Others again said that he was a good-for-nothing and had just got the idea into his head, pulled out his gun and fired so that people would talk about him with awe, repeating how Kalayji had killed Bekir Effendi. Still others, who knew Kalayji Osman well, said that ever since childhood he had hated Bekir Effendi and was helping Ali Safa Bey only because the other villagers had always loved Bekir Effendi and disliked him. Bekir's wedding, with such celebrations and joy in the village, had been too much for Kalayji Osman and he had killed his cousin out of spite and envy. However, there had been no particular reason for

Kalayji to shoot Bekir Effendi. All these various reasons had played some part in Kalayji's mind.

After that Kalayji became a weapon of terror and intimidation in the hands of Ali Safa Bey. The most ruthless brigands roaming on the mountains joined his band. Like a plague, a curse, he fell upon all the poor people of the Chukurova who ever resisted Ali Safa Bey.

But even after the shooting of Bekir Effendi Ali Safa was still unable to wrest another yard of land from the villagers of Karadut. Kalayji could no longer enter the village. For all his shooting, the villagers of Karadut did not look upon Kalayji as a brigand or even as a man, and were utterly unafraid of him.

Then the whole Chukurova was suddenly astir with the name of Slim Memed on the lips of all. After he had burned Aktozlu Memed became a legend. Countless villagers flocked to see Aktozlu. Among themselves and to all those who came from neighbouring villages, the women and children of Aktozlu said: "He's a giant of a man. He took a huge pine log in his hand and went from house to house, setting each on fire. He rushed through the village like a whirlwind. If the fire of one of the houses subsided, he would dart forward and set it alight again. You should have seen this Memed! His eyes flashed in the darkness of the night. One moment he was tall as a poplar, then small again. Bullets can't harm him. We kept firing at him, but it was all of no avail."

In all the other villages of the Chukurova varying versions of the event and new tales of Memed's feats were being repeated.

When Ali Safa Bey met Kalayji at their usual meeting-place in the cave of the Teacher's Vineyard and suggested that he should get rid of Memed, Kalayji was very pleased but refrained from showing his pleasure. "That'll be hard work, Ali Safa Bey," he said. "It'll be difficult to cope with a man like that."

"Memed's name has become a legend in the Chukurova. If you kill him you'll become famous throughout the country. What an opportunity! If you destroy Memed, all the Chukurova will be ours."

"It's difficult," Kalayji repeated.

"Don't be afraid," said Ali Safa, slapping him on the shoulder. "I'll make it worth while for you."

"We'll see. Perhaps we'll find a way."

"You must. However brave he is, he's still a greenhorn and doesn't know the ways of the mountain. You only have to lay an ambush for him."

"We'll see."

Kalayji left Ali Safa Bey, returned to his men and said: "We've a job to do. It'll bring us good money, easy money too."

His men stood there waiting for instructions.

"There's an upstart, the one they call Slim Memed, who set fire to Aktozlu village. We have to get him out of the way."

Kalayji's band felt that to kill Memed would be as easy a job as eating or drinking. Since he had taken to the mountain, Kalayji had already disposed of three rival bands. It was said that he had now killed more than forty men, including Bekir Efendi.

Kalayji Osman was a short man, with strange, death-like, frozen eyes, green as a serpent's skin. His sparse beard, stiff as the prickles of a hedgehog, was yellow. In spite of his broad shoulders he was slim, and his neck was as red as if it had been roasted over a fire. He wore blue trousers with silver-embroidered pockets and cartridge-belts all over his chest, some of them even fastened round his legs, silver-mounted and glittering. Pistols with mother-of-pearl handles, daggers and knives were scattered everywhere on his person. Field-glasses hung from his neck. From beneath his purple fez, yellow locks fell over his brow.

Neither audacious nor brave, only cunning, he never fought face to face with anyone and always struck from behind. In his many ventures he may have seemed to be Ali Safa Bey's tool, but Ali Safa Bey was also Kalayji's tool. So far Kalayji had only come up against the police once or twice. As soon as the police set out on his trail, Ali Safa Bey's network of messengers would immediately warn him. Kalayji spent his winters in Ali Safa Bey's house, in a special room built for him, leading a luxurious life. Only when he tired of staying in that room would he go off to the mountains and rejoin his band, which also had quite comfortable winter quarters. When the snows set in they would settle in some inaccessible mountain village forcing the villagers to regale them with their choicest lambs, while they themselves would relax till spring. All this freedom and comfort they owed to Ali Safa Bey; they were ready to do anything he ordered.

"Does anyone among us know Slim Memed?" asked Kalayji.

Horali was leaning against a tree, his eyes closed. He looked up. "I know him well, Agha. We were together in Durdu's band."

"Then come and sit by me, Horali!" called Kalayji.

Horali rose and came over. Kalayji took him by both shoulders and shook him. "Tell us, what sort of man is this Slim Memed."

Horali swallowed and moistened his lips before speaking. "Well, at first glance he's not much to look at. Small, thin, with a big head and wide-set eyes, he looks about twenty, a boy who always seems to be thinking. Anyone who hasn't seen him shoot or been beside him in a skirmish cannot understand his character. But can he shoot! The day he joined our band—and you know what a good marksman Durdu was—Memed proved himself a better shot than Durdu. Now he can shoot through the eye of a needle. He's very bold. In that quarrel by the nomads' tents he could have killed Durdu and all of us. But he didn't. If he hadn't been that kind of man, would Durdu have put up with this affront? Durdu was afraid of him. . . ."

"That's praise, Horali! Has Memed hired you to sing his praises?"

"No," answered Horali. "You asked me to explain and I've told you what I've seen with my own eyes. Memed is that sort of man."

Kalayji sat down, held his head between his hands and began to ponder. A couple of hours later he called Horali again. "Listen carefully, Horali. Does Memed trust you?"

"No, he doesn't."

"Why?"

"When he defied Durdu, I sided with Durdu. In any case he doesn't trust anyone, not even Jabbar, who's with him now."

"You talk of that greenhorn as if he were as experienced a brigand as Gizik Duran," Kalayji taunted.

"I know him."

"You don't," Kalayji replied abruptly. When Kalayji was angry he would pick at his nose and pluck hairs from his nostrils. He was doing so now. "So you want to make out that this Memed doesn't let himself be trapped and doesn't ever get shot?"

"That's not what I mean. There's no man who doesn't fall into a trap, and Memed is still green. It depends on the kind of trap."

"I'm relying on you, Horali. You're a resourceful fellow. There's no more experienced brigand than you left on these mountains. I'm leaving this job to you!"

"All right, Agha, but there are two of them."

"Who's the other?" asked Kalayji.

"Jabbar."

"Jabbar's a fine brave lad."

"What can we do? He'll have to go with Memed."

"Let him go," answered Kalayji. Suddenly he added: "Listen, Brother Horali, we'll find out first where they are. Then you'll go to Memed and invite him to join our band. If that doesn't work, we'll find some other way."

"Perhaps he'll accept. Then we'll settle the business easily. If he doesn't suspect a trap, he might come."

"Is that agreed?"

"All right."

"Can we find his lair easily? Have they any definite hide-out?"

"He's a greenhorn," smiled Horali. "It'll be easy to find him."

XIX

It was very dark, with only a few stars twinkling feebly, though dawn was approaching. For days, running, hiding, hungry, they had passed through forests, over rocks, up and down mountains, exhausted, both of them bent double beneath the load of ammunition supplies on their backs, so weak that their hands trembled, as if from cold.

Suddenly there was an uproar and Jabbar started. "What's that?" he asked in astonishment.

"The spring," answered Memed. "You know, when we first came . . ."

"I remember. Let's rest for a while."

"No." Paying no heed to his own weariness, Memed would not stop anywhere but plodded steadily on. "How far do we still have to go, Brother Jabbar?" he asked, pointing. "See, we're nearly there." He took a deep breath and stopped, then started again. "We'll rest when we get to the village. We must reach it before dawn. Yes, Jabbar, we can't stop now, after coming so far. Soon we'll be in the village, won't we?"

"Agreed," answered Jabbar.

Memed did not speak again. As they approached the village he began to walk so rapidly that Jabbar needed all his strength to keep up with him.

Thin rays of light were appearing in the east as they entered the village, greeted by the barking of dogs. Memed paid no heed to them. Walking ahead at a brisk pace, he soon came to Durmush Ali's house.

"Uncle Durmush Ali!" he called.

Durmush Ali answered at once: "Is that you, Memed?"

"Yes."

"I'm coming. Welcome, lad. What have you done with that infidel? We heard you'd burned Aktozlu village and roasted Abdi Agha alive."

When the door was opened Memed asked excitedly: "Who brought you this news? Has all the village heard?"

"We've all heard, lad. You did well. We were all glad. One should not rejoice at anyone's death, but he deserved it. Even his wife was pleased. 'He's got what he deserved,' she said, without shedding a single tear. Come in, lads." Then he asked anxiously: "Your other friend, what have you done with the old man?"

"Don't ask," Memed sighed.

"God have mercy on him," said Durmush Ali. "I'll light the fire for you straight away. You're sure to be hungry."

Memed had not forgotten his question. "Uncle Durmush Ali, who brought you the news?"

"Don't you know, lad? Don't you know that Lame Ali has become Abdi Agha's man? It was he who brought the news. He stood outside Aktozlu and watched. When the village was all on fire he went and brought Abdi's bones from inside the house. Even the bones were charred."

"So Lame Ali has become his man?"

Durmush Ali was stirring the glowing embers from under the ashes on the hearth. "That's right, lad," he said gloomily. "Man is a base creature, suckled on raw milk . . ."

Memed laughed.

"Don't you believe it?" asked Durmush Ali, looking into his eyes.

"Uncle, how quickly you forget!"

"Eh, when you get old . . ."

"It doesn't matter," said Memed, stroking the other's shoulder. He sat down by the fire, Jabbar beside him.

Puffing and blowing, Durmush Ali kindled the fire. "Well," he laughed. "What other news do you bring?"

"Nothing," said Memed.

The first rays of morning soon began to come through the window, slowly lighting up the room.

Durmush Ali's old wife was fluttering about Memed in a fever of excitement. "Roasted, eh?" she kept repeating. "What a good deed that was! Say it again, my Memed. So he was roasted alive, was he?" She took the soup off the fire, melted the butter and poured it sizzling into the soup, filling the house with the smell of butter. "Roasted, eh? They say his bones were charred too. Good! They say Aktozlu was burned to ashes. Let it be!" She set the table in front of them, filled a big bowl of soup and placed it in the middle. But her tongue never stopped wagging and she cackled endlessly. "Roasted, eh? Roasted alive!"

The spoon lay idle in Memed's hand. He seemed to be unable to dip it into the soup or to put it down on the table. Jabbar noticed this, their eyes met and they remained silent.

Durmush Ali stopped eating and began to stare at them anxiously. Then Memed suddenly dipped his spoon into the soup and ate hurriedly. A sharp point of light had come back into his eyes. He seemed to be under a spell; his head swimming. The yellow sparks flashed through his mind. A fire, tall as a mountain, was rolling across the thistle fields, on and on.

He raised his head and sat upright. His sun-tanned face and his eyes were bathed in light. "Listen, Uncle Durmush Ali," he said.

Durmush Ali's eyes questioned. "What do you want to say, my son?"

"That infidel's dead now," Memed began in a trembling voice, then fell silent.

They cleared away the table and stirred the fire. The children of the house sat in a corner, staring at Memed with wide-open eyes. Durmush Ali was still waiting for Memed to continue. When Memed had said, "He's dead now," it was clear he was about to announce something important.

"Well, go on," cried Durmush Ali, unable to contain himself any longer.

"I have an idea," Memed began slowly. "I don't know what you'll say about it." He was silent again, then spoke very fast: "The fields of this village and of the four other villages, all the fields . . . However much each man sows, all of it to each . . . You know the rest. I'll keep watch over the villages with my rifle and we'll burn the thistle fields. . . ."

"Eh, Memed," said Durmush Ali, astonished. "God bless your eyes, but talk a little more slowly. I didn't understand anything."

Memed bridled his excitement. "What I mean is this. These lands don't belong to that infidel." Durmush Ali reflected. He

257

scratched his head as Memed explained: "These fields are everybody's. That infidel didn't create them, but five villages worked like slaves for him. There are no Aghas in the Chukurova. You should listen to Corporal Hasan!"

"There was a time, long ago, when these fields were everybody's," Durmush Ali agreed, "before this infidel's father appeared. He stopped at nothing to wrest the land from us. Before that, everybody cultivated his own land just as he liked."

"That's it," Memed burst out. "It'll be like that again."

"If only it were," murmured Durmush Ali, his eyes full of tears.

"It will. I want to ask a favour of you. Send word to the notables of the five villages to come here. I'll speak to them and distribute the fields. They'll be saved from slavery. What everyone sows he can then reap as his own. The oxen they have shall be their own."

"If only . . ." exclaimed Durmush Ali.

"Send word for them to come."

Durmush Ali's wife, leaning against the pole that bore the roof, had been watching all this as she worked her hand-spindle. The spindle now fell from her hand and her arms hung idle. A spider was spinning its web on the sooty wall. The old woman suddenly pulled herself together and threw herself on Memed. "God bless you, lad, is this true? Will you really do it?" she asked, kissing his hands over and over again. "We shan't give up half or two-thirds of our crops to anyone?"

"Slavery is ended," declared Memed decisively. "Until I die I'll watch over the fields, with my rifle in my hands . . ."

The woman let go of Memed's hands and retired into a dark corner. There she sat weeping quietly for a long time.

Durmush Ali went out, hesitated, then came in again. He stared at Memed, whose face looked like a rock. "Whom shall I call, son?" he inquired.

"Whoever you think has enough sense."

"All right . . ."

He went to Hüsük's house and explained the matter to him. Hüsük said nothing. He too was hesitant. Then they went round to all the men in the village. Some were pleased at first, then began to ponder. The villagers were at a loss.

People gathered in little groups all over the village and talked fearfully, without daring to look into each other's eyes. An excited crowd shifted quietly from house to house, filled with hope. After a while the crowd gathered by Durmush Ali's door, waiting without stirring. Even the infants held their peace.

Memed heard the crowd outside and asked Durmush Ali's wife: "What's going on outside, Mother?"

Wiping her tears, she answered: "All the village is gathered outside. Their eyes are fixed on this door. I don't know . . ."

She went outside and all eyes were focused on her. She felt crushed beneath the weight of their collective gaze and was angry. "What do you want?" she shouted. "Why are you all here?"

Not a sound came from the crowd.

"Why are you silent? If it's Memed you want to see, he's inside."

Still no one uttered a word.

"Perish the lot of you, why do you stand like that? Why are you all there as mournful as if there had been a funeral in each one of your homes? Look at them! Those are supposed to be men!" She turned to the women. "And you, you call these creatures men and take them in your arms and go to bed with them! What kind of women are you? Why do you stand there like blocks of stone? Play, laugh, make merry!"

The crowd seemed frozen.

"May God perish you! Haven't you heard? Memed has roasted Abdi Agha alive!"

A wave of excitement passed through the crowd.

"Roasted him . . . Burned down Aktozlu village, from end to end. Haven't you heard? He came to us yesterday. He's inside now. Haven't you heard? There's an end to your working only to make Abdi Agha richer. The fields are ours! Roasted alive! The oxen are ours too! Roasted, and Aktozlu village destroyed!"

The crowd swayed. A murmur arose, then grew louder. Everyone began to speak at once. The village was filled with an incredible roar. The dogs barked, the cocks crowed, hens scurried hither and thither, the children snivelled. In the stables the donkeys brayed, the horses neighed. Never in all its existence had such a tumult been heard in Deyirmenoluk.

Soon the village was filled with a cloud of dust and the merriment began as drums and pipes played and the people sang Memed's praise.

"Our Slim Memed!"

"It was clear from his childhood he would become a man like this!"

"And the oxen will be ours!"

"The men will sow as much of the fields as they wish. There's no more giving up two-thirds of the crops. No more hunger in the winter!"

"No more begging like dogs."

"Our Slim Memed!"

"No more selling the cows . . ."

"No tyranny!"

"Everybody can go where he wishes."

"Everyone can have guests in his own home."

"Everyone his own master!"

"Our Slim Memed!"

"Abdi Agha roasted alive, and a great village destroyed!"

"Roasted, roasted!"

"The Chukurova is quaking with fear."

"Our Slim Memed!"

"Roasted! Roasted!"

"He'll fetch Hatché out of her prison and all five villages will celebrate their wedding!"

"Our Slim Memed!"

For two days and nights the drums and pipes played ceaselessly. The other four villages were also celebrating and the deep booming of the drums resounded there too. At night all the plain of thistles was filled with lights. A mad gaiety poured forth, seeming to bring to life even the rocks, earth, water and trees.

The notables of the five villages were at Durmush Ali's house with Memed. They stared at him, some doubtfully, some fearfully, some gratefully, some fondly.

On the afternoon of the second day Memed expounded his plan. "Aghas, now is the time for ploughing. I have something to suggest."

"Yes, Memed."

"Before ploughing the fields, why don't you think first of burning the thistles?"

"We never thought of it!"

"Wouldn't the ploughing be much easier?"

"Of course," they replied.

As Memed rose, all heads were raised towards him. "We'll set fire to the thistle fields," he said. "After that we'll plough them." He girded his rifle and cartridge-belts and went out, followed by the notables.

"To the thistle fields," roared Mistik. "With drums and pipes to the thistle fields . . ."

"The oxen won't get wounded by the thistles any more," said Durmush Ali.

Solemnly Memed walked ahead, out of the village, his head high, his eyes half closed, behind him Jabbar, then the villagers. Women and children had climbed on to the roofs to see him. The drums and pipes were silent. Not a sound could be heard.

They plunged into the thistle fields. Autumn winds were blowing gently down from the mountains on to the Dikenli plain. Memed stopped and the villagers stopped too, waiting for a sign from him as he stood there. He turned his head. The villagers behind him were still waiting.

Before him stretched the plain of thistles, milk-white as if it had been snowing. A rustling arose from the millions of tiny white snails clinging to the thistles and weighing the stems down to the ground.

"Jabbar," called Memed softly.

Jabbar cut his way through the thistles and came to his side. "Yes, Brother?"

"Why couldn't they have first burned the thistle fields and then ploughed, when I used to drive the oxen?"

Jabbar smiled.

The crowd stirred. Some of them began to cut down the thistles and stack them in a heap. Others joined them and soon there was a great mound of thistles that steadily grew into a small hill. Durmush Ali leaped forward. "That's enough," he shouted excitedly. He took a piece of resin-wood from his pocket, lit it and thrust it into the mound of dried thistles, which slowly caught fire. Soon the whole mound was wrapped in whirling flames, fanned this way and that by the wind. The villagers withdrew in a semi-circle and stared at the fire leaping from the mound to the plain and running ahead of the wind. Then the drums and pipes began to play. Songs, shouts and gaiety spread across the plain as the crowd followed the flames, dancing in groups. Jabbar was firing shots at the sky.

But Memed waited silently in the middle of the thistle fields until sunset.

The wind was driving a great ball of fire across the plain at full speed. Wherever the ball of fire passed, the ground was coal-black. The fire was following the sun towards the west. The thistles crackled as they burned, singing like birds ahead of the fire.

Gravely, Memed walked back towards the village. All dressed in greens, reds, and blues, the women and children who had been making merry on the thistle fields followed him.

All night, until the morning, the fire raged across the Dikenli plain from Kinalitepe to Yildiztepe, from the spring to Kabaaghach and on to the other villages, as far as Churukchinar. A great brightness enveloped the plateau. Then a huge ball of fire appeared on the peak of Alidagh, scattering sparks like the morning star. The peak of Alidagh was as bright as day. The villagers were awed at this sight, so was Memed. It was the first time a fire had ever been seen on the peak of Alidagh.

The seven who had borne false witness against Hatché now came and stood in front of Memed, not daring to speak.

"Speak up," said Memed.

"Forgive us, Memed . . ." they muttered.

"You're forgiven."

"We were forced to do it, Memed."

"I know."

With heads bowed and tears in their eyes the seven withdrew silently.

All night Memed had been too happy, too exhilarated, and also too sad for Hatché, ever to sleep.

A bright, fresh, clean, white day, light as a feather, dawned over Deyirmenoluk. The village was in a sparkling dream, its trees were bathed in light, the thistle fields still burning. The white plain had turned black from one end to the other.

News came that Lame Ali had been seen on the road, on his way to the village. Memed waited for him eagerly. Lame Ali arrived, dragging his lame foot wearily. He stood before Memed. out of breath, sweating and exhausted.

"Come, Ali Agha, come!" smiled Memed as he went up to him, held his hand and patted it affectionately.

Ali did not speak. His face was ashen and creased. In a few days he seemed to have aged fifteen years.

Memed could bear it no longer. "Why are you so gloomy, Ali Agha?" he asked.

"Don't ask," moaned Lame Ali dismally.

Memed realised that he was trying to conceal something with this "Don't ask," uttered in such deep weariness, sorrow and anger. "Is there something wrong?" Memed asked, wide-eyed.

Still out of breath and with trembling hands, Ali repeated: "Don't ask! Don't ask . . ."

"Don't frighten me, Ali Agha!"

"What's done is done. But it nearly killed me," he moaned.

"Speak!" said Memed, leaning towards him.

"The infidel," said Ali. "He . . ."

"Well?"

"He's escaped!"

"What!"

Memed was speechless. He swayed, his eyes saw only darkness, then his whole body became tense.

"I've spoken to him," Lame Ali explained. "Now he's taken a house in town and will settle there. He sent me to his house here."

Seeing Memed now in such a state, Jabbar was afraid. "It doesn't matter, Brother Memed," he said, trying to console him. "He won't escape from our hands. He can't. If not to-day, then to-morrow . . ."

Durmush Ali's wife uttered a scream. She went into a dark corner, wailing and beating her bosom. "Oh, my troubled head! Did this have to happen too?"

"What are you worrying about?" asked Jabbar. "Whatever happens, he'll never dare to set foot in this village again. The fields are yours and the oxen too. As long as we're alive . . ."

But she continued to wail.

Soon the villagers had all heard the bad news. Not a soul remained in the alleys as they shut themselves up in their houses. The dogs stopped barking and the cocks crowing. It was as if there were no longer a single living creature in the village, as if all the people who a few hours before had been so noisy and gay had gone off to another land.

Silence reigned everywhere until the middle of the afternoon. Durmush Ali had collapsed, his head buried between his old shoulders. His wife crouched in a corner, her cheeks pale and sunken. Memed, his forehead wrinkled, sat thinking, his head resting on his gun.

Late in the afternoon there was a slight stir in the village. First a cock climbed on to a dung heap, flapped its wings and crowed. The cock's green, red and purple feathers gleamed in the light. Then the dogs started barking again. Finally the people came out of their houses and began to gather in little groups. A murmur ran from end to end of the village.

"He's come down from his mountain and thinks he's become a man, that Memed!"

"That pauper Ibrahim's son!"

"He's become a man and is distributing our Abdi Agha's fields!"

"Look at the size of him!"

"The idiot!"

"He's become a brigand and burns villages!"

"He can't even carry a gun . . ."

"He's become a brigand and wants to hand out our Agha's fields and oxen as if they were his own!"

"He used to fawn at our Agha's door like a dog."

"That pauper Ibrahim's good-for-nothing son . . ."

"Strutting about arrogantly, the good-for-nothing!"

"And that poor girl rotting in prison because of him!"

"He's burnt all the thistles so that we can plough without hurting our legs!"

"Coming to this village and boasting that he'd killed Abdi Agha."

"Our Agha would kill a hundred dogs like him with one shot!"

"Our Agha!"

Afterwards all the villagers crowded into the courtyard of Abdi Agha's house and congratulated his wives and children.

The murmuring lasted till midnight. More than half the villagers supported Memed and lamented Abdi Agha's escape, but kept to their houses. Durmush Ali was like a corpse. His wife was ill and had taken to her bed, not uttering a word. Memed, too, had kept silent ever since he had received the bad news. Only Jabbar moved around, talking endlessly, trying to convince the villagers. "Abdi Agha won't be able to set foot in this village again. Don't be afraid. In any case, he'll die soon, you can be sure of that. I swear he'll die, don't worry, he'll die, I tell you!"

But no one listened to him.

They left Durmush Ali's house before daybreak. Memed could scarcely raise his head. It was bowed, almost lifeless. Jabbar walked slowly beside him, equally silent. As they were leaving the village one or two dogs barked after them. Memed paid no attention and Jabbar threw stones at them.

The thistle fields had stopped smouldering. The cracked earth was covered with black ashes. Memed stood there tensely on the edge of the wide plain, Jabbar not daring to say anything to him. He waited, but Memed did not move, so he went and sat down on a rock, with his rifle in his lap. The sun rose. Memed was still standing motionless, his shadow stretching out towards the village. It was mid-morning, but still Memed had not moved. Jabbar could bear it no longer. He went up to Memed and shook him.

"Don't grieve, Brother Memed," he said. Memed suddenly stirred. His eyes blinked as if he had been asleep.

"Don't worry, Memed. Men are base creatures, suckled on raw milk. As for him, we'll get him sooner or later."

Memed gritted his teeth. "Sooner or later . . ." he exclaimed, the words coming sharp as a knife. Then he stared across the broad burned plain into the distance.

XX

The deep green of the myrtles reminds one of a julep that makes people drunk, but madly drunk. The slopes of Sulemish are covered with myrtles, clinging to the ground in thick clusters. If you follow the goat-tracks you can detect their sharp, heavy perfume that brings on drowsiness, laziness.

The lower slopes of Sulemish end in a high valley. Not a stone can be found there. The soft earth is as fine as sand, covered from end to end with pomegranate trees. In spring the red flowers blossom and the whole valley is like a blanket of red flowers. They call it the Pomegranate Garden.

On the lower side of the Pomegranate Garden flows the Savrun, a river that bubbles forth from a spring far up in the Taurus Mountains, at first as a tiny wild stream that leaps foaming from rock to rock. But here it rests a while, spread over the plateau like a lake, only ankle-deep, with small islands of silt and sand scattered there. Most of them are half bare. Warm-smelling agnus-castus trees and purple-trunked tamarisks with their needle-shaped leaves also stand there all alone, and oleanders with big pink flowers by the water's edge.

For years melon and water-melon had been cultivated on Bostanjik, one of the largest of these islands. Memo the Kurd had rented it from one of the great land-owning Aghas. The finest melons and water-melons of the Chukurova grew on Memo's Bostanjik.

Horali was the watchman of this garden. His hut, built on piies above the ground, was surrounded with melon rinds that could hardly be seen for the bees swarming over them. The bees were of all kinds, honey-bees, black bees, blue bees with their colour shining in the sun and turning green. The heaps of melon rinds were proof of Horali's generous nature. No one could come to Bostanjik and leave without having eaten melon.

Horali's origins were unknown, but he fitted into Bostanjik and seemed to be just as much at home on this island as the tamarisks.

No one knew whether Horali liked Bostanjik or not. Did the tamarisks growing on Bostanjik like it? It was the same with Horali.

He made a good livelihood there and Bostanjik had its pleasant sides. While he was sweating through the hot summer nights, the Savrun would flow gurgling under his hut and the pebbles would shine in the moonlight.

One spring day the labourers came back to till the garden on Bostanjik, but what did they find? There was no more Bostanjik, only water. The flood had washed the island away. After that Horali disappeared for a year or two. In those days brigandage was a kind of fashion. A man would take to the mountains at the slightest provocation. Then it was suddenly heard that Horali had joined the brigands and all were astounded.

This same Horali was now searching high and low for Slim Memed in order to lead him into an ambush. But something was troubling him, grief in the secret places of his heart. He did not know why.

First he asked the villagers of Deyirmenoluk. "His lair is on Alidagh," they said. Horali wandered fruitlessly about Alidagh for several days without finding Memed. Wherever he asked, the villagers he approached stared stupidly into his face and said: "Memed? We haven't seen him; we don't know him."

Every mountain villager had heard of Memed and loved him. People who knew where he was hiding would never tell. Such had always been the custom of the mountain peasants. It was never easy to find the lair of a brigand who was popular among them.

But Horali did not give up hope. He wandered from mountain to mountain, searched and searched, then found a new approach. "I'm from Slim Memed's band," he would say to those he met. "After the village was destroyed I became separated from them."

Slowly this trick began to work, and Horali finally discovered that Memed had established his base at the source of the Savrun, but that he sometimes stayed in the village, spending the night there.

The region near the source of the Savrun was full of little groups of brigands and robbers. Memed did not mix with them or talk to anyone and the ill-will and envy that other brigands bore him increased. But they were also afraid of him. Memed stalked around the source of the Savrun like a dark fear.

If he did not sleep in the village he would make his bed on a branch of one of the big pines while Jabbar kept watch below. When his turn came to watch, he would not climb down but sit up there with his gun in his lap. He had arranged his tree like a hut, making it comfortable. He used to say to Jabbar: "Come and see." But Jabbar refused ever to climb the tree.

One of the villagers who used to give shelter to Memed brought Horali to the foot of the great pine. Jabbar was glad to see him and embraced him. "It's good that your wound has healed, Horali. Where are you now?"

Memed climbed down at once to greet him. "Welcome, Brother Horali! We've often wondered where you were."

Horali was taken aback at this warm reception. "There's nothing to say," he murmured, not knowing how to explain his presence. "Nothing!" he repeated, then pulled himself together. "I'm with Kalayji's band now. I joined them after Durdu was killed. We wander around, that's all. What else do you expect? What's written is written. It's fate. . . ."

"What's up, Horali?" asked Jabbar, laughing. "You look worried. What's the matter?"

"Don't ask," sighed Horali.

They squatted down, leaning their backs against the tree.

"Where's Sergeant Rejep?" asked Horali, his eyes searching all round.

"May you live long. He's dead," answered Jabbar. "That wound finished him."

"Poor Sergeant Rejep," exclaimed Horali sadly. "Such is the way of this world!"

"A false deceitful world," burst out Jabbar angrily. "The black earth is where it all ends."

Memed had been musing. Suddenly he asked: "We heard

about Durdu's end, but tell us about it yourself. You were there."

"Don't ask, Brother Memed. Don't ask," moaned Horali. "It was a pity for all those fine lads, a great pity."

"Well, come on, tell us, Horali," said Jabbar. "Don't leave us in suspense."

"After you left us Durdu became more and more enraged and we began to kidnap women from the villages, to carry them off to the mountains and to have a good time with them."

"When a brigand does that it's the end," commented Jabbar. "There's no escape for him."

"If it were only that!"

"What else?" demanded Jabbar.

"He began to tax the villages. Every village, every house, had to pay him a tax, according to their riches or poverty. . . ."

"What next!" exclaimed Jabbar.

"There's more," said Horali.

"What?" asked Jabbar, his eyes opening wide.

"He would sit over the pass at Deveboyun and, whatever living creature passed, would shoot the right leg of each animal and the right arm of each man."

"Completely mad!" cried Jabbar.

"He shot the right arm of over a hundred people. Some of them died."

"And then?" asked Jabbar.

"Then, let me tell you, Brother. One day we went into Aksoyut village. We made the women come out of the houses and brought them into the square, all of them, even the old women, and we forced them to dance. Poor things, they huddled together like sheep, trembling all over. Durdu terrified one or two of them into doing the belly-dance a little. After that Durdu started cursing the village, cursing endlessly. The men were shut up in their houses and couldn't come out. All of a sudden, I still can't figure out how it happened, everything was lost in a cloud of dust. Durdu had disappeared and I found myself on the roof of a house. I had lost my gun. For half an hour that cloud of dust concealed everything. Then it cleared up and the crowd was seething down below, a tired, death-like crowd. I climbed down from the roof, shaking with fear. Why did I climb down? I still don't know why. I stood there and watched the crowd as it scattered slowly. No one saw me. Perhaps they saw me and took no notice. They had no energy left. There were no corpses anywhere but Durdu and the other bandits had simply been trampled to death, with no trace of them except a few rifle-stocks in the dust and one of Durdu's boots. That's how it was. When I came to my senses I fled!"

"So that's how it was, eh?" said Jabbar. "So! They never told us it was like that."

"It was to be expected," commented Memed. "And Durdu knew that it was coming to him. That's why he'd lost his mind and committed such outrages."

"Your Kalayji is another one of that kind. He too . . ." said Jabbar.

"He's not like Durdu," answered Horali. "He's cowardly, a treacherous cheat. He wouldn't let himself be caught easily!"

"Let me give you some brotherly advice. He'll disappear too, in the long run, and end up just as badly. Keep away from him, Brother. You've kept out of trouble so far. I would be sorry if anything happened to you."

Memed had scarcely listened to them, but now turned round. "I'd be sorry too, Horali," he said, taking Horali's hand. "Now tell us. Why were you looking for us? Is there something, have you a message for us?"

Horali stared at them stupidly for a while, lowered his head, blushed and turned pale. "Kalayji has invited you," he said, speaking very quickly. "He wants to meet you. He's very curious about Memed. He asked me about you and I praised you. 'I know him,' I said. 'He's my friend, my brother. I'll go and find him and bring him here.' Then I searched high and low for you."

Memed and Jabbar exchanged glances, as if to say, "There's something behind this."

"So?" said Memed. "Is that all?"

"Yes," stammered Horali.

"So you've been looking for us for a long time?" asked Jabbar.

"Very long."

"What would Kalayji want with us?" asked Jabbar.

"I praised my brother Memed . . . 'Go and find him and bring him here, since you've praised him so much,' he said."

"You did well, Brother Horali," Memed concluded. "Thanks."

Jabbar glanced angrily at Memed.

"Let's go," said Memed. "In any case, I wanted to know him too. Where is he waiting for us?"

"On Mount Konur."

"Come along! If I didn't accept his invitation, whose would I accept?"

Jabbar was puzzled. He went over to the man who had brought Horali and, taking him aside, asked him: "How was it he came to you, this brigand?"

"He was asking everyone he met about Memed. They brought him to me. 'I'm from Memed's band,' he said. 'We got separated. I haven't been able to join up with him since. Take me to him.' So I brought him here. He was very insistent about it."

"I see. You can go now."

The man started off, then turned back to stare.

"Brother Huseyin," Memed called after him. "We'll be back in a few days. Good luck to you. Thanks for bringing our friend."

"Good-bye," said the man.

Mount Konur was far from where they were, more than a day's journey.

Towards midday they reached Siyringach and, as night was falling, the Stream of the Monks. They obtained some food from a village nearby and, after a couple of hours' rest, set off again. As day was breaking they reached Akkale, where they drank from a mossy spring. All the time they walked Memed went ahead, with Horali in the middle and Jabbar in the rear. They climbed to the white-rocked peak above Akkale, where they would stop to sleep. For some reason, as they came to the peak, Horali was lagging a long way behind. Jabbar made the most of this opportunity.

"Memed, do you realise what he's up to, Brother?"

"I know," Memed smiled.

Jabbar could not contain himself. "Then why are we going?"

"Don't you see, Brother?" said Memed. "He's sent a man after me, to set a trap for me. Someone who knows me. He invites me. How can I refuse to go? If I didn't he would say I'm afraid to go. He thinks he's leading me into a trap . . ."

"We'll surely fall into it. There are ten of them."

"If they were a hundred, there's still no other way."

"Then let's kill Horali," suggested Jabbar.

"No. I must see Kalayji. I want to see what kind of a man he is."

"All right, let's see him, come what may."

"Just look at Horali's face, changing from one minute to the next. It's the face of a man who regrets something and is ashamed of what he has done. It seems to me he'll suddenly empty himself and tell us everything. He can't look us in the eyes for even a moment. He's probably praying hard in his heart that we refuse to go to Kalayji. When he comes up, look at his eyes."

Horali then caught up with them and they were silent.

"Well, Horali," said Memed, patting him on the shoulder. "So that's all there is to it?"

"Yes," answered Horali with trembling lips.

On the mountain-top there was a grove of huge walnut-trees. They went and sat in their shade.

"Lie down and sleep," said Jabbar. "I'll keep watch."

In turns they slept and kept watch. It was almost evening when they left Akkale and entered the rocky area east of Andirin. Then they plunged into a thick forest. The smell of pine, wild mint and penny-royal filled the air. Over the babbling of a stream, the cooing of a turtle-dove could be heard.

"We must be coming to the Cloudy Rock," said Jabbar.

"That's right," replied Horali. "To-morrow morning we'll be at Kalayji's. They'll be waiting for us on Mount Konur, by the Gokche spring."

"So?" said Memed, clenching his teeth. Then he controlled himself. He could not think why Kalayji should want to set a trap for him and felt confused. He had indeed thought of Abdi Agha, but could not make out the connection between Abdi and Kalayji.

A many-hued dawn broke over Kayranli Peak. The mist was slowly rising from the soil and the trees when they reached Mount Konur.

"You can rest here," said Horali. "I'll go ahead and tell the others."

Memed and Jabbar sat down, leaning against a tree.

"Do you think they'll open fire on us, Jabbar?" asked Memed.

"No, man. They won't kill us before they've given us roast lamb to eat."

"You're right. Kalayji isn't brave enough for an open fight. If he's the Kalayji we've heard about and know, he'll first take our guns away and set us down to eat and only then kill us. Easy work. But I don't understand why he wants to kill us."

"Easy," replied Jabbar. "He's Ali Safa Bey's man."

"Well?"

"I'm surprised you don't understand, Memed. They're all dogs of the same breed. Do you see now?"

"So it's Abdi, eh?"

"It can't be otherwise."

Just before midday Horali returned. They rose and walked towards Gokche spring.

As they came out of the woods on the lower side of Gokche, Kalayji appeared on the far side. It was clear that he was waiting for them.

Memed threw himself down and immediately began firing at Kalayji. From behind him there was a cry. Memed turned for a moment and saw that Jabbar had shot Horali, who now lay sprawling on his back in a pool of blood.

"I did well," shouted Jabbar. "I waited till the last moment to give him a chance to speak and save his sweet soul."

"Kalayji's disappeared," grumbled Memed. "I fired too soon. I don't think I hit him." Then he shouted at the top of his voice: "Kalayji! Enough of your tricks. If there's any manhood in you, come out in the open. Don't be afraid. Ali Safa's dog! Filthy butcher! Come out in the open."

Jabbar was shouting too: "You thought we'd run away? Come out, if you're a man."

But not the slightest sound came from the other side.

Soon a volley of shots was fired on them from all sides. Memed laughed. "Kalayji's grown brave. I'll show him."

The skirmish lasted till the middle of the night.

XXI

It was soon the talk of the Chukurova, from Kadirli to Kozan, from Jeyhan to Adana and as far as Osmaniye. At the prompting of Abdi Agha and Ali Safa Bey, Kalayji was reported to have set a treacherous ambush for Memed, who had escaped from it without a scratch, wounding Kalayji and killing two of his men.

In the Chukurova and on the Taurus mountains Memed's adventures were repeated, much exaggerated, from mouth to mouth, everyone supporting Memed's cause. The mountain people, in spite of the danger they incurred, were ready to protect him against all his enemies at any cost.

"Slim Memed?" they would say. "People think he's just a slip of a boy, but he's all courage, from top to toe. His mother's blood will be avenged on Abdi Agha and Ali Safa Bey can no longer escape retribution for his misdeeds in Vayvay village."

The immediate consequences of Memed's fight with Kalayji were felt at once in Vayvay. It was evening when the news reached the village. People left off work and collected in the square to rejoice. At last the village had found a champion. They were elated and all began inventing tall stories about Slim Memed, who soon assumed legendary proportions in their eyes. They told of so many heroic deeds and fights that the lives of ten men would not have sufficed to perform them all. But the villagers were in no mood to stop and think about such considerations. Memed had stood up against their enemy, against Kalayji. For two years they had not been able to leave their homes for fear of Kalayji, while Ali Safa Bey had been steadily taking over their fields. They were even cut off from the town and could no longer go there to seek protection of their rights. In another six months all the fields would have been Ali Safa Bey's and the villagers would have become his serfs.

Big Osman sat down on the stone well head in the middle of the square. "Memed, my hawk!" he kept repeating. He could say nothing else, only "Memed, my hawk!"

Big Osman was a man of eighty, thin and short, with slanting green eyes and a sparse beard. There were only some fifteen white hairs on his chin. He had ten sons, now gathered around him together with other villagers, all waiting to hear what he would say.

After repeating "Memed, my hawk!" once more, Big Osman rose to his feet. "My hawk doesn't rob the people, does he?" he asked.

"Would Memed ever rob the people?" they answered.

"Get my horse saddled, sons. Collect what money you have and let me go to my hawk. He must need money in the mountains. Everybody must give as much as he can."

As soon as it was warm and the dew of the Chukurova earth turned to steam, Big Osman rode his horse towards the Taurus mountains, still wrapped in blue mists, rising above the plain.

Everywhere he inquired after "Memed, my hawk!"

It took him three days to reach Deyirmenoluk. He was ready to fall off his horse from sheer weariness, when he dismounted in the village. Leading the horse by the bridle, he hobbled through the village and stood breathless in the square, his mount bathed in foam.

The children left their games and stared at the old man who stood there puffing and blowing. Big Osman raised his head. "Children, come here!"

The children all gathered round him.

"Where is Rose Ali's house?"

The boldest of the boys answered: "He's been dead for years, before I was born . . ."

"And Slim Memed's?"

"Aren't you a strange uncle!" cried the bold boy.

Big Osman roared out angrily: "What's the matter with me, boy?"

"Memed's become a brigand. Haven't you heard?"

"How would I know, child! I'm from the Chukurova. Hasn't Memed any relatives? A father, a mother?"

The boy shook his head.

275

"Where does he stay when he comes down to the village?" inquired Big Osman.

"With Uncle Durmush Ali."

"So Memed's become a brigand?"

"Aye, he's become a brigand. He came to the village saying 'I've killed the Agha,' and distributed all our Agha's fields to the villagers, just as if they were his father's property. Then he burned the thistle fields, but our Agha will now see to it that he is killed. No one likes him in this village. Only Uncle Durmush Ali's wife loves him, and our Agha will drive him out of the village."

"Where is Durmush Ali's house, son?" asked Big Osman.

The child made a sign with his head. "It's there."

Big Osman pulled at the bridle of his horse and set off in the direction of Durmush Ali's house.

"One of God's guests," he called out as he stopped and announced himself by the door.

Durmush Ali came out in his white underwear and with his neck bare. His back was bent and his milk-white beard seemed to reach to his knees. "Welcome, God's guest, welcome!" He took hold of the bridle and led the horse into the stable.

A big fire was burning inside. Durmush Ali came and sat by the fire opposite his guest. "Greetings!" he said, pushing a rusty cigarette-box towards Big Osman.

The old man leaned forward. "Come nearer and lend me your ear," he began. "Have you any news of Slim Memed? Where would he be?" he asked fearfully in a low voice.

Durmush Ali laughed uproariously. "Why do you ask about Memed so timidly? There's nothing to fear."

"Memed is my hawk. How would I know? I'm looking for him." Big Osman then explained in detail why he was looking for Memed and what he wanted. Durmush Ali's wife came and listened too.

Big Osman could not refrain from repeating, "Memed, my hawk." These words were like balm on his tongue.

"Memed is our hawk too," said the woman. "You'll see, he'll soon kill that bald Abdi and come back to distribute the fields again. Ungrateful villagers! The things they did to my Memed, Brother! Let the time come and I'll go out in the middle of the village and tell them just what I think of them. I know what I'll say to those worthless villagers who've made my boy a wanderer.

Go, Brother, say this to Memed. Tell him to kill that infidel, Ali Safa Bey too. Let him cut off Kalayji's head and send it down to the Chukurova. Tell him his Aunt Hürü said so."

"For God's sake, woman," cried Durmush Ali, "be silent a while! Let's attend to our guest's business."

"Oh, you!" she answered in disgust. "Lame Ali was going off to see Memed in any case. Memed is in Chichekli valley. We can send our guest with Ali."

"Is it far?" asked Big Osman hesitantly.

"Quite far," replied the woman.

"Then let me stay the night here, please, and I'll go there to-morrow."

"Stay here to-night, Brother," said the woman. "I'll send for Lame Ali. He's Abdi's steward, but he's still on our side . . ."

Durmush Ali glared angrily at his wife. She fell silent. Then they noticed that Big Osman was leaning back against the wall and was already asleep, with his head drooping to one side.

Durmush Ali smiled. His wife smiled too. "Poor old man," she said. "Who knows how many days he's been in the saddle!"

XXII

They were climbing a narrow path that led to the upper reaches of Chichekli valley. Ever since morning Big Osman had been asking Lame Ali: "What sort of a man is my hawk?"

Lame Ali had replied: "He has big hazel eyes, stiff hair like a brush, a bitter expression on his face, a pointed chin. His complexion is dark and he's of medium height. He can fire a shot through the eye of a needle. He's swift and brave and faces dangers or death with his eyes wide open."

"So?" said Big Osman. "And does my hawk always hide on this mountain peak?"

"No," replied Lame Ali. "But it looks as if he'll stay here this year. Chichekli valley is near the town . . ."

"Well?"

"You know that Hatché is in prison there. The witnesses have withdrawn their evidence, but still the Government won't set her free."

"Ah, my poor hawk!"

"That's how it is."

They reached a green meadow, covered with grass that was short as if it had been trimmed. Black and white autumn clouds were gathering in the sky.

"How much farther is it to my hawk's nest?" asked Big Osman.

Lame Ali pointed to a rocky slope covered with trees.

"It's there."

"Let me see my hawk just once before I die!"

Towards evening they came through a wood to a low mud hut. Lame Ali whistled. Jabbar appeared on the roof of the hut.

"Jabbar!" shouted Ali.

278

Jabbar called into the hut: "Brother Memed, look who has come!"

Memed came out in turn on the roof. "Ali Agha! Welcome!" They embraced each other.

"Forgive me, Memed," said Ali. "I've been looking for you for a long time. I had some news for you but I couldn't reach you. It's a good thing you escaped out of Kalayji's ambush. So it was that son of a whore Horali? I would never have expected it of him. I've known him ever since he looked after the garden!"

While they were talking Big Osman stood smiling. His horse was behind him, its right foreleg, as always, drawn up against its belly. Its coat was dishevelled and damp.

Memed asked Lame Ali in a low voice: "Who's that?"

"He's from far down, from Vayvay village. He keeps on calling you his hawk."

Memed walked slowly towards the old man and held out his hand: "Welcome, Uncle!"

"I'm glad to be here, my son. Are you my hawk?"

"Who?"

"Slim Memed."

Memed smiled a little shyly. "I am."

With unexpected agility Big Osman rushed forward, threw his arms around Memed and began kissing him. "Slim Memed, my hawk!" He was kissing him and weeping at the same time.

Jabbar came and drew the old man away from Memed. Osman sank down on a rock, his face in his hands. "Slim Memed, my hawk!" Jabbar then led him into the hut. The interior was lined with bear-skins. Cartridge-belts, grenades and guns were hanging on the walls.

"I can't believe it, my boy," the old man kept repeating. "I can't believe my eyes. Truly, you are my hawk? Is it really you?"

"Excuse me, Uncle," said Memed, blushing and embarrassed. "This is the mountain. We can offer you no coffee."

"May you live long, my hawk!"

Memed had gained some weight. There was colour in his cheeks. His black moustache was longer. His expression had become harder, as if he were ready at any moment to meet an attack. He was more sun-tanned, blackened, dried up, and seemed taller than before.

"Well!" exclaimed Lame Ali. "I must say that since I've seen you . . ."

"May God never bring famine to Chichekli valley," laughed Jabbar. "They feed us well here. Memed is the Agha, the judge and the government of the whole valley. People here don't go to the Government any more with any of their requests. Memed attends to all their business, and is just in all his decisions. That's how things are since we've last seen you."

Lame Ali smiled. "It's well that you escaped from Kalayji. I heard everything, how Abdi went and threw himself at Ali Safa Bey's feet and how Ali Safa then summoned Kalayji to town to arrange for him to kill you. I came to warn you, but you weren't to be found. 'Oh,' I said to myself, 'Kalayji has eaten up my Memed!' So I set forth again and heard at Akkale that you had come up against Kalayji and wounded him, killing two others. I threw my cap in the air for joy and went back to the village. A month later I heard you were in Chichekli valley. Big Duran said so . . ."

"My hawk," said Big Osman. "I'm the ambassador of the villagers of Vayvay. Kalayji is Ali Safa's dog. There isn't a man in the village who hasn't had to suffer at his hands. Ali Safa was wresting our land from us and would turn Kalayji loose on us when we tried to defend our rights. Then I heard . . ."

Interrupting him, Memed turned to Lame Ali. "So all this was Abdi Agha's work? I guessed it was . . ."

"We'd heard that you, my hawk, had wounded Kalayji," Big Osman interrupted Memed. "If only you'd killed him!"

Calmly, without any excitement, Memed answered: "News reached us yesterday that his wound didn't heal and, a few days ago, he was carried off to hell."

Big Osman threw himself on Memed, kissing his hands. "Is it true? Is it true, my hawk? At last our fields will be ours! Is it true, my hawk?"

"It's true," answered Memed. "I had been wondering how it happened that my shot hadn't killed Kalayji. I had taken good aim."

"God grant all your wishes. Amen!" exclaimed Big Osman. Then he opened his saddle-bag and produced a large pouch which he gave to Memed. "The villagers sent this, my hawk. Thank God

Excuse me, but I must go now and bring the good news to the village. They'll make a great celebration!"

He hurried off to unfasten his horse from the tree, mount it and ride back to the door. "Good luck, my hawk. Just let me get back home with the good news. Then Uncle Osman will come to see you again. Good-bye, my hawk!" He spurred the horse and was off.

Memed was puzzled by Big Osman. "Strange," he said.

"Eh, lads, I was anxious," declared Lame Ali. "How on earth did you find this Chichekli valley, in heaven's name?"

"We found it," smiled Memed.

"Tell me how you came across the place?" insisted Lame Ali.

Memed pointed to the wall, where a long-necked Turkish musical instrument, a *saz*, was hanging.

"And so?"

"It makes all sorts of sounds," said Jabbar.

"Are you making fun of me, Jabbar?" scowled Lame Ali.

"Ali Agha," said Memed. "This *saz* belongs to Poor Ali, the minstrel. We met him at Mazgach. He was sitting on a rock playing his *saz*, his gun lying beside him. He joined us. He's been a brigand for a long time."

"Poor Ali is a wonderful minstrel. You should hear him sing," added Jabbar.

"I understand. Poor Ali is a brigand and a fine minstrel. But how did you come to choose this place?" asked Lame Ali.

"This is Poor Ali's village. His uncles are the most powerful men there. Do you understand?" said Memed.

"Poor Ali will be coming soon," said Jabbar. "He's on the peak of the mountain now, composing songs. Who knows what about? As soon as he comes down from the mountain, all out of breath, he'll take the *saz* in his lap, crouch over it and start to play. That's the kind of fellow he is, as merry as a wedding." Then Jabbar turned to Memed. "Well, Memed, open the pouch that old man brought us and let's see how much money the people of Vayvay have sent us."

Memed slowly opened the pouch. The money was all in wads.

"Is it all money?" asked Jabbar wonderingly.

"All . . ." answered Memed.

"We're rich," exclaimed Jabbar.

"It looks as if we are . . ."

"Long live the old man!"

"And there'll be more to come," said Lame Ali. "You'll see. That old man won't leave you in peace. Every couple of months he'll collect more money from the villagers and bring it to you. He's a fine man, he is."

"He must have suffered a lot," said Memed. "Who knows what cruelties Ali Safa and Kalayji inflicted on them?"

"You need no longer worry about money," added Lame Ali. "Behind you stands all of Vayvay village, as firm as a mountain."

"Like a mountain," agreed Jabbar.

"Big Osman liked you," said Lame Ali to Memed. "Even if Kalayji hadn't been so vexatious, he would still have brought you the money. That's the way of such men. You're his 'hawk' now, you can go down to his house, take his son and kill him, and he won't say anything to you. They're like that."

"So you can go on being a brigand till Doomsday. You can't come to any harm," said Jabbar.

"Don't talk like that, Jabbar," replied Lame Ali. "Do you think Ali Safa Bey will just stand idle? Kalayji was his soul and now you've deprived him of his very soul. He won't let you get away with it."

"He'll try not to," agreed Memed.

"Let him try!" exclaimed Jabbar.

"Well," said Memed, "as Poor Ali says, 'Have we ever seen a day that was not followed by night?'"

Poor Ali then came strolling by with his gun slung over his shoulder. He went straight to the *saz*, took it down from the wall, sat down where he was and began to tune the instrument. Suddenly he started to sing. He had a low, deep voice. It was as if the sound did not come from within him, but from a thousand years away, from afar, from the mountains, from the Chukurova, the sea, laden with the salt-tang of the sea, the resin of the pines, the scent of the wild mint. "Come to me," he sang, "and soothe my affliction, sovereign healer of this world's woes." He stopped singing as he strummed louder on the instrument, playing the refrain. Then he continued: "Wherever I looked, I saw only my love."

He finished the song and remained crouched over his *saz* as if asleep. Then suddenly he raised his head and his hand flew over the strings of the *saz*, plucking them with his plectrum, "Mountains, rocks and flying birds . . ." He played and sang like a wild force of nature, a tempest:

> "Ask my name and I'll say that I'm Poor Ali.
> If I'm wise one day, I'm mad one hundred days.
> I'm the white-foamed torrent in the spring
> And I come from the snow-capped mountain peak."

He stopped and remained motionless, spent. Gently he laid the *saz* aside.

Memed, too, had remained motionless. A steely gleam had come and settled in his eyes. A ball of yellow light flashed, sparkling through his head, and the sun-drenched Chukurova plain rose before his eyes. He quietly pushed Lame Ali aside. "Ali Agha . . ."

"Yes?"

Memed signalled to him with a nod to go outside. Lame Ali rose and walked to the door, followed by Memed. Behind them Jabbar approached Poor Ali and nudged him. "Listen, Ali," he said. "Listen to me . . ."

"What's the matter?" asked Ali, roused from his dreams.

"Memed's taken Lame Ali outside. Do you understand?"

"I understand," laughed Ali.

"He's mad. He's taken leave of his wits. Do you know what he's saying to Lame Ali now? He wants Ali to go down to town with him."

"What else would it be? He tells everyone he meets, 'I must see Hatché once more in this world, then God can take my soul. I'll go to the prison and see her; even if the town were a burning fire I would go.' It's being repeated all over Chichekli village."

"He's looking for his death! I do my best to deter him, but he then gives me such evil looks as if I were his enemy," complained Jabbar.

"There's nothing you can do," said Poor Ali.

"Perhaps," said Jabbar. "But Memed is a fine man, a good man. There's never been a man like Memed on these mountains, nor will there ever be another like him. He's a fine fellow, a saint."

The north-east wind was raging outside, heralding a snowstorm. A flock of cranes had passed over the mountains only a little earlier. Winter had come, its tang already in the air.

The fallen pine-needles whirled in the north-easter. Memed held Lame Ali against the pine-tree and forced him to sit down. "Sit there."

When Lame Ali looked into Memed's face he was astonished to see his lips trembling. He waited anxiously.

Memed squatted beside him. "Ali Agha," he began. "You're an intelligent man, but you've been the cause of all these troubles of mine and you know it. I've realised long ago that you had no choice in that business. You're a good man."

"I'm sorry, Memed . . ." pleaded Lame Ali.

"I'm no longer reproaching you, Ali Agha."

"What is it, then?"

Memed stopped to think for a moment. His face was taut, as if some great pain was tormenting him. "I'm going to see Hatché to-morrow," he said at last.

Lame Ali was astounded. "What?" he cried.

"I'm going to see Hatché to-morrow," repeated Memed, his voice low but firm.

"How?"

"I've said enough. I'm going."

Taking his head in his hands, Lame Ali hesitated. "Difficult," he sighed. "Very difficult. You'll be courting death."

"I have written death on my forehead," said Memed, his features drawn by his suffering. "Here, right in the middle of my heart, there's a great fire. It's destroying my heart. I must go. I can't bear it any longer. To-morrow I'll be up at dawn and on the road to town."

"And if they catch you?" asked Lame Ali. "All my own hopes and the hopes of a whole village are founded on you."

Memed's face darkened. "The hopes of a whole village? What kind of a village?" He spat angrily on the ground.

"Don't be angry, Brother," said Lame Ali quietly. "You mustn't bear them a grudge. They pretend to back the Agha out of fear, but their hearts are all with you. The hopes of a whole village, of five villages, are founded on you."

"I'm going," interrupted Memed curtly. He rose and went towards the mountain-top, swaying as if drunk in the winter wind, with its tang of dry pines.

Bewildered, Lame Ali rose and went inside the hut.

"What did Memed say to you?" Jabbar asked anxiously. "Tell me, Brother Ali?"

"To-morrow, before dawn, he's going off to town."

"The man's mad," shouted Jabbar. "We'll have to tie him up. They'll catch him and kill him. We must tie him up. Where's he gone now?"

"He went up the mountain. He was like a drunken man."

Jabbar ran up the mountain after Memed. The north-easter was breaking branches in the trees. The air smelled of early snow. The clouds had turned black and were whirling across the sky. Suddenly everything became dark and huge warm drops began to fall.

Jabbar found Memed seated on a rotten trunk under a bare pine-tree. Memed was lost in thought, not even noticing that Jabbar had come. Jabbar sat down beside him. "Brother," he said gently, "don't do this. You've told everybody. There's no one who hasn't heard about it in Chichekli village. They'll surely have heard about it in town too. They'll catch you. Don't do it!"

Memed raised his head and looked straight into Jabbar's eyes. "True. You're right, Jabbar. But come and ask me. Ask me what I'm suffering. It's as though two hands were squeezing my heart. I can't go on without seeing Hatché. If I don't see her I'll die. So I might as well die seeing her. Will you do one last brotherly act for me?"

"There's nothing I won't do for you, Memed. We've said we're brothers. We've said we're as one man, body and soul."

"In that case, find me some tattered old clothes. That's all that I ask of you."

Jabbar did not answer. His head sank forward.

XXIII

Big Osman entered the town one morning at a gallop, his horse's bit dripping with foam. He dismounted in the market-place, passed the horse's reins over his arm and paced from one end of the square to the other, smiling. "Greetings!" he called to all in a loud voice. "Greetings!"

The town had heard of Kalayji's death and understood why Big Osman was now parading around so proudly.

He strolled up and down the market two or three times, searching for someone whom he did not seem to find. Then he left the market and turned towards the low ground by the stream. He came to Tevfik's coffee-house and stood there, in front of his horse, his face red and his hands trembling. He leaned his forehead against the window of the coffee-house and peered inside. His eyes lit on Abdi Agha, seated in a corner. Big Osman rejoiced. Tying his horse to the acacia tree in the square, he went inside and approached Abdi Agha. The Agha raised his head. Their eyes met and Big Osman smiled. Abdi Agha went pale.

"Greetings," Osman called in a loud voice and without waiting for Abdi Agha to return his greeting, turned on his heel and walked off, leaving Abdi gaping after him.

He untied his horse from the acacia, jumped into his saddle and set off at a gallop for Vayvay village, which was two hours from the town.

After Big Osman had left the coffee-house, Abdi Agha was tense with fear. His white-handled pistol was in its holster on his right hip. He kept his hand on it all the time. Playing backgammon, counting money, eating his food, his hand was always there. He was all the time expecting to meet an invisible enemy.

He went off hurriedly to the letter-writer. Politician Ahmed was a strange character who spoke as if his mouth were full of walnuts knocking against each other. He was also the deadly enemy of the other letter-writer, Mad Fahri, and Ali Safa Bey's special henchman. He had profited from Kalayji just as much as Ali Safa Bey and had been the bandit's active agent in town. That is why he, too, had been much upset by the news of Kalayji's death.

Abdi Agha rushed into Politician Ahmed's shop. "Write, Ahmed Effendi. If the Government is a government, let them show it. Write just as I tell you. The brigands are holding all the mountains and passes and have set up their own government under every bush. Write that! Even fifteen-year-old boys have taken to the mountains. They are burning the villages. They even raid the town. Our lives and goods are no longer safe. Write that! Even the women have taken to arms. It's rebellion, a rebellion covering the whole region. The laws remain on paper. Write that! Write it! Let the military come and dig them all up by their roots!"

Politician Ahmed's dark face became even darker. He took the black felt cap from his head, laid it on the table and began to mop his brow with the handkerchief he had pulled out of his pocket.

"Do you really want me to write what you've just said?" he asked.

"Exactly, word for word, write what I said. These policemen just cannot cope with such brigands. A regiment of them would not be able to contend with Memed, let alone with the others. Write that the Government should send the military. Write that there's a rebellion. A twenty-year-old boy is a brigand chief, my own labourer, known by the name of Slim Memed. Write exactly as I've told you. Memed drives me out of my own village and distributes my fields to my own labourers. My five villages! I'm even afraid to walk about the town. I've taken a house just opposite the police station and placed sandbags against the windows to protect me from their shots. I've blocked the flue of the chimney to protect me against bombs. The other day they came to shoot me. If we hadn't had warning, if there hadn't been a guard, they would have dynamited my house. 'I'll dynamite the whole town,' Memed has said. There! Write exactly that!"

Politician Ahmed snivelled. "How can I write such things? They'll cut my hand off! And supposing I did write it, there's the honour of the town to be considered too. We mustn't compromise the good name of our town. Besides, Kalayji may well be gone, but Ali Safa Bey is still alive. He'll build up another robber band. Ali Safa wouldn't agree to your writing to the Government like that."

"Do as I tell you," burst out Abdi Agha angrily.

"I can't."

"I tell you to write, Brother, write!"

"I can't."

Abdi Agha rose to his feet in a fury. "Then I'll get Fahri Effendi to write it."

"Get it written wherever you like, but it won't do you any good."

Abdi Agha went immediately to Mad Fahri, who heard his footsteps from afar and slowly raised his head from the table to greet him.

XXIV

Towering over Chichekli valley is the Hawk's Rock, a high, steep, smooth and mossy cliff that rises abruptly to the sky. The Hawk's Rock is often mentioned in stories and legends of these parts. Towards the summit of the cliff is a little spring called the Hawk-Rock Spring, surrounded by green shrubs and fragrant wild mint. Their perfume spreads from a spot which is set at the height of three poplars and from which the bubbling water falls down the steep face of the rock.

In olden times there was once a youth who had a passion for hawks. A wild hawk had nested here in a hole in the face of the rock and, when the time came for the hawk's chicks to hatch, the youth decided he must have a young hawk. But the hawk's nest was in the middle of the smooth steep rock and he could not reach it from below, nor from above. So the youth tied a thick rope to the stoutest tree on the summit and climbed down, thus reaching the hawk's nest. There he seized a chick and concealed it in his breast. But the mother-hawk, realising what was happening, flew to the rescue in an angry rush and beat against the rope with her wings, cutting it as if with a sword. The youth and the chick concealed in his breast both fell and were dashed to pieces. That is how the rock came to be called the Hawk's Rock.

Memed had set off in the night. When he came to the foot of the Hawk's Rock he stopped to rest. Hearing a slight stir behind his back, he turned and saw Jabbar staring at him, his shirt open and the sweat streaming between the hairs of his chest.

For a long while Jabbar stood there while Memed lowered his eyes and stared at the ground. Then Jabbar came and sat down by Memde. Gently he stretched out his hand and grasped Memed's, squeezing it several times. Memed did not respond but continued to look straight ahead.

"Brother!" whispered Jabbar in a hoarse, trembling voice. He said it with so much feeling that Memed was forced to turn towards him. Jabbar took his hands in his own. "Don't do it, Brother!"

Memed shook his head reproachfully. "If you, too, don't understand my sorrow, Brother Jabbar, it would be better for me to die."

"Memed," moaned Jabbar. "I understand your sorrow. But the time's not ripe. Your sorrow is my sorrow too."

"In that case, Brother Jabbar, don't try to dissuade me. Let me go to Hatché. If I get caught, it's my fate. If I don't get caught ——" Then he was suddenly angry and his expression changed. "No one shall catch me," he said firmly.

"It's as if you were placing your wrists right in the handcuffs. Supposing someone recognises you? Abdi Agha, for instance. You'll be lost in town."

"It's fate," said Memed. The light in his eyes grew brighter. "I won't get caught."

"Well, my brother, may your road be clear!"

"Thanks," said Memed.

"I'll wait for you here three days, in Kurd Temir's house. If you're not back in three days, I'll know you've been caught."

Memed rose and set forth. Until he was out of sight Jabbar repeated to himself: "We've lost you too, Memed! These mountains will never see anyone like you again."

From Chichekli village Memed had obtained a pair of torn sandals and the clothing of a fifteen-year-old boy. The clothes were of hand-woven cotton, the coat dyed with pomegranate skins, the white *shalvar* trousers dirty and torn, as well as too tight, so that they made him look smaller. He had a thick shepherd's crook in his hand and wore a torn and greasy cap. His weapon and ammunition were fastened inside his trousers to his legs, the strings that bound them tied round his waist.

He went as fast as he could, his eyes seeing nothing about him, his head swimming as though he were rolling in some vacuum. The world no longer existed for him.

Towards midnight he reached the outskirts of the town. The dogs were barking among the houses. What should he do? He would no longer find an inn open at this hour; besides it would be too dangerous for him to stay there. The grinding of a mill rose from below. He turned and walked towards the mill.

Its roar was deafening and he could detect from afar the smell of warm flour.

To-morrow was Friday, visiting day at the prison. He had one great worry, Hatché's mother. Since Abdi Agha had settled in town she had come to visit Hatché every Friday, supposedly to bring news of Memed. But she invented the most unimaginable stories about him, though no longer about his wickedness, only about his virtues. She had told her daughter about the distribution of the fields and the burning of the thistles, exaggerating and expanding every detail to five times its real proportions. "Memed," she had said, "has grown taller and fatter. He's just like a minaret." Hatché was overjoyed. The prison was no longer a prison; it had turned into a paradise. Every now and then she would throw herself into Iraz's arms and kiss her. Iraz was filled with the same joy. Since Memed had settled in Chichekli valley news and money had come from him every few days.

Dusty flour sacks lay all around him now. Four heavy round millstones were turning, scattering flour in every direction. One could also hear the splashing of water. The miller was a man with a greyish white beard and a cast in one eye. Some fifteen villagers were seated in a ring around a fire they had lit in the middle of the mill. Memed came and greeted them. The others made room for him and he settled down among them. After a time they went on talking, forgetting all about him. They spoke of the fields, the crops, poverty and death. Then someone told of how a merchant had been robbed in Deveboynu. Some said that Slim Memed had done this job. The mention of Slim Memed's name led to the question of the distribution of the land. An old villager asked in amazement, "All right, he distributed the land, but what did he want to go and make the villagers burn the thistles for, the madman?" The others gave all sorts of fancy explanations for the burning of the thistles. Memed cursed them beneath his breath. Not one of them gave the right reason, which did not seem to occur to them. When his anger had passed he laughed to himself. What did the Chukurova villagers know about thistles? What could they know about that plague?

Then the men curled up to sleep where they were, Memed too. When he woke it was broad daylight. A villager was standing beside him. "Eh, boy!" he cried. "It's morning. Bestir yourself. There you are under the very hoofs of the horses and donkeys. Get up!"

Memed rose in a daze and set off at a quick pace towards the town. He was soon there and passed through the market, exactly as he had last seen it. The brass-ewered sherbet-seller was wandering around and Blind Haji was lovingly and eagerly hammering the horse-shoes. As Memed passed his smithy he was singing the song of Kozanoghlu to the beat of his hammer on the anvil. The smell of *kebab* rose from the shops where village women in black *shalvar* trousers were coming and going.

Timidly Memed stopped a villager who was going past the town-hall garden and asked him the way to the prison.

"Go straight up this street and through the stone gate opposite," replied the villager and went his way.

Memed came through the gate. A squad of guards was standing at attention, waiting for the sergeant. It gave Memed a strange feeling to see so many policemen at once. He suddenly felt like turning back and running off to the mountains. Never before had he felt such a weight oppress him. Beyond the men was a low windowless building, its walls covered with moss, before which two or three village women were waiting.

Memed hunched his back, making himself look as small as possible. He had guessed that this was the prison, from seeing a guard walking up and down on the flat roof. He had listened to many tales of prison life and this was just what he had expected. Slowly he walked towards the hut.

A bad-tempered guard accosted him roughly. "What do you want, boy?"

In a whining voice, Memed answered: "My sister's here, a prisoner!"

"Who is it, Hatché?" asked the guard harshly.

"Aye . . ."

"Hatché! Hatché!" shouted the guard through the door. "Your brother's come."

When Hatché heard the word "brother" she was puzzled and came out perplexed. Memed's face was pale and he was squatting at the foot of the wall.

"There he is," said the guard.

As soon as Hatché saw Memed she stopped dead. Not a sound came from her mouth. She staggered forward and sat down beside him, leaning against the wall. For a long while they sat side by side, like two mutes, staring into each other's eyes. Then Iraz came. She was amazed at Hatché's worn expression, nor could she understand why they were speechless. She approached Memed. "Welcome, son."

Memed muttered something inaudible. Iraz could make no sense of it.

Towards midday the guard came up to them. "Come, that's enough. Be off with you." he shouted.

Memed rose slowly, making himself as small as possible. From his pocket he drew his purse which he threw into Hatché's lap. Then he turned and walked off. Until he had disappeared through the big stone gate Hatché remained staring after him.

"What's up, girl?" asked Iraz. "Who was it?"

"Come inside, Iraz," moaned Hatché.

They went inside and Hatché threw herself, utterly spent, on her bed.

Iraz was puzzled. "What's the matter with you?"

"Memed . . ."

"What?" shouted Iraz in astonishment.

"That boy was Memed."

"May I be struck blind," cried Iraz, beating her breasts. "May my eyes drop out of my head! I didn't even have a good look at my lion's face . . ."

They were silent. Suddenly the two women, their eyes streaming with tears, began to embrace each other, swaying this way and that. "Our Memed!" they repeated again and again.

They sat down on the bed side by side, smiling.

"Yuregir plain . . ." said Hatché.

"Our house!"

"I'll spread red earth on the walls. And thirty acres . . . I won't let you do any of the rough work."

"No," objected Iraz. "We'll all work as hard as we can."

Now a new door of hope had opened for them. For days in the prison there had been talk of an amnesty. A deputy who had come from Ankara was reported to have said that it would soon be proclaimed. The prisoners had made up songs about the amnesty and hummed them day and night. There was an elderly man, Mustafa Agha, among the prisoners, and everybody listened to him because he was wise and learned. Every day Hatché would go to him and ask: "Uncle Mustafa, when they empty the prisons, will Memed be granted a pardon too?"

"Not only Memed, but every wolf and bird on the mountains will be granted a pardon."

Hatché was thrilled. Her joy grew day and night.

The soil of Yuregir plain is warm and fertile. From prisoners who knew about Yuregir, Hatché learned of every village and hamlet there. "We'll settle at Karatash," she would say. "Won't we, Iraz?" And Iraz would reply: "Yes, at Karatash . . ."

Hatché went out, ran to the men's section and shouted: "Uncle Mustafa!"

Mustafa came towards the door. "What do you want, my wild girl?" he asked in his soothing voice. He knew what Hatché would say, but he still asked.

"And Memed too?"

"Even the wolf and the bird of the mountain. If there's an amnesty, it's like that. And there will be, in honour of the Government."

"I kiss your hands, Uncle Mustafa."

"Wild girl," smiled Mustafa Agha as he always did, returning to his cell. It was like this every time.

"The amnesty will be proclaimed," said Iraz. "But they're taking us to Kozan on Wednesday. They can't pronounce the sentence here. That's what the court decided. If only the amnesty would come, then we wouldn't have to go to Kozan. It worries me . . ."

Hatché was very upset. "If only . . . Memed won't be able to come to Kozan. If only I'd spoken to Memed! I was tongue-tied and couldn't speak. To-day's Friday. How long is it till Wednesday?" She began counting on her fingers. "Saturday, Sunday . . . five days till Wednesday. If only I'd told Memed we were going."

"Had I known it was Memed, I'd have told him straight away," said Iraz.

"Will the pardon come, Iraz?"

"Mustafa Agha's a wise man. He has connections in Ankara. If he doesn't know, nobody knows."

"We'll have a weeping willow in front of our house, with its branches hanging down to the ground, won't we?" exclaimed Hatché.

"Yes."

"And calves! Purple-brown calves."

When Memed left the prison, his head was spinning. He went to the market-place and flung himself down on the white stone in the middle. After a while he recovered his senses. There were piles of oranges in the market and stacks of cabbages like small hillocks. He rose from the stone and walked towards Tevfik's coffee-house, where a crowd was gathered. The men were wearing long cloaks and carried shovels on their shoulders. A short man with a silken cord round his neck kept cursing them. This surprised Memed. "There are men like Abdi Agha here too," he thought, while the short man cursed repeatedly. No sound came from the men, who just hung their heads without moving. Then the man who had been cursing suddenly began to speak more softly. "Brothers," he began, "you are more precious to me than my life." Memed could make no sense of this. The men with the shovels on their shoulders slowly moved off, their heads still bent, walking towards the stream. Some people said: "They're going to the rice fields." This puzzled Memed even more. He went back through the market. From the door where he had eaten on his first visit to the town there drifted a smell of *kebab*. He went in, faint with hunger.

"Quick, Brother," he said to the waiter.

"Fan the brazier up," the other called to the cook.

When Memed looked about him he could not believe his eyes. Sitting there behind him he had seen Lame Ali. But it was no hallucination. Lame Ali smiled surreptitiously. Memed said nothing, a hundred terrible possibilities flashing through his mind. Lame Ali did not speak but went on smiling. Then he stood up and came and sat down in an empty chair beside Memed, leaning towards him. "Don't worry, Brother," he whispered. "It's all right. We'll talk later."

The *kebab* was served. They ate together and left the shop. The brass ewered sherbet-seller was going his customary round of the market.

"Sherbet-seller, a sherbet," said Memed.

While the sherbet-seller was filling the glass Memed caressed the copper ewer with his hand. The sherbet-seller laughed. "It's made of gold, boy, gold!" he said.

"It was Jabbar who told me you had come to town," said Lame Ali. "So I got on my horse and hurried down to see that nothing should happen to you. I waited for you at the door of the prison. How is Hatché? Is she well? Well, you madman, how dare you come down to town without a horse? If something happened and you were forced to flee, there'd be no escape for you. That's why I've been following you everywhere with a horse. Somebody may recognise you and, if anything happens, you can jump on to the horse and hurry off to the mountains."

Memed's eyes filled with tears. "Thanks, Ali Agha."

"You're our Slim Memed. Thanks be to you, Brother!"

"May I tell you something, Ali Agha?"

"Yes."

"Hatché and I sat opposite each other, both of us tongue-tied. We couldn't utter even a word. When I saw her there I couldn't bear it. I can't go again. If I do I'll be tongue-tied again. You must go to her. Ask her if she has anything to say to me."

"All right," said Ali. "Wait for me by the coffee-house in the market. The horse is tied beneath the mulberry-tree at the far end of the market. If anything happens, jump into the saddle and ride off."

"I'll ride off." He felt a strange, inexplicable shiver go through him. Something cold was running down his back. He felt uneasy, bursting with impatience. He wanted to run away, to break something, smash it. He felt something akin to sadness or fear, a conflict within him.

He walked quickly to the horse. Those who saw him took him for some bewildered village boy. The horse's nostrils were full of straw. He took some green grass from the ground and cleaned the horse's nose. It was an iron-grey horse, dappled with big bluish spots. Along its rump it was reddish. He caressed the horse's head and went over to the coffee-house and ordered tea. Hatché seemed to appear before his eyes. She had greatly changed. Her face had filled a little, but it was sallow and she had large black circles under her eyes and was obviously weak and weary. It tore his heart. Tears began to fall from his eyes on to the table. He was sitting sideways, on the alert. He drank his tea, his eyes fixed on the road impatiently.

Ali appeared at the end of the street. His face was downcast. Memed went to meet him. Together they returned towards the horse.

"What did she say?"

"Don't ask!"

"Is it bad?"

"Well, it isn't good . . ."

Memed's heart was bursting. "Tell me! I knew it! My heart was troubling me. It wouldn't let me rest. Tell me!"

"They're taking Hatché to the Kozan prison this coming Wednesday. 'Let Memed forget about me,' she said. It seems that she will be condemned to a heavy sentence and the court at Kozan has to decide. They're taking Iraz with her too."

Memed was as if thunderstruck for a long while. When he recovered his wits he had forgotten Ali and was smiling. In his mind's eye he saw the Chukurova, its trees, grass, stones, earth and towns bathed in sparkling brightness. He continued to smile. Then he suddenly jumped on to the horse. He had changed and become a completely different man.

"Go ahead of me, Ali Agha. I know what we have to do."

They left the town hurriedly, passed by Binbogha and came to the upper regions of Dikirli, where Karajali Osman now had his orange orchard.

Ali seized the horse by the bridle and stopped it. Looking into Memed's eyes he asked: "What do you want to do? Tell me!"

Memed dismounted and, still smiling, took Ali's hand. "I'll watch the road and take Hatché away from the police."

"Are you mad?" asked Ali angrily. "To take a prisoner out of the hands of the police in the middle of the Chukurova, in broad daylight? Are you mad?"

XXV

Memed returned to the hut elated. Jabbar had never seen him like this, nor had Poor Ali. It filled them with pleasure to see him in such a cheerful mood.

Memed was singing gaily as he wandered around the hut:

> "There were five pears on the branch,
> The eastern sky was growing light.
> Her mother would give her no cover
> So her white breasts were cold."

They had never believed it possible that such a song could be heard on Memed's lips.

"Poor Ali," roared Memed, in a tone that contrasted with his usual calm and measured manner, "take down your *saz* and play us some cheerful tunes!"

Poor Ali took the *saz* from the wall and began to play and sing a cheerful tune:

> "I came and saw the bolted door
> Her black hair plaited all with gold . . ."

Memed joined in the song and, seeing Lame Ali by the door, put his arm through his. "Play us a dance," he said to Poor Ali as they began to whirl around the room until Memed was out of breath and stopped, leaning his back against the wall. But he could not keep still and his fingers moved ceaselessly.

"Jabbar!" he said.

"Yes, Brother?"

"This is the day!"

"What's the matter with you? Has anything happened?"

"This is the day, the day to prove our manhood . . ."

"Don't talk riddles, for God's sake!"

Memed took off the boy's clothes he was wearing and threw them into a corner of the hut. Then he put on his own usual clothes. The upper part of the shoes he was wearing was of thick Marash leather, wrinkled and deep red. The soles were cut from the rubber tyre of a car. His *shalvar* trousers were of brown serge. He had taken them from a merchant they had robbed. After the encounter with Kalayji, Memed and Jabbar had spent several weeks on the Marash road, robbing people. All their money, clothes and ammunition came from there. They were very pleased with the results of their robberies and intended to hold up the Marash road again. Their belts and rifle-straps were silver-mounted, finely worked. Memed had discarded his fez and now wore a blue silk 'kerchief. The nomad chief had sent him his pistol and its holster, which were both embossed with gold. Memed's finely-worked cartridge-belts were fastened crosswise on his chest, in a double row, also a present from the nomad chief.

"What is it, Memed? Out with it!" said Jabbar, his curiosity now roused.

"To-day's the day."

Lame Ali was leaning in the doorway, smiling all the while.

"Tell us, Lame Ali," said Jabbar.

"On Wednesday they're taking Hatché to Kozan. He's going to kidnap her from the police on the road. That's what he's so pleased about."

Not a word came from Jabbar, whose face fell. Poor Ali was silent too. In any case he never meddled in this kind of business.

Memed sensed what Jabbar's silence meant, but pretended not to notice. Let Jabbar disapprove! He did not expect anyone's help. Come what may, his mind was made up.

During the early days of their association, Poor Ali had often recited a ballad about Koroghlu, describing the youth of the legendary outlaw. For days now this tale had been haunting Memed's mind. This is how the ballad went: "Once upon a time, in Bolu town, Koroghlu had seen a very small dog in the street, as small as your hand. Four or five huge dogs converged on that little dog and attacked it, but the little dog did not run away and defended itself and even defeated the others, forcing each in turn to slink off with its tail between its legs. Koroghlu had watched the fight and learned his lesson. Such a tiny little dog, but with such great courage! After that Koroghlu became the fearless Koroghlu of the legend and, when troubles overcame his father, took to the mountains to become a brigand."

Memed had been fascinated by this tale. After listening to it he had sworn again that he would kill the Agha.

"Why are you looking so sour, Brother Jabbar?"

"It's nothing."

"Don't be afraid. I shan't drag you into this business."

"I haven't said anything. I'm only pitying you."

"Jabbar," cried Memed angrily, "you're always pitying me."

"You're a valiant man. That's why I pity you."

"But why?"

By now Jabbar was really angry and began to shout. "In the middle of the Chukurova, on the plain, in broad daylight, among all those villages, you expect to capture someone from the police! Whoever goes down into the Chukurova fails to come back alive. That's why I pity you. More than that, you don't know the Chukurova. If you had someone like Sergeant Rejep with you, well it would be something. Does one go down into the Chukurova groping as one does in the dark?"

Memed was tense. "So you won't go with me?"

"I can't just walk knowingly into a trap."

"Speak frankly, leave all this talk about traps. Will you go or won't you?"

"I can't go."

"Good. You speak, Poor Ali. Will you go with me?"

"I don't know the Chukurova, Brother. I'm afraid of it. I wouldn't be of any use to you. I'd be a nuisance. But if you wish, I'll come. Out of friendship only . . ."

Jabbar shot a look at Poor Ali as if he could kill him.

"So that's how it is," said Memed and fell silent.

That evening they didn't eat their meal together. Each one retired into a corner, sulking and uncommunicative. The gayest amongst them was Lame Ali.

When it was time to sleep Jabbar said: "You can all sleep. I'll keep watch."

Memed and his two companions slept.

At midnight Jabbar approached Memed and shook him. Memed sat up angrily. "What do you want of me, Jabbar? You've shown no friendship. What more do you want of me?"

"Brother!" said Jabbar. He took Memed's hand between his own.

"You've shown your friendship," laughed the other.

"Forget about this business. In any case they'll release Hatché. Haven't the witnesses all withdrawn their former testimony? Aren't they all ready to testify in her favour? Haven't they testified that it was you who killed Veli? They'll let her go."

"They denounced their previous testimony, but that's worth nothing. If it was, why are they sending Hatché up to the Criminal Court? They're sending her there now. Do you understand? Because of me she'll drag out her life in prisons. I'll die or save her. I can't ask you to come. It's better if you don't. This is almost certain death. A man in his senses doesn't court death."

"I'll do everything for you, Memed, but this is absolute folly. It's just throwing yourself into the fire with your eyes wide open. It's a pity for us and for you, Brother. Come, take my advice. Please, Memed, don't reject it. It'll break my heart if you die so stupidly. Don't do it, Brother!"

"Jabbar, don't waste your breath. If I knew for certain that I was going to die, I would still go. How can I continue living like this?"

"Do as you like, then," said Jabbar. "He who falls by himself does not cry." He dropped Memed's hand.

Saturday, Sunday, Monday, Memed and Jabbar still avoided looking each other in the face, each evading the other's presence. Memed rose each day very early and went off on the mountain, returning to the hut only after nightfall.

On Tuesday morning Memed rose before daybreak and woke Lame Ali. "I'm going, Ali Agha."

Ali rose at once to his feet. "This business can't be done alone, especially with your not knowing the Chukurova. I'll come along too." He laughed. "But don't think that I'll do any shooting! You'll do that job and I'll only watch from a distance. I'll hide somewhere and watch. I'll find a good horse for you in Chichekli village and one for myself too. I'll go ahead and do your scouting while you wait in ambush for the police close to the mountains, in the reed-bed by Sitir. Wait now, while I go down to Chichekli village. Is that all right?"

Memed's eyes sparkled with pleasure. He threw his arms around Lame Ali and kissed him. "How can I ever repay you for this, Ali Agha?"

"I'm just trying to put together what I've broken," answered Ali, shaking his head sadly. He walked off hurriedly.

A couple of hours later, in broad daylight, there was a noise at the door of the hut, the sound of a horse that had been ridden hard and was breathing heavily. Memed rushed out. "Ali Agha!" he cried out, laughing. "Bravo!"

"This is a horse for a wedding. I've decked it out."

Round the horse's neck hung blue beads and ribbons of all colours. The saddle and bridle were embroidered with silver thread.

"Yes, a horse for a wedding!"

"And I've brought a saddle-cloth," said Ali. "There'll be heavy rain. It can both protect you from the rain and . . ."

"Eh?"

"It can also conceal your gun. If you draw it over you, only your head can be seen. Come on, don't let's waste any time."

Memed jumped into the saddle. Lame Ali mounted his horse too. Jabbar stood motionless on the threshold, staring after them, his face deathly pale, as rigid as a carved Hittite figure.

Memed rode back towards the door. Without looking Jabbar in the face he called in a broken voice: "Farewell and forgive me, Brother Jabbar. Farewell to you, too, Poor Ali!"

Jabbar remained motionless as a statue.

"Farewell, Brother," said Poor Ali.

They rode at a brisk pace across the meadow.

For a long while Jabbar stood there without moving.

XXVI

It was drizzling, though the sun was shining. The drizzle would stop every once in a while and then begin again gently. The reeds were wet, the rain trickling off them and forming drops on the leaves, which glistened in the sunlight.

In those days a huge reed-bed spread below Sitir, and the road used to pass across the myrtle-covered slopes of the mountain above it. They rode down to the reed-bed from above the village of Küchük Chinar. As the sun was setting the rain ceased.

"Didn't I do well to bring the saddle-cloth?" asked Lame Ali.

"Certainly."

"It's no longer raining."

"But it'll begin again."

"In all the Chukurova there's no better place than this reed-bed for an ambush."

"Ali," Memed teased him. "Where did you learn all these tricks? You seem to know the Chukurova stone by stone."

"When I was a boy I used to steal horses from the Chukurova and bring them up to the mountains. Now you know why I can still find my way so easily in the Chukurova!"

"I understand. Are you sure they'll come along this road?"

"You can go to Kozan by two roads," replied Lame Ali. "By the Chukurköprü road or by this one. It's a good thing it's been raining. They won't be able to get through by the Chukurköprü road because of the mud. So they're sure to come by this one. This is a good spot; you can't find a better for an ambush. Do your job fast and make off for the mountain. If Jabbar had known it would be like this he would have come too."

Memed's face became taut at the mention of Jabbar.

"I swear he would have come," repeated Lame Ali. "He was afraid. He thought we'd get surrounded in the middle of the plain in broad daylight."

Again Memed was silent.

"He was afraid," Ali continued. "And cautious too. He knows that none of the brigands who have ever come down to the plain have been able to return to the mountains."

"Not one has ever returned?" asked Memed in astonishment.

"Not one."

Opening their bag of food they began slowly to eat.

"I'll go along the road that leads to the town and then ride back behind them. You can go up the mountain and sleep. At dawn you must come down into the reed-bed, tie your horse somewhere near here, where it can't be seen, and come up close to the road. I'm off now. To-morrow afternoon they'll be here."

Lame Ali mounted his horse and hastened along the road towards the town.

As soon as he was out of sight Memed rode up the mountain. He dismounted by a well sheltered quarry like a cave. Even if it rained, he would not get wet here. He tied the horse to a big oak-tree by the quarry. Water had collected in the hollow of the quarry, so Memed piled up a few large stones and, wrapping himself up in the saddle-cloth, settled down on them. He slept fitfully.

At dawn he rose, mounted his horse and rode down to the reed-bed, driving the horse into the middle of it and tying it securely to the roots of a clump of reeds.

Ever since the previous evening he had felt strange, his whole body aching. He now sat down, his back against a clump of reeds in which a swarm of wasps had hived. Spiders' webs were spun all over the reeds, which grew in feathery clumps. The sun was shining on these clumps of reeds.

Nothing can be harder than to wait. Memed waited. How long? It was already noon and a humid heat had spread over the plain. Then it was afternoon and the shadows of the mountains opposite began to stretch towards the east. Memed took his rifle, which had been leaning against some roots, and went over to a hollow by a huge clump of reeds, close to the side of the road, straining his eyes as he gazed towards the town, but not a single human figure could be seen. He bit his lip. He felt like firing his rifle, come what might, if only to relieve his tension. He felt like firing at the reeds, at the road, no longer able to bear the suspense.

Then he pulled out his knife and began digging a hollow. He dug with all his strength, piling up handfuls of earth on the edge of the hole. Breathless, he ran to the road. Still there was nothing in sight. His hands fell to his sides as he stood there and lost all hope. He fetched his gun from the hollow, then settled in the middle of the road.

The sun was almost setting. Suddenly, far along the road, a group of dark figures appeared in outline against the light. Slowly they drew nearer. Memed's heart began to beat wildly, but still he did not go and hide among the reeds. Then he distinguished two women walking ahead of four men in uniform. Reluctantly he slipped back among the reeds. The sun was now almost hidden behind the mountain opposite. Aiming at the leg of the tall police-men at the rear, he pulled the trigger. Screaming, the man spun round and fell to the ground. Memed fired right and left repeatedly, like a machine-gun. The police escort had been taken completely by surprise.

"Men, you're up against Slim Memed," he cried. "Leave those women and be off."

Another man fell screaming. The last two threw themselves into the waterlogged ditch by the side of the road and tried to fire back at Memed. Darkness was falling and the rain had begun to drizzle gently. The women just stood where they were, trembling like leaves, until they sank down in the mud in the middle of the road.

"Come on, men, be off on your business. Don't put up a fight! Even if you were a whole squad, you wouldn't get anywhere."

The air was loud with the cries and groans of those who had been wounded.

"Take your wounded comrades and be off," Memed ordered.

The men stopped firing for a while. The women were recovering from their first shock.

Iraz nudged Hatché. "Don't be a fool," she whispered. "Let's slip quietly over to Memed."

"Did this, too, have to happen to me?" Hatché moaned. "Let's go."

They crawled silently along the road.

"Memed!" whispered Hatché. "You've come?"

It was pitch-dark. Memed jumped out of the hollow on to the road and came straight to the women who were tottering like shadows in the darkness. He held their hands and pulled them down among the reeds by his horse. The guards were still firing wildly. The horse gave a long whinny at the sound of their steps. Memed untied it. "Mount," he said. "Mount, both of you, and follow me."

As they left the reed-bed the guards stopped firing and were attending to their wounded comrades.

A rider passed at full speed, going towards the mountains, sparks flying from his horse's shoes as they beat the stones. But he soon turned back. "It must be Lame Ali," Memed said to himself.

A voice called softly: "Memed! Memed!"

"We're here, Ali, come!" called Memed.

Ali came up to them, quite breathless, and dismounted.

"Brother Memed, take the horse back to Chichekli village. Don't linger in these foothills but go straight to Akchadagh. To-morrow Sergeant Asim will be after you with all the men he can muster. Don't get caught. I'll keep in touch with you. By to-night you must make it to Chichekli village. From there on to Akchadagh. Don't stop on the way. God be with you!" He turned and disappeared in the darkness.

"I won't forget your help, Ali Agha," called Memed.

He jumped on to the horse Lame Ali had brought. "Come up behind me, Hatché."

Hatché dismounted from the other horse and climbed into the saddle behind him.

In the darkness they rode at full speed towards the mountains. Several times they found that they had taken the wrong road, but they reached Chichekli valley before sunrise and rode straight into the village, stopping there in front of a house.

Memed called to the occupants of the house to come out. A youth of about eighteen opened the door. When he saw them he smiled and came to hold the bridles of their horses. The horses were flaked with foam as he led them to the stables.

Hatché and Iraz were huddled together and trembling. In the

grey light of dawn their faces appeared vague, distraught, puzzled. They entered the house, where the women lit them a fire and spread mattresses for them by the hearth. Memed and his two companions sat down wearily on these mattresses.

"Friends," Memed announced. "I have a two-days' hunger."

"Presently, presently, Slim Memed," his hosts replied.

XXVII

Abdi Agha was utterly demoralised. He had grown thinner and his cheeks were sunken. In the coffee-house, from morn till evening, the only talk was about Slim Memed. It enraged him, but what could he do? The mouth of the people is not like a purse that you can draw tight.

He was in such a state of anxiety that he could not keep still but shuttled continually from Mustafa Effendi's shop to Tevfik's coffee-house, from Tevfik's coffee-house to Remzi's fruit-shop, from there to the stand of the letter-writer, Politician Ahmed. Everywhere he would talk for hours without letting anyone else utter a word.

"Do you see now what kind of a man he is? You said he was just a boy. Don't I know him, that devil's son? And he won't stop at this! Don't say Abdi didn't warn you. He'll form a government of his own in the mountains. This man distributed to the villagers my own fields, the deeded lands I had inherited from my father, and did it with gay celebrations too. If he isn't a government, what is he? He'll soon proclaim his own government. I've sent telegrams to Ankara, perhaps a thousand, but nobody answers them or even inquires what's really happening. It's a strange thing, my friends, this government business, leaving all these honest citizens at the mercy of a brigand in the Taurus mountains instead of sending a regiment of soldiers and cutting the evil out at the root! With all due respect, I'm not sticking my tongue out at the Government. I would never do that, Effendi! But why does it allow a few brigands to make slaves of us all? It's a crying pity, isn't it, a sin? . . ."

On the morning of the second day after the fight they brought the wounded guards into the town. The story spread from mouth to mouth. Abdi Agha was in the market-place rushing in his agitation here and there. He had lost his head and could barely speak, repeating only to all whom he met, acquaintance or stranger: "Didn't I warn you?"

He came to Tevfik's coffee-house, laid his head down on a table and remained motionless. He forgot to order his lunch. As he was dozing, one of Ali Safa's servants came up to him. "My Agha wishes to see you," he said.

"What?" asked Abdi wearily.

"Ali Safa Bey asks you to come to his house."

Abdi rose. He had a splitting headache.

Ali Safa Bey met him at the door and took him by the arm. "Come in, Agha, come in! I see you've forgotten us."

Abdi Agha raised his head. His eyes were bloodshot. "Didn't I warn you?" he said.

Ali Safa Bey smiled. "Come inside, man. We'll talk about it."

"Didn't I warn you?"

Pausing now and then to allow Abdi Agha to breathe, they climbed the stairs. Abdi Agha threw himself exhausted on the divan and sighed: "Didn't I warn you?"

When they brought coffee he looked as though he would drop the cup. As he drank the coffee trickled from his lips down his chin.

Ali Safa Bey sat down beside him, stroking his beard. "For God's sake, Abdi Agha, you'll ruin this town with all your petitions. The Government will send an army. Wouldn't it be a pity if the name of our town were trampled in the mud because of a couple of ruffians on the mountain?"

Drawing a deep sigh, Abdi Agha moaned and shook his head.

"Doesn't Abdi know what he's doing, Ali Safa Bey, my son? He'll kill me. He won't let me live. I'm at a loss what to do. My health is failing. I'm not afraid of dying. What troubles me is that a huge government cannot get the better of that slip of a boy. And more than that, you don't know what's really troubling me, Ali Safa Bey! He went to the village and distributed my fields to the villagers, saying 'Abdi's dead, I've roasted him alive.' That's what's killing me. I'm not worried about my death, Ali Safa Bey, I've already one foot in the grave. If not to-day, then to-morrow. No one lives for ever. But to-morrow another man of the same kind will arise and distribute your fields too. The next day, another and another and another! That's what I'm afraid of."

Ali Safa Bey patted his shoulder: "No, Abdi Agha, no. Set yourself at rest. They'll get their deserts. Don't worry."

Abdi Agha's eyes flashed and his beard stiffened. The blood rose into his cheeks. "To-day it's me, to-morrow it'll be you. That's what frightens me. Let there be as many brigands on the mountain as you will. What's a brigand anyway? But this frightens me, this land business. If it once gets into the heads of the peasants, there'll be no stopping them. This is what I'm frightened of, not being killed. You can do as you like, Ali Safa Bey, but that man must die, if you ask me, before another day goes by. What he has done has been like putting a water-melon rind in the mind of a donkey. We mustn't waste time. Don't forget about that water-melon business. Even the people of Vayvay go to him for protection now."

Ali Safa Bey laughed. "I understand, Agha, I understand, but don't be afraid. If not to-day, then they'll bring his head and throw it before your door to-morrow. Don't be afraid. A squad of policemen under Sergeant Asim and Black Ibrahim with fifty other volunteers is already after him. The policemen may be fooled, but Black Ibrahim is an old brigand who knows these mountains and all the tricks of his trade. I told them: 'Cut off Memed's head, stick it on a pole, bring it down and plant it before Abdi Agha's door.' They'll do it."

"He mustn't live another day. Let's hope it'll be as you say . . ."

"Hope? Why, he's as good as caught! Do you know Black Ibrahim?"

"I know him."

"He's the one to do the job!"

Abdi Agha was calmer now. The door of hope was opening. "We can trust Black Ibrahim to get the better of him. But how's your business at Vayvay progressing?"

Ali Safa Bey cut him short. "Since Kalayji died, things have been bad. They're no longer afraid of me. If it goes on like this!"

"We must get rid of Memed . . ." said Abdi Agha.

"We will!"

XXVIII

The police set on Memed's trail had received positive orders: "Dead or alive, bring him back, otherwise . . ." There was a grim threat in that "otherwise." The men who had received such orders created havoc in every place they entered. Men, women and children were questioned and beaten. A constant sound of lamentation rose from all the mountain villages, but no one seemed to know where Memed was and no one went out to search for him. Those who gave any indication of his whereabouts systematically put the policemen on the wrong track. Story after story was told in the mountain villages about how Memed had saved the innocent girl from prison. People talked of nothing else. In one day perhaps ten songs were composed about Hatché's rescue from the guards.

Two days after the events in the reed-bed the police raided Deyirmenoluk. They were so sulky that they seemed ready to tear a fly to pieces if it settled on their faces. They went straight to Durmush Ali's house, dragged the old man out in front of the door, and cross-examined him, but could not extract a word from him. They questioned and questioned, threatened and threatened, all to no purpose. They began to beat him with the butts of their rifles. His wife kept hopping around the old man as he was being beaten, screaming at the top of her voice, till one guard silenced her with a blow of his rifle-butt.

They left the two old folk bathed in blood in the courtyard of their hut and went off to other houses. Until evening they beat up the villagers one by one and then stayed that night as guests in Abdi Agha's house. The next morning they rose early and began beating the villagers again. In the end, weary and weak from their efforts, they set the villagers to beating each other.

Memed had withdrawn to Alidagh, a mountain of terrifyingly steep precipices, the lair of long-horned violet deer. Its rocks there are as sharp as knives. One cannot clamber over them, they cut so deeply into a man's flesh. There is a legend about a mountain of flint; Alidagh is such a mountain. Towards the peak the trees thin out and cease far below the peak, a naked rock, capped with snow all through the year. Memed had often stalked deer there and knew every stone, rock and cave of Alidagh.

On the peak there is a cave to which no track leads. To reach it one has to climb over five hundred yards of bare rock, clinging to its surface.

After leaving Chichekli valley, Memed and the two women found themselves threatened with encirclement. News soon reached them that Black Ibrahim was on their trail. Shepherds, farmers, wood-cutters, everyone brought news to Memed, so that he was informed of any new development the same day. Iraz and Hatché were very weary, their feet so swollen that they were forced to rest several days on the mountain near Chichekli valley.

Black Ibrahim and the guards were systematically combing the Chichekli mountains, from the valleys to the peaks. A shepherd who worked for Poor Ali's uncle came to warn Memed. "They're encircling you. Escape or you'll be killed." But they could no longer escape. The attack began at dawn. They were completely surrounded. Memed used his ammunition very carefully, aiming only at those who tried to edge forward and then firing at them. Sergeant Asim was constantly calling on him to surrender, but Memed called back "All right," and would then fire again. The police could not move from their cover.

Memed's rifle jammed and a shot remained in the heated barrel. He buried it in the earth to cool it and continued firing with his pistol. Hatché was trembling with fear. Memed laughed at her. He was black with dirt, bathed in sweat which poured from his armpits and back, leaving a streak of white salt where it dried.

Iraz helped Memed. In a few moments she cooled the rifle and removed the shot from the barrel. Memed was pleased to have the rifle back in his hands. Towards evening the others stopped firing. This was one of Black Ibrahim's tricks. He would behave as if he had withdrawn and given up the attack. Those who were surrounded would then try to escape and he would fall upon them. But Memed understood that he would have to rout them. Shouting wildly he leapt up and rushed into their midst. Hatché let out a scream but he took no notice. The encirclers were taken completely by surprise and suffered a complete rout under Memed's withering fire. As they rushed downhill, Memed pursued them until sunset, and it was midnight before he got back. Hatché threw herself into his arms weeping.

Iraz caught hold of her and pulled her away. "What are you crying for, you little fool? Is it the end of the world? What's the matter? This is a bandit's daily life! A brigand's wife must bear with everything. Stop whining! Has the boy saved you only for you to make trouble for him?"

"I've something to say to you," said Memed breathlessly.

"Say it!" said Iraz.

"Listen, we're lost. We must escape and manage somehow to put them off our scent. You must make an effort and we'll walk as far as Alidagh. There's no other way. We have a week's supplies and in two days we can reach Alidagh. It'll be a home for us. I know a good place there and no one else knows it. When I was hunting a wounded deer I once fell there and that's how I found it. We'll live there until the end of our days if necessary."

"Not until the end of our days, only until the amnesty. Next year there'll be an amnesty on the anniversary of the setting up of the Republic."

"An amnesty?" asked Memed. "But we can't, unless this business . . ." He stopped. Not a sound disturbed the night. "I'll attend to this business before the amnesty."

"Of course. It can't be otherwise. Even if he hides in a squirrel's hole . . ." said Hatché.

"We'll settle his account," replied Memed. "Get up, let's be on our way."

They set off, shivering with cold. The sky was light and the stars and the whole firmament seemed frozen, polished. The branches of the trees were damp and their clothes became wet as they brushed against them. Hatché sighed but pulled herself together, remembering that a brigand's wife must grit her teeth. They stepped cautiously, slowly, without making a sound. The

313

branches tore at their faces. Memed went ahead, Iraz behind him, with Hatché in the rear. They descended Chichekli mountain as day was breaking. Memed gazed into Hatché's eyes. Iraz left them where they were, went ahead and disappeared behind a rock, leaving them alone

XXIX

It was a difficult climb to the peak of Alidagh. The rocks were sharp, cutting their hands and feet. Down below, the Dikenli highlands lay among the clouds, the size of a hand. The five villages of Dikenli stood out like small dots in the distance.

Their heads seemed to swim as they stood at the foot of the precipice which would bring them to the cave. Memed could have climbed it and returned ten times, but how would these two women get there? It was a difficult task.

"Rest here while I take our things there and settle them in the cave. Then I'll come back and fetch you."

The two women were amazed at the ease with which he climbed up the face of the smooth rock wall.

Half an hour later he was back again. His eyes were smiling: "It's better than a house, it's a real stronghold. There are eagles' nests beside it. Our neighbours will be the eagles." He took Hatché by the hand and began to drag her up. "Come along, Iraz can wait for me here. I'll take you up as food for the eagles."

"Must I climb that wall?" asked Hatché, aghast.

"You'll hold on to me, not to the wall," said Memed. "Come on!"

As they climbed, once or twice Hatché felt dizzy and screamed. Memed scolded her. They finally reached the top.

Without waiting for Memed, Iraz rose and started climbing the rock. She was so tired that it seemed to her as if her hands would fall off, but when Memed turned back he found her at the top of the rock.

"You must have been born a brigand," said Memed.

"Yes," she replied proudly.

The mouth of the cave was just wide enough for them to enter.

The cave itself was deep, its floor of earth as black as coal-dust, as soft as flour. Its surface was thick with bird-droppings and the walls of rock were streaked with white veins.

"No man has ever set foot here," declared Memed.

"All the better," said Iraz.

"It's our village," said Hatché.

"Our home!"

Hatché's eyes were moist with pleasure. "Come, let's clean house."

"I'm going down to the village," said Memed. "Take this pistol. What do you need for your home?"

"A mirror," said Hatché. It was the first thing that entered her mind.

"You vain little thing!" laughed Iraz.

"Two mattresses, two blankets, a wooden bowl, a saucepan, a griddle, flour and good health." Hatché then added, "You can think of the rest."

"Keep well," called Memed.

By midnight he reached Durmush Ali's house. The old woman opened the door, guessing that it was Memed. "Sssh! Sssh!" she warned.

Memed crept in. "What is it, Mother Hürü? What's happened?"

"Sssh!"

Memed did not utter a word as she lit a piece of resin-wood, closed the windows tightly, went out and searched around the hut to make sure that no one was watching or overhearing them.

"My son, how did you manage to come? The village is full of policemen. They've beaten up Durmush Ali shamefully. They pulled the poor thing by the beard and dragged him around the village streets. All the villagers have been beaten. It's all that goat-beard's doing. How is it you haven't killed him yet? They asked Durmush Ali where your lair is and when he answered he didn't know, they set about him so harshly that he's still bed-ridden. They beat me too. I'm black and blue all over. You must kill that infidel."

"What's the news of Lame Ali?" asked Memed.

Angrily she raised her voice. "Memed, they should cut your throat with a blunt knife! Didn't I tell you to kill him when he fell

316

into your hands? Now he's become the Agha's man. Abdi has given him your old house. If only you'd listened to me and killed Ali! Now he's with the police on your trail once more. He collects tithes for Abdi Agha and gets the police to beat the villagers. You're to blame, Memed, believe me!"

"Where's he sleeping now?"

"Where would he sleep?" she shouted in anger. "In your house! He brought his family yesterday and settled there. His filthy slut of a wife is settled in my fine Deuneh's house! I sat and watched it and my heart bled. It withered up within me!"

"I'm going there," said Memed as he rose.

"It's full of policemen. But if you go about it carefully you can still kill that infidel and get away."

Memed went to his old house. A strong smell of milk and of calf reached his nostrils.

"Ali Agha! Ali Agha!" he called softly.

Ali leapt out of his bed at the sound of Memed's voice. "The man's mad," he said to himself. "Surely he's mad." Precipitately he came outside. Putting his hand over Memed's mouth, he said in a loud voice, "You did well to come to me. Thanks, Brother. So Memed's gone to Akchadagh? It's well you told me as we were planning to search the region of Akkale to-morrow, all for nothing . . ." Then he whispered: "Go to Durmush Ali's house. I'll be there at once."

He went inside and told the policemen: "One of my men just came and told me that the rogue has gone off to Akchadagh. You can hunt him there like a partridge. The job's easier now. At last we're really on Memed's trail. On Akchadagh you'll encircle him and that'll be that. I'll go to Abdi Agha's wife and cheer her up with the news."

The night was dark. He was amazed at Memed's boldness.

When Lame Ali came in Hürü was taken aback. She looked witheringly at Memed, as if to say that there really was no use in ever warning him.

"Mother Hürü, we've business to discuss," said Memed.

"You can talk," said Hürü. "Anyway, I'm not eager to see that lame pig's dirty face. Talk."

Lame Ali laughed. "For some strange reason Hürü has always been against me. What have I done to her?"

317

Hürü shook her head and gnashed her teeth at him. "I know what you've done, you lame pig! Now you're hand in glove with the police too. If our Memed weren't here, do you think I'd let you into this house? I'd break your neck. I'd take a stone and . . ." She withdrew, muttering threats and curses.

"Eh, Memed!" exclaimed Lame Ali. "How did you come here in all this tumult?"

"We've come."

"Black Ibrahim is on your trail. Abdi sent him. Abdi and Ali Safa Bey thought that Black Ibrahim would get the better of you. But he's no longer the Black Ibrahim we once knew. He's grown old and fat. He's watching the mountain pass with his men, thinking that sooner or later you'll go through there and he'll be able to shoot you. So be careful and avoid that pass. Then, let me tell you, I'm Abdi Agha's favourite now. It's Lame Ali this and Lame Ali that. He comes to me for everything. He didn't die, the wretch. If only you hadn't let that woman in when you burned the house down!"

"How were we to know, in all that confusion?"

"Ali Safa Bey has promised Abdi Agha that they'll bring your head and exhibit it in front of Abdi's house in town, next to the police station."

"Take no notice of that talk. Now, I need two mattresses, two blankets, a mirror, a saucepan, a wooden bowl, a pail of flour. Load it all on a horse and let me have it. Salt, pepper and butter too."

"Easy, with Abdi Agha's help! His house is at your service! We'll get whatever you want."

XXX

A squad of policemen under Sergeant Asim and accompanied by Black Ibrahim's band stayed in the mountains all through the autumn and winter. Every villager gave them a different report. They searched Akchadagh, the Goksun mountains, Beritdagh, Binbogha, Aladagh, Kayranlidagh, Konurdagh and Meryemchil pass. Not a stone did they leave unturned, up hill and down dale, but not a trace of Memed could they find. He seemed to have vanished from the face of the earth. They spent the winter in Deyirmenoluk and left no hole unexplored on Alidagh, where they would often stalk the deer. They even passed close to the cave but found nothing.

Lame Ali went ahead of them. "We'll certainly find him," he would assert, as he led them off to Binbogha or some other place.

"What's happened to your famous gift for finding clues, Ali?" they taunted.

"Old age," Ali would reply with a sigh. "I can't see as clearly as I once could."

Far from ageing, however, Lame Ali seemed to be younger, keen as the wind, with a fire of hope burning in his heart.

After they had roamed the mountains and valleys at random all through the autumn and winter, they returned weary and exhausted to the town, having destroyed two big bands of brigands, but not having found Memed. In town the Aghas were in despair.

Black Ibrahim seemed to have grown ten years older. "I've never seen the like of it!" he said. "This man has a secret gift; he's simply disappeared. But I'll find him and come to grips with him. There's no escape. I've an account to settle with him. In the fight at Chichekli valley I must have fired a hundred shots, thinking I had aimed at his head, but nothing happened to him. Bullets don't touch him, otherwise I would have settled his account long ago."

The rumour spread. "Bullets don't touch Slim Memed!" From mouth to mouth it reached Abdi Agha's ears. The old man seemed to be melting away. Long days and nights of waiting for news of Memed's death had reduced him to mere skin and bones. Every once in a while he would call on Ali Safa Bey. "Well, my son Ali? What with watching and waiting, my two eyes have increased to four and from four to eight. What's the result?" Ali Safa Bey would answer: "Be patient. With patience even bitter aloes can turn sweet. I've given you my word. I'll have his head brought and planted in your own yard. Be patient!"

But when Abdi Agha heard the rumour about bullets not touching Memed, he lost his head and rushed straight to Politician Ahmed's shop. Ahmed's expression became even more stupid, his speech even more confused and unintelligible.

"Write," said Abdi Agha. "Write to the Government in Ankara that a bloodthirsty brigand is ruling the mountains, killing children and carrying off young virgins to rape them. He's formed a government of his own in the mountains and his influence is spreading steadily. He distributes lands and this has gone to the heads of the villagers. Now write all that clearly. Let them really understand! Underline it heavily. When he's raped the girls he's kidnapped he cuts them to pieces and hangs them on the trees, piece by piece. His bandits have settled on the Marash-Adana road and allow no one to pass. Write, Politician Effendi, write Brother! Whatever skill you have, put in this letter so that whoever reads it in Ankara will be lost in amazement. Let them send an army. I'll go and get the stamps," he concluded as he left.

The town was in a turmoil. "Slim Memed, a boy as big as your finger. That he should do all this and not be caught!"

To all whom he met Abdi Agha poured out his woes. With the intrigues of Ali Safa Bey the whole business grew in importance. Then the reinforcements arrived the week that the squad of policemen returned to town, and Sergeant Asim was forced to set forth again in search of Memed. Black Ibrahim also went into the mountains with his own band, swearing oath upon oath to Abdi Agha that he would bring him Memed's head.

XXXI

The stalks of the yellow crocus are so short that one scarcely sees them. The flowers seem to rest on the ground, spread among the rocks like a yellow carpet the colour of the sun. The purple hyacinths grow knee-high. The little violets glisten like tearful eyes. The red flowers that bloom here are like no others, a crystal red, pure and warm in the midst of the green grass, that gushes like a spring from the ground. From Alidagh it looked as if green rain had fallen. The rocks were dappled, decorated in various hues. The air was light, scented with the sweet smell of flowers. Towards the foothills the rocks of Alidagh turned a purple red. White clouds touched the mountain and passed by, cradling Alidagh.

On the slopes facing Binbogha a spring bubbles among the scattered green pines. Memed used to bring their water from there.

The sunlight filled the world. Dikenli was bathed in light. Everything, trees, thistles, stones and rocks, seemed to have turned to light, melted into light.

Hatché lay with her head resting on Iraz's knees, at the mouth of the cave. Iraz was picking the lice out of her hair.

They had spent the whole winter in the cave, furnished it like a house, more pleasant than that of many a rich village Agha with its floor spread with pine-needles over which they laid hand-worked nomad rugs, their colours suggesting spring. The chief of the Black-haired tribe, Kerimoghlu, had given them these rugs as a wedding gift. The walls of the cave were hung with the skins of big-horned deer. The horns seemed to have been polished and the fur glistened like gold.

It had been a difficult winter. When the tempest was raging on Alidagh and the blizzard gave them no respite, they ran the risk of freezing to death each night, in spite of the fire that they kept burning till morning. For a month and a half Memed had worked to pierce a smoke-hole through the rocks, but it made no difference, the cave was still full of smoke. In the snow, the tempest, the blizzard, they were often forced to open the door and go outside for a breath of fresh air. But their hands and feet would soon be numb with the cold and they would rush back into the smoky cave.

They snuggled close together, covering themselves with all the deer skins, blankets and rugs they had. Only with the coming of day did they separate. Memed would go hunting deer while the women cooked their food and knitted stockings. The skins on the walls were those of the deer Memed had shot. They would eat the meat and dry the skins. All through the winter they had never lacked meat.

Lame Ali would bring them flour, oil and salt, which he left in a cave in the foothills where Memed would collect it. Even Lame Ali did not know their hiding-place. In order to leave no tracks in the snow they dragged a thick branch of blackthorn brush behind them. Blackthorn is best for covering tracks, passing over them and effacing them. In half an hour all traces would be gone. However much Alidagh was searched, they thus never came to harm. How could the police suspect anything? On all sides they saw only virgin snow, smooth and spotless.

"Well?" Hatché, at Iraz's knees, asked. "Where's the amnesty? Mustafa Agha was a liar."

"It'll come," answered Iraz. "Be patient, girl. A day dawns behind every hill."

They had grown thin and dark and their skin clung to their bones. Their eyes were twice as large as usual, but they were healthy and bright.

"Dear Iraz, if only one day dawns behind one hill, it's enough. If only one day would dawn! I don't ask for more."

"Be patient."

"On the mountaintop!" said Hatché. "Think of all the things that have happened to us. I go about as if in a dream. I just can't believe that I'm really Hatché and that Memed's really Memed."

When they had nothing else to do Memed would spend all day teaching them how to shoot. Iraz soon became quite a good shot, but Hatché could not manage it at all. She hated the very sight of a weapon and of ammunition, feeling sick at once. "If only we could get away from all this," she now sighed.

"By now the green crops are knee-high in the Chukurova," said Iraz. "The ears are ready to burst open. The ants are pouring out of their nests on to the paths, spreading out under the sun." Iraz's eyes filled with tears. "The land of Adaja . . ." she said. "Let Memed kill my Riza's murderer before the amnesty comes. I would like to kill him with my own hands. Then we'll go and settle in the Chukurova. We'll sow and reap our own land at Adaja. My Riza's father used to earn a good living with that land."

"The land of Adaja," repeated Hatché, closing her eyes. "The narcissus grows in thick patches among the rocks of Adaja, isn't that true?"

"Yes."

"The land of Adaja gives back forty-fold what one sows there. With a year's earnings a man can build himself a home. In any case, if we go there we'll have enough money for a home."

"We'll have the title-deeds drawn up in our Memed's name. The land at Adaja must be his. The amnesty will come and if it doesn't, we'll go off to some place where we're not known. If we could make Memed forget about Abdi we could even go now. We would change our names. A day will come when Memed will also kill Riza's murderer. No, I must kill him with my own hands. That's why I learned to fire a gun."

"Oh!" exclaimed Hatché. "How difficult it all is!"

"Very difficult . . . But sometimes I feel quite happy and say to myself that I've found a son in Memed to replace my Riza. But sometimes, too, my girl, I seem to become mad. The breasts from which my Riza sucked his milk cry out for vengeance. My heart says 'Take your gun, go down to the village, kill that murderer Ali, and then let them do what they like.' Ah, just you wait, my girl! That Ali, I'll make mince-meat of him! Cursed Ali, how could you have killed my boy?"

"A day dawns behind every hill, be patient. I know it will dawn but . . ."

"Again?" exclaimed Iraz. "You're eating away at Memed. You'll kill him with your worrying."

Hatché hung her head. "It's a whole week since he went away. He has never stayed away more than three days. Ah, this brigand's life, these mountains, this fear! I'm afraid, Iraz, I can't help it. My heart is all tight and tense. Did he ever stay away more than three days? Something has happened to Memed. I want to go down as far as that village. Let me go! Memed would have been back long ago if something hadn't happened to him." She was weeping bitterly. "Let me go, Iraz."

Iraz frowned. "You'll stay right here, you silly little fool," she shouted. "If you move a step from here I'll shoot you. You'll only bring trouble on his head. One of these days the lad will get himself shot because of you. He's sure to be all right, you'll see."

Hatché rose and ran into the cave, throwing herself down on the floor. Her body shook convulsively as she sobbed for a long while.

Iraz went and sat by her. "My girl, my beautiful Hatché, why are you eating yourself up like that? It's doing you no good. Nothing can happen to Memed. He would get the better of a hundred men. Why do you cry like that?"

"Iraz," said Hatché, as she dried her eyes, "if only you were right . . ."

The mist was rising from Dikenli. A few black clouds were scudding across the sky when Memed rushed into the cave, sweating and breathless, his hands and face dripping with blood. When Hatché saw him, she threw her arms round his neck and began to weep again.

"Stop, Hatché," said Memed. "Listen to what I have to tell you!" He caressed her hair.

Exasperated, Iraz grasped Hatché's arm and pulled her away sharply. "For heaven's sake," she shouted. "You'll worry the lad's head off with these doings."

"Stop, let me tell you what happened," said Memed, smiling. "As I was coming from Kerimoghlu, Black Ibrahim lay waiting for me in the Sarija highlands. He's a strong man, brave and intelligent, and pursued me right up to the foot of the mountain. For three whole days we played hide and seek. I ran off in front of them, then doubled back, going as far as Sarija again, but they kept after me. We played a real cat-and-mouse game. My only worry was not to let them learn about Alidagh. Then, with Jabbar's help, I gave them the slip in the foothills and came here. We won't go out for a week. Now tend my wound."

The two women set to work to undress Memed. He was wounded in the shoulder. As they were extracting the bullet, Memed was seized with fever and, with his knees pressed against his stomach, began to tremble. Hatché lost her mind. She no longer knew what she was doing.

Memed's fever lasted a whole week. His wound had festered and swollen. It was only after another week that he at last came to himself and began to recount everything as it had happened: "Before I reached Sarija I came up against the police. There were ten of them, Sergeant Asim leading them. We began firing. God knows, Sergeant Asim will meet his death one of these days at my hands, he comes at me so openly. 'What's this, Sergeant Asim?' I called. 'Are you tired of life?' I raised my weapon and when he saw me so close to him he threw himself down with a scream. 'Don't be so scared, Sergeant Asim,' I said. 'I have nothing against you. If I'd wanted to, I could have shot you ten times over. Go your way!' He then rose from where he was lying, smiled at me, collected his men and went off without a word. Then someone was to bring me ammunition to Sarija. When I reached the place we'd agreed on I was met by a volley of shots. It was Black Ibrahim, firing away like a hailstorm. Before I could fire twice I was wounded and they pursued me for two days, as far as the mountain. Suddenly I heard a voice that sounded like Jabbar's. Then I realised that Jabbar had somehow heard of my plight and was attacking them to relieve me. We drove them back together, but they came back after me. In the end Jabbar drew them all on to himself and I escaped. But I never caught a glimpse of Jabbar, though I'm sure he got the better of them. Still, we should not stay here much longer. They're hot on our scent now, and Ali Safa Bey is the cause of all our misfortunes."

He lay in bed another week. In the foothills they could hear the sound of shots every other day as Memed's wound slowly healed.

XXXII

That autumn on Dikenli, the people were working joyfully. This year the soil's yield was good, the ears full and heavy.

Mother Hürü was like a whirlwind, rushing all over Dikenli. Like a tongue of flame, she talked endlessly and cursed furiously. The ribs on her right side still ached from her beating. She wore a plaster and when she breathed deep her face would still wrinkle with the pain.

"May their eyes drop out, what did they want with an old woman like me?" she would complain bitterly and then add persuasively: "Hey, you villagers! Abdi Agha isn't coming back to this village. Since he won't come, you won't have to give him two-thirds of the crop. You would be fools if you did. Say that the crop hasn't been good this year. We can't just die of hunger, you'll say. We would have nothing left for ourselves! Will you take our lives? There's nothing, nothing, man. The earth was parched and the crops dry. They all dried up . . ."

From Deyirmenoluk she would go to the neighbouring village and from there to the next, always muttering to herself. As soon as she saw someone threshing or reaping, she went over to him: "Give thanks to Memed. Bless him day and night. Do you realise what you owe him? If it hadn't been for him, Abdi Agha would still be preying upon us like a bird of evil. Thank God, he's no longer in the village. Don't give a single grain to him! What has he ever done to earn it! He's taking his ease in town."

People thought about it, shook their heads and took their caps off to scratch them. "What will be the end of all this?" they wondered.

The harvesting was over and they took the crops back from the fields to their homes. Nobody gave a single grain of wheat to Abdi

Agha. Lame Ali and the Agha's other stewards went from house to house in vain.

"We would gladly give our souls for our Agha," the villagers would answer. "There's no one like our Agha. Would we have him living there so miserably in a strange town? But what can we do, we haven't harvested a single grain. What can be his share of nothing? Next year, if God is good, we'll give to our Agha! That infidel Memed has driven our dear Agha from the village. God willing, there'll be a good crop next year, then it can all be our Agha's. We'll be hungry and it can all go to our Agha. There are five villages on Dikenli. All five will help our dear Agha."

"Why," would argue Abdi Agha's stewards. "Dikenli has seen its best harvest in years! You're all liars. Why don't you say openly that you don't recognise any rights and won't give him his dues?"

"Ah!" replied the villagers. "May our eyes drop out! With our Agha driven away to a strange town, would we refuse him his dues? Is it possible! We'd give our soul for our Agha!"

Hürü was beside herself with joy. All her activity in the summer, all her chattering had not been in vain. She dyed her white hair with henna and tied round her head the green and red silk 'kerchief that young girls wear at marriages and feasts. Her dress was of silk too. She took out of her trunk the beads she had worn as a girl and wore them too, binding a silk sash from Tripoli around her waist. Her face was wreathed in smiles as she went from house to house singing. "Hürü's young again," they said. Every young girl who heard her indecent and ribald songs would blush.

When he heard that the villagers refused to give him his accustomed dues, Abdi stormed off to Politician Ahmed again and made him write another pathetic telegram to Ankara, pouring out all his woes. Then he rushed around the town repeating everywhere all that had happened. He went to the governor and to the chief of police and wept and complained. The governor and the chief of police decided that something had to be done and sent fresh policemen to Deyirmenoluk to question the villagers. They locked Mother Hürü up in a hut. But not a word could they get out of anyone. The villagers submitted to being beaten, cursed, driven from pillar to post like a flock of sheep, but not a sound escaped their lips. The whole population of five big villages was speechless.

Things reached such a pitch that the district governor had to go up to Dikenli in person, but even that was of no avail. The villagers all stared at him with empty eyes and half-witted faces.

Lame Ali was the first to speak. The villagers were all astounded when he declared: "We would all gladly sacrifice ourselves for our Agha," he explained. "Who does that brigand Memed think he is? Does he think he can order us about? If we had harvested a single grain we'd have given it to our Agha. This year there's a famine. If we don't all die it'll be a miracle. Ask me, I'm the Agha's steward. I'll go hungry too."

Lame Ali let his eyes wander over the crowd, huddled like a flock of sheep.

"Tell them," he said. "If we had harvested a single grain, wouldn't we have given it to our dear Agha?"

The crowd stirred slightly and muttered: "We would have given it all."

"If he wants our lives . . ." prompted Ali.

"We would give them too."

"And if Memed comes to the village?"

"He can't come."

"But if he comes . . ." insisted Lame Ali.

"We'll kill him."

The district governor did not believe a word and began to search the village, house by house, but was unable to find a single grain. Where had the villagers hidden such a store, what had they done with it? It was unbelievable.

News of all this reached the town the same day and it seemed that the door of Dikenli had at last been opened on to the world.

Abdi Agha tore at his hair in rage and despair. Memed was clearly responsible for all this. Only his death would put an end to it. When Huseyin Agha in Aktozlu was then shot one night in his bed, it was like rubbing salt into a wound. Who could have killed him? Only Memed.

Sergeant Asim was courageous, a good man, a mountain wolf, but not capable of catching Memed. He received reprimand after reprimand from his chief and was so ashamed that he could no longer hold his head up as he walked through the market. Some of the gossip about him had reached his ears. "Memed's just a slip of a boy, but he can twist this big sergeant round his little finger." Sergeant Asim felt deeply humiliated.

XXXIII

The rocks, the trees, the grass, the flowers, the ground, all of Ali-dagh was covered with snow. Even the sky was white, an endless expanse of it stretching from Alidagh to Dikenli, from there to Akchadagh and Chichekli valley and down to the Chukurova, without a single blemish.

The sun shone down on this boundless expanse and a million flashing sparks seemed to rise to the sky, dazzling one's eyes. Only rarely did the shadow of a cloud darken the endless unsullied white as it passed.

The situation in the cave was bad. They had run out of food and wood, Memed's hair and beard were all matted, Iraz was thin and grimy, and now Hatché was pregnant and about to enter her labour. "If not to-day, then to-morrow," said Iraz. Hatché had grown pale and her black hair was dull and tangled.

Sergeant Asim allowed them no peace. Ever since autumn he had been prowling all around Deyirmenoluk and wandering up and down the slopes of Alidagh.

Iraz drew Memed outside the cave. "There's no blizzard to-day, son. Let's decide what we're to do. This girl will give birth to her child any moment now. Are we to go down to the village or should we try to look after her here? Let's decide."

"We can't take her down to a village," said Memed, his face wrinkled with anxiety. "They're in all the houses. She'll have to give birth here."

They went back inside. Hatché was sitting with her back against the wall of the cave, staring fixedly ahead. Her eyes seemed frozen.

"Hatché," said Memed, "Iraz and I are going down to the village. Load your gun and wait. We'll be back by night."

"I can't stay alone," said Hatché.

329

"What are we to do, Hatché?" asked Memed.

"I'll come too."

"Don't be foolish!"

"I can't stay here."

"Let Iraz stay too," he suggested.

"No," she replied curtly.

"Why are you so cross?"

"It's how I feel."

"Stay, girl," pleaded Iraz.

"I can't."

"You've grown contrary since you came to live on the mountain," said Iraz.

"That's how I am," Hatché snapped back.

They were silent. Memed sat down on a stone outside the cave, his face between his hands. An eagle circled overhead, its wings spread out. Memed was angry.

"You two stay here," he suddenly shouted as he started downhill, going faster and less carefully than usual.

"What do you want of the lad?" Iraz burst out after he had left them. "Hasn't he enough troubles on his head already? The police won't leave him a moment of peace, and now he has you nagging him besides!"

Hatché did not open her mouth.

Later in the afternoon Iraz went out and saw to her horror that Memed's blackthorn brush lay outside. Madly, at the top of her voice, she called after him, but Memed had gone long ago. She called and called, and then went inside and threw herself down beside Hatché.

"The worst," she cried. "I fear the worst is coming. He's forgotten the blackthorn and there's no blizzard to cover up his tracks. The air is quite still. If I were to go out to cover his tracks, I would never be able to pass where he goes . . ."

On the evening of the second day Memed came back. His cheeks were pale and he was crushed beneath the burden he bore.

"I was scared," he said. "Once I got down I remembered I had forgotten the blackthorn. If I had turned back it would have been night. The police don't give Lame Ali any peace. They're forcing him to follow me. That's what I'm afraid of. If he finds a trail he can't help himself, he just has to follow it. He said to me, 'For

God's sake, drag the blackthorn brush behind you!' I knew then he couldn't help himself. I'm afraid, especially now. It's a bad business."

"Lame Ali would never do it," said Iraz. "Don't be afraid, lad. He would give his life for you."

"I know, but if he sees a track, he can't help himself. I should have killed him on the very first day. . . ."

XXXIV

Sergeant Asim was in despair. "That devil Memed has descended like a plague on my head. If he would only slip off and attend to his own business somewhere else, I would be a free man again."

His men were worn out and disheartened too. "Every blessed day of this cruel winter we've been out on the mountains! What will be the end of all this?" Wherever they saw a track that looked at all human, wherever the snow had been disturbed, they would comb the mountain for days. In their search for Memed they had already disposed of several other bands of brigands.

For the past month they had been combing Alidagh because a shepherd-boy they had questioned and beaten had admitted seeing Memed there. Alidagh was in a state of siege, as if sentinels had been posted everywhere to watch. Sergeant Asim could not believe that Memed was living on Alidagh in such a severe winter, but refused to abandon the search after obtaining this information from the shepherd-boy.

One day a mounted policeman, breathless with excitement, brought news. "Sergeant, we've seen him," he said, "dragging a blackthorn brush over his tracks. He was going up to the top of the mountain. When he saw us he ran off without firing a shot. But his trail cannot be missed, even if he drags blackthorn over it. The surface of the snow is frozen and dragging blackthorn is now of no avail. We examined his trail; it's an old one."

Sergeant Asim was exultant. At last they were really on Memed's track. He sent a man to Abdi Agha's house to summon Lame Ali.

"We've found his trail," he told Ali, "and you'll follow it."

"My eyes betray me in the snow. I have to be able to see earth."

The villagers agreed. "Lame Ali can't follow a trail in the snow. He'll lead you astray," they said.

But Sergeant Asim was adamant. "Even if you can't do the job, you've got to come."

Ali began to tremble like a leaf. "I kiss your feet, Sergeant, but don't drag me out in this cold weather."

"You're coming along," the sergeant said with finality.

Lame Ali stood there, hanging his head as he leaned for support against a wall.

The police, with the sergeant leading them, set forth for Alidagh.

The whole village was in an uproar. "Memed's trail has been found!" Men, women and children followed the police in a crowd as far as the foot of Alidagh, staring at the tracks in the frozen snow.

Ali saw the tracks and his heart tightened with sorrow. "Why didn't he drag the blackthorn behind him, the fool?" he muttered to himself, bewildered and dismayed. "They're sure to find him now, with such a clear trail."

Sergeant Asim seized Ali by the arm and led him to the beginning of the trail. "What are you muttering there? Tell me, are these his tracks?"

"No," answered Lame Ali. "This is some shepherd's trail. Besides, it's a month old."

Sergeant Asim was in a towering rage. Seizing Ali's arm, he flung him down in the snow. "You villain," he shouted. "You're the Agha's steward, you eat his bread, and at the same time you're hand in glove with Memed. One and all, you're each another Memed, waiting for a chance to pounce on a victim!" Then he gave his men the order to follow the trail.

Freezing in the snow, their hands frost-bitten, they followed the trail for two days and came out on the peak, which they encircled completely.

The villagers were already mourning. Lame Ali hung his head and wept. "They've found him," he said. "They've found our Memed!" He threw all precaution to the winds.

Mother Hürü was furious. "Let them find him," she cried. "They'll see what kind of reception they'll have. Let there be a thousand policemen! My Memed will slip through the fingers of a thousand!"

The first skirmish took place towards evening. The police had found the path to the cave and spotted its opening. Without intermission they hurled hand grenades at the mouth of the cave from above. When they came too close Memed began firing in a circle around Sergeant Asim.

They might still have escaped and saved themselves, but Hatché was in travail, giving birth to her child in the cave. When she heard the shots she began to weep.

"Didn't I tell you?" said Iraz. "It's because of the blackthorn."

"Yes, but they wouldn't have found us by themselves," said Memed. "Lame Ali couldn't avoid tracking us down again. I should have killed him. If only a blizzard would start, they wouldn't be able to stay here. Once they've gone, it will be a week before they come back."

Sergeant Asim called in a friendly voice, "Memed, my boy, surrender! We've cornered you at last and you can't escape. Soon there'll be the amnesty. Surrender! I don't want your death."

Memed's reply was a bullet that split a stone in front of the sergeant.

The onslaught became more furious. Both sides fired without respite.

"We'll wait here a week or a month," called Sergeant Asim. "Your supplies of ammunition will run out."

Gritting his teeth, Memed at last replied. "I know, Sergeant, I know," he shouted. "That's how it will be. But I won't have left a single one of you alive. I'm not surrendering. In the end you'll bring my dead body out of the cave. Do you understand, Sergeant?"

"It's a pity for a man like you. If you kill all of us, they'll send more police. What can you gain? The amnesty will come this year. Surrender now, Memed!"

"Don't waste your breath, Sergeant," shouted Memed. "I could have killed you many times, but this time I'll do it. You should have stopped following me."

The noise of bullets drowned their voices and they soon ceased to taunt each other.

The heap of empty cartridge cases around Memed grew steadily. He had two more bags of cartridges but he was worried. He was being forced to fire too fast.

Iraz was busy with Hatché, who kept on moaning. "That it should have happened on this day!" exclaimed Iraz. She left Hatché for a moment, seized her gun and ran to help Memed, firing until Hatché began screaming again. Then she went back to her.

Hatché's forehead was covered with beads of sweat as she lay writhing on the ground. "Mother," she cried, "Mother, you should never have brought me into the world!"

Memed and Iraz were both smeared with soot from the smoke in the cave, which stank of their sweat.

Suddenly Memed cried, "I'm wounded." Then he regretted it and bit his lip until it bled.

Hatché had heard him and rose like an arrow from where she lay; she dropped down beside him. "Memed, are you wounded? I'll kill myself."

Iraz came and unfastened Memed's coat. "You're wounded in the shoulder," she said as she began immediately to tend the wound while he kept up his fire on their assailants.

Sergeant Asim was astonished that a bandit should have such a supply of ammunition. Some of his men had been wounded and he slowly began to lose hope.

Hatché uttered another long scream. Iraz held her up. "Hold tight!" she said. Pain disfigured Hatché's face. Suddenly a baby's cry rang out. Memed turned and saw the child still covered in blood, Hatché's face as white as paper. He looked away. His hands were trembling and the rifle slipped from his grasp. Iraz picked it up and began firing. Hatché lay there as if dead, but Memed soon pulled himself together and said as he reached for the gun: "Give it to me, Iraz."

Iraz handed it back to him and went over to clean the child and rub it with salt. "A boy," she said.

A bitter smile crossed Memed's face. "A boy!"

The fight continued until late in the afternoon. Memed managed their defence single-handed. Iraz loaded his rifle while he used a stone as a support and fired with only one hand.

Suddenly Iraz hung her head, exhausted. "There's no more ammunition," she said.

Memed had forgotten about ammunition. A harsh sound escaped from his throat, as if he were being strangled. He collapsed over his gun, then rose and staggered towards the child. For a long while he stared at it in wonder, before turning back to the mouth of the cave. He was smiling.

He picked up his rifle, pulled his handkerchief out of his pocket, and fastened it to the barrel like a flag.

He turned to Iraz, who was seated under an overhanging rock, weeping all by herself, utterly exhausted. "Iraz," he said.

She raised her head and looked at him.

"Listen. They won't leave me alive. Call my son Memed."

He went outside and, brandishing his rifle in the air, shouted: "I surrender, Sergeant Asim!"

Sergeant Asim was strongly built and handsome, with a bushy moustache, large eyes and a good-natured expression.

He was astounded when Memed announced his surrender, unable to believe his own eyes and ears. "Do you really surrender, Memed?" he shouted back.

Memed answered in a weary voice: "I surrender, Sergeant. Your wish has been granted."

The sergeant turned to his men. "Don't come out of cover. I'll go. Perhaps it's a trick."

He was soon at the entrance of the cave. He came in and took Memed by the hand. Smiling, he said: "Better luck next time, Memed!"

"Thanks."

"I still can't believe in your surrender, Memed!"

Memed was silent. He held out his hands for the handcuffs.

Iraz, who had been crouching in a corner, suddenly leapt forward. "Sergeant," she cried, "do you think it's you who have made Memed surrender?"

She pulled the blanket away and exposed the baby, its eyes half closed. "Here's who made Memed surrender. And you boast that you're a man!"

Sergeant Asim had not expected this. He looked first at Hatché, then at Iraz, then at Memed. The smile froze on his lips. He stretched out his hand to Memed and took off the handcuffs. "Memed!" he said, then was silent.

They stood, eyeing each other. "Memed!" His voice was

hoarse. "Memed, I'm not the man to accept your surrender under these conditions." From his waist he pulled out five rounds of ammunition and threw them on the ground. "I'm going. Shoot after me so as not to make a fool of me in the eyes of the others," he murmured.

He rushed out of the cave, shouting.

Memed fired after him.

When he reached his men Sergeant Asim said: "Would that outlaw ever surrender? He played that trick only to shoot at me. If I hadn't thrown myself down, I'd have been hit. It's good I was going carefully. There's a storm coming. Let's go down or we'll all freeze to death here."

Weary, exhausted, the men turned round for a last look at Memed's cave as they started downhill.

Black clouds were swirling around the peak of Alidagh. It began to snow heavily. Soon a wild blizzard was blowing. All that night it swept from rock to rock over Alidagh, which was lost in an expanse of white, no longer distinguishable from the sky.

XXXV

The news spread from village to village, from them to the town. "Memed has been killed. When the blizzard clears up on Alidagh they'll bring down his corpse."

The eyes of Deyirmenoluk were fixed on the storm-swept peak of Alidagh, the mountain of mountains, in all its majesty. Alidagh had defeated Slim Memed.

The villagers remained in their homes, expecting Abdi Agha to return as soon as the news of Memed's death should reach him.

The villagers of Vayvay had meanwhile been wresting their fields back from Ali Safa Bey piece by piece. Big Osman now looked fifteen years younger and was defying Ali Safa openly.

The news that "Slim Memed, my hawk," had been killed reached Vayvay. Big Osman remained quite still, as if paralysed; even knives would have failed to pry his mouth open. Tears streamed from his eyes when at last he spoke: "My hawk! What a gallant man was my hawk! Such large eyes, such brows, such slim fingers! And so tall, like a cypress! My hawk! He said to me, 'Uncle Osman, one day I'll come and be a guest in your house.' But this was destined never to be. My hawk! And his wife was with him. What will the poor thing do now? Listen, villagers, my hawk saved us from that infidel's hands. Let's bring his wife down to the village, give her a field and care for her. If she goes to prison, we'll care for her there too. Is that agreed?"

"Agreed," said all the villagers. The fear of Ali Safa Bey came and settled in their hearts again.

Lame Ali had brought the news to the town and came to Abdi Agha. "Your enemy's life is just so much, Agha," he said. "Finished. A shepherd, who came down from the mountain, said

338

he'd seen the body with his own eyes. Sergeant Asim had cut off its head. I said I must bring the news quickly to my Agha, so I hastened here without delay."

At first Abdi Agha could not believe it. Then he was wild with joy. For three days everyone who came from the mountain confirmed the news that Lame Ali had brought.

Abdi Agha hastened first to Ali Safa Bey, who was not at home. His wife said: "You see, Abdi Agha? One pays for one's sins. I congratulate you!"

"Thank you, my daughter," said Abdi Agha as he left.

He went to the governor and, kissing his hand, said in servile tones: "May God never bring adversity upon the Government, Governor. Sergeant Asim is a hero, a brave man! I'm ready to do anything for him!"

"Congratulations, Abdi Agha. You've complained so much about the Government that if it hadn't been for Ali Safa Bey you would have brought shame on the town's good name. Luckily Ali Safa Bey never let them send your telegrams."

Abdi Agha's eyes opened wide. "Not even one? Not a single one?" he exclaimed.

"No, not one," laughed the governor. "If they had gone, these telegrams would have sufficed to hang you and me too. Were you mad? Does one send such telegrams to Ankara?"

Abdi Agha pondered, then began to laugh heartily. "It's as well they didn't go, Governor. I was just nervous. They would have made our town's good name worthless. When a man gets angry he forgets everything. I just couldn't bear to see a great government unable to deal with a miserable boy! Believe me, it went against the grain. But what was I thinking when I sent all those telegrams? Madness! Governor, forgive me."

After the governor he called on the commanding officer of the police to whom he likewise expressed his joy and thanks, inquiring if he should give Sergeant Asim a present and asking that Memed's head be exhibited in front of his house in the village, not here in town. The chief of the police granted his request.

Returning home, Abdi Agha summoned Lame Ali. "If Sergeant Asim ill-treated you a little," he said, "you must not bear him a grudge. He's a hero, a gallant man. See, he's wiped out our enemy." Then his bitterness overflowed. "Those villagers," he snarled. "Those beggarly, ungrateful villagers! When I wasn't there for a year they didn't turn in a single grain. To-morrow I'll go up to the village. So there was a famine last year, was there? Dishonest, beggarly people! Tell me, was there really a famine that you didn't give me my dues? So you relied on Memed? Take your Memed. Take his head and do what you like with it. Have you seen your Memed now? Now I'll show you what famine really means. I'll show you!"

He took Lame Ali's hand: "Ali!"

"Yes, Agha."

"This year's crop was better than any year's, wasn't it?"

"Twice as good as any other year's."

"Ali!"

"Yes, Agha?"

"How shall I punish those villagers?"

"You know best, Agha."

Abdi put on his best clothes, rubbed perfume on his rosary, went to the barber's and got a shave. He could not control himself for joy. He came to Mustafa Effendi's shop and smiled as he entered it.

"One should not rejoice at anyone's death, Abdi Agha, even at your enemy's," said Mustafa Effendi. "You never know what may happen . . ."

After he had wandered all round the market, from one shop to another, showing his joy, after each one had congratulated him, after he had mounted his horse and was setting off for the village, it happened. The bad news came: "Wounded as he is, Memed has escaped from Sergeant Asim!"

"Who said so?"

"Sergeant Asim said so."

"Where is Sergeant Asim?"

"He's coming. I saw him at Shabapli."

Abdi Agha turned his horse's head and went back to town.

Sergeant Asim and the policemen entered the town, weary, exhausted.

Abdi dismounted, almost falling off his horse, in the courtyard of his house. He made his way listlessly to Mad Fahri, the letter-writer.

"Write, Brother," he said. "Write to Ismet Pasha himself. The governor, the telegraphist, Ali Safa Bey, the chief of the police and the brigand Memed are all hand-in-glove. Write! Pasha, of all the telegrams I wrote you, they didn't even send one off! Write that!"

XXXVI

"My hawk," Big Osman exulted. "He's broken the back of the Aghas. Ali Safa Bey is still trying to send men up the mountain. Let him send as many as he likes, my hawk will devour them all!"

They had gathered under the great mulberry-tree at the back of the village. The autumn leaves were yellow, ready to fall.

"We've regained our fields now, haven't we?"

"All."

"Thanks to whom?"

"To Slim Memed."

Big Osman rose to his feet. "Ali Saip Bey, the deputy, has news from Ankara," he said.

The villagers were all ears.

"He's spoken with Ismet Pasha. At the national holiday this autumn, at the Government *bayram*, there'll be a great amnesty. In fifteen days or a month Memed will be pardoned too. He has a child. Let us give him a field. Let him settle in our village. What do you say?"

The villagers answered as one man. "Let him settle here," they said. "His place is with us. Our fields are his and our lives too."

Big Osman set aside a hundred acres of the village's most fertile land. These hundred acres belonged to the Widow Eshe. They collected money among themselves and bought the field from her. Collectively the villagers ploughed the hundred acres and sowed them with wheat.

Big Osman took a handful of the soft ploughed earth. It slipped through his fingers like water. "If I die I shall die in peace at last," he said. "Ali Saip Bey doesn't tell lies. What he said will certainly happen. He's Ismet Pasha's own man."

But a new storm now burst over the town. They had failed to

catch Memed and Ali Safa Bey accused the governor and the chief of police of protecting the brigands. He sent telegram after telegram to Ankara.

The governor then received sharp orders to catch the brigands and sent the captain of the police out in person to do the job.

The Taurus villages had had enough, not so much of the brigands but of the police. Memed could not take shelter in the villages any more. For days he and the two women remained on the mountains with the child, hungry and thirsty. Several times they nearly fell into ambushes which Captain Faruk had laid, but still managed to escape. If Kerimoghlu had not been there to help, Memed would have been lost. Wherever Memed was, Kerimoghlu brought him ammunition, food and money. The money from Vay-vay village was also brought by Kerimoghlu, who was waiting for the *bayram* as impatiently as Big Osman.

Deyirmenoluk and the other villages of Dikenli were not at all pleased with the prospect of the amnesty. If Memed came down from the mountain they feared that Abdi Agha would return to the village too.

"What is this amnesty? If a brigand's a brigand, his place is on the mountain. If I were in Memed's shoes, I would never come down. Why should he be a villager like us and live miserably? Now the whole world is afraid of him and he's much better off!"

XXXVII

"Have you heard, Memed?" asked Lame Ali.

Memed laughed with bright eyes. "No."

"Didn't I tell you what kind of a man Big Osman was in Chichekli valley? Ali Saip Bey has come from Ankara and announced that the pardon will be proclaimed at the big *bayram*. Then Big Osman gathered the villagers round him and spoke to them. 'Slim Memed is our hawk,' he said. 'Let him come and settle in our village.' The villagers replied: 'His place is among us!' They've bought a hundred-acre field for you. Big Osman chose it himself. He said that Ali Saip Bey cannot be wrong and that you should be careful to keep out of danger until the *bayram*. 'I'll bring the news of the pardon to the hawk myself,' Big Osman said. Well, what do you think of it?"

"This captain doesn't let us breathe. He's left all the other brigands in peace, all those bloodthirsty murderers, and comes only after me. We've already had at least ten fights. Whatever happens, if we meet again, I'll shoot him."

"Don't, there's the pardon. Wait a while and try to keep him at bay," said Lame Ali as he left.

Alayar has soil red as blood, as red as if you took a red watermelon, cut it down the middle and put it in the sun. For three days they had been hiding on the red land of Alayar. Although Captain Faruk hovered over them like a bird of prey, they were happy. Since she had heard about the pardon Hatché could not sleep for joy. She and Iraz sang all day. The child had been named Memed. He had grown fat and strong and could hear all day the loveliest lullabies.

Hatché tossed little Memed in the air and caught him again.

"Iraz," she said, "just see what God has done for us. We talked of thirty acres. He's given us a hundred and a house besides!"

She was as full of jokes, of childish tricks and nonsense as a girl of twelve. Every so often she would turn to Memed. "Well, Memed, the pardon is coming. We have our house and field. Go on, laugh a little!"

But Memed would only smile bitterly.

That night they were surrounded by Captain Faruk at Alayar. "Slim Memed," the captain called. "I'm not Sergeant Asim. You'll see."

Memed did not reply. He had learned how to escape from the police and was firing in such a manner as to distract his assailants. It was night and they would soon slip through the cordon that encircled them and escape. Iraz was more agile, a better shot and braver than the most renowned of brigands. She could keep the guards at bay by herself for three whole days.

Captain Faruk was furious. One man, two women and a baby!

"Slim Memed, you can't escape."

Memed had made up his mind. He fired with the intention of killing the captain, and moved forward into the very midst of his assailants. It was the first time he had been so neglectful of precautions.

"I'm hit," Hatché cried to him from behind. Memed stopped dead, rooted to the spot, but did not turn back. He fired a circle of shots round the captain. This did not satisfy him and he began to hurl one grenade after another. Then, like an arrow, he ran to Hatché's side. She lay on the ground, lifeless, the child beside her. She was almost smiling.

Memed turned back and began firing all round him like a machine-gun, constantly tossing out hand grenades.

The captain was wounded. His men could hold on no longer.

Iraz had collapsed, weeping on Hatché's dead body. Her face was as it had been that first day in prison.

Memed sat with his gun on his knees, his head bent, weeping.

Iraz raised her head from the dead body and stared at the sky. Far above, a flock of cranes was passing.

Hatché's blood was mingled with the red earth of Alayar.

Then the child began to cry. Memed took him and pressed him to his heart. To quieten him, he sang a lullaby.

"I'll go to the village," said Iraz, "to see that they bury Hatché."

Memed remained motionless as a stone, his face tense and terrible to look at, his eyes fixed on the dead body, the baby in his arms.

When the villagers heard the news, men, women and children came and stood by the body. "Ah," they moaned, "Slim Memed's ill-starred Hatché!"

Memed summoned the headman and gave him some money. "Bury my Hatché with all due ceremony," he said.

He looked at Hatché for a long time. She was smiling. He took the child in his arms. "Let's go, Iraz," he said.

Iraz followed him as they began to ascend the mountain.

Near the peak they found a cave. They sat on a rock at the mouth of it. The leaves were falling from the neighbouring trees. A bird was singing. From the rock opposite a cloud of white pigeons rose. A lizard climbed up a tree-trunk. The child, which had been sleeping in Memed's arms, awoke and began to cry.

Iraz came, took Memed's hand, and looked into his eyes. "Brother!" she said. "Brother! I must tell you something, my Memed!"

Memed waited without stirring.

"Brother, give me this child and let me go off to the villages around Antep. He'll die in these mountains. I've given up thinking of avenging Riza's blood. In my Riza's place there's this boy now. Give him to me and let me go. I'll bring up the boy."

Memed slowly handed the child to her. Iraz took it and pressed it to her breast. "Riza!" she said. "My Riza!" With one hand she stripped off the cartridge-belts that she wore and piled them all up in one spot. "Good luck, Memed," she said.

Memed came and took Iraz by the arm. The child had stopped crying. For a long time he fixed his eyes on the child's face. "Good luck."

XXXVIII

Its rump could not be said to be round, but long, like an egg. Its ears were slim, a long white blaze on its forehead, its legs short compared with the length of its back, its colour neither red nor bay, neither russet nor grey, but a dappled iron-grey.

The horse stood waiting in front of Big Osman's house. It neighed and stamped the ground. Its back was thin. Its eyes were bright and sad like a girl's eyes. Its tail swung down as far as its hoofs. Its mane fell to the right. When it galloped the mane curled in the wind with the shape of a reed-pipe.

The pardon had been proclaimed with the great *bayram*. Most of the brigands on the mountain had come down and surrendered their guns. The courtyard of the police station was full of brigands waiting there.

Big Osman stroked the horse's mane. "It's fine enough even for my hawk," he said. "This horse is fit for my Memed!"

"It's fit for him," said the villagers.

Big Osman jumped on to the horse's back. "In less than two days I'll be back with my hawk. Go and summon the drummers from Endelin village. Let the drums beat in pairs! That's how Vayvay village must greet Slim Memed. Other brigands come on foot, but our Memed must ride in triumph on an Arab steed!"

Big Osman drove his spurs into the horse and rode off at a gallop. The Taurus mountains were blue, turning to purple.

Jabbar had brought the news of the pardon to Memed. The two old friends embraced and sat down side by side without speaking. "I'm going down to surrender," Jabbar said at last as he left.

Memed had not opened his mouth. He entered Deyirmenoluk one day at noon. His face was dark, his eyes hollow, his brow creased. He was bleak as a rock, but there was an obstinate glint in

347

his eyes. It was the first time in a long while that he had entered the village in broad daylight. He rolled drunkenly, as if he had no control over his body. The women put their heads out of their doors and were watching him with awe. The children walked with him, but some distance, behind, fearfully.

They told Hürü that Memed had come into the village. She hurried to meet him in the square and seized him by the collar. "Memed!" she shouted at the top of her voice. "You let them get Hatché, and now you're going down to surrender to them? Abdi will come back and settle in the village again like a Pasha. Are you going to give yourself up? Coward! This year for once Dikenli plateau has not gone hungry. For once we've eaten our fill. Will you let Abdi Agha swoop down upon us again? Where are you going, you woman-hearted Memed? To surrender?"

By this time all the village had collected in the square, standing there motionless in deathly silence.

"Woman-hearted Memed! See all those villagers staring at you. Will you go and surrender? Will you bring Abdi upon us again? My fine Deuneh's bones protest in the grave. My beautiful Hatché's bones . . ."

Memed turned pale and he trembled as he stared at the ground.

Hürü let go his coat abruptly. "Go and give yourself up, woman-hearted boy," she said. "The amnesty has come!"

Big Osman rode at full speed into the village. "Slim Memed, my hawk," he said. Cutting through the crowd, he came to Memed and embraced him. "My hawk! Your house is built, ready for you. I've had your field sown. This horse is a present from our villagers. Unlike any other brigand our hawk will be welcomed with drums and pipes by Vayvay village. Let Ali Safa Bey and Abdi Agha burst with rage! Mount the horse and come along!"

A rumble rose from the crowd in the square. "Curse the old man! Curse him . . . Curse him. . . ."

Memed took the horse's reins from Big Osman and jumped into the saddle. Lame Ali was standing at the other end of the crowd. Memed rode straight towards him. With a nod of his head Memed ordered Lame Ali to follow him. Then, spurring the horse, he galloped off in a cloud of dust. The murmuring crowd remained staring after them, all the villagers as still as statues.

Memed drew rein at the Hawk's Rock and dismounted. He led

the horse to a plane-tree and tied it there. The plane had shed its leaves and stood deep in a pile of yellow-golden and red-veined leaves.

It was green all round the spring at the Hawk's Rock, crystal green.

Memed sat down on a rock and rested his head in his hands.

When Lame Ali caught up with him, breathless and anxious, he sat down beside him and wiped the sweat off his brow with his forefinger. "Brother, I'm dead tired. My breath won't come." He was silent for a while.

Memed raised his head slowly. Again there was a glint in his eyes as a yellow burning spark flashed through his head. "Brother Ali, will he be in his house at midnight? Can I find him?"

"You'll find him as if you had put him there with your own hand. He's afraid to take a step out of doors at night."

"Explain the lay of the house to me again clearly."

"You know the prison, don't you? Well, on its right you'll see the police headquarters. A little beyond at the other end of the street, there's a single blue-washed house. As you're going at night you won't notice its colour, but it stands alone. It has a tall chimney, like a minaret. You can guide yourself by that, it strikes your eye immediately. It has two floors whereas all the other houses around there are single-storied. Abdi Agha sleeps alone in the room on the west side. The big entrance door is bolted but has a crack. Stick your knife through that crack and you'll lift the bolt. It'll open."

Without another word Memed rose, went straight to his horse, untied it, mounted and set off at a gallop. The horse went like the wind, its mane curling up like a reed-pipe.

When the whir of the lower windmill reached his ears, he reined in and halted, listening. Then he rode the horse on slowly while he loaded his rifle and his revolver. He passed through the centre of the market. The oil-lamps of the coffee-houses were still burning. A few men looked at him strangely. But it was not surprising to see an armed man in those days and they took no notice. Memed hardly even saw the men, and went up the street past the mosque, and found the house with the tall chimney to his left.

He dismounted in front of the house, tied the horse to a low branch of the tall dark mulberry-tree in the courtyard, stuck his knife in the crack of the door and forced it open. A light was burning upstairs. He went up the stairs three at a time. When the women and children saw him, they started screaming, but he went straight to the room on the west side. Abdi Agha lay stretching himself sleepily, his arms wide open. "What is it? What's the matter?" he asked, still stretching. Memed went up to him, took his arm and shook him.

"Agha! Agha! I've come!" he said.

Abdi Agha opened his eyes. At first he could not believe what he saw. Then his eyes remained wide open. Even the pupils turned white.

Outside there was complete confusion.

Memed raised his gun and fired three shots at Abdi Agha's breast. With the blast of the bullets the lamp in the room went out.

Like lightning Memed dashed down the stairs, mounted his horse just as the police became aware of what was happening and began firing towards the house. He rode the horse at full speed towards the Taurus. Shots poured after him like sand in a storm as he left the town.

At sunrise he galloped into the village and drew rein in the middle of the square. The horse was grimy with sweat, its sides heaving like bellows, its neck and rump covered in foam. Memed was perspiring too, the sweat streaming off his back. His face and his hair were all wet.

The shadows stretched out endlessly towards the west. The sweating horse was bathed in light, shining all over.

The villagers saw him there in the square, like a rock, upright on his horse. Slowly all the people gathered round him, forming a big circle. There was not a sound. Their eyes were fixed on him, hundreds of eyes. They kept obstinately silent.

The upright, rock-like rider in their midst stirred a little. The horse took a couple of steps and halted again. The rider raised his head. His eyes swept over the crowd. Mother Hürü, pale, dried-up, bloodless, her eyes wide open and fixed on him, stood waiting for some word, some sign from him.

The horse stirred again as Memed rode towards Mother Hürü, then stopped. "Mother Hürü," he said. "It's done. Now you have no more claims on me!"

He turned his horse towards Alidagh, galloped through the village like a black cloud and was gone, lost to sight.

It was the season for ploughing. The inhabitants of the five villages of Dikenli gathered together. The young girls wore their best dresses. The old women donned white 'kerchiefs, white as snow. The drums were beating. It was a merry feast and even Durmush Ali danced, in spite of his failing health. Early one morning they all went off to the thistle fields and set fire to them.

No news of Slim Memed was ever heard again. No sign or trace of him was ever found.

From that day on, each year, the villagers of Dikenli made a practice of burning the thistle fields in the course of a merry feast before they began ploughing. The fire rolls each year over the plateau for three days and three nights, devouring the thistles that seem to shriek as they burn. With this fire a ball of light appears on the peak of Alidagh and for three nights the mountain is white, as bright as by day.